ForeWord Reviews

FICTION: FANTASY

Eternal Nights - Book One: Redemption

Richard Spegal

iUniverse

978-1-4502-2044-6

Four Stars (out of Five)

Redemption is the first book in the occult fiction trilogy Eternal Nights by Richard Spegal.

Much more than a simple tale of evil vampires pitted against the forces of good, it is the tale of two ancient vampires in search of redemption.

John Wolf and his wife, Danielle, are a lovable, nine-hundred-year-old couple who possess unmatched supernatural powers, along with a vestige of humanity. Defending their immortality, they must go head-to-head with the Sword of God, a militant arm of the Catholic church dedicated to eradicating demons. After spending centuries futilely hunting the undead, the Sword of God enlists werewolves—sworn enemies of vampires—to assist them in their mission.

Fierce battles ensue between vicious werewolves and the vampires. There is no paucity of bloodshed in the battle scenes that follow. A warning to the faint-hearted: the book contains graphic scenes of decapitation, disembowelment, and blood drinking by the gallons.

Spegal deftly avoids the tropes of the often predictable tale of good battling evil, as is typical of the occult genre. This story's antiheroes, John and Danielle, decide to fight back through political destruction. They sneak their way into the Vatican, fully intent on killing the pope. Instead, however, John and Danielle find themselves in the company of an understanding pontiff who allies himself with the couple to work toward destroying the Sword of God. There are more surprises in store for the unsuspecting reader that, in the end, add up to a twisting and turning storyline that is sure to satisfy. This is not your typical, one-dimensional occult book.

Redemption is as much a lesson on the secrets of the kingdom of the undead as it is a tale of good versus evil. Ghouls (the loyal minions of vampires), werewolves, and other creatures of the night populate this tale to create a panoply of occult characters whom readers will find both interesting and compelling.

Underneath the blood and guts lies a cleverly constructed story. Unlike the vampires typically depicted as clinging "to their immortality with every drop of blood in our bodies," these vampires are torn between the bloodthirsty, bestial satisfaction of blood drinking and the deep wish to be forgiven and granted redemption in the eyes of God.

In the end, the forces of the Sword of God close in on the vampires' haven. Is an ancient marriage and nine hundred years of immortality about to come to an end? After reading *Redemption*, readers will anxiously await the next tale of "undead enchantment" to follow in Book Two.

Gary Klinga

ETERNAL NIGHTS
BOOK I
REDEMPTION

Richard Spegal

Eternal Nights
Book I
Redemption

gatekeeper press

Columbus, Ohio

This book is a work of fiction. The names, characters and events in this book are the products of the author's imagination or are used fictitiously. Any similarity to real persons living or dead is coincidental and not intended by the author.

The views and opinions expressed in this book are solely those of the author and do not reflect the views or opinions of Gatekeeper Press. Gatekeeper Press is not to be held responsible for and expressly disclaims responsibility of the content herein.

ETERNAL NIGHTS
Book 1: Redemption

Published by Gatekeeper Press
2167 Stringtown Rd, Suite 109
Columbus, OH 43123-2989
www.GatekeeperPress.com

The editorial work for this book is entirely the product of the author. Gatekeeper Press did not participate in and is not responsible for any aspect of this element.

Library of Congress Control Number: 2022938520

ISBN (paperback): 9781662928628
eISBN: 9781662928635

To my parents for always helping
when I really needed it, and for not when
it wasn't truly necessary.

To my wife for keeping me fed,
and pretending to understand why I spend most
of my time staring at a computer screen.

Lastly, for my children
for proving beyond a shadow of a doubt
that demons are among us.

Prologue

1089 AD

DANIELLE AWOKE with a start next to her new husband. She was confused and slightly disoriented. With the workout her husband had put her through earlier, she should have had no problem sleeping until well into the day. A quick glance out the window, however, confirmed that it was still the middle of the night. What had caused her to wake? She looked at her husband, John. He seemed to be lying in the same position he had collapsed into earlier and was breathing softly. With the elimination of that possibility, her feelings of uneasiness mounted.

Perhaps it was just where they were. Her husband was the best sword master in all the land. Years ago, he had fought for, and won, a position as the captain of the king's personal Elite Guard. As a reward for his years of loyal service, the king had allowed him the use of one of his hunting lodges for a fortnight after the wedding.

It was a wonderful wedding gift but being alone in the forest took some getting used to for Danielle. The unfamiliar surroundings and noises were peaceful but different. She was about to dismiss her uneasiness when she heard it. Footsteps.

They were so soft that she almost thought she had imagined them. Just as Danielle was about to blame them on her nerves, she heard them again. There was no mistaking it this time. There were footsteps coming from inside the lodge, and they were coming closer.

She was almost paralyzed with fear. No one would ever come into one of the king's personal hunting lodges uninvited—at least not with good intentions. Her fear continued to grow until she remembered that she was sleeping next to one of the most feared men in the entire kingdom.

John awoke after a moment of gentle shaking. He turned toward her, his eyes full of love. Danielle quickly put a finger to her lips, to forestall anything he might say. He looked surprised but didn't speak, recognizing the look of fright on his beloved's face.

Danielle was about to whisper what she had heard, when John's head snapped in the direction of the sound. When he turned back, Danielle nodded to confirm that this was why she had awakened him. He nodded his understanding and crept out of bed. Since he would be fighting the intruder indoors, he chose a short sword to take with him.

As she watched his lean, well-muscled body, armed with one of his favorite weapons, moving toward the intruder, Danielle began to feel better. Her biggest concern now was that her husband was a very messy fighter when angry. It would probably take her all day to clean the mess he was about to make of the intruder, but it would be impolite to leave bloodstains inside the king's lodge.

The quiet night was suddenly split by John's signature battle cry. There were a few loud crashes, a heavy thud, and then nothing. Danielle resisted the urge to get up and run to her husband. It was more proper for a noblewoman to await her lover's return.

There were footsteps approaching her once more, but now they were expected. However, within a few seconds, Danielle knew that something wasn't right. The footsteps sounded very light. There was no longer any reason for John to be sneaking around, and his normal footsteps were much heavier than that.

There was something else as well. A heavy scraping sound, as if someone was dragging a very large bag of feed, accompanied the footsteps. As the sounds drew closer, Danielle's heart once again filled with fear.

It was dark, too dark for her to see very much. With shaking hands, Danielle managed to light a pair of candles next to the bed. She looked up in the renewed lighting and froze.

At the foot of her bed stood a normal-looking man with long dark hair. It may have just been the flickering light, but there was something about his face and skin that didn't seem right to her. She looked down at the man's hands, and that's where any resemblance to a human ended.

The fingers on his right hand looked more like long claws, and they were clutching something. It took Danielle a moment to focus through the shock and fear and see what the stranger was holding. When she realized what it was, the fear in her heart redoubled in size, and she knew there was no hope for her.

The man was holding onto the back of her husband's neck. He had been dragging John's lifeless body across the floor toward her. Although the creature—it certainly wasn't a man—had a slight build, he was holding John, with no apparent effort, with one hand.

Seeing her dead husband in the creature's claws shocked Danielle out of her stupor. She grabbed one of the many knives within reach and lunged forward.

"Demon!" Before she was even within arm's reach, the creature locked his gaze on her.

"Stop." The single word was spoken very softly, yet it froze her instantly. She fought with all her strength but couldn't move. She tried to scream, but her voice would no longer obey her.

The creature grinned, dropped John's body, and came toward her. She fought furiously against the invisible restraints yet accomplished nothing. She struggled to scream until the muscles in her throat bulged, yet no sound accompanied her efforts. She was powerless.

The creature plucked the dagger from her hand and dropped it to the floor. As he grabbed her naked body and pulled it closer to him, one of his clawed hands closed around her hair and pulled her head back.

Tears spilled from her eyes as she looked up at the creature's face. He hovered over her, his foul breath invading her nostrils. Now, not even in her mind could she muster the will to resist.

A wave of weakness rippled through her body as the creature's fangs pierced the skin on her throat and her life's blood began to flow from the wound. With darkness closing quickly around her, she had time for one final thought.

At least I will be rejoining you soon, my love.

* * *

ONCE THE CREATURE finished feeding, he observed his handiwork. It had been quite a satisfying night, and if all went well, it would be a few days before he would need to feed again. In addition, he had finally found what he was looking for.

These two would make excellent additions to his coterie. His inhuman speed was the only thing that had saved him from the male. As it was, he had lost a nasty chunk of flesh to the male's sword.

The woman had proved quite formidable in her own right. Somehow, she was nearly able to break his hold over her. That had never happened before—and shouldn't *ever* happen with a mere mortal. He was convinced that she was unable to detect the level of strain he had been under in order to maintain his hold, but he knew how close she had been to breaking him.

They were a perfect pair. He was an amazingly skillful fighter, and she had the potential for extraordinary mental prowess. When he explained the circumstances to the others, he was certain that no one would argue with him about turning them both.

They were both alive but only barely. Should he turn them or finish them off? He had to make a decision soon. He shrugged to no one in particular. His mind had been made up from the start. Tucking one body under each arm, the creature left the lodge and disappeared into the night.

Chapter 1

2009 AD

THEY LEFT THE THEATER, arm in arm, and began to walk down the street. Sharing an affinity for Shakespeare, they made it a point to see as many of his plays as possible. It was interesting to see the many different interpretations different theater groups would come up with. So far neither of them had seen a remake that could compare to the originals, the ones that Shakespeare himself had directed, but they still enjoyed them.

"That was one of the better showings of *Hamlet* that I've seen in quite a few years. What do you think, love?" Danielle snuggled closer to her husband as they continued to walk.

"It was okay, but the one in London was better."

"Agreed, but that was over eighty years ago, and I clearly implied that I was using recent performances as comparison," came the mock-serious retort.

"Really? Wow, it seems like no more than a decade or two." She had a point. It was becoming more and more difficult to keep track of when certain events took place. Every now and then, John had to stop and think to remember what century it was. Living over nine hundred years had a way of doing that to you.

They found a bench on the sidewalk and stopped to wait for the theater crowd to die down. If they were going to eat here, they'd have to be patient.

Huddled next to each other on the bench, they appeared to be nothing more than a pair of young lovers enjoying a night on the town. There was no conversation between them. After over nine centuries together, neither one was uncomfortable with long periods of silence. At times they would go days or weeks without speaking to each other, aside from the occasional "I love you."

John Wolf found himself thinking, once again, how lucky the two of them had been. He had learned everything he could about what had happened to him and his wife and what they had become, and according to that knowledge, the situation that he shared with Danielle was impossible.

Their sire had agreed with that assessment, all those centuries ago. He treated them very well after he turned them. He worked hard to teach them about what they had become and to train them in their many new abilities. Unfortunately, it was nothing compared to what he had done to them.

As soon as they had decided they couldn't learn anything new from their sire, John and Danielle destroyed him. The rest of his coterie met the same fate when they tried to take vengeance for the death of their leader. It was then they realized why everyone had been so nice to them.

John and Danielle were much stronger than they should have been. They destroyed a total of ten vampires, all of whom were far older than they. It shouldn't have been possible, yet they had done it. They then ran off together, away from what passed as civilization in those times, to contemplate what they had become. Cursed and despised creatures. They were vampires.

It couldn't be, and yet it was. Even after spending years with their sire's coterie, they hadn't truly accepted what they had become.

It wasn't until those first dark and lonely nights together that they had let themselves believe it.

During that time of grieving the life that was lost to them, it was only their love that had seen them through. It was their love that had helped them to accept the unacceptable. It was their love that kept them alive to this day, for more than once they had tried to meet the dawn with open arms and end it all, but they just couldn't face losing each again. The odd thing was, it was also their love that was the solid impossibility.

As vampires, they were in essence nothing more than walking corpses. They were corpses with unbelievable powers and abilities, but corpses nonetheless. However, since vampires were still conscious beings, they did have emotions and feelings. Unfortunately, vampires were also demons.

Vampires waged a near constant battle to keep their own beast at bay. The best way to put it into human terms would be to say that the beast was comparable to adrenaline. Any activity that would cause a human's adrenaline to peak would cause a vampire's beast to awaken.

Occasionally the beast reached the surface. When this happened, the vampire was temporarily held in the grip of pure, primal emotions. Most would enter a frenzied state, where they would kill anything around them, friend or foe.

As vampires aged, they lost more and more of the humanity that they had in life. This made dealing with the beast more difficult the older a vampire got. As a result, many vampires that managed to live more than a century were little more than bloodthirsty animals.

So why would love be impossible for a conscious being capable of feeling emotion? The problem was that even when a vampire was calm, the emotions that he or she felt always leaned toward the negative side. Even the most controlled vampires were, at best, very cynical creatures. Having to live in an eternal night, not to mention being forced to feed on human blood to stay alive, didn't do much to help a vampire's outlook on life.

Love was something that vampires just didn't feel for other creatures. They could care about things, and some could even fall in love with them. It was not too uncommon to see an old vampire shed a tear of blood over a painting or sculpture. Monsters could be art lovers too, after all.

Wolf, however, had heard that vampires simply could not transfer a feeling of love to another living thing. It was something about the nature of the beast within them that wouldn't allow it to happen. A vampire saying that he loved a mortal because she was delicious (in the literal sense rather than the figurative one) didn't count.

Wolf had never heard of another vampire even claiming to love another living or *un*living being. Yet, in over nine hundred years of unlife, the love he and Danielle had for each other had never even wavered. If anything their love had grown stronger.

His theory was that it was because they were husband and wife. They were turned at the same time and had no one or nothing else to cling to. A young vampire usually held tightly to something from their mortal life for many years, sometimes even decades. They thought that by doing so they could deny what they had become.

Since vampires did not sire very often, and when they did it was almost never more than one at a time, they were probably the only married couple to ever be turned at once. When you considered that, their situation no longer seemed that strange. It made sense that a vampire couldn't fall in love, but they were already in love before they were turned.

Their love for one another made it much easier for them to hold on to their humanity. In truth they were actually quite happy most of the time, even after over nine centuries. Once they had accepted what had been forced upon them, they decided to make the best of it.

What could possibly be better than spending the rest of your immortal life with the one you loved? Not to mention the fact that they never aged. Imagine being able to spend eternity with your wife, and she never aged beyond twenty-eight. Neither of them looked much different than the night they were turned, over nine hundred years ago. Yes, there were definite benefits to immortality.

A lifetime of soldiering for the king had kept John in excellent shape while he had been alive, and he retained his lean, athletic build into death. Danielle had been the daughter of a minor noble, but her family had not quite been important enough for their relationship to be "proper." Dark features were uncommon in the area where she lived, however, and they gave her a beauty that many found quite exotic. Her skin tone had been just dark enough to raise the eyebrows of every man who saw her walk by. She played to the strengths of her attributes and made sure that no woman was her equal. Her physical prowess was eventually enough to make up for any slight difference in their social standing. John actually shared her dark features, albeit not her skin tone, which gave her the appearance of having a light tan and drove men at the time wild. They had made an excellent match, and once the king had given them his blessing, no one would dare question their union.

While their bodies may have retained their youthful appearances, it was difficult to hide the evidence of age in their faces. It wasn't anything physical—their skin and features remained as perfect as ever—but a person simply cannot hide age. Experience gives a person a certain look that is evident to anyone who gives them more than just a passing glance. If the eyes were the windows to the soul, John wondered what someone would see if he or she were to look into the eyes of two ancient vampires. For this very reason, they did their best to avoid extended contact with people in general—a task made easier by the fact that most people who encountered them were more interested in examining their "other" features.

Their love, though an oddity, was understandable once you considered the circumstances. The strangest part of their relationship, something that even they admitted to each other as being odd, was their continued physical intimacy. When they were affectionate in public, it was mostly for the purpose of blending in. It made them seem harmless and human. In truth, however, they actually derived physical pleasure from doing it.

This was what never made sense to either of them. They were dead. They could still love each other, and do so very deeply, but their bodies were dead. It wasn't possible to feel pleasure from your dead flesh.

It was true that vampires could still have sex. They could redirect blood flow to certain areas of the body and make a very convincing show of it. This was used as a very effective means of luring prey, however, not something done for pleasure.

Very young vampires sometimes would try over and over, for the purpose of pleasure. They hadn't yet accepted what had happened to them. To a vampire, sex simply involved mashing his or her body against a human's until the human was sufficiently subdued. Then the vampire fed and left. A dead body was impossible to stimulate sexually, at least from physical sex. Many vampires found that they entered a state of ecstasy while they fed, although that was due to the power that the blood held over them and it was the closest vampiric equivalent to a living human's physical pleasure.

Despite the fact that they knew it was impossible, John and Danielle could still stimulate and please each other physically. The whole young lover act wasn't just an act. They still had sex and enjoyed it as much as one would expect from two newlyweds.

The only possible explanation had to be the love they shared. Any married couple would tell you that sex was far more than just physical. Perhaps their intense emotional bond fooled their minds into thinking that their bodies were being stimulated normally. Whatever the reason, it happened, and it allowed them to tolerate immortality.

* * *

ONE LOOK AT HER husband and Danielle could tell he was lost in the past. It always amazed her that he could do that so easily. She didn't really want to disturb him, but the crowd would be completely dispersed before long.

"John," she whispered and gently nudged his shoulder. He reflexively tensed almost immediately. When he realized that there was no danger, John merely sat up a little straighter and looked in the direction of the theater.

Where there had once been a mob of people, only a few now lingered. They would have to make their decision soon, or else it would be made for them. It would do them no good to have waited this long only to have inferior prey forced upon them.

"What about her?"

John looked at the woman Danielle indicated and shook his head.

"No, she's not big enough to feed the both of us; besides, you know you're the only woman for me. The fat guy over there should be good enough though." Danielle playfully shoved her husband

and agreed his choice would definitely provide more blood than the woman. They got up and resumed walking down the sidewalk.

The fat man was standing on the corner and looking at what appeared to be a bus schedule. He was looking back and forth from the schedule to his watch, and he didn't seem very pleased. They were closing the distance, but the man was apparently too annoyed to spare a glance at the two strangers.

John and Danielle began talking excitedly to one another. They did their best to sound as irritating as any young couple can sound to an older man. Their efforts were rewarded when they got within ten feet of their prey.

"I'm sorry, but would you mind keeping it down?" The man had turned to look at them in annoyance.

"Oh, I'm sorry, sir." John did his best to sound respectful and apologetic. "We didn't realize how loud we were talking." The man didn't respond. He merely went back to reading his bus schedule.

It didn't matter what they had said to one another. The instant the man turned his gaze on the pair, Danielle locked eyes with him and took control of his mind. He didn't know it, of course, but he was now a puppet.

They left him at the corner and continued down the sidewalk. A quarter mile later, John noticed the entryway into a large alley, decided it was the perfect place for their meal and a sudden burst of inhuman speed sent the pair into the darkness. If anyone had been watching, they would have seen the couple blur and then vanish.

They moved deeper into the alley, and John positioned himself to where he could defend his wife if the need arose. It wouldn't, but one should always be cautious. When he was ready, he signaled to Danielle to bring the prey.

* * *

FRANK PATTERSON was not in a good mood. The play, while enjoyable, had run twenty minutes longer than it was supposed to, causing him to miss the eleven-thirty bus. There wouldn't be another going in his direction for an hour, and he lived too far away to walk. To make matters worse, it was unseasonably warm this evening.

He was annoyed enough before that couple had disrupted his thoughts with their lousy happiness. At first, he was able to ignore them, but they were talking just too damned loud. Didn't they have any respect for a person's right to be miserable?

Well, he had showed them. They probably never expected that an older gentleman like himself would confront them. Well, they had never met Frank Patterson. He had been polite but stern, and the man had apologized. Frank noticed that when they resumed walking, they were much more quiet and respectful.

The knowledge that he had taught those two kids to respect their elders began to brighten Frank's mood. He was feeling good about himself, and maybe even a little tough. Maybe a nice walk would do him some good. After all, his home wasn't really that far, and the moon was full and beautiful tonight.

His mind made up, he took his suit jacket off, threw it over his shoulder, and began strolling down the sidewalk. Once his legs had a chance to stretch out, he started feeling even better. He had a surprising amount of energy for some reason, and before he knew it, Frank found himself humming a tune.

It was a nice night for a walk, and a cool breeze had begun to blow. It was so nice that Frank didn't even care that he was walking in the wrong direction. It seemed like a perfectly good idea to turn into the alley, and when he saw the two shadowy figures descending upon him, he tried to wave. Even as they took his body down and their fangs pierced his throat, he couldn't have been happier to be alive.

* * *

AS JOHN FELT the sudden warm rush of blood flood down his throat, he flattened his tongue and elongated his lips to make sure that he didn't spill any. Something stirred deep within him. The beast. The scent of blood and the possibility of a fresh kill had awakened it and it tried to overwhelm him, to make him drink more and more. It seemed to scream for him to finish off this poor excuse for a mortal.

All in all, it was a pitiful attempt, and John was easily able to battle the beast back. He drank for a few more seconds before withdrawing his fangs and licking the wound closed. He checked the man's pulse. It was weaker than before but still steady.

"I took about a pint and a half. You should be able to take about two without killing him." Danielle nodded her understanding and bent down to feed.

He had left more for her because she had done most of the work. Vampires used blood as a source of energy for everything they did. Merely existing required a small amount of blood, but the cost was much greater when they were using their abilities.

They could control the distribution of blood throughout their bodies with a thought. If a vampire wanted to punch through concrete, for example, it was a simple matter of moving blood into the desired fist to power the punch.

Danielle had been expending blood the entire time she had the fat man under her control. It hadn't been too costly because she was very old, and the older vampires got, the more control they had over their blood usage. Still, she had used more blood today than he had, so it was only fair that she should get to drink more.

Older vampires were also able to hold far more blood in their bodies. When first turned, their bodies had held about the same amount of blood as when they were mortal. When coupled with the fact that they went through blood much faster back then, it was obvious why, as younger vampires, they had fed much more often. Now, unless they were actively using their powers, John and Danielle hardly went through any blood at all. In addition to that, they could each hold nearly ten times as much of it in their bodies. It made no logical sense to them, but that's just the way it was.

It was an unbelievable advantage over younger vampires that might have a grudge against their elders. As a pair, John and Danielle could fight as long and as hard as dozens of other vampires combined. That didn't take into consideration the additional powers they had learned over the years.

John watched as Danielle finished her meal. She withdrew her fangs, licked the new wound closed, and checked the man's pulse again. They tried their best to not kill mortals unless they posed a threat to them. She nodded to John and then went about cleaning up the scene.

She did the same thing every time they finished feeding. First she would place the body in the most comfortable position she could. Then she would recite as many protective incantations as she knew. Unfortunately, until their prey awoke and returned home, he or she would be very vulnerable. To counteract this, Danielle would cast protective magic over the body before they would leave.

It wasn't a perfect solution, but the incantations were more than powerful enough to protect their prey from anything mortal. Beyond that, there was nothing they could do. That was life, or rather *un*life.

"What are your plans for the rest of the evening?" John asked as his wife finished.

"There's a new weapons shop opening down the road from here. They're supposed to specialize in knives and swords. I was going to go check it out. See if they have anything worth adding to our arsenal. Care to join me?"

"Sounds tempting, but maybe another time; I've got to go check in at the blood bank and make sure everything's okay. Then I'll probably just go back to the haven."

Danielle understood perfectly. Everyone that worked in their blood bank was fiercely loyal to them, but blood was too important to just trust loyalty.

Vampires had another ability that came in handy when one needed manpower. They could create their own minions. It was a very simple process that John and Danielle had been using more and more in the last two centuries.

All a vampire had to do was feed some of his or her own blood to a healthy mortal. The vampiric blood would work many changes in the mortal's body, producing a creature known as a minion, a ghoul, or any of a dozen names they had been given throughout the centuries. A ghoul wasn't nearly as powerful as a vampire and had no special abilities. The vampiric blood worked to enhance the abilities they already possessed, not give them new ones.

They made the perfect servants. They were not hindered by sunlight, and they were more powerful than the strongest of humans. Most important was their unmatched loyalty. Any ghoul would simply sacrifice his own life so that his vampiric master could go on living.

They had no choice but to be loyal. The instant a human was ghouled, he or she became dependent on the blood of his or her master. If the vampire did not continue to give the ghoul blood at regular intervals, they would die. So if the vampire was destroyed, every ghoul it had would die as well shortly thereafter.

At first, neither John nor Danielle had cared for the idea of ghouling someone. As time wore on, however, it became evident that they needed eyes and ears during the day. In these modern times, it was hard enough to just stay undiscovered.

Presently, they each had dozens of ghouls. All of Danielle's ghouls worked at the hotel where their main haven was located. John's ghouls operated a private blood bank, which had been another ingenious idea.

While it was true that they used very little blood for what could be considered vampiric day to day activities, combat was another story altogether and with advanced age came advanced abilities. They could go days without consuming blood if they wanted, but when they did need it, they needed *a lot* of it. It would take too much time to hunt for blood in those quantities, and stealing it was too dangerous. A decade ago, John had the idea to set up a private blood bank. The credentials were all falsified, of course, and the facility was staffed exclusively by ghouls.

A mortal could walk in, donate a pint of blood, receive twenty dollars, and be on his way. Officially, the blood was used to test new medications and disease identification methods. In reality, the blood was simply stored until it either went bad or John asked for some to be delivered to the haven.

The blood was tested before being sent out. Diseases did not concern vampires, but foreign substances did. If the blood a vampire drank contained drugs or alcohol, the vampire would become intoxicated. Vampires were extremely weak against intoxication of any kind, and John knew from experience that the results were not pleasant.

The blood bank made hunting completely unnecessary. They hunted because they liked it, not because they needed to. There was no substitute for warm, fresh blood, and they indulged themselves whenever they could.

The blood bank served an additional purpose. Every time John stopped in, he would gorge himself on blood. He would simply drink until he couldn't drink any more. Within a few minutes, the fresh blood would integrate into his system, and then he would allow his ghouls to drain him of most of it. This blood would be stored for distribution among the ghouls as needed. John would then drink a bit extra right before he left, since he didn't like the idea of running close to empty. Danielle went through a similar procedure for her own ghouls.

All of the ghouls' blood distribution was handled by Samuel Robinson. As the oldest and by far most powerful of either vampire's minions, he was in overall command of both groups. He had fought side by side with John and Danielle on a number of occasions. John even believed that he was strong enough to bring down most fledgling vampires on his own.

Sam was trusted with such an important task because he knew, better than any other ghoul, the price of failure. He knew that despite over a century of loyal service, neither vampire would hesitate to rip his throat out at the slightest sign of betrayal. He had seen what had happened to his predecessor, when he had gotten too greedy.

In addition to that, John had promised to make him a full vampire one day. It was something most ghouls aspired to be. John would have already fulfilled his promise if Sam hadn't been so useful. As a full vampire, he would lose the ability to be out during the day. Who else but Sam could John trust to take care of his and Danielle's safety during the sunlight hours?

John knew that as soon as Sam found a suitable replacement, he would ask for fulfillment on the bargain they had made. John wouldn't even hesitate to do so. Just as he wouldn't hesitate to eliminate him if his loyalty so much as wavered, not that Sam had ever shown any signs to be concerned about.

"Okay, so we'll meet back at the haven about an hour before sunrise?" Danielle offered.

"Sounds good, love." With that, they embraced and went their separate ways.

* * *

THOMAS ANDREWS was a Templar in the Sword of God, and he was as arrogant as they came. To be fair, he had good reason to be arrogant: he was almost as good as he thought he was. He was the best in his chapter, he was sure of that much, and with any luck he'd be making arch-Templar soon.

He knew that the pair of individuals he had been watching were vampires. Even a novice was taught to sense the undead, no matter what form they took. He had been out for a simple walk when it had hit him like an awful smell.

Thomas began to follow the "scent," and his instincts, through the city. It was over five miles before he tracked down the source of the assault on his senses. He was the best in the area, and this was the first time he had sensed an undead from over a mile away. That should have been the first indication he should just leave, or at least call in for help.

Unfortunately, he was too arrogant to ever ask for help. He knew that these vampires were older than any he had ever encountered, and if he could bring down at least one by himself, the priests would name him the next arch-Templar for sure. The only question was how to proceed. How did one go about attacking vampires as powerful as these two obviously were?

Thomas was still trying to make up his mind when he had a stroke of good fortune. The two vampires separated. They had been talking to one another, and then they just wandered off in different directions. He chose the female and began his pursuit.

She was strong enough that she could easily have sensed him following her if she were trying. It was obvious that she wasn't, but Thomas was prepared to flee the instant she showed signs that she had detected his presence. If he were a normal human, she wouldn't have even had to try to detect him. Fortunately for him, he wasn't normal.

All warriors of God were trained in many abilities useful for combating the undead and one of these was masking their presence. Thomas was one of the best, and fledgling vampires never detected him, whether they were trying or not. He knew, however, that his abilities were nothing compared to those of the creature he pursued. He would have to act quickly before she thought to check her surroundings.

He continued to follow her for another few miles, wanting to make sure that when he killed this one, the second vampire wouldn't sense it right away. He needed time to get away. The male could be dealt with later.

Thomas saw that they were moving into a very secluded area. It would have to be done now. No innocents could be endangered. He drew his favorite weapon and ensured that it was fully loaded. When he was satisfied, he took a moment to center his mind and say a short prayer.

The weapon he drew, a sawed-off shotgun, had always been his favorite. Stakes were only used in emergencies or when you caught a vampire sleeping. Hunters that got close enough to vampires to use a stake usually got torn to shreds. The shotgun was not much longer than a proper stake, and it was easily concealed and carried within his standard-issue trench coat. The other main difference from a standard shotgun was that his weapon fired phosphorous rounds. One blast to the head would destroy a fledgling vampire. This vampire, however, would most likely absorb several shots before she died.

Thomas knew he would have to start by firing a round into the back of her head. She would survive, but would undoubtedly be stunned for a moment. He would pump the remaining five rounds into her head and chest. That should give him the few seconds he would need to draw his sword and take her head. Decapitation would kill any vampire, no matter how old or powerful.

Thomas estimated the distance between him and his target to be about thirty feet. No professional marksman could miss such a perfect shot. In one smooth motion, Thomas brought his weapon up, took aim, and pulled the trigger. Nothing happened.

It took a moment for him to realize why his weapon wouldn't fire. He was no longer holding it. As a matter of fact, he was no longer even standing where he had been a second before.

Thomas had been slammed against a wall about twenty feet from where he had been standing. The female vampire he had been tracking was standing in front of him, studying him the way a child would study a curious-looking insect. She was holding his shotgun in one hand, while the other was clutched into a fist.

In another few seconds the pain registered, and it took all of Thomas's discipline to not scream in agony. His back felt as though it were on fire, and his whole upper body seemed to be one big bruise. What had she done to him—and in so short a time?

The vampire appeared to now be studying his weapon with true interest. His life was forfeit, and he knew it. He had drastically underestimated her, and for that he would pay the ultimate price. The only thing he could do now would be to go down fighting.

With all his remaining strength, Thomas tried to force himself into a crouch. He would lunge at her in one final, desperate attack. He never got the chance. The instant the vampire noticed him trying to move away from the wall, she raised her empty hand and pointed at him.

An invisible force slammed him back against the wall. This time the vampire did not lower her hand, and Thomas could feel himself being held in place. He made the intelligent decision of staying completely still and accepting his fate.

The vampire seemed to divert her attention back to the weapon. She removed one of the rounds, sniffed it, and then loaded it back into the weapon. She looked almost as if she couldn't make up her mind. Thomas took some comfort in the fact that if she fired at him, death would be very quick.

She removed her jacket, lifted the weapon, and aimed it at his head. Apparently, she had come to a decision. Thomas closed his eyes and waited for death. When nothing happened, he opened his eyes and saw that the vampire was grinning wolfishly at him. She swung the weapon to point it at her own bare arm and then pulled the trigger.

The noise from the shot was deafening. Stunned by the vampire's actions, Thomas stared at her in disbelief. Midway between her elbow and shoulder, her left arm was now halfway severed. Large chunks of flesh and bone had been blown away, and there was blood everywhere. As bad as the damage was, however, Thomas knew that it should have been much worse. How powerful was this creature?

He noticed her begin to examine the wound herself, as if surprised that she suffered any injury at all. Perhaps she had expected normal rounds, and not phosphorous. Thomas took grim satisfaction in that. Satisfaction that quickly evaporated when he saw what happened next.

The vampire displayed her ruined arm to him, as if she was showing it off. Within seconds it began to heal. The bone reformed, the flesh began to knit together and fill out, and new skin began to form over it. In under a minute, all traces of the injury were gone.

It was impossible. No vampire could heal from an injury like that so rapidly! She was deliberately flaunting her power. It had been believed that most elder vampires had been hunted down and destroyed. Some would always slip through the cracks, of course, but surely none this powerful!

He was desperately trying to hold on to consciousness now. The others had to be warned. It was only logical to assume that the male was at least as powerful as she was. This was bad. The Sword of God had not dealt with elders this powerful in nearly three centuries. He couldn't die.

The vampire went back to studying him and his weapon. Then, suddenly, she raised the weapon over her head in one hand. He guessed that she had decided to club him to death.

She brought the weapon down, but not onto his head. Instead, she threw it, as though it were a knife, at his right leg. The throw had so much force behind it the barrel went right through his leg and buried itself over three inches into the sidewalk. The shock was so great that Thomas was temporarily spared the pain.

He looked the monster directly in the eyes, and something told him that he had only seen a small example of her power. He wondered what she would do next, but in an instant she was gone. Seconds later, the full pain of what his body had been through hit him, and he blacked out. It was less than two minutes from when he had originally drawn his weapon.

* * *

EVEN AS SHE departed the scene, Danielle couldn't help but wonder about the oddities of her brief conflict. After parting company with John, Danielle continued on down the road. The store was a few miles away, but with an evening so pleasant, she saw no reason to hurry and waste blood unnecessarily. Instead she merely strolled along at a normal walking pace.

She didn't sense the threat that the man trailing her posed, which was the first of many things she found concerning. Perhaps if Danielle had been actively trying to identify threats, she would have sensed him in an instant. It may have also been that her powers had sensed him and had just decided that one attacker posed no threat to a nine-hundred-year-old vampire.

Whatever the reason, Danielle had remained clueless about what was happening behind her. It wasn't until the stranger raised his weapon and began to pull the trigger that she had become consciously aware that something was wrong. When she did, her reaction was too fast for her to even realize what she was doing.

All she knew was that, out of nowhere, her mind exploded with a single word. *Danger!* Before she could even think, she had reflexively spun around and threw out a wall of force by swinging her arm in an arc. Everything that had been behind her, including a man who was holding a shotgun that had been aimed at her head, flew backward.

She remembered watching as he crashed into a wall about twenty feet back and lay motionless. It took her less than a second to cover the distance and disarm him. She remained standing there, simply looking at him. Why did this mortal attack her? Was it random? Did he just simply pick the wrong victim this time? Of course, now that she had time to think she knew how absurd that sounded. People generally didn't trail each other with the intent of simply gunning one another down on the open streets at random. Well, not normally anyway.

Once he did open his eyes, he seemed very confused. When he realized she was standing over him with his weapon, he did not panic. He attacked, or at least he tried to. As soon as Danielle saw him try to get up, she raised her free arm and sent another bolt of force into his chest. His failure to panic was additional proof this had not been a random attack.

He smashed against the wall much harder than the first time and wisely decided to remain still. It was curious that he was still not panicking. He didn't even seem to be in shock. John would have told her to kill him. He had attacked her and therefore had forfeit his life.

Danielle, however, had seen no reason to kill him. He no longer posed a threat to her, but she had thought to give him another example of her power. She examined the weapon he had been holding. It was a standard shotgun, sawed-off to be more easily concealed. It would do quite nicely.

Normal shotgun rounds would barely even penetrate her skin. It would be a shocking display of power. Not wanting to ruin her leather jacket, Danielle removed it. She then aimed the shotgun at her attacker's head. She was only teasing him, but he didn't know that.

She began to pull the trigger but quickly switched targets. Instead of firing at his head, she fired at her own upper left arm. The thunderous discharge had been expected; however, an unbelievable wave of pain immediately consumed her, and she had almost dropped the weapon and cried out. Something was wrong.

Danielle looked at her arm and was shocked to see that it had nearly been severed above the elbow. Realization came to her quickly, and she now understood why the rounds had smelled odd to her before. *Phosphorous!* She hadn't recognized the smell before, but phosphorous was the only thing that could eat through her flesh and bone like that. It was then that she had realized beyond the shadow of a doubt that her attacker was a vampire hunter of some sort. It had been one more powerful argument to kill him, and be done with it, but Danielle had always preferred using fear and manipulation.

She displayed her arm so that her would-be killer could see the injury more clearly. It began to heal automatically, but she had concentrated on forcing it to heal faster. The effort was costly in blood, but the effect was more than worth it. Within about thirty seconds, the wound had completely healed. The mortal had finally begun quivering in fear, his skin turning ghostly white. The only thing left to do was to immobilize him.

She lifted the shotgun and tossed it like a throwing knife at his right thigh. The barrel went through his leg and into three inches of concrete. Danielle waited for him to look away from her and at the wound on his leg. The instant he did, she vanished in a blur of speed.

In retrospect she really should have killed the fool for attacking her, but there was no use worrying about it now. She had already decided to not tell John about what had happened. He would not have approved of how she had handled the situation. He would have killed the attacker immediately, drained his blood, and disposed of the body. But there was no sense in them arguing over something as foolish as the fate of one mortal.

It would be a good idea for her to hunt some more before returning to the haven. The blood she had used during the brief conflict needed to be replaced. She would half-drain a few people on the street and then return to the haven as if nothing had happened. Besides, what possible threat could one half-dead mortal pose to them?

Chapter 2

SIMPLY PUT, the Sword of God was a branch of the Catholic Church that was created by Pope Gregory IV in 842 AD. It was founded and maintained for the sole purpose of combating the physical manifestations of evil. These included anything that could be considered abominations in the eyes of the Lord. Unfortunately for the rest of the world, the individuals responsible for labeling creatures as abominations or demons were far from infallible.

The SOG, with its very selective membership, was the Catholic Church's most carefully guarded secret. Only the pope and his closest advisers knew of its existence. After a few decades of study and preparation, its members were ready to take the fight to the abominations' doorsteps in a holy war of purification.

At first they were remarkably successful. Many types of abominations were completely wiped from the face of the earth. In fact, of all the different types of demons, only vampires and werewolves escaped major harm. Their ability to blend in with mortals made both groups very difficult to identify until it was too late. The werewolves, however, rarely fought with the mortals, unless they were defending themselves. It was the vampires that turned the tide of the holy war.

The amazing successes that the SOG had won were quickly turned around once the vampires began actively fighting back. It began slowly and quietly. Operatives would fail to report in, and entire teams would disappear without a trace, but no one would admit the cause.

Everyone preferred to believe that the war was being won. Then, one night, that all changed.

Elder vampire Mikiael Nightstalker walked into a major cathedral during a midnight service on Christmas Eve, which was something the SOG's propaganda insisted was not possible for a demon to do. He pointed at the archbishop conducting mass, and the congregation watched as the archbishop exploded in a bloody mess. He then waved an arm in the direction of the tabernacle and the crucifix, and both simply melted. Finally, parishioners began attacking one another, their minds bending to Nightstalker's will.

There had been two dozen well-armed and elite SOG soldiers present, and they were all dead in seconds. Vladimir finished by raising his arms and destroying the building itself. The entire incident lasted less than three minutes. Over three hundred innocents lost their lives, and Nightstalker escaped unharmed. There was no longer any denying it: the vampires were fighting back, and the mortals didn't stand a chance.

The Inquisition brought about a reversal that saw the humans once again winning the war. The Church had taken a risk and exposed the vampire's existence to the common people. Faced with a hostile population and fewer places to hide, vampires were destroyed in scores.

By the end of the Inquisition, very few elder vampires were left, and those that survived went into deep seclusion while they rebuilt their numbers. The SOG knew that they had only bought humanity a brief respite, for mortals were simply unable to match the strength of the vampires. If humans were ever going to gain an advantage, they would have to come up with a different approach.

Someone suggested employing werewolves to help with the vampire problem. Like vampires, werewolves could easily blend in to a crowd since, until they changed form, they appeared as everyday people in every way. No one knew why, but werewolves and vampires had a deep-seated hatred for one another, so the promise of being able to kill vampires would likely be enough to get most werewolves to agree to help the SOG.

The idea was very simple, at least in theory. Once werewolves were identified, approach them while they were in human form. Offer them full employment with the SOG, in exchange for their being the main enforcement arm of the organization. If they declined, leave before the werewolves got angry. If they agreed, bring them directly to the nearest SOG base for additional information.

Having werewolves fight on their side gave them a chance. Individually, the average werewolf was far more powerful than the average vampire. They could be out during the day, and when not in wolf form, they were indistinguishable from normal humans. Unfortunately, they did have a few weaknesses.

Werewolves could live up to five hundred years, but they were not immortal. After the first few centuries, age began to very slowly degrade a werewolf's abilities. Vampires were immortal, and they grew stronger with age. A trained vampire was also able to use heightened senses to smell the difference between a normal mortal and a werewolf in human form.

Another disadvantage was the animalistic nature of a werewolf's abilities. Their strengths were purely physical, and most didn't use weapons. Once vampires reached a certain age, they were able to master many abilities that would allow them to put down a werewolf from a distance.

Finally, werewolves were living creatures. They could take an unbelievable amount of punishment, but they suffered from all of the same weaknesses as the rest of the living. Heart, brain, spinal cord and organs were easy targets for the more powerful vampires to exploit with relative ease.

A powerful vampire could take on two and even three werewolves. The SOG deployed them in groups of four. Each group of four werewolves was further supported by a dozen heavily armed soldiers. While the werewolves charged in, the soldiers would hang back and fire their weapons at the enemy. If the werewolves were not enough to take down a pack of vampires, the hail of ranged fire would surely finish the job.

All in all, having werewolves working for them gave the SOG the punch it needed to stay ahead in the war against not only vampires but all abominations. Since the werewolves cooperated willingly and happily, there was no need for extra security to keep them in line. There were problems, however.

When the idea was first brought to the attention of Pope Pius II, he steadfastly refused. His reasoning was that they could not use one abomination to fight another. That would make them just as tainted as those abominations that they sought to destroy.

With every defeat that the SOG suffered; however, the arguments about using werewolves became more and more demanding. Eventually the pope came to the decision that the entire SOG was a mistake. It was not the Church's place to wage war on anybody, he decided, even if it was the spawn of Satan that they were fighting against. History being fraught with religious wars, his opinion was the exception rather than the norm for church leaders.

The SOG did not go quietly, but they eventually bent to the will of the Church, or so it seemed. What the pope did not know was that the SOG had anticipated such an occurrence and had made preparations. They did not disband; rather they merely went into hiding to consolidate their forces.

In the centuries that followed, the Church never suspected that the SOG still existed. Most of those that had been privy to the knowledge of their existence forgot in time. Eventually, the SOG became nothing more than a legend.

In reality, however, the SOG grew quickly. They developed their own priesthood, which was based on Catholicism but with a combative twist. No longer bound by the restrictions the Catholic Church had placed on them, they recruited from everywhere. This included the enlistment of werewolves. They even spread secret bases across the world.

By the twentieth century, the SOG was arguably the most powerful organization in the world, thanks to the werewolves they employed. They had multiple bases, research centers, industrial plants, and strong points in almost every major country. Their members numbered in the millions, but less than a few hundred knew who they really worked for. In addition, they had thousands of werewolves in their service. All of this power, and no one even knew that they existed.

So, they fought on in secret, using technology and skills developed to assist in locating and destroying the demonic vampires. The war would continue to be waged for a long time to come, but it finally looked as if humanity stood a chance.

* * *

ARCHBISHOP JENKINS was in command of, and responsible for, all SOG activity on the eastern coast of the United States. It was a very prestigious post, and the archbishop ran a tight ship. It was with great pride that he took his seat of power each morning to dispense new orders. He glanced now at one of the strongest Templars in his entire diocese, but it was not pride that filled him this time. It was fear.

Thomas Andrews, senior Templar of the Sword, was laid out on the hospital bed before him. He was covered nearly head to toe with bandages, and there were IVs and tubes running into both of his arms. The doctors had assured him that Thomas was out of danger, but he looked ready to die at any moment.

He had been found in a back alley, severely beaten and with his own weapon pinning his leg to the sidewalk. His back had been badly broken, and he had serious internal injuries and a major concussion. To make matters worse, there had been no way to move him without killing him. The shotgun had been buried too solidly, and Thomas had already lost too much blood. One of the doctors had to sever Thomas's leg about six inches below the hip joint. Thomas obviously didn't know about it yet, but he wouldn't be happy when he found out.

"Thomas, what happened to you?" The machines monitoring Thomas's condition beeped in response, but the Templar remained silent. What kind of monster would have done such a thing? Even vampires usually killed their victims. They didn't leave them broken and still breathing.

Jenkins was not naive enough to think that his Templars were the most powerful beings on the planet. Thomas's loss was not what frightened him. What frightened him was the fact that there was basically no evidence of a struggle.

They had found neither bodies nor pieces of bodies, and there was no damage to the surrounding area. All they had found was some blood that they believed to be that of Thomas's attacker. The test results had not come back yet, but he was certain that they would prove the blood to be vampiric.

Thomas may be arrogant, but he really was one of the best. More importantly, he was smart and always traveled well-armed. Powerful vampires attracted attention, and none had been believed to be in this city. The entire situation was very inconclusive, and Jenkins didn't like uncertainties.

He motioned for a nearby doctor to join him. It was time to see if he could get some answers.

"What do you wish of me, Your Excellency?" The doctor spoke as he executed a deep bow. Even after he completed his bow, he kept his eyes averted from the archbishop's.

"Please, my son, do not look away from me. It is I who should be bowing to you this day. The skill and speed displayed by you and your staff was what saved one of our most powerful warriors from falling victim to the demons. You have done your Church a wonderful service. I give you all my personal blessing." He made the sign of the cross in the air over the doctor's head.

"Thank you, Excellency. We are all just servants of the Lord," the doctor answered, his face beaming with pride. The archbishop didn't want to issue his next order, but he had no choice. The doctor would just have to understand that.

"There is something more I require of you, my son."

"Anything, Excellency, I'm yours to command."

"I need you to wake our fallen comrade." The doctor appeared to be shocked at the suggestion.

"Excellency, if I wake him, the chance of complications arising in his condition will increase significantly. I do not wish to risk his life." Jenkins sympathized with the man, but he needed answers.

"I understand how you feel, my son. If there were any other way, I would not be asking this of you. We must discover exactly what happened, as soon as possible. Others may die if we remain ignorant. You know that Templar Andrews would agree with us if he could. The preservation of innocent life is worth whatever it takes." The doctor began to slowly nod in agreement.

"I will do it, Excellency, but please, I beg of you, keep him awake only as long as is necessary."

"You are the expert here, my son. I will certainly honor your request." Satisfied, the doctor manipulated a few controls. Thomas began to stir, but he did not wake. The doctor gently slapped him on the cheek until he opened his eyes.

"Please, my son, leave us," Jenkins ordered when he saw that Thomas's eyes were opening. "Remain outside of the room. I will summon you when we are finished."

"Of course, Excellency." The doctor bowed deeply, turned, and left.

Jenkins moved into Andrew's field of vision. The Templar noticed him and began blinking rapidly, as if trying to focus his vision.

"Excellency," he gasped as he realized who was standing before him. He appeared to be trying to stand.

"Relax, my son. You are in no condition to move." Jenkins gave him a moment to compose himself. "I have come here because I need your help."

"Anything, Excellency."

"Our men have examined the place where you battled. They found very little. Other than some blood on the pavement, there was nothing that even hinted that a struggle had taken place there." It looked as if Andrews wanted to interrupt but lacked the strength to do so. The archbishop motioned for him to speak.

"The reason it looked that way, Excellency, is because there was no battle. There was no struggle. There wasn't even a disagreement. I drew my weapon and took aim, and then it was over. She tortured me for a few moments and then vanished." The intensity with which Andrews was speaking sent him into a violent fit of coughing. There was little that the archbishop could do to help, so Jenkins placed a comforting hand on his Templar's shoulder.

"Easy, my son, you must try to remain calm until your strength returns. I need you to tell me what happened. What did this to you? How can we stop it?" Andrews nodded, took a deep breath, and began his tale.

* * *

IT TOOK NEARLY half an hour to explain what had happened. The archbishop asked many questions, and Andrews did his best to answer them. He made sure to point out that there was at least one other vampire in the city, a male that was most likely at least as powerful as the female.

"I must admit, my son, your news troubles me. It has been a long time since the Sword of God has dealt with a vampire as powerful as this, let alone two of them. I am merely a soldier on the battlefield of the soul. You, my son, are a true warrior. What should we do about this threat?" Andrews felt a moment of pride at the realization that the archbishop was seeking his counsel.

"Divide and conquer. It is by far the safest, most efficient way of dealing with enemies this powerful, Excellency. I can give excellent descriptions of both vampires. If we can discover where they spend their time, we can set an ambush for onc of them. Once the first one is destroyed, we can send all of our resources after the second.

"I wouldn't bother even trying to locate their haven. They didn't survive this long by being careless. An ambush would have the best chance of success. I would use an entire team of werewolves, and at least two squads of our best men." Andrews wanted to give a much more detailed battle plan, but his strength was failing rapidly. Jenkins seemed to notice this and signaled for him to stop.

"Thank you for your advice, my son. I will send some artists to you, when you have regained your strength, so that we may have pictures to work from." Andrews lacked the strength to respond, but he smiled at his archbishop's obvious enthusiasm in planning to destroy the demons.

* * *

THE ARCHBISHOP spent a few additional moments congratulating Andrews on doing the Lord's work before deciding that the man could stand no more excitement for the time being. He gave his senior Templar one final blessing before turning to leave. Once outside, he motioned for the doctor to approach him.

"I believe that I may have taxed his strength a bit too much. Please see that he gets the rest that he needs. In about eight hours, I'll be sending some men to speak with him briefly. I also need you to have someone on your staff go find Templar Robinson and send him to me." Jenkins read the look on the doctor's face.

"That's right, my son. We're fighting back. In no more than three days' time, we will be striking back at the demons." The smile on the doctor's face showed that he clearly approved of the archbishop's intentions, and with a deep bow he excused himself and set off to complete his tasks.

Chapter 3

IT WAS HIGHLY irregular for Danielle to be wandering the streets by herself, as often she had been doing the last few nights. Definitely irregular enough to draw John's suspicion, which explained why she had been leaving and returning before he woke. Her intentions were good, but she didn't want to ruin the surprise by answering questions.

The night Danielle was attacked, she had continued on to visit the weapons shop. For the most part, she was unimpressed with the shop's selection, which consisted mostly of simply decorative pieces. She was looking for something she could use.

As Danielle was about to leave, the shop's owner had engaged her in conversation. Through speaking to him, she found out that he had actually made all the weapons that he was selling. At that, she took a chance and described what she wanted.

She wanted a Japanese-style *katana*, but with a blade a foot longer than normal and made properly from folded steel. The pommel was to be carved in a design that depicted a battle they had fought against a trio of werewolves. Most importantly, she wanted it ready in one week.

When she finished giving him directions, the owner laughed at her. He stopped laughing when Danielle tossed several hundred dollar bills onto the counter. He slowly counted the cash, got up, locked the door, and hung up a "Closed" sign. Once he sat back down, they got into some serious negotiating.

It didn't take long. Danielle told the owner she would give him two thousand dollars now and ten thousand more upon the completion of the weapon. He agreed that the amount was more than enough motivation to complete the weapon to her specifications.

Danielle thanked the owner for his cooperation and told him she would stop in periodically to check on his progress. He had mumbled something in return, apparently still trying to recover from the shock of the transaction he had just completed. Feeling that her weapon couldn't be in better hands, she left the shop that night very pleased with herself.

She had checked back with the owner every night since, to ensure that he was making acceptable progress. So far she had been impressed with his work, given the difficulty of what she had asked him to do. Apparently, he had a friend that did all of his carving, which allowed him to concentrate on the blade.

Perhaps if Danielle had been paying more attention to her surroundings, she would have been more prepared for what was about to happen. After the night of the attack, Danielle had vowed to not allow herself to be taken by surprise again, especially not by a mortal. It was difficult, however, to not allow yourself to grow at least a little cocky over the centuries.

It was that cockiness that nearly got her killed once, and it was that cockiness that allowed her to walk straight into the ambush that now awaited her. If it hadn't been for the amount of time she spent honing her skills to a razor's edge, the attack would have been a complete success. As it was, she barely survived the initial assault.

Danielle had been walking down the sidewalk, unaware that anything was amiss. It was just another beautiful night full of the same city smells she had come to love so much over the years. Although warmer nights did tend to bring out the smell of garbage a bit more, at least it wasn't the middle of summer. Out of nowhere, however, her senses peaked. Eyes everywhere, over a dozen pairs altogether, and all fixated on her. Her senses exploded with the word *DANGER!* much as they had the last time she had been attacked. The only difference now was that the feeling was far stronger and coming from every direction.

Danielle responded instantly and with superhuman speed. She ran forward and leapt. Shots rang out, and the area where she had been standing an instant before was peppered with phosphorous rounds. A few rounds managed glancing blows off of her clothing, but none penetrated to her flesh.

The clothing that Danielle and John wore looked normal, but looks can be deceiving. The fabric was made with Kevlar and other metallic fibers. The clothing was very expensive and heavy, but it was as if each of them were wearing a suit of full-body armor. That extra armor allowed her to survive the initial assault uninjured, although the outer layers of her protective clothing had melted mostly away.

She took quick stock of her situation. There were multiple attackers, who seemed to know exactly what they were attacking. It was doubtful they knew how powerful she really was, but it was obvious they knew she was a vampire.

They were also excellent marksmen. Even as fast as she had been moving, over half her jacket had been melted away by their phosphorous rounds. Like it or not, she had walked right into a trap. The best thing for her to do would be to just run. No mortal could track her, and she could be back here with John in minutes.

She plotted her best escape route, but before she could get away, four men stepped calmly in front of her. She paused out of curiosity. They carried no weapons but didn't seem the least bit concerned about blocking her path. This was obviously another part of the trap, but a small amount of the cockiness which had gotten her into this mess began to return. Being stealthy and setting a successful ambush was one thing, but directly standing in her way in to challenge her escape? That was simply not allowed. So instead of easily changing direction, she met the new threat head on.

The men didn't smell like normal mortals, but it was obvious that they weren't vampires. It wasn't until Danielle looked into their eyes that she knew how much trouble she was in. *Shit! Werewolves! So much for escaping.*

One werewolf was no match for her, but there were four of them—plus over a dozen mortals, who were armed to the teeth. More importantly, she might not be able to outrun four werewolves. Whatever she was going to do, she had to decide now. It was only a matter of time before the shooters reacquired their aim, and the werewolves were beginning to advance. There was only one thing for her to do. Get away. Unfortunately, the only way for her to escape was to fight through the werewolves. As soon as she realized what would have to be done, Danielle sprang into action.

The instant she moved, the werewolves leapt into action. They quickly morphed into their true forms, and Danielle began to truly fear for her life. At least one of the werewolves was an elder.

Danielle's form was a blur as she leapt from corner to corner, from rooftop to street and back to rooftop. All at once, she was everywhere and nowhere. She threw out a bolt of force whenever she acquired a target, but it wasn't enough.

It seemed that no matter where she moved, there was always someone close enough to shoot at her. She had managed to find and kill four attackers, but there were many still firing. Worse, the werewolves had completely vanished.

She leapt to a rooftop and took a moment to scan her surroundings. No one was shooting at her, although she still sensed danger everywhere. So far, Danielle had still not been injured, although her armor had taken a few more rounds and her jacket had all but disintegrated. The absence of the werewolves bothered her, but escaping was still her best option.

Danielle ran and leapt for the next rooftop, but she collided in midair with a werewolf that had jumped up to intercept her. The two went down in flurry of fur, flesh, and flailing limbs. The impact with the cement cracked several of her bones, but Danielle managed to get one of her arms free.

She drew her sword, quickly decapitated the werewolf, and moved down the street in a blur. She had been lucky. The werewolf had been very young. His claws and teeth had not been strong enough to get through the remnants of her reinforced clothing.

As Danielle searched for her remaining attackers, she used some of her blood to knit her bones back together. A trio of mortals stepped in front of her and fired. All three rounds hit her in the chest. Lacking any substantial protection, they easily burned through her mildly reinforced shirt, and she could feel the phosphorous eating away at her flesh and bone.

Less than two seconds after the mortals fired, they were all dead. Danielle once again took to the rooftops, where she used even more blood to heal the hole that had been burned in her chest. Things were not going well for her.

She was using too much blood, and her attempts to escape didn't seem to be accomplishing much. As if that weren't enough, she began to notice a familiar feeling welling up from deep inside. It was the beast. The prolonged fight, as well as her rapid use of blood and multiple injuries, was causing her beast to awaken.

At the moment she could handle it, but she knew that if she went into a frenzy, it would all be over. The only way for her to survive this situation would be to maintain total focus. Unfortunately, focus alone might not be enough. She was not alone.

Sharing the rooftop she had landed on were at least eight mortals and the three remaining werewolves. Somehow she had managed to circle back around and collide with their main attack force. She was surrounded.

Danielle didn't hesitate for an instant. She began reciting an ancient incantation and called upon the full power of her blood. Charging the werewolves was her only chance, and the elder would have to be destroyed fast. As she charged, streams of fire poured from her body in every direction. More fire erupted from the tips of her fingers as she aimed them at her attackers. Using fire was dangerous for a vampire, but it was also a very potent weapon.

A few mortals were reduced to ash, and others screamed out in agony. Danielle saw one werewolf bounding away in pain and terror, its body ablaze. One of the drawbacks of being covered in fur was being extremely flammable.

Unfortunately, the elder werewolf was not the one that had been set afire. It had simply disappeared again. Danielle briefly considered trying to run again, but that hadn't worked so far. *No,* she thought to herself, *I have to fight.*

Danielle charged the remaining werewolf. It didn't look overly powerful, so she decided to attack it physically. It would take a few seconds longer, but she simply couldn't afford the blood to use magic.

What little remained of her blood reserves had to be saved for when she was forced to engage the elder.

Sword drawn, Danielle attacked. It was a gamble. She was betting that the remaining mortals would not fire at her, for fear of hitting the werewolf. She was wrong.

As the werewolf defended itself against her sword, Danielle felt her side explode. They were firing at her once again. The first round was followed quickly by several more. Most either missed completely or hit the werewolf. A few, however, succeeded in causing more damage to her flesh.

The shock of her new injuries, the brutality of her battle with the werewolf, and the amount of blood she had already used all contributed in strengthening the beast within her. She tried valiantly to hold the beast at bay, but it was no use. Her senses were filled with blood fury, and Danielle lost control.

There were few sights more horrific than a nine-hundred-year-old vampire entering a killing frenzy. She threw her sword aside and attacked the werewolf with her bare hands. The young beast was no match for her fury.

The problem for Danielle was that she was no longer interested in death. She wanted blood. She could have easily killed the werewolf, but instead she latched onto it. Ignoring the injuries that the werewolf was inflicting on her already-mangled body, she sank her fangs deep into its neck.

As the blood poured down her throat, it served to both satisfy the beast and increase its yearning. Werewolf blood was much more potent than the blood of mere mortals. As pint after pint of the thick, warm fluid flowed down her throat, she was in ecstasy.

Warm blood had never tasted so good, and it was the only thing in the world. All else was nothing. She would continue drinking until this werewolf was nothing but a husk. Of course, the five remaining mortals with shotguns had a different plan for her. She was about to pay the price for losing control.

Feeding on the werewolf was an excellent method of destroying it. Unfortunately, it required Danielle to remain relatively still. Since the werewolf was no longer struggling, she didn't have to move at all. The beast didn't care, so long as it got the blood it craved.

This had been just the opening that the mortals had been waiting for, and they were quick to exploit it. All five fired as one, and they quickly emptied their weapons into the unmoving vampire before them. The results were devastating.

Danielle was firmly in the grip of the beast. All that mattered was the blood she was drinking. Even so, over a dozen phosphorous shotgun rounds striking her in the back in rapid succession was enough to get the beast's attention. She glared at her attackers, eyes filled with pure fury, and they simply ceased to exist.

The mortals were no longer a threat, but the damage had been done. Danielle collapsed, the phosphorous continuing to burn an enormous hole through her back and into her chest. Her spine had been destroyed, and she was unable to get back to her feet.

As she lay battered, broken, and bleeding on the rooftop, the beast began to recede. She was dying, and that realization was enough to shock her back into partial control of herself. Not that it would do much good.

Danielle knew she was out of immediate danger from her attackers, but there was still an elder werewolf out there somewhere. She had to get away. Her wounds began to heal automatically, but it wasn't enough. Moving her head slightly, she was able to bring her wounds into view.

There was a jagged hole where her ribcage used to be, and if not for her advanced age, she would already be dead. Her wounds immediately sealed, which stopped her blood loss, but they wouldn't heal on their own. She would have to focus her remaining power.

It would have been so much easier to just lie there on the rooftop and die, and the only thing keeping her from doing just that was her love for John. She wouldn't abandon him without a fight. There had to be a way out this.

She had just drained a werewolf completely. Much of that blood had been splattered across the rooftop, but several pints of it still remained inside her. She focused on the potency of that blood now and the power it represented. She forced it through her body, forced her flesh and bone to regenerate.

Slowly but steadily, the hole in her back and chest closed. Danielle could feel her bones gradually reforming. A few moments later, she was able to stand, and most signs of her injuries had vanished. She was no longer dying, but she was far from out of danger.

Odds were that the elder werewolf wasn't going to just let her escape. She had barely enough blood to stay alive, let alone fight a battle. Perhaps she could charge back in the direction of their haven. If she got close enough, John would be able to help. It probably wouldn't work, but it was the only plan that she had.

Then Danielle heard the sound she had been dreading, a low rumbling growl that was slowly gaining strength and volume and she realized her plan had come too late. The elder werewolf was back.

Spinning around, Danielle saw the beast moving slowly across the rooftop toward her. She held no illusions that the monster may be injured or even afraid. Most likely it was just being cautious after seeing what she had done to its friends.

There was no way out. She no longer had the power to even think of outrunning the wolf, and her body held too little blood to support her magic, which left her few options. The beast didn't know how weak she was, or it would have attacked her already, but it would find out soon enough.

"Don't suppose you'll let me walk away, huh?" The werewolf answered with an unbelievably loud roar and raised itself to its full impressive height. "Didn't think so. Well, here goes nothing," she mumbled to herself.

Danielle drew her remaining sword and attacked. She still possessed nine centuries worth of skill in hand-to-hand combat. As long as her sword could pierce the beast's hide, she had a chance.

The werewolf slashed and clawed at Danielle's throat and chest. She ducked low and attempted to drive her sword into the beast's heart with the strength that only an ancient vampire could muster. The sword didn't even penetrate a full inch before snapping.

No! The beast's hide was too tough for normal bladed weapons. Danielle should have tried to run, but she fought on. As she blocked and evaded the werewolf's constant attacks, her right hand changed, the fingers becoming six-inch claws. Bladed weapons may not work, but nothing would stop a vampire's claws or fangs.

It seemed like a good idea under the circumstances. Unfortunately, it was also Danielle's final mistake. Elder vampires were superior to werewolves because they were smarter. They knew that you did not kill werewolves hand to hand. You killed werewolves at a distance, with mind control or with magic. If you insisted on attacking a werewolf physically, you did so with superior weapons. John may have been able to defeat the beast hand to hand, but that was because he had always specialized in that type of fighting.

Danielle would have been hard pressed to win this fight, even if she was in top form. She didn't care. There was nowhere left for her to go. If she had to die, then she would go down fighting. All this ran through Danielle's mind as she raised her arm for a strike at the beast's throat.

The werewolf saw the attack coming and moved quickly to defend against it. It was close, but the werewolf's claws were faster. They easily severed her right arm at the shoulder, and the arm turned to dust before it even hit the ground.

Pain and shock hit Danielle like a sledgehammer. Precious blood poured from her shoulder, and she lost control. The beast did not take control of her; she was too close to death for that. She merely lost control of her powers.

Danielle's left hand was locked onto the werewolf's right arm, holding it in place. A stream of fire unexpectedly exploded from her hand, igniting them both, and both warriors were blown back by the force of the explosion.

The fire spread across the werewolf's fur quickly, and the beast desperately tried to douse the flames. As Danielle's skin began to melt, she knew that she wasn't much better off. As a final act of desperation, she threw herself from the rooftop.

Once Danielle hit the pavement, she managed to roll around enough to extinguish the flames. As she lay there, staring at the sky and unable to move, she knew she was finished. It was too much to hope that the fire had destroyed the werewolf. Once it recovered from the flames, it would come back for her and there was no longer anything she could do to defend herself.

Danielle knew that she wasn't completely drained of blood. If that had been the case, she would have already turned to dust. Unfortunately, she didn't have enough blood left in her system to actually do anything other than just stay alive. Even if the werewolf didn't find her, the sun eventually would. *John won't even recognize the pile of ash that I'll be.* That brief thought gave her pause. She would never see her husband again.

She held no doubts that all vampires eventually ended up in hell, and odds were that hell wasn't very accommodating to lovers. *Oh, John! I don't want to die.* A single tear of blood slowly trickled down her charred cheek.

* * *

JOHN WOKE SUDDENLY and with a start. A moment's check revealed that Danielle wasn't in the haven. What had caused him to wake so suddenly? Something was very wrong.

Closing his eyes, John began to concentrate. He focused the full power of his mind, just as Danielle had taught him. Almost instantly he doubled over in intense anguish and pain.

At first it seemed as if the pain was his own. It didn't take long, however, for John to realize that he was merely sensing it from someone else. It was also fairly obvious who that someone else was.

John didn't waste another second. He grabbed a thermos and a sword, and he was gone. He didn't even bother to stop and dress first, not that anyone would notice at the speeds he would be moving.

The thermos was a precaution. If Danielle was in trouble or in danger, it could only be because she needed blood. Lack of blood was the only thing that could cause vampires of their age to be in any danger. Of course, the thermos only held two quarts, but it would hopefully be enough to offset whatever trouble his wife had stumbled into.

Time was of the essence, and John used large amounts of blood to increase his speed. He scoured the city, extending his senses for any clues he could find. At the same time, he reminded himself to stay cautious. Anything that could threaten Danielle's life was not to be taken lightly.

Finally John picked up a pair of suspicious smells charred flesh and the unmistakable stench of a werewolf. By themselves not overly strange, but together these smells were worth investigating. Werewolves didn't have the ability to set their prey on fire, but his wife did.

It took John another fifteen seconds to follow the smells to their source. What he saw was enough to cause him to set the thermos down and draw his sword. An elder werewolf was moving slowly down an alleyway toward an odd black shape.

The werewolf was huge but missing most of its hair. Wisps of smoke were coming off of its body, which led John to believe that the hair had been burned off. The werewolf was also favoring its right arm and didn't seem to notice John standing behind it.

He had to act fast. It seemed obvious what was happening. John just hoped he wasn't making a fatal mistake. If Danielle had attacked this werewolf and been unable to kill it, then it had to be much more powerful than it appeared. John's logic was sound; he just had no way of knowing that Danielle had been battling many attackers.

John charged forward, attempting to cut the werewolf's spine. Unfortunately, the sword snapped before even cutting into bone. He threw the useless pommel to the side as the werewolf turned to face him.

John's hands became claws as he traded blows with the beast. The outcome was never really in doubt. The werewolf simply wasn't fast enough. In less than a minute, John finished the fight by punching through the werewolf's chest and squeezing its heart until it burst.

An elder werewolf's blood was very potent, and John didn't waste a drop as he drained the beast. Once finished, he tossed the dried-up husk aside. He still didn't know where his wife was, but he decided to check out the black shape that the werewolf had been moving toward. It was probably just an unlucky mortal, but maybe John could put him out of his misery.

As he got closer to the body, John's bad feeling returned. He needed to hurry and finish off this mortal so he could continue searching for his wife. Of course, from the looks of it, the mortal wouldn't need any finishing.

The body was barely recognizable as human. One of the arms was missing. The flesh was charred and half-melted away. The body also seemed to be half-crushed, as if it had fallen from the top of one of the surrounding buildings.

The stench was horrible, especially to someone with heightened senses. John was about to leave to continue his search, but something was still nagging at the back of his mind. There was something odd about the corpse's face.

Looking very closely, John saw what looked like a dried, red trail leading from the corner of the corpse's eye. Given how badly burned the surrounding flesh was, it was difficult to be certain of what he was seeing. It looked like a tear trail, but red? He touched it, and a piece of red flaked off onto his finger. A taste revealed that it was blood.

An icy hand gripped John's undead heart. There was only one creature in the world that cried tears of blood. He reached forward slowly and gently parted the charred lips, an act which caused small pieces of flesh to flake off the area. Gleaming, white fangs showed in sharp contrast against the blackened lips that had covered them. There was no doubt in his mind; this blackened husk of a corpse was his wife.

Oh my God, I'm too late. Even as he thought it, John knew that it couldn't be true. Danielle was over nine hundred years old. If she had died, she would have immediately turned to dust, and this realization did wonders to lift his spirits.

Of course, his wife was still in grave danger and could die any second. The fact that she wasn't responding to him, but wasn't a pile of dust, meant that she had just enough blood to survive. The instant that blood ran out, she was finished.

John wasted no more time on reflection. He immediately retrieved the thermos, unscrewed the lid, and carefully poured some of the blood into Danielle's open mouth. When she had a mouthful, he stopped pouring and waited to see what would happen.

For a few seconds, there was no response, but then John saw her throat muscles begin to flex. It was difficult to see, since the skin was melted and charred. Slowly, the level of blood in her mouth began to recede.

John continued feeding her blood, mouthful by mouthful, until the thermos was empty. A half-gallon of blood wasn't enough to even begin repairing the damage that had been done to her body, but it was better than nothing. It should be enough to at least let her be more responsive.

Danielle's eyes slowly opened, and she began to move her remaining hand. John placed his hand on top of hers and held it in place. He then placed a finger over his lips. The message was clear. *Don't move, don't speak, just drink.*

John turned one of his fingers into a claw and slashed open his forearm. He directed the blood pouring out of his arm into Danielle's mouth. As the seconds ticked past, she grew stronger and was able to swallow the blood fast enough to not waste any.

After several minutes, John stopped her and allowed the gash in his arm to heal. He guessed that he had poured several pints of blood into her. It would be dangerous for him to give her any more, since his own supply was running low.

Looking at Danielle's body, John wasn't able to see much of a difference. She didn't look quite as crushed as she had before, so some of her bones must have reformed, and she was able to move under her own power again, but that was all.

John was stunned. So much blood and that was the only difference in her condition? Neither of them had ever been this wounded before. He had to get her back to the haven. There, and with the help of their ghouls, they had access to an almost unlimited supply of blood. He carefully lifted his wife off the ground and carried her back to safety.

John had been far too distracted by Danielle's near death to pay any attention to his surroundings. Since he had no idea what had happened, he merely assumed that the werewolf had been the only threat. He hadn't noticed the eyes that had been observing them from the other side of the street. Eyes that closed now as their owner hurried off to report to his master.

Chapter 4

"SO YOU ARE certain that the vampire survived, my son?"

"Unfortunately, Excellency, yes. It was difficult to believe, even after seeing it with my own eyes. I believe that I was lucky to have escaped with my life."

"If I may ask, my son, how did you manage to escape?" The young soldier looked nervous, as if he were afraid that the archbishop would be angry that he failed to fight to the death.

"I'm not certain, Excellency. The female was not destroyed, but she appeared to be incapacitated. At the end, she made no move to defend herself against the approaching werewolf.

"If the male had not arrived when he did, the werewolf would have finished her. It was strange. Once the male dispatched the werewolf, he seemed to be consumed with grief and concern for his partner. He appeared to share some blood with her and then grabbed her and left.

"I didn't think that vampires could actually feel concern for one another, but I am thankful that he did. His preoccupation with his partner's well-being was probably the only thing that kept him from sensing my presence. Forgive me, Excellency, if I acted in error, but it seemed more important to get this information to you than to commit suicide by attacking them both."

"You made the right decision, my son. Thank you for your foresight. You are dismissed." The young soldier bowed deeply and left.

Archbishop Jenkins was deeply troubled. That young soldier had been the sole survivor of the force that had successfully ambushed the female vampire. They had all drastically underestimated her power, and now four werewolves and sixteen good men had paid the price.

The only positive thing about the entire engagement was that they had proven that the monster wasn't invincible. If the young soldier's report was accurate, then the vampire had wiped out the entire attack force but at a severe cost. If it hadn't been for the intervention of the male, the monster would have been destroyed.

That caused the archbishop even more concern. How did the male find her at just the right moment? One thing was certain. These vampires were far more powerful than he had originally guessed. They also acted differently than vampires were supposed to.

It was always possible that vampires more powerful than the two they now faced existed, but he didn't know of any. It had been centuries since the SOG had dealt with more than one elder vampire in the same area, and Jenkins prayed that he had the necessary resources to deal with them now. He considered it fortunate that they were even able to discover their presence.

The only reason he had even been in the area was that he was in the middle of conducting his annual inspections. It wasn't required, but Jenkins would, at least once a year, pay a visit to the various cities that he was responsible for protecting. When he wasn't touring his area of operations, the archbishop ran things from his base in New York City.

It seemed that God had placed him at the right place at the right time. That was the only logical conclusion that the archbishop could reach. He was not one to believe in coincidences.

That thought helped to harden his resolve. *God may help me to see, but He will not do my work for me.* Jenkins knew what must be done. All he had to do was carefully consider all the information at his disposal.

He had learned some important information, which he would use to plan his next move. First and most important was the fact that it would be nearly impossible to ambush either vampire individually again, since the element of surprise had been lost. Secondly, the male vampire had to be considered at least as powerful as the female had proven to be. Lastly, and the only positive information so far, the ambush had proven the monsters' power had its limits.

Archbishop Jenkins had access to literally thousands of men and dozens of werewolves along the eastern coast. All he needed to do was call them in. There were no other major concerns anywhere in his area of responsibility. There were always suspected vampires under investigation, or other minor rogue demons to destroy, but nothing even approaching the magnitude of what they now faced. He would call in a full battalion of his best warriors and werewolves. They could all be in the city by the end of week.

At the same time, Jenkins would devote a significant portion of his intelligence resources to discovering the demons' haven. Investigating blood banks and blood donor centers may also prove helpful. *Yes,* the archbishop thought to himself, *we may have suffered a small setback, but the Sword of God will always triumph in the end.*

Jenkins sent a courier to inform his superiors of the current situation, and then he set about putting his plans into motion.

* * *

IT HAD BEEN five days since the ambush. Five days since John had barely managed to rescue his wife. Five days and nights that she had remained submerged in a bathtub filled with blood, and five days and nights that John had stayed at her side.

They say that necessity is the key to invention, and John's little bathtub idea was proof. In the alley John had been able to give Danielle several pints of his own blood in a short amount of time. She had latched on to his forearm and drank quickly.

It must have been a reflexive act of desperation, for once he had gotten her back to the haven, he had tried the same method without success. The blood merely filled her mouth and quickly spilled over. The strength that she had exhibited in the alley was gone.

John did not understand how to help her properly. They had been injured many times in the past nine hundred years. He had also seen countless other vampires die. Neither of them, however, had experience with injuries this severe. He did not know how a vampire would react to being brought to the brink of death.

They had both heard stories of elder vampires going into a deep sleep, similar to a human coma. Supposedly, it was a response to severe injury, blood loss, or simply being tired of their current existence. Their bodies would simply shut down, rather than running out of blood and turning to ash, and they would reawaken days, years, or even decades later. That is, if the stories were true.

Danielle had still been able to swallow blood, but only one mouthful at a time. At the rate of only a mouthful at a time, it would take weeks to feed her enough blood to heal herself. They did not have that kind of time, although it was hopeful in that it meant the "vampiric coma" theory was not true in this case. Probably.

John needed her healed as soon as possible, so they could find out who was responsible for the attack. He placed her charred and broken body in the bathtub and tried to decide what to do. It was then that the idea came to him.

John figured they didn't have anything to lose by trying, so he instructed her ghouls to fill the bathtub with as much blood as they could. It took them about twenty minutes, but when they finished, Danielle lay submerged in blood. He then dismissed the ghouls and sat back to see what would happen.

It took several hours, but eventually the level of blood in the bathtub began receding. As soon as the blood receded enough, John ordered the ghouls to refill the tub. It seemed that his idea would work, so all that remained was for him to sit and wait for his wife to finish healing.

Throughout the last five days and nights, the ghouls that ran the hotel all came to lend their support to their fallen master. Every one of them appeared to be sick with grief. This caused John to realize a problem he had not foreseen. All the ghouls that worked in the hotel were Danielle's.

John's ghouls had come to the hotel once already to drain him of the blood necessary to keep them alive. Unfortunately, Danielle could not be drained at the moment. Every drop of blood that she was absorbing right now was being used to heal her.

The ghouls that were coming in to visit their fallen master didn't look sick from grieving; they looked sick because they were dying. John could do nothing about it except hope that his wife finished healing soon. It had taken them decades to assemble the number of ghouls they had now without raising any suspicions.

If all Danielle's ghouls were to die, the hotel would no longer have a staff and the same could said for their blood bank. They would have to move to another city, and John did not think that moving was a good idea right now, not with something apparently hunting them. John's experience being a hunter for nearly a millennium told him that running away never worked in real life. Real hunters never quit until they either caught their prey or were killed themselves.

He had been given much time to think over the last five days, and he no longer believed that his wife's attacker had been only a single werewolf. No werewolf could have done this kind of damage to a nine-hundred-year-old vampire. A werewolf could possibly have killed her, certainly, but not beaten her this badly and thoroughly *without* killing her. It simply wasn't possible. There was something out there seeking to destroy them, and until his wife recovered enough to tell him what had happened, he was clueless as to what it might be.

John looked over to where Sam had fallen asleep in his chair. He had insisted on being allowed to remain with his master at this time of grief. Unfortunately Sam was still mostly human, and had to succumb to sleep eventually.

A common misconception about vampires was that they had to sleep during the day or else fall victim to the sun's rays. This well-known "fact" was almost a complete myth. It was true that the rays of the sun would destroy a vampire, even one as powerful as John, but they didn't have to sleep during the daylight hours.

Most vampires did, in fact, sleep during the day. This was because of the extreme weakness that came over them. They also healed much faster when they were asleep. So, it was a more convenient time for them to rest, but by no means was it a necessity of their existence.

However, John had opted to forego sleep for the last five days so that he could better monitor any changes in his wife's condition.

"Sam, wake up." John spoke quietly. Sam stirred slightly but remained asleep. John stood up and walked over to where he was sleeping. Sam woke after a slight shaking of his shoulders, although it took him a moment to realize who was waking him.

"I beg forgiveness, master. I was only resting my eyes. They grew tired from observing your glory for so long." Sam appeared properly chastised and sincere, but John knew better. His face split into a grin as he returned to his seat.

"It's not my fault you were born a human, Sam. Oh, and it's not considered resting your eyes after over seven hours; it's called sleeping on the job. If your eyes are that tired, because of my glory, then it is only fair that I correct the problem.

"I'll gouge both your eyes out and buy you the best glass eyes on the market. It's the least I can do for my most faithful servant." Any of his newer ghouls would be cowering in fear by now, but not Sam. Sam merely laughed briefly, winked at his master, and began to stretch the sleep from his muscles.

"Seriously though, sir, what's up?" Sam joked around with both John and Danielle a lot, but he knew that his master wouldn't have awakened him unless he had a task.

"Just a few questions. You pay attention to our logistics a lot better than I do, Sam. How much longer can Danielle's ghouls survive without more blood?" All traces of humor on Sam's face were instantly replaced with a look of seriousness.

"Not long, sir. Unfortunately, the timing couldn't be worse. The day she was injured was the day she was scheduled to be drained, and our stocks had already been depleted. The first ghouls won't die for another three days, but they'll be unable to function properly in about another twenty-four hours. I don't have to tell you what that means, sir." It meant that they were in a lot of trouble.

Their haven was the entire top floor of the hotel, but all the other floors were rooms for regular humans. It was excellent cover, but it did present interesting problems. If the hotel staff began to act strangely, someone would notice. Word would quickly spread, and people would begin asking questions.

He doubted that it would go so far as to someone figuring out what they truly were, but it didn't have to. Whatever was hunting them already knew what they were. Problems with the hotel would make it easier for them to be discovered.

"Honestly though, sir, how much longer could it possibly take?"

"I don't know, Sam. Neither of us has ever been this badly injured before. All I know is that the last few times her body was exposed, it looked healed, at least on the outside. It shouldn't be too much longer." They stopped talking as another ghoul entered the room to refill the pitcher of blood John had been drinking from.

John looked at the ghoul's face closely. Her eyes were bloodshot, and her skin was ghostly pale. There was also what looked like a bad rash spreading across her face and trailing down her chest. The ghoul left before John could say anything to her.

"She is one of the worst cases, sir. So far there aren't too many that are that bad, so we have been able to keep them out of sight of the human guests here. Twenty-four hours from now, however, there will be too many like that to hide them." John nodded in understanding as he drank from his pitcher.

He stared at the bathtub full of blood that concealed his wife. Occasionally he could detect a small ripple on the surface, but that was the only change. *C'mon, love, what's taking so long? Come back to me.* As if in answer to his silent request, blood was suddenly thrown everywhere.

Danielle's upper body had broken the surface as if from a large convulsion. With eyes closed and fangs bared, she hissed, sounding like an animal in intense pain. She immediately straightened herself, opened her eyes, and scanned the room.

The instant her eyes locked onto John's, she leapt out of the bathtub, splashing more blood across the room, and went straight for his throat. John didn't know what was going on. If the beast had retained control over her, Danielle wouldn't hesitate to sink her fangs into his throat. Sam immediately got over his shock and drew his weapon, ready to come to the aide of his master.

John was about to signal him to attack when he realized he hadn't been bitten yet. Danielle wasn't attacking him, she was clinging to him. A second later he realized that she wasn't trying to bite him either, she was kissing him. He responded to his wife in kind and then remembered Sam was still ready to attack.

"It's fine, she's okay. Get some towels and a robe," John looked around at the blood that covered almost everything in the room, "and get this place cleaned up." Satisfied that his master was not in any danger, Sam put his weapon away.

"Yes, sir." With that, he left the room, and John could hear him handing out orders as he ran to one of the hotel's many supply closets. Satisfied that the situation was well in hand, John turned back to the wife that had been returned to him.

"I thought I lost you," he whispered softly into her ear.

"You did," she answered, "but then you found me." She pulled back slightly and allowed her husband to look her over. It was hard to believe that the beautiful creature standing before him had been nothing but a charred, broken corpse a few days before.

Her smooth skin was covered in blood, and her long hair was soaked with it. John could also see fresh blood pouring from her eyes in small droplets that traced fresh streaks along her cheeks. *She's crying.* As much as they wanted to just stand there and hold each other for the rest of the night, they both knew that there were things that had to be done.

"My love, I have to tell you what happened."

John shook his head and held up a hand to stop her protest. "Later. First we need to get you cleaned up. Then you have to feed your ghouls." Danielle's shocked expression told John she had just realized that they couldn't feed while she was healing.

"How long?"

"Five days."

"Did we lose any?"

"No, but there a few that are very close. Once we get everything stabilized here, you can tell me what happened. Sam and I want every detail. Then we'll start to come up with some plans." It wasn't odd that John wanted Sam to be present for her explanation. Sam had been with them for over a hundred years, and they kept him posted on everything they did.

Keeping Sam in the loop was the best way for him to command their ghouls properly. Combined they had over one hundred ghouls, and Sam was in command of them all. That many ghouls represented a very powerful force to contend with. It allowed them to possibly plan a daytime strike against anything that threatened them. More importantly, Danielle liked Sam. He was a nice guy.

"Agreed. I'll take care of my ghouls, love. Why don't you get some rest. When I'm finished, I'll come wake you." John nodded as several ghouls entered the room and began cleaning.

"Sam?"

"I know, sir. I'll keep an eye on everything here. You need to get some rest." John nodded his thanks and went to bed.

* * *

"THAT'S EVERYTHING I remember." It had taken a few hours for Danielle to get cleaned up and feed all of her ghouls. Afterward, she had awakened John and found Sam, and now the three of them sat around a table with drinks while she related everything she remembered about the ambush. Danielle also decided to tell John about the surprise attack that was made on her a few nights before the ambush.

John was not pleased to hear that she had withheld this information. The only explanation was that the attacker she had left alive had belonged to whatever group was hunting them. He must have simply noticed her during his nightly travels and tried to take her down alone.

When Danielle proved to be far more powerful than he had expected, he reported the situation to his superiors. Then, they had set up the ambush that had nearly killed her. They had to assume that they knew she was still alive. The real question was what were they going to do next?

"Mortals and werewolves working together? I don't like this. Sounds like something far more organized and well-established than some random group of vampire hunters. They organized a powerful ambush against you, and only three nights after the first attack." John shook his head. "No, I don't like this at all."

"I agree that the situation doesn't seem very good, my love, but there are other things that I don't understand. In order for them to do what they did, it would have been necessary for them to observe us, or at least me. It's obvious that they haven't found our haven, or else they would have attacked us here during the day.

"So if they know who we are, or at least what we look like, they are most likely observing us out on the street." John nodded, following her logic so far. "Well, why haven't we noticed? The only two times that I have noticed anything wrong in the last few weeks was right before each attack.

"These people are just mortals. There is no way a werewolf could stalk us without us smelling it, so it has to be the humans that are doing the stalking. How could any mortal even stare at us without us sensing it?" She threw up a hand in frustration.

"Good question. I haven't noticed anything wrong at all, but they also haven't tried to attack me yet. I suppose it's possible they don't know about me, but I'd guess that they do. If either of us were to notice that something was wrong, it would be you. The fact that you haven't concerns me. I can't explain it."

"If I may?" Sam set down his glass of brandy and appeared ready to say something.

"Of course." John was willing to hear any suggestion at this point.

"I don't know the entire problem. These mortals are obviously better trained than normal humans, and it seems they were trained specifically to hunt vampires. That would make a big difference if you two were both fledglings, but you're not.

"No amount of training should be able to help a mortal conceal themselves from you, at least not by itself. Unfortunately, I have noticed something over the last several decades, but it was never a problem, so I continued to mind my own business. I was also afraid that you would be displeased with my observations, and I would get my throat ripped out.

"We are facing a well-organized, well-established, and well-trained organization of unknown size and power, and they have chosen to hunt you two down. Are we all in agreement so far?" John and Danielle both nodded. "Okay, in light of this information, I feel I must mention what has been bothering me more and more over the last few decades. Please, don't kill me." There was no humor in his voice or expression. Sam actually feared that what he had to say would displease his master to the point of his own execution.

"You know better than that, Sam. Speak your mind. That's why we keep you around. Besides, anything you can tell us that might help would be useful." Sam took a deep breath and looked his master straight in the eye.

"Okay, you've gone soft. You both have." The shock was visible on both vampires' faces. To have a mortal tell them that they'd gone soft was preposterous. "Please hear me out. Remember back when we spent those twenty years in Asia?" They both nodded.

"We ran into everything. Cults, werewolves, pickpockets, other vampires, and a few things I still don't know what they were. I was still young for a ghoul, but I was old enough to have gotten over the delusions that you two were gods. Even so, I was amazed by you both for those twenty years. I've never seen either of you as good as you were back then.

"Since we left Asia, we've traveled through all of Europe, and North America together, and you both finally decided to settle here. Since we left Asia, I have also noticed a steady decline in your alertness. But it's understandable.

"Europe and North America are both run by politics and businessmen, not superstition, like those areas in Asia were. There aren't nearly as many threats here to worry about, and you both know it. Back in Asia, it seemed like everyone we talked to knew you were vampires just by looking at you, and we had to watch our backs at every turn. Here, almost no one truly believes that demons and vampires even exist.

"I think that it's a combination of having very few threats standing in your way and being complacent because of your power. Whatever it is, it's obvious to me, and it may be what has kept you from noticing that you're being spied on. You haven't been trying to notice because you don't think that it's possible."

John took a moment to consider what Sam had said before responding. His first reaction was to be angry, but the more he thought about Sam's words, the more they made sense. Danielle met his gaze and gave a slight nod. Apparently, she agreed with Sam.

"Well, I hate to admit it, Sam, but you may be right. I honestly don't consider anything around here to be threatening to me, so I don't pay as much attention as I should. You'd think I'd have learned better in the last nine centuries."

"You're not the only one, love. I admit that I suffer from the same problem. At least it is something that is easily rectified. Now that we have an idea as to why we haven't been able to detect their spies, we'll just pay more attention to our surroundings. Thank you for pointing this out to us, Sam."

"Yeah, thanks for being blunt."

When Sam realized that neither vampire was going to kill him, his humor came back in force. "Someone has to look out for you two, what with you being so old and all."

Both vampires grinned, but John was quick to steer them back on track.

"Okay, so we can most likely prevent ourselves from being spied on. That's good, but we need to find out more info on them. Whoever these people are, they will eventually defeat us if we do not take the offensive. They have too many resources, and they know exactly what they are up against." Danielle nodded in agreement but didn't offer any additional information.

"I have an idea, sir." John motioned for Sam to continue.

"Well, we basically just established that if you two are paying attention, you'll know the instant that you are being spied upon, correct?"

"Basically, yes. Then we can easily find and eliminate the spy before he can report any more information about us." Sam shook his head.

"You could find and eliminate the spy, but then he or she wouldn't be alive for you to track to his base." Realization dawned on John's face, and Danielle merely grinned wolfishly.

"Well, I'll be damned." After realizing what he had just said, John quickly added, "No pun intended."

"What I propose, sir, is that the two of you continue doing exactly what you've been doing. When you notice that you're being spied on, find the spy and then conceal yourselves. I don't care how well-trained they are, no mortal can track elder vampires who are purposefully concealing themselves.

"Whoever is spying on you will just assume you've left, and eventually he or she'll return to base. Once you see where it is, just hurry back to the haven, and we can make plans to attack the following night. We can even have a few ghouls help out, just in case the spy doesn't make it back to his base before dawn." Sam picked his drink up and leaned back in his seat, a sure sign that he was finished.

"Actually, that sounds like an excellent plan. Since we'll actually be trying from now on, it'll be easy to keep ourselves hidden when we want to. Also, until this is over, neither one of us is leaving this haven alone. No more of your midnight strolls or whatever it is that you've been doing, love." Danielle made an agreeable noise but looked disappointed for a reason John couldn't fathom.

"Okay, love, I agree that this is the best plan we have. When should we start?"

"It'll be dawn in an hour or so, so we should wait until tonight. And then we'll keep trying, every night until it works. Anything else?"

"One more thing, sir. While you two are asleep today, I'm going to try and scrounge up a few remote transmitters for the three of us to wear. I want to be able to stay in contact with you at all times.

"I'll have twenty armed ghouls ready to move at a moment's notice. If something happens, just tell me where, and we'll be there as soon as possible." Leave it to Sam to find some way to include himself into the action.

"Good idea, Sam. You're on a roll today," Danielle hadn't said much since she delivered her explanation of what had happened, but something in her voice told John she had something more to add. "One final thing. Don't underestimate them."

"Agreed, my love, as long as they have werewolves working with them, we must remain careful."

"I was talking about the humans. We cannot afford to underestimate them."

"I don't understand, ma'am. Other than the werewolves, what possible threat could a few mortals pose for the two of you?" John didn't say anything, but he had a look of confusion on his face. *What is my wife getting at?*

"First of all, Sam, we have no idea how many mortals we are facing. Secondly, we know they are trained to fight vampires. Until we discover just what abilities they have, we need to be wary." John had a feeling he had figured out where she was going with this.

"Sam, you have seen firsthand the power of the magic that both my husband and I wield. We never told you where we got that power, did we?"

"Uh, no, ma'am, I just assumed that it came with being a vampire." She smiled at him.

"No, Sam. Many of our powers do come from beings vampires, but the actual magic does not."

"Then how " She silenced him with a raised hand.

"Let me tell you a story, and maybe you'll see why you should never underestimate a trained human."

Chapter 5

1142 AD

THEY WANDERED aimlessly through the forest. John and Danielle both needed to feed, and they needed to feed soon. Neither of them had ever gone this long without blood before, and they were unprepared for the effects that the hunger had on them. They had been like this for days, ever since the fight with that ... thing, whatever it was.

It had been just over fifty years since they had become vampires, but neither of them was keeping track of time very well. With the exception of their old coterie, which they had destroyed, they hadn't run into single vampire, and they began to fear that they were even more alone than they felt. Only recently had they begun to accept and attempt to embrace their new existence.

The first few decades following their time with the coterie were a blur. They consumed just enough blood to stay alive, and they refused to feed on humans. This was common for many younger vampires, but they had held on to their past longer than most.

However, once they decided that they would not kill themselves, things began to change. They began to slowly come to grips with what they had become, and to experiment with the new abilities they had acquired since becoming vampires. The only thing that they had not yet accepted was the need to feed on humans. They both insisted on using animals instead. Animals provided enough blood for them, if they hunted enough, but the blood was of a lesser quality. John and Danielle were still too young to understand exactly how the blood worked in their remade bodies.

They were always hungry because the lesser quality of animal blood caused it to be used up much faster. It caused them to have to spend most of their time hunting. One positive thing about their situation was that nearly constant hunting gave them both ample opportunities to master their skills.

Things had been beginning to look up for them over the last few years. They had decided that immortality together was a blessing, not a curse. There were many things that they still did not understand, but they decided to just discover them together.

At the moment, however, things were not looking positive at all. In fact, they were both certain that they would not live through the night. It had been three nights since that horrible thing had attacked them, and they still didn't fully understand what happened.

They had been wandering through the forest after a good night of hunting. With several hours left until sunrise, they had been trying to decide where they wanted to visit and what they wanted to see. What good was immortality if they didn't take advantage of it? It was in the midst of this good-natured debate that they had heard growling from up ahead, but they weren't the least bit concerned. In fact, this sort of thing happened all the time. They would end up strolling through some random animal's territory, and whatever animal it was would get angry and attack them for the intrusion. They would simply kill the animal, get some extra blood for the evening, and continue on their way. Sometimes, Danielle would use the opportunity to practice the mind control abilities that she had recently discovered.

This was just another one of those times, or so they had thought. This animal had sounded quite large, but that didn't bother them at the time. This deep into the forest, it was not uncommon to encounter several varieties of large animals that most had never seen. In reality it was rather exciting.

"You can have this one, love," Danielle had told him. She had then backed soundlessly into the undergrowth to his right. This would hopefully cause the animal to ignore her and charge John instead. It was, after all, his turn.

They both carried a pair of swords and several knives they had acquired throughout the decades. One of the only useful things their sire had told them was that even though they were now vampires, they should make sure to always be armed. Vampires that went into battle unarmed would most likely die. Immortality did not make them indestructible.

John decided against drawing one of his swords. It was, after all, just an animal. He instead forced a bit a blood into his hands, turning both sets of fingers into long, razor-sharp claws. Once ready, he simply stood there, waiting for an attack that never came.

John waited for a few moments, but all that answered him was a disturbing silence. As he was about to decide that the animal had simply left, he heard a series of loud roars, growls, hisses, and crashes from somewhere off to his right. Concern grew within him. He recognized the voice behind some of those noises, and from the sound of the roars, whatever was attacking them was very big.

John quickly turned his right set of claws back into a normal hand and drew one of his swords. An instant before he jumped into the underbrush to come to his wife's aide, the largest monster he had ever seen stepped out in front of him. Monster was the only word John could think of to describe the beast that now stood before him, and he was momentarily stunned by its appearance.

It stood on its hind legs and was nearly twice his size. Muscles seemed to bulge from every possible place over its entire body, and claws that rivaled his own extended from both of the creature's hands. The only thing about the monster that didn't seem right was the shape of its jaw. It was very odd. When John realized why, he was horrified.

Its jaws were perfectly normal. The odd shape was due to the body of his wife, which was clutched between the creature's teeth. The creature tossed its head from side to side a few times before releasing its hold on Danielle, sending her limp form cartwheeling through the air before crashing into a large tree.

It was enough to shock John out of his stupor, and he charged the monster with everything he had. He might have no idea what the creature was, but its scent confirmed that it was a living being, and it would pay dearly for attacking his wife. It would pay with its life.

The battle was brief and incredibly violent—simply a blur of fangs, claws, fur, and metal that was too fast for mere human eyes to track. John was receiving much more damage than he was dishing out, but the beast seemed to be losing ground. He didn't understand why, but that didn't stop him from taking advantage of it.

John was very young for a vampire of that time period. He had no idea that he was fighting a werewolf, and an elder werewolf at that. No one ever explained to him that werewolves existed, and that they hated vampires more than anything.

* * *

THE WEREWOLF, on the other hand, knew exactly what he was fighting—two very young vampires, so the battle should have been quick and simple for him. However, luck had not been with him this night. The vampire had scored a lucky hit on him, which would doom him very soon if the situation did not change.

The werewolf's one major weakness against vampires this young was his mortality. The vampire, on the other hand, only had to deal with blood loss; no other type of injury would significantly affect its combative abilities. Unfortunately, the same could not be said for the werewolf himself. In addition to blood loss, broken bones, internal injuries, and fatigue were grave dangers for him.

To his advantage, the vampire's sword was next to useless against his strong hide. This information allowed the beast to concentrate on defending himself against the vampire's claws.

A vampire's claws, much like a werewolf's, could slice through anything. The vampire obviously did not possess this information because he continued to concentrate on using his sword instead. He didn't seem to notice that even solid blows with the weapon were doing little more than slicing off clumps of fur.

Unfortunately, even with the werewolf's advantages and knowledge, there was one thing that he didn't know. He was not simply fighting a young vampire. He was fighting one who had just seen his wife nearly ripped apart.

The vampire managed to deliver one solid hit to the werewolf's right side. The claws bit very deeply, cutting through muscle tissue, tendon, and bone as if they were nothing. By itself, that one successful attack would not be nearly enough to even the odds. But that was when the beast realized he was very unlucky today.

Two of the werewolf's severed ribs punched several holes into his right lung, and that changed everything. As a mortal creature, the werewolf needed to breath. With only one working lung, it was impossible for the beast to draw in enough air to fuel his entire body.

So the werewolf began to fall back. He needed to buy time until he could heal his internal injuries. This shouldn't have been difficult for the healing abilities of an elder werewolf, but the damn vampire just wouldn't let up. He seemed to have realized that his sword was useless, because the weapon was now lying on the ground and he was using two sets of claws.

The werewolf knew that if he wanted to live, the fight needed to end now. Focusing all of his remaining strength, he wrapped a massive clawed hand around the vampire's chest and squeezed. This froze the vampire in mid-attack.

The werewolf used the momentary interruption to get his jaws around the vampire's neck. One final bite and it would be over. This would not be a fight that he would care to reflect on in the future. Being brought this close to death by a single young vampire? What was wrong with him?

* * *

JOHN KNEW THAT he was in serious danger. He seemed to be doing well, despite the extensive damage that he had taken already. For some reason his sword was useless, so he discarded it and used his claws instead. With two sets of claws, John was doing even better against the beast, but that's when it all changed.

The beast struck out faster than John thought possible and wrapped its claws around his entire chest. When he felt the monster begin to squeeze, John forced as much blood into his chest as possible.

It was a struggle between powers, but he thought he would be able to recover easily. It was then that John realized he had been tricked.

He noticed too late the jaws that were beginning to close around his throat. The strike to his chest had simply been something to distract him, and he had fallen for it. The beast was easily open to attack, but he would never be able to strike fast enough. John didn't know much about vampires, but he knew that decapitation would kill him, and that was what was about to happen.

What hurt worst wasn't the injuries he had suffered. It wasn't even the knowledge that he was going to die very soon. What hurt the worst was the fact that he had failed. He had failed his wife, the only thing left in the world that he cared about.

He closed his eyes, tears of blood flowing freely from them, and waited for death. Instead of death, however, something strange happened.

John didn't see what, but something happened that made the beast let go. One second he could hear the monster's growls, smell its foul stench, and feel the press of its fangs. In the next instant, instead of biting down, the beast suddenly pulled its fangs away from John's throat.

When John felt the clawed hand around his chest slowly relax its grip, his confusion grew. He slowly opened his eyes to see what had happened, and relief swelled within him. The monster's headless corpse was slowly collapsing in front of him. The head lay off to the side, its jaws locked open in death. Standing behind the beast's body was Danielle, her claws slowly returning to a normal hand.

John could hardly believe that his wife had survived the attack. Looking at her body, however, it was clear that it had been a close call. Her chest was a mess of deep wounds and loose flesh, where the beast had clamped his jaws down on her. Her upper body also seemed to be at an odd angle, compared to the rest of her. The impact with the tree must have broken her spine in several places.

"Danielle, you're alive!"

"Of course I am. Someone had to save your ass, my love, but that was still a little too close for my tastes. What the hell was that thing?" They both hobbled over to a large rock and rested against it.

"I don't have a clue, but it's dead now. Now might be a good time to heal, but then let's get the hell out of here. There might be more of them." Danielle nodded agreement, and they began recovering from the battle.

At the time neither of them realized how much danger they were really in. They had been able to fully heal, but in doing so, they depleted their supplies of blood. They hadn't been too concerned, since they both assumed hunting would solve their problems. Neither of them realized they had battled a werewolf, so they obviously didn't know what it meant to be in a werewolf's territory.

Werewolves are very territorial, especially as they age. When a werewolf takes up residence in the wild, which most of them did in those times, they stake out huge areas of land to call their home. They hunt, kill, or chase out anything that is in what they consider their territory.

Eventually the surrounding wildlife gets the idea and gives the beast whatever space it wants. Since John and Danielle had stumbled into the werewolf's territory, and since they were both vampires, the beast attacked them immediately. John and Danielle were victorious, but they killed the only living thing for miles around.

It didn't occur to either of them to feed from the body of the werewolf, so they confidently began to hunt. Three nights later, they were in much worse condition and far less confident. With no excess blood in their systems, their appearances began to suffer. They began to actually resemble walking corpses.

After three nights of hearing birds and insects but no other wildlife, they realized that they were missing something important. Of course, by then it was far too late. John stopped walking, sat down, and signaled Danielle to do the same.

"I don't understand why, but, except for birds and insects, this whole area is dead. It's time to admit that we're in serious trouble." Danielle nodded her agreement. In addition to their other problems, their beasts were also awakening. They were still too young to really understand how to suppress this reaction, and they both felt like they were slowly losing control.

"So what do we do now? I'm so hungry. I've never felt like this before." His wife's voice sounded a little too animalistic for John's taste. They didn't have much longer.

"I don't know, love. We should pick a direction and move as fast as we can in a straight line. We have to get out of this area. Maybe then we can find something, anything, to feed off of."

"But we don't know how big this area is. I can barely remember where we've been the last few nights."

"I know, but do you have a better idea? I refuse to give up. Not now, not after finally accepting what we've become." Danielle looked frustrated, but she didn't have an answer. John was about to suggest that they get moving when his wife spun around.

"What is it?" He drew a sword and began to scan the surrounding area. Danielle was turning in circles, sniffing fiercely at the air.

"Do you smell that?"

"What?"

"Blood."

John immediately put his sword away. "Of course I smell blood. There are birds everywhere, but we can't catch them. And we already know that you can't use your mind control on them." She turned on him, her face a mask of animalistic desire.

"This is different. Stronger. More powerful." She pointed into the night. "That way, and not too far. How can you not smell it?" John faced the direction she was pointing and concentrated.

"Well, I'll be damned." He *could* smell it. Now that he had caught the scent, the smell consumed him. They must be weaker than he thought if they hadn't noticed it before.

"We already are. Now let's go." Without waiting for a response, Danielle disappeared into the night. John followed quickly behind, drawing his sword for a second time. If the scent was stronger, it may be because the creature was stronger as well. They were in no condition to fight a serious battle, but there was no stopping Danielle.

Less than fifteen minutes later, they came in view of a small cabin. It looked deserted, but the source of the scent was definitely inside. They both crouched in the undergrowth, deciding how to proceed.

"I say we just walk in. We don't have time to be careful; the sun will be up soon." His wife was right.

"You do realize that you are suggesting we feed off of a human."

"Yes," she looked at him with eyes full of despair, "but I don't see as how we have much choice. We may not last another night without more blood. I'm not suggesting that we kill whoever is inside. We just need to drink enough to last us a few more nights. Then, we can get out of here and find better hunting grounds."

"Agreed, but remember, no killing."

"Yes, John." They shared a brief kiss before quickly approaching the cabin's front door. John carefully tested it and found, to his surprise, that there was no bolt or chain keeping it closed.

The irony of the situation was not lost on him. Wasn't this how it had all started; in a different cabin, in a different forest, all those years ago? A glance at Danielle told him that she was thinking the same thing. He shook his head in an attempt to clear his thoughts and nodded to his wife. She responded in kind. It was now or never.

John quickly opened the door and charged through it, sword at the ready. Danielle was right behind him, and she immediately moved to his right side. The cabin seemed far larger on the inside, and they were standing at the beginning of a long hall.

There was an old man at the other end of the hallway, working at a table. He was wearing an odd red and black robe, and there were candles everywhere. He looked up slowly and smiled at them.

They both bared their fangs and charged down the hallway. John's first thought was that they wouldn't get much blood from an old man, but it was better than nothing. His next thought was that he couldn't move. He shifted his eyes as far to the right as he could and saw that Danielle was still next to him, also not moving.

"Can you move?" he asked her.

"No. What's going on?"

"No idea. Ask him." The old man, who had been sitting at the table an instant before, was suddenly standing less than three feet from them, the smile still plastered to his face.

"I would welcome you to my humble home, but I must admit that I don't like vampires very much."

"What is this? What are you?"

"Just an old man who doesn't appreciate being considered food. Oh, and don't bother trying to move; it won't do you any good. Isn't magic wonderful?" John didn't like being toyed with, but that seemed to be exactly what the old man was doing.

"Damn you." The old man simply laughed.

"Don't worry; it'll all be over soon. I've dealt with your kind before." With that, the old man raised his hands. Lightning shot from his fingers and consumed both John and Danielle. He was obviously very pleased with himself and his self-proclaimed ability to destroy them.

John's body convulsed, and he almost growled in agony, until he realized that there was no pain. It was very odd. He could still see Danielle out of the corner of his eye, but it was impossible to tell if she was doing any better or worse than he was.

Suddenly, Danielle shocked both John and the old man. She simply walked up to him and buried her fangs into his throat. John regained control of his body and joined his wife in feeding. They didn't have to discuss that the no killing rule had been abandoned.

They both drank until the body was nothing but a husk, which Danielle quickly tossed aside. John was about to ask his wife what had happened when he noticed something very strange. He expected to feel better, since they had finally fed, but he didn't expect to feel so powerful.

They had each probably gotten about half a gallon of blood from the old man, but that shouldn't have been nearly enough to make them feel this powerful. John could tell from looking at her that Danielle felt the same way.

This was the first time they had fed from a human, so they did not realize that a human's blood was much more potent than what they were used to. They discussed their discovery for a time and then came to a decision: it was time to go back to civilization.

They would live normal lives, and they would feed exclusively from humans from now on. They agreed that they would not kill anyone who did not pose a threat to them, but they couldn't overlook the power that human blood gave them. Of course, they would have to continue feeding from animals until they found civilization again, but that was unavoidable.

"Now that everything's taken care of, you mind telling me what the hell just happened?"

Danielle grinned. "Of course not, love. It's simple. We ran into someone who had the ability to use magic, but he was just a man. When he froze our movement, it startled me. You probably reacted the same way." John admitted that he had.

"Well, I tried to break free, but after a few seconds I stopped trying. I accepted that I didn't understand what was happening, so I relaxed until I could figure out what to do. When he shot us with that lightning, I realized something was wrong. It was obvious that he was trying to hurt us, but the attack simply didn't hurt.

"I felt a little stinging sensation, but that's it. It made me think that maybe whatever barrier he was using to freeze our movement wasn't as strong as I thought. I concentrated and just walked through it. The look of fear in his eyes told me that there was no trap, so I started feeding.

"His powers may have been very effective against another human, but I think he was bluffing when he said that he had dealt with our kind before. It was our shock, not his power, that stopped us."

"Okay, I'll go along with that." With the threat dispatched, John began to take in their surroundings. "Hey, let's look around a bit." They started rummaging through the cabin, their curiosity getting the better of them. "Danielle, look at this." John was looking over the items on the table where the old man had been working.

There was a scattering of old scrolls and books covering the surface of the desk. John turned his attention to a few of them, but he couldn't make sense of whatever language they were written in. Danielle didn't seem to be having any better luck, but they were both able to guess what they were looking at.

"I'm guessing this is the stuff he studied to learn his magic."

"Looks that way," Danielle agreed.

"Do you think we could learn it too?"

"Hmmm, I don't see why not. We would have to translate it all first. Of course, since we're vampires, the magic may be stronger for us." That definitely sounded good to John. Anything that might increase their power or abilities would also increase their chances for survival in the years ahead.

"Okay, let's take all this with us. I'm sure that we'll be able to find a way to translate it eventually." They found three bags containing various supplies, which they immediately emptied out onto the cabin floor. Anything that appeared to have something to do with magic was tossed into the bags, and after less than an hour, all three bags were filled.

"I think we got everything, love."

"Looks like it. You want to stay here today? The sun will be up soon." It was true that dawn was rapidly approaching, but Danielle didn't want to stay in the cabin. It felt ... odd.

"John, I don't want to stay here a second longer than I have to."

"All right, we'd better get moving then." Danielle nodded, and then they both grabbed the magical supplies that they had gathered and disappeared into the night.

* * *

IT WAS YEARS LATER before they were able to master even the simplest of magical abilities. They discovered that there were many types of magic throughout the world. The magic the old man had been using was known as elemental magic.

Elemental magic had four different versions: fire, water, earth, and wind. Fire was the easiest to learn, and it was also the most powerful. Unfortunately, fire magic was also by far the most dangerous, especially when you were nothing but a walking corpse.

Water and wind were both difficult to learn and, by themselves, not terribly useful in combat. As a combination, however, John and Danielle realized that they could control certain aspects of the weather. A well-placed lightning bolt could easily turn the tide of a battle.

Earth was the most difficult to learn, and it wasn't very useful in a city environment, at least not if you wanted to keep a low profile. Away from civilization, on the other hand, it was very useful in combat. Earth was also far safer to use in combat than fire.

Throughout the decades and centuries, they both encountered many other types of magic. It took time, but they learned to master everything that they could. Danielle had also been right about magic being more powerful when done by a vampire.

They learned how to use the power of their blood to fuel their new magical abilities. As they aged, they also grew in power. Their magic gave them an edge in every battle they fought.

What they didn't know at the time was that almost every elder vampire had magical abilities. When you lived that long, it was only natural to encounter that sort of thing eventually. They very rarely encountered other vampires, especially other elders, and when they did, they didn't exactly hang around to listen to their life stories.

They encountered many interesting opponents throughout the centuries, but they never forgot the lesson the old man had taught them—never underestimate your foe.

Chapter 6

THOMAS WOKE to the sound of footsteps approaching his bedside. He opened his eyes and was instantly alert, thanks to years of difficult training. It had been several days since his encounter with the vampire, and he had completely recovered from his injuries, with the notable exception of his missing leg.

The whole situation had put him in a foul mood. He wanted to fight, but instead was stuck lying in bed trying to sleep. No one had told him yet how the ambush had turned out, but he was sure that it had been a success. Even if it had been, however, he was certain that the SOG had taken casualties. They were his friends, and he hadn't even been able to fight at their side.

Thomas was in no mood to be disturbed, and it was probably just some initiate bringing him his evening meal. They wouldn't even let him do that himself. He rolled over in bed, ready to make his displeasure known, when the words caught in his throat. Standing at his bedside was Archbishop Jenkins. He got over his momentary surprise quickly and was out of bed, bowing a greeting to the archbishop, in seconds.

"Good evening, Excellency. How may I help you?"

Jenkins smiled, but it seemed strained. "The first thing you can do for me, my son, is sit back down." Leaping out of bed on one leg as quickly as he had, had made Thomas feel a bit dizzy, so he was more than happy to comply. "Tell me, my son, has anyone brought you word of the results of our ambush?" Thomas's interest was piqued.

"Not yet, Excellency. I thought perhaps we were unable to track the beasts down to stage the attack."

There was no question that Thomas was indeed telling the truth, and it surprised Jenkins. News of such a negative nature usually spread quickly.

"In that case, my son, I'm afraid that I bring you bad tidings." The archbishop spent the next thirty minutes telling Thomas everything he had learned about what had happened. When he finally finished, there was a look of total shock on Thomas's face.

"An entire werewolf element, led by an elder, and over a squad of our men? Excellency, how is this possible?"

"The vampire turned out to be even more powerful than we had thought."

"This is all my fault." Thomas cradled his head in his hands.

"How can you say that, my son?"

"Excellency, the ambush plan was my idea. It was a mistake that cost many good men their lives."

Jenkins nodded. "It is true that they lost their lives, but their souls are free. That is much more than can be said about the creature that killed them. It is not fair to blame yourself, my son. The ambush was a very good idea.

"The problem was that we never expected to face elder vampires this powerful ever again. We lost the battle, but we gained information. The female was nearly destroyed, so we know that we possess the capability to destroy them. We simply need a new strategy."

Jenkins then explained to Thomas the steps he had taken thus far. As Jenkins spoke, Thomas merely responded with curt nods and the occasional "Yes, Excellency." There was no reason for someone of Jenkins's station to be explaining such things to him, and Thomas was afraid that he knew why the archbishop was doing it. His fears were confirmed within moments.

“My son, you may have already guessed why I am telling you all of this. I seek your counsel again. The information we now possess is very useful, but I lack the skills necessary to apply what we have learned. We need a refined plan, but I’m not qualified to come up with one.” Thomas cradled his head once again.

“Excellency, please, I can’t. My last idea got too many killed. How can I think of something new that may result in the same?” Jenkins moved to sit beside the troubled Templar. Placing a hand on his shoulder, he spoke as gently as he could.

“The Lord tests us from time to time, my son. I believe that He is testing us right now. If it was easy to do these things, then it wouldn’t be much of a test, now would it?” He waited for Thomas to slowly shake his head.

“You are the most experienced warrior here. We need your help. We need your advice, but I can’t force you. The Lord gives all men the freedom of choice. You must choose to help. Not to exact revenge for your injuries, but because it is His will that we do.” Jenkins waited several long moments for an answer, knowing all along in his heart that Thomas would stay true to His task. When he finally did speak, Thomas’s voice was quiet but firm in its resolve.

“The first thing you must do, Excellency, is request twice the number of men and werewolves that you already have to aide us. Do not plan any more ambushes because they’ll never work. We can no longer hope to engage the abominations separately. Elders of their age will never make such a costly mistake more than once.

“Our new strategy must be subtle, thorough, and implemented over time. We must target their resources first, and when they are weakened and forced into the open, we may strike at the abominations themselves.” The plan sounded good, but Jenkins didn’t understand it.

"My son, what do you mean by targeting their resources? And what do we need with so many men of our own?" Thomas surprised him with a grim, feral smile.

"We need the extra men for our own protection, Excellency. Vampires have been hunted throughout the ages. Most of them run and hide and eventually make mistakes that end in their destruction. A few vampires learn that the only way to survive being hunted is to destroy the hunter. If the hunter dies, then the prey no longer has anything to fear, until the next hunter comes along.

"The elders that we now face must belong to the group that fights back. It is the only way that they could have survived for so long. They know by now that something is after them. They may not know much about us, but they have to realize that whatever is after them is a very well-organized group. The female also must have noticed that werewolves and regular humans were working together.

"As old as they are, it stands to reason that they have accumulated a variety of resources. I'd stake my life on the fact that they are now focusing every one of those resources on discovering what is hunting them. Once they have enough information to come up with a tangible target, they will attack it.

"At this point, destroying these particular vampires isn't just God's work. It's the only way to prevent being destroyed ourselves." The full implications of what Thomas had just said began to sink in, and Jenkins grew even more afraid. It is not that Jenkins feared death—his soul was prepared—but he feared failure.

If the monsters defeated him and his men, it would mean far more than just their deaths. It would mean the vampires would then have access to all of their information. They would learn everything they needed to know about the SOG—where their bases were, what covers they used, and much more. Two vampires would never be enough to topple the SOG, no matter how powerful they were, but what if they joined with others?

Jenkins refused to pursue that train of thought any further. The Lord would never allow that to happen. Or would he? God gave men free will, which meant he gave men the chance to make the wrong decisions, the chance to fail. *No!* He couldn't think that way. His purpose was to prevent those things from happening, and that was what he was going to do, no matter the cost.

"Okay, my son, I understand. We must stop the abominations, but we cannot attack them directly. At least not yet, even with extra men. So we need to attack and destroy their resources—the same resources that they are now using against us. This will put them on the defensive, and then we can keep building the pressure until they make a mistake." Thomas's smile was now one of pleasure.

"Exactly, Excellency." Jenkins returned the smile, satisfied with his ability to keep up so far.

"I'm still not clear on what resources they have. How do we find them, and how exactly do we destroy them?" Thomas shifted to a more comfortable position.

"Well, Excellency—"

Jenkins raised a hand to interrupt him. "My son, this will go much faster if you refrain from calling me 'Excellency' every other sentence."

"Okay, but only if you agree to go easy on the 'my sons.' It's only fair."

Jenkins nodded. "Agreed."

"Well then, as I was saying, their most important resource is obviously blood. I don't know much about the inner workings of vampires, but I remember being taught that the older a vampire is, the more blood it is able to hold. We've agreed that these vampires are very old, a few centuries at least.

"If they hunted for all of the blood they used, we would have discovered them before now. As it is, the only reason we discovered them now is because I happened to be in the right place at the right time. They must be getting most of their blood from another source. They may have a storage facility of some kind." An idea came to Jenkins.

"What about a blood bank?"

Thomas's eyes widened at the obviousness of the suggestion. "Of course! That has to be it. I would recommend conducting a thorough investigation of every blood bank in the city. It might be a good idea to include any bank within twenty miles of the city, to stay on the safe side." The archbishop considered it for a moment.

"An excellent plan, but it may take considerable time to find what we are looking for."

"Yes, but since we know what to look for, we *will* find it. We can narrow the list of possibilities by ignoring banks owned and operated by major companies or relief organizations such as the Red Cross. Privately owned banks that are a bit more low profile would be the best place to start.

"The other main resource they have, one that will cause problems for us, is their minions. Who knows how many innocents they have ghouled. They could have an entire army, and we'd never know until it was too late.

"Their ghouls might not be anywhere near a match for our werewolves, but most of our regular soldiers would be outmatched. We lack the experience for this kind of battle." Ghouls were also even more difficult to identify than vampires were, but Thomas saw no reason to add what they both already knew.

"Do you have any suggestions?" Thomas sipped from a glass of water that had been sitting forgotten at his bedside.

"It's safe to assume that whatever blood bank they are using is staffed entirely with ghouls. It's simply foolish to trust something that important to anyone not completely dependent on you for their survival. Once we discover the proper bank, we destroy it and everyone inside.

"It may not get them all, but we'll be able to eliminate some of them. If we're lucky, the ghouls inside the bank will call for help, and that'll bring us more of them. We destroy everything that shoots at us, and when the smoke clears, the vampires will have lost their main blood supply and a sizable portion of their minions." It was a good plan, but not perfect.

"There are two major flaws that I see. First, what if we are wrong about the facility having only ghoul workers? Secondly, if they call for help, won't the vampires come to protect their supply?"

Thomas saw the objections coming and was prepared. "We can take care of the first problem with additional investigation. When we find the right bank, we study the profile for every worker we can find. Unfortunately, that information can all be falsified. The best we can honestly do is to simply use caution.

"If you were the average man, minding your own business at work, what would you do if a group of armed men attacked your place of business?"

"I would pray," was Jenkins's automatic answer, to which Thomas arched his brow. "No, I wouldn't. I would run or hide or maybe even beg for my life."

"Exactly, but what would you do if you were a slave dependent on your master for survival, and your master's most precious possession came under assault?"

"I would fight the attackers. No matter what the odds, I would fight with everything I had, because if I lost the fight and survived, my life would be over anyway."

Thomas leaned back in satisfaction. "That is how we tell the difference. We initiate the attack and then simply kill anything that fights back, which is why I would suggest not using werewolves. They are to indiscriminate once they change forms. Two squads of our own men should do the trick. We can have more men and werewolves on standby to help deal with any reinforcements."

Jenkins considered the proposal very carefully. "That is good, but innocent life may still be lost. As you said, our men are inexperienced. Who knows how they will react. The ghouls themselves may start killing innocents in retaliation to our assault."

"I admit that is a possibility," Thomas's voice grew soft, "and I don't care for it. Unfortunately, I don't see as how we have much choice. Once we attack, it has to be quick and total. Our men will be at a disadvantage and must use the initial surprise for as much as they can.

"I honestly don't see how we can defeat these abominations without endangering innocent lives at some point. I believe that we must accept this and move on. It's nothing compared to the damage these vampires can cause if we sit idly by. All we can do is try our best to minimize innocent casualties as much as possible."

Jenkins didn't like the sound of that at all. "What about my second question? If the vampires come themselves, they will most likely wipe out our entire attack force."

"That problem, at least, has a simple solution. We attack during the day."

Of course, why hadn't Jenkins already thought of that? He still didn't like the plan, though, but it was the only one they had.

"We will proceed with the investigations you suggested. I shall meditate on a solution to prevent innocent casualties, but if I cannot find a better one, we will use your plan. What else can we do?"

"There isn't much more that is plausible for us. We can divert a portion of our resources to searching for their haven, but I wouldn't expect too much in way of results. Keep the vampires under watch, and when we destroy what resources we can, see how they react and go from there."

Jenkins nodded and rose. "Thank you for your counsel. Trust in your faith, for we will emerge from this darkness with new strength." The archbishop turned to leave, but Thomas called after him.

"Please, I have a request."

Jenkins paused and turned back. "You have more than earned the right to one. Name it."

"I want to help."

The request confused him. "I don't understand. You have already helped a great deal. You just finished outlining an excellent strategy for us to pursue."

Thomas shook his head slowly. "That's not what I meant. I want to actually do something. Please."

Jenkins considered this for a moment, and it began to make sense to him. Thomas was a warrior. He wouldn't be satisfied merely handing out information. His warrior instincts and nature would demand that he take action. The injuries he had sustained would only increase that need, not lessen it.

The question was should Jenkins let him? Thomas had already suffered enough. His injuries would guarantee that he would never be the warrior he once was. That knowledge alone would be difficult enough for him to accept. What right did Jenkins have to ask more of him? Of course, he wasn't asking anything. Thomas was offering to do whatever he could, of his own free will. Free will was given to men by God Himself, so who was Jenkins to stand in its way? With that final thought, his mind was made up.

"You may have your choice of two jobs. You may head up the investigations we will be starting, or you may take charge of training our soldiers."

Thomas smiled and considered his options. "I would prefer to lead the investigations. When can I start?"

"Tomorrow." Jenkins raised his hand to forestall the objections that he knew were coming. His demeanor made it obvious that there would be no further argument on the subject, and after a moment, Thomas nodded his agreement. Jenkins watched as he slowly and very carefully stood up and gave him a deep bow.

"I thank you, Your Excellency."

Jenkins nodded and gave a quick blessing. "Sleep well, my son."

Chapter 7

"YOU KNOW, sweetheart, eating three rare steaks isn't very ladylike."

Danielle paused briefly between bites. "This coming from someone currently eating his fourth steak?"

John grinned and signaled the waitress to bring another helping.

A bar might not normally be considered the best place to order a good steak, but the fare at Mike's Bar and Grill was top-notch. Of course, it could simply be because it was the only place that would accept their definition of "rare." Whatever the reason, Mike's had been their favorite restaurant since it opened, six years before. Of course, being vampires, they didn't frequent too many eating establishments.

Vampires were not required to eat, but they were still able to if they so desired. The problem was that a vampire's body couldn't store anything but blood. One of the first things that happens to vampire after being turned is the body purging everything that isn't blood. It's a very painful process of retching that can last anywhere from hours to days. It is not uncommon for a new vampire to actually lose an organ or two during the process, at least the first time it happens. Very few vampires would voluntarily repeat that process.

John and Danielle, on the other hand, were exceptions. They knew that every steak they ate, and every glass of beer or sangria they drank, would exact its toll on them later. In spite of that, however, they had two good reasons for continuing to eat on occasion. They had learned through painful personal experience that out in the open was the best place for two very old vampires to hide. Who would think that vampires would go to a bar and eat something other than the other customers?

The second reason was much more unusual, at least from a vampire's point of view. They simply liked the taste of good steak and excellent beer, or in Danielle's case sangria. Vampires could still taste things normally, but the pure ecstasy and power imparted by the consumption of blood made all other tastes seem bland and pointless. John and Danielle had no explanation for why they were different. Perhaps it was because they had been able to retain much more of their humanity than was usual? Neither of them cared what the reason was; things were simply the way they were. Their palettes were terrible compared to the average human, but they were willing to take what they could get.

It was the third night since they had decided on their current strategy, and it finally seemed to have paid off. They had been eating for about thirty minutes when they noticed that a group of three men at the bar had become very interested in them. To their credit, the men had done nothing to give themselves away. It was simply vampiric sense that had allowed the elders to notice them.

Throughout their entire meal, John and Danielle had been chatting away about several subjects. They talked about anything that you would expect a young couple to talk about. At the same time, they talked about the men at the bar. Of course, for that portion of their conversation, they used voices that couldn't be overheard by mortal ears.

"Sam, you see the ones we're talking about, right?" Sam had gotten involved in a series of games with some of the bar's more regular patrons, and John could hear the cheers and clinks of glasses coming from the direction of the establishment's dart boards and pool tables. John only hoped Sam remembered to not win too much or too often.

"Of course I do, sir. They're the only three people at the bar not drinking alcohol," came the reply through John's earpiece. Sam insisted on certain formalities while actually working. His observation had caught both John and Danielle by surprise. They had failed to note that difference, trusting in their extra senses to do the work for them. Of course their pursuers wouldn't be drinking. Only a fool would dull their senses with alcohol while trying to track vampires.

"Okay, I think we've been here long enough. Is everything ready?"

"Yes, sir. I have a dozen armed ghouls on standby, and my two best trackers are ready to take over if it gets too close to dawn." John couldn't help but grin at that. Even though Danielle and he had created all of the ghouls, and the ghouls depended on them for their continued existence, Sam always referred to them as his.

"Well, hon, are you ready to leave?"

"Sure you don't want any dessert, dear?"

"I'm stuffed. I'll be lucky to make it to bed before collapsing."

"Guess we better get going then." Their banter briefly attracted the attention of the few surrounding tables. Reactions ranged from annoyance to appreciation of the obvious love that they shared. John signaled for the check and gave the waitress enough cash to include a 50 percent tip for herself.

She wasn't surprised by the amount of money, and didn't insult him by asking if he wanted change. They didn't come in too often, but when they did, they always asked for her. She knew what they always ate and would bring it to them without being asked. Then she would simply keep it coming until John signaled for the check.

John watched her count out the cash and then smiled when she had finished. They rose to leave, and as always, Meg walked them to the door, opened it for them, and bid them good night. She had begun doing that after the third time they had requested her. John guessed that it was her way of saying thank you. It was definitely preferable to his own body's way of thanking him for the meal. They were both strong enough to postpone the inevitable, but nothing could stop it. Sometime tomorrow night, they were both going to be very unhappy for about twenty minutes.

Once they left the bar, they picked a random direction and started walking. John couldn't help but grin at what they must have looked like; anyone that had known what to look for would have seen two elder vampires being followed by three hunters, who in turn were being followed by a ghoul, who was being followed by a dozen more ghouls. It was certainly an odd procession.

"Time to turn the tables. Everyone ready?"

"Aye, love."

"Ready, sir." Upon receiving Sam's confirmation, John and Danielle simply turned around and walked back toward their pursuers. They had decided earlier to stay close enough to whomever was following them to not only track them, but listen to what they said as well. Their methods may have seemed foolish, since they were simply walking right next to their pursuers, but they were nonetheless very effective.

The two ancients were using their powers for all they were worth to conceal themselves. Few other vampires would have been strong enough to see them, much less a trio of humans. So they both walked right next to their pursuers, John on their left and Danielle on their right. They only complicated part of the plan was the two of them simply staying out of the way. The street was still rather busy and being effectively invisible did not make you immaterial. They planned to continue until they either found out what they wanted or had to return to their haven to escape the approaching dawn.

“We’re in position.” It was more of a risk to actually speak, but John was confident that he could conceal his voice as well.

“I’ll take your word for it, sir.” There was no way for Sam to know where they were now, so he would have to just trust his master.

* * *

AS THE MINUTES passed, the hunters began to grow visibly nervous. Finally, the one John had picked as the leader stopped them.

“We’ve lost them.”

“How is that possible, sir? They were right in front of us.”

The leader seemed annoyed, but he was otherwise doing a good job of controlling the situation. “It is unfortunate, but not entirely unexpected. We are dealing with beings of great evil, and evil has always been able to conceal itself from man. The only question we face is did we simply lose track of them, or did they discover they were being followed?” It was obvious that the leader had already made up his mind and was only testing his men’s perceptions. It was a leadership quality few possessed.

“I think, sir, we simply lost them. I believe that if they had discovered us, we would already be dead. It is easy to see how two abominations as powerful as they are could evade us, although it is odd how it happened—so suddenly and seemingly for no reason.” The second man agreed, and the leader considered their statements.

“I believe that you are both correct and have raised an interesting point. We were tracking them just fine a moment ago. If they didn’t discover us, why would they have changed tactics so suddenly?” Obviously more testing.

“Perhaps they are hunting.”

"Possibly. That would explain why they would suddenly want to cover their tracks. Assuming that is the case, what do we do about it?"

"We could continue searching. If they are hunting, then there's an innocent life at risk."

"Even if we did find them in time, we can't possibly stop them."

"We have a duty to at least try."

"But—"

The leader silenced the growing debate with a raised hand. "You are correct. We have a duty to preserve innocent life, but we have a greater duty to our brethren. At least one of us must live to report what little we have learned. Besides, our intelligence suggests that they don't kill their victims. They have lived here a long time. If they killed every victim they hunted, we would have discovered their presence long ago.

"We will continue searching, but we will not interfere with anything we happen to find. If we do find anything, at least we will be able to lend immediate aid and comfort to any surviving victims. We'll search until the beasts flee the coming dawn, but remember that you are both under orders to not engage."

"Yes, sir."

"Aye." The men both agreed, but it was obvious that they were unhappy with not being allowed to engage the abominations. Still, they were both soldiers of God, and they would follow His will, wherever it may lead.

* * *

"Did you get all that?" John had keyed up the sensitivity on his earpiece in the hopes that Sam would be able to listen in on their pursuers' conversation as well.

"Yes, sir, I heard it all, and I must admit that I find much of it very odd."

"So do I, but we'll discuss it later. We're going home, so report whatever you find to us tomorrow night."

"Aye, sir." Most of what the men had said to each other had raised some very interesting questions. Unfortunately, they had only learned one definite fact: their pursuers would be continuing to search until dawn. There was no point in following them if they knew their pursuers wouldn't be returning home tonight.

John trusted Sam and his ghouls to do the job. He even knew that if Sam found anything good, he would make plans on his own and just present them to him when he awoke the next night. It was hard to remember what they ever did without him and their other ghouls. There was one additional reason to get back to the haven as soon as possible.

It was very possible that they would be attacking something tomorrow night. It wouldn't be very good for all of the steak and alcohol they had consumed to force its way back out in the middle of an assault. If they got back to the haven in time, they could force all of it now and be done with it.

"Ready to go, love?" At the moment they were still following the hunters.

"Can't we just take one of them? The others wouldn't even notice until we were long gone."

"Yes, but eventually they would notice. Then they would know, without a doubt, that they had been discovered. We can't let that happen until it's too late."

"Yeah, I know, but look at them just walking around as if they're still hunting us. Maybe if we nab one, without the rest noticing, they'll see what we're capable of and leave us alone."

"I wish. Think about how much damage you did by yourself when they ambushed you. They're still hunting us in spite of that, so one more death won't change their minds."

"Fine, but we better have plenty of blood left in the fridge, 'cause I'm thirsty as hell, and I want first dibs on them tomorrow."

John grinned at his wife. "We have plenty of blood, and yes you may. After all, you still have a score to settle."

"Okay, okay, let's get going then." They moved as one, and barely thirty seconds later, they were back in their haven, trying to regurgitate dinner.

* * *

"FIND ANYTHING useful, Sam?" John had just risen for the evening and was roaming the haven in a black silk robe. He eventually found Sam in the office, poring over what seemed to be a blueprint of some sort. It had been a restful day, and he was feeling surprisingly good after recently having several pounds of steak and beer exit his body the same way it had entered. Now it was time to get back to work.

"I believe we did. We tracked those three until nearly noon. Whoever they are, they're very professional. They wandered around randomly for hours before finally going home. Seriously, this only worked because it was our plan from the start, and we still nearly lost them once," Sam's face had a look of annoyance mixed with professional appreciation. "Anyway, we managed to track them back to here, but only because of how many ghouls we were using." He slid the blueprint across the table so John could read the title.

"Lori's Bed and Breakfast?"

Sam nodded. "I did some checking, and I don't think this place is a normal bed-and-breakfast. I couldn't find it anywhere on the Internet, and they were booked solid for two months when I checked in person. It is possible; however, that it's nothing more than where some of these people sleep. If that's the case, we may be tipping our hand for no real gain. Your call, boss." Unfortunately, Sam had a valid point.

One way or another, after this attack, the enemy would know that they were on to them. The target they chose needed to be worth it.

"Honestly, I don't think we have much choice. I'm not waiting for another target; we need to take the offensive now. We'll just hope that this bed-and-breakfast, or whatever it really is, provides us with some answers. I think it's a good risk though. If you think about it, the cover these people are using is good, except that the building is a fake. That is an obvious flaw that no one could have overlooked. Hell, this haven is a real hotel that is filled with guests all the time, all to maintain the cover. So there must be something there that is too valuable to risk people stumbling upon. Can we attack tonight?"

"Of course," Sam replied after thinking about what John had said. "If that's what you want, I would suggest any time after ten, so that gives us about two and a half hours. How do you want us to handle the assault?" John took a long swig from a glass another ghoul had handed him before answering.

"Danielle and I will go in, with you and about a dozen ghouls covering our backs. We're going to try and maintain surprise for as long as possible, so make sure that the ghouls have plenty of bladed weapons. One in every three ghouls should carry some kind of heavy weaponry, since we may run into werewolves at some point. Danielle and I, of course, will carry everything we can.

"Tell the ghouls not to attack anything unless they are instructed to or are attacked first. With the exception of that rule, you can handle the ghouls however you wish as long as you remember to keep them behind us." Sam jotted down a few notes.

"Got it. It'll take about twenty minutes for us to be ready. When do you want to leave?"

"So, what are you boys talking about?" Danielle was leaning, arms crossed, in the doorway. Her robe was the same color as John's, but that's where the similarity ended. John's robe was fairly loose and floor length. Danielle's, on the other hand, was extremely tight and very... revealing.

Danielle had long ago realized that one of her most powerful weapons in a world dominated by men had nothing to do with her being a vampire. She had always been aware that she was extremely attractive, but when she was still mortal, she was careful to hide it. It wasn't proper for a woman to flaunt her body back in the eleventh century. Somewhere in the nine hundred years since then, Danielle had definitely tossed that habit aside.

Now not only did she not hesitate to flaunt her body, she enjoyed doing it. John got used to it after a while. It took a few hundred years for him to be able to see other men's reactions to his wife without wanting to rip their throats out, but that passed as well. Jealousy wasn't really a factor after over nine centuries of marriage. That explained why John laughed at Sam's reaction to Danielle's appearance instead of killing him.

You'd think Sam would've gotten used to seeing her walk around the haven in outfits that generally contained less total fabric than a normal person's shirt by now. Perhaps it was more difficult to get used to when it was a woman you could never have, rather than your wife. In any event, since it didn't bother John, he usually just let Danielle have her fun.

"Come on over, love. Sam and I were planning our assault for later tonight."

"Ah, so can I assume you found us a nice, juicy target there, Sam?"

"Well, target, yes, but not so sure about the juicy part yet." They spent a few minutes filling her in, and then all three of them went over the blueprints together.

"So there are only three actual exits from the building itself, here, here, and here?" Danielle pointed out all three exits on the blueprints, leaning forward far more than necessary.

"Yeah, it looks that way: the main entrance, the rear entrance, and what looks like a side entrance for maintenance purposes or something like that."

"Okay, I say we go in through the back door. Cut the phone lines first, but leave the main power on. We station a team of four ghouls to block off and guard the two exits we won't be using. That still leaves Sam, plus four ghouls, to directly guard our backs." Sam and John took a moment to consider Danielle's insight.

"I like it, but what about alarm systems? Won't leaving the main power on allow them to call for help?"

"Screw it. Let 'em call for help. The police's response time in this city sucks, and any confusion caused by the alarms will only aide us. I'm only concerned that whatever organization we're about to attack might call for assistance from their own. Unfortunately, I seriously doubt cutting the main power would stop that, so we'll just have to move fast."

"Agreed, but I say we take eighteen ghouls, instead of just twelve: twelve to guard the three exits, and six to move inside with us. We don't want too many going inside, since it'll mostly be close-quarters combat, but I would like the extra firepower since we'll be going in blind."

Sam nodded. "Okay, I'll get it set up. When do you guys want to leave?"

"Quarter after ten sounds as good as any time, right?" Danielle agreed.

"Okay, I'll be back at ten with the other ghouls." Sam gathered up his things and, with a nod to them both, set about his tasks.

"Love, may I ask you a favor?"

"Of course."

"I have an errand that I must run alone. It will only take me about twenty minutes, and I promise I'll be careful."

"Why must you go alone?"

"It's a secret."

Danielle could tell that didn't sit very well with him. "Please." She put on her best pouting face.

"You know those puppy dog eyes don't work on me. They stopped working about five hundred years ago."

"Oh really." She untied her robe, allowing it to flutter open and closed on its own. "How about now?" She had him, and worse, she knew it.

"Damn it, I can't believe that still works on me. Twenty minutes, but no longer."

"Thanks, love. Maybe in another five hundred years."

* * *

LESS THAN TWO minutes later, Danielle was standing outside the weapon's shop she had visit on the night of the first attack. In all of the current excitement, she had almost forgotten her deal with the owner. Of course she was very late, but hopefully he had finished, and not simply assumed she was never coming back. There was only one way to find out.

The shop was closed, but she could hear the owner inside. Carefully, she entered without damaging the lock or the door itself. Not wanting to startle the old man, Danielle rang the bell and stood quietly just inside the door.

"We're closed. Come back tomorrow." The owner came out from where he had been working, and seemed surprised to see someone inside the shop, despite the fact that he had obviously heard the bell. "I'm sorry, ma'am, I thought I had locked the door already."

"Jason, it's me." Danielle hoped he recognized her. The owner was fairly old, and he illustrated that point by squinting at her while reaching for his glasses. His glasses in place, Danielle noticed his eyes widen slightly in recognition.

"Ah, Danielle. You're late." She bowed slightly at the waist.

"My deepest apologies, Weapon's Master, but I was unavoidably detained in the hospital for several days."

Concern touched the corners of his eyes. "Nothing serious I hope."

"Not at all. I sustained a few chest injuries in a car accident. Fortunately, it is all concealed by my clothing, and eventually I won't even have a scar. They kept me for so long merely as a precaution. If you have completed what I asked for, I will be sure to compensate you for my tardiness." He nodded, and the concern in his eyes turned to excitement.

"I was concerned when you didn't show, but I knew you'd be back eventually. It's just as well, ma'am, because it took me three days longer than we agreed on to finish. It is done though, and I even went ahead and made something else to go along with it. Actually, you're just in time, since I didn't finish the second piece until yesterday. Come, come, I'll show you." Jason began leading Danielle toward the rear of the shop.

It wasn't necessary for her to feign surprise or excitement. Danielle couldn't wait to see what he had accomplished. She was also curious about the second piece he mentioned. The deal they had made was for a sword and nothing more. So what else had he come up with? She could, of course, just read his mind, but that would take all the fun out of it.

"This is where I do most of my work." Danielle had to admit, she was impressed. She didn't know anything about manufacturing weapons, but she recognized most of the tools and hand-operated machinery that filled the large room.

"I was wondering why this place looked so big from the outside. This is quite a setup you've got here." Jason took a large amount of pride in his work, and he thanked Danielle for the compliment.

"Still one more room." He led her to the back wall and unlocked a final door. This let them into a much smaller but far less cluttered room that was filled with weapons racks and testing equipment.

Jason moved over to the closest rack and retrieved a cloth-wrapped bundle. He seemed barely able to contain his glee as he handed it over to Danielle. She thanked him and carefully unwrapped the item. One glance at the weapon was enough to render her speechless.

"Do you like it? I daresay it's the finest weapon I have ever made." To say the sword was acceptable would have been an enormous understatement. It was beautiful. Every aspect of the weapon showed that it had been crafted by a master.

"Jason, it's ... it's incredible. Although, I never asked you to paint the blade black." She wasn't complaining; it was merely an observation.

"Ah, but it's not painted."

"What do you mean?"

"Well, I decided to use a bit of initiative. The only reason for someone to want a weapon like this is that you plan to use it." Danielle started to say something, but he stopped her. "It's none of my business, ma'am.

"Anyway, light glinting off the metal blade is a dead giveaway if you don't want to be seen. A black blade will prevent that from happening."

"So you painted it black?"

"No, that wouldn't have worked. Paint would chip off; the edge would lose all of it almost right away. How much do you know about making weapons?"

"I'm an expert in the use of all weapons, but I admit that I know next to nothing about making them."

"Okay, I'll spare you the details. Basically, I heat the steel a certain way and add a few special ingredients, and the end result is black steel. That's why, as you can see, even the edge is completely black. It's the steel itself, not paint. Call it a trade secret, since I'd rather not see too many others like this one on the market." Danielle had no idea what he was talking about, but it sounded impressive.

"Well, I must say, I'm impressed. Mind if I test it out?"

"Please do. I'd consider it an honor and a privilege to watch you." Danielle spent a few minutes going through some moves and testing out the sword's strength.

"Amazing, Jason, and I mean it. I am curious though; didn't you say something about a second piece?"

"Ah, yes. I got so caught up in watching you enjoy your purchase that I forgot all about the surprise I have for you." He grabbed a second bundle and handed it to Danielle. She carefully set the sword on a nearby rack and unwrapped the new bundle.

It was a scabbard. Looking at it made Danielle realize that she had forgotten to ask for one. It seemed much simpler than the sword itself, but the quality was no less. There were straps for carrying the weapon on your back, but it looked as if they could be adjusted to carry the blade wherever you wanted.

"This is very nice. I can't believe I forgot to ask you to make one." It didn't seem possible, but his smile grew even more.

"I made it special for that sword, so no other blade will fit properly in it. The inside is lined with thin steel to keep the sword from damaging it. The outside is simply tough leather, although I treated it, so it should stand up to the elements better than normal." Danielle wished that she could stay and speak with him longer, but she was quickly approaching the deadline she and John had agreed on.

"This is all wonderful work, but if I don't leave soon, I'll be late for an important appointment."

"Of course. I don't want to delay you any longer."

"I believe that I still owe you ten thousand dollars," she mentioned as she began counting out bills.

"That was the original deal, ma'am."

"Well, here's the ten thousand I owe you, plus," she counted out more bills, "five thousand more for your extra work and my tardiness." It was surprising, but the man looked almost horrified.

"No! That's too much. I cannot accept that much money."

"Don't argue with me, Weapon's Master. I like to reward excellent work. Obviously money is of no concern to me, so why shouldn't I pay you as much as I want? Besides, I've been doing some checking on the Internet, and swords of this quality can sell for much more than what we agreed on. I almost feel like I am shortchanging you." She sheathed the sword and strapped it to her back.

"Actually, ma'am, that has a lot to do with age as well. It takes a great deal of skill and considerable time to make a sword a sword like this, but the actual cost in materials is quite lower than you would think. Quite frankly, almost no one makes swords like this anymore, so if you're looking at a sword of this quality somewhere else, it is probably also very old."

"Semantics. Now if you'll excuse me, I really must be going."

He walked her back to the front door. "Good evening to you, and thank you for your incredible generosity."

"It's been my pleasure. If this weapon performs as well as I think it will, I'll be back." Danielle thanked him once again, unlocked the front door, and left.

* * *

JASON IMMEDIATELY bent down to relock the door when a thought occurred to him. *If she had to unlock the door to leave, how did she get in?* He quickly glanced down both sides of the street, but she was nowhere to be seen.

* * *

"I WAS STARTING to worry about you, love." Danielle found John in the kitchen, gorging himself on blood. "Did you do what had to be done?"

"Yep. Didn't have any trouble, and no one saw me."

"Gonna tell me where you were?"

"Eventually, but not right now." John merely shrugged and went back to drinking. "Where do we stand?"

"Sam has all the ghouls ready and waiting. We'll be leaving soon, so you should start drinking." Danielle agreed and went to the fridge. They were about to go into battle blind. It would be foolish for them to not drink as much blood as possible first. There was no telling what kind of resistance they would encounter.

"You seem overly excited."

John bared his fangs. "Of course I am. It's been far too long since we've gone into battle on our own terms. It's time to show these jokers what it means to be hunted."

Danielle smiled. "Payback's a bitch."

They toasted the sentiment with fresh glasses and went back to drinking.

Chapter 8

"WHAT DO YOU make of them?" They had spent about an hour getting to Lori's Bed and Breakfast, in order to allow their ghouls to follow carefully, and another fifteen minutes checking it out. All three entrances looked perfectly normal. They had circled around to the back, leaving two teams of ghouls behind to guard the other doors. It was at the back door that they finally encountered something that could be considered resistance.

Two men were lounging near the back door, chatting quietly with each other. If John and Danielle didn't know better, they would have dismissed the men immediately. They weren't doing anything odd, but it was still possible that they were guards. John stared at them carefully, trying to find something definite. It took nearly a full minute before something hit him.

"You see those chains they're wearing?" They were each wearing a gold chain with a small crucifix hanging from it. "The men we were following yesterday each had one."

"Hmm, the one who attacked me the first time had one, but I didn't notice if the mortals in the ambush were wearing them. It's safe to assume that they were."

"Great, just what we need—a band of organized religious nuts." Danielle laughed but didn't discount the seriousness of the statement. They had dealt with their fair share of fanatics over the centuries, and while most of them were barely more than simple amusements, organized groups of them could be very dangerous. “Let’s take these two out, nice and quiet, and then go in.” As he began to move, Danielle held him back.

“Wait! Yesterday you said I could have first blood.” John merely nodded and motioned for her to continue. Danielle smiled and vanished, and then both guards suddenly dropped dead. John’s eyes were able to keep track of what happened, and he felt little sympathy for the mortals. Danielle had simply charged them while morphing both hands into claws. Once within arm’s length of both guards, she thrust a single claw upward through the underside of each chin and deep into their brains.

It was one of the quickest and quietest ways to kill a mortal. Simply slitting the throat didn’t work as well as it appeared to on television. A slit throat caused several sounds that tended to echo in the dead silence of night. Stabbing a man under the chin, through the jaw, and up into the brain was an instant death. There wasn’t even the risk of a final death scream, since death came far too fast for one.

Danielle quickly searched both bodies and turned up several concealed weapons. These men had definitely been guarding something. She glanced around for more targets but found none. Uttering a sigh of displeasure, she waved the others forward. The final team, from the first squad of ghouls, took up positions to guard the door, while the rest of the entry team took up positions to guard their masters.

“That’s odd.”

John turned to face his wife. “What?”

“Touch the cross on one of their chains.”

John was hesitant to do so. They were far too powerful to have anything to fear from blessed holy relics, but it still hurt like hell. After a moment he nodded, crouched down, and cautiously brushed his fingers across the crucifix.

"What the hell?" He felt nothing other than the normal cool touch of metal. Most of all, his beast remained silent. It was just a simple religious trinket, but if it had been blessed, it should have had some effect on him.

One of the most potent weapons mortals possessed against vampires was faith. It could be used in the form of personal faith, blessed objects or weapons, or even entire holy areas. Faith could be used to cause a vampire some pain, but that was merely a side effect. Faith made a vampire suddenly and uncontrollably angry. Vampires were demons, and when a demon was confronted by the belief and trust in God represented by faith, there could only be one reaction.

The sudden anger caused a vampire's beast to awaken and gain strength. If the mortal's faith was strong enough, or the vampire was too weak, the beast could easily overcome them. A vampire in a frenzied state caused by faith, referred to as a faith-frenzy, was overcome by a sense of self-preservation, rather than the thirst for blood that a normal frenzy caused. When in a faith-frenzy, vampires ran, killing anything that got in their way, including friends. It wasn't the best way to actually kill a vampire, but it was an excellent way to chase one off, allowing the mortal plenty of time in which to flee.

When it was used in conjunction with more destructive weaponry, faith was a good last-ditch defense. When a vampire hunter wore a crucifix around his neck, its purpose wasn't just to show their allegiance to God. It was supposed to afford them some extra protection in case their attack failed. However, every experienced vampire hunter knew that it would only work if the crucifix was properly blessed. That raised some interesting questions about the men they had just killed.

"Maybe they just don't know any better. Not everyone knows all the rules." John knew it was foolish to think that, even as he was saying it. These people had demonstrated that they knew exactly what they were doing. It didn't make sense that they could know what they did, and not know something as simple as that.

That could only mean one thing. The crucifixes were blessed, just not by anyone with the true ability to do so. Unfortunately, that raised many more-disturbing questions. Who blessed them, and did these people know that their artifacts were blessed by someone without the true ability to do so? A single glance at Danielle was enough to tell John she was thinking the same thing.

"What the hell is going on here?"

"Good question, love, but we're not going to find the answer standing out here. Sam, cut the phone lines now. We have to move." Sam nodded toward another ghoul, who immediately came to attention and ran off. Thirty seconds later the ghoul returned and gave Sam a thumbs-up.

"Phone lines are cut, sir." John grunted in satisfaction and nodded toward Danielle. She moved to the door and demonstrated one of the few powers she possessed that John had not yet mastered himself. He watched as she mumbled a few words, shimmered, and turned to mist. The mist slid silently through the crack under the door. A brief moment later, John heard a click, and the door opened silently.

John wished that he was able to do that as well as she could. He was able to turn himself into mist, but he wasn't able to extend the transformation to his clothing and weapons. It wouldn't do him any good to travel somewhere as mist if he would be naked and unarmed when he changed back. John's thoughts were interrupted as Danielle waved the entry team forward.

Thirty minutes later it was all over, and John let out a growl of disappointment. They had cleared every room on every floor of the bed-and-breakfast. Twenty-two people had been found wearing small crucifixes, and six people had been found without them. It was more people than they had expected to find in a building that size, but that was of little concern or interest to them. The ones wearing crucifixes were killed immediately, but the other six were left alive. They bound and gagged them and then locked them all in various closets, but they wouldn't kill people who might be innocents. Unfortunately, that was all they found.

There were a few positive results to the assault. First, John and Danielle were able to gorge themselves on fresh blood. Secondly, they reduced the enemy's numbers by another twenty-four soldiers. Finally, they collected a small armory's worth of weapons and phosphorous ammunition for their own use. As for answers to their questions, however, they struck out. All in all, they tipped their hand for merely small gains. The assault was a failure.

At the moment, the entry team was performing a final search, while John and Danielle sat in the lobby and discussed what to do next. So far, it didn't look as if anyone had been able to get out a warning. John was about to call off the entry team, to try and cut their losses, when Sam made his report.

"Sir, I think we found something."

"Where are you?"

"In the basement."

"Okay, we're on our way." John looked up and saw Danielle put away the magazine she had been reading. It was almost comical. They had just broken into a building and killed almost everyone inside, but Danielle just had to put the magazine neatly away in its proper place.

John gave her a questioning look, but she merely shrugged and took off toward the basement.

They linked up with Sam a few seconds later. He had the rest of the entry team holding position, weapons drawn, around what appeared to be a trapdoor in the floor. When Sam saw them enter the room, he went to meet them.

"Congratulations, Sam, you found a door."

"Yes, well, it's not on any of the blueprints, sir."

"Really?"

"Yes, sir. The blueprints show this as being the building's bottom floor." John could see that Danielle was thinking the same thing he was. *Perhaps this mission wasn't a failure after all.*

"Okay, open'er up." One ghoul put away his weapon so he could open the door, while the others fanned out and got ready. As the door opened, John and Danielle's anticipation grew.

What had looked like a simple wooden trapdoor was four-inch-thick solid steel. Add that to the fact it wasn't on the building's blueprints, and there simply had to be something down there worth hiding. Thankfully, the ghoul was strong enough to handle the door. John doubted that a normal mortal would have been able to do it alone.

Once the door was completely open, the ghoul moved back with the others and drew his weapon. Everyone waited, weapons ready, their attention riveted on the new opening in the floor. When nothing happened after two minutes, John took it as a sign that they remained undetected. He signaled to Sam, who stacked the entry team into a straight line behind the two vampires, their weapons alternating between the regular and low ready positions. Sam gave his master a thumbs-up when his ghouls were ready, and they all disappeared into the opening.

A stone stairwell descended about fifteen meters before leveling off into a narrow hallway with poor lighting. The vampires moved through the hallway slowly, allowing their senses time to give them an idea of what lay ahead. There was no point in concealing themselves, since it wouldn't help the ghouls. They had to simply rely on sensing the enemy first.

The team had just gone through the hallway's third twist when John held up his hand to signal a halt. He glanced over to Danielle, who answered with a quick nod. They must have both sensed it at the same time. Mortals. A lot of them, and they were close by. A series of hand signals informed the ghouls of what they had sensed, and they moved on.

Since it was hard to tell how close the mortals actually were, they were advancing much slower now. John had a good idea on straight-line distance, but the hallway had too many twists and turns in it for that to make any difference. When dealing with professionals, it was always best to err on the side of caution.

Eventually the hallway came to an end at a large metal door, which looked completely out of place. While the stairwell had been very dark and dank, the door looked new and had a fluorescent light directly above it. There was also an electronic lock in place of a door knob. It looked as if it required a keycard of some sort, and the input of a code, in order to open it.

They didn't have a keycard or a code, although it would be easy enough to get a keycard from one of the many bodies they left in the main building. He dismissed the idea, as it wouldn't help him with the code part, and he was tired of sneaking around. It would be more fun to just break the door down, especially since it looked pretty expensive.

Once he made up his mind, John looked every member of the team in the eye until they each nodded that they were ready. It wasn't necessary to discuss the plan, since everyone knew what was going to happen. When he was satisfied that the entire team was ready, John called upon the power of his blood to strengthen himself. It only took one blood-strengthened kick to break the door open and send it soaring through whatever room was on the other side. The entry team burst through the opening, took up attack positions, and froze in disbelief. They had definitely discovered something, and whatever it was, it was huge.

They found themselves on one side of an underground chamber that could have easily fit Lori's Bed and Breakfast inside of it and have room to spare. The chamber appeared to be divided into several different sections, although there were no actual walls dividing them. One of the larger areas was made up of a few dozen computer stations, and there were mortals working at about one-third of them.

They were the only mortals in the entire chamber, most likely due to the late hour. At the moment, however, not a single one of them was getting any work done. They were all staring at the entry team with the same looks of disbelief that the entry team wore.

The groups simply stared at one another for what seemed like an eternity. Finally, one of the mortals moved, as if reaching for something. That was all the entry team needed to be snapped out of its disbelief. The air was instantly filled with thrown weapons. Thankfully, the ghouls didn't need to be told not to use their various projectile weapons. They all knew that they wouldn't get much information out of the computers if they riddled them with bullets.

The range was about four times what a normal mortal could handle with thrown weapons. Fortunately, John, Danielle, and their ghouls weren't normal, and their aim was very good. Within seconds, every mortal had been dropped, various shaped blades finding their eyes, throats, and in some cases both.

"We might've just hit the jackpot, guys. Get moving." John figured there wasn't much sense in sticking to hand signals anymore.

"On it, sir." Sam and three ghouls put down their weapons and took out small stacks of blank discs and empty flash drives. They each went to a different computer station and began copying any and all files they could find, while two other ghouls began gathering up any hardcopy files they could locate. A single ghoul remained behind to guard the hallway they had come in from. It was tempting to collect all of the weapons as well, but that would take too long and there was a limit to what even they could carry.

"Let's move a little faster, people; we have to assume that these men got a warning out." Danielle went to a station and began working on her own. She didn't have any discs, but she could read over ten times faster than any mortal, and she would be able to memorize it all. Every little bit helped, and after all this nonsense, John wanted to leave with something good.

* * *

INITIATE JONATHAN Reynolds was furiously typing away at his keyboard, looking for anything he could use. He was part of the team assigned to the task of locating the vampires' haven. The only solid leads they had to go on were several clear pictures and a list of every location where they'd been spotted. Reynolds was currently going through every city record he could find, looking for other pictures of the vampires or anything that would give him a clue. It was a long shot, but it was only one of many plans Templar Andrews had put into action.

Reynolds was in the middle of scanning pictures taken the previous New Year's Eve when he was startled by what sounded like an explosion. He looked up in time to see their brand new door crash into the wall on the opposite side of the room. Half of his mind was in shock, since that door weighed over half a ton. The other half of his mind begged the obvious question. What could send a half-ton metal door hurtling that far and not completely destroy the surrounding area? Unfortunately, the answer soon became clear.

Nine figures burst into the room as Reynolds watched in horror. He didn't recognize seven of them, but he doubted that there was anyone in the room that didn't recognize the other two. The two abominations were responsible for the majority of his fear. Grief threatened to join his fear and overwhelm him once the full implications of seeing them here sank in. In order for them to be here at all meant they had gone through the building above. All those brave men, most of which were his friends, were all dead. Instead of overwhelming him, however, the grief seemed to cancel out his fear. He attained a sort of mental detachment and was suddenly much more aware of everything around him.

Reynolds was aware that, even though the two enemies faced each other, nothing was happening. The lack of response from his fellow workers was understandable. They were researchers, and did not possess the physical ability or the mental discipline to deal with what was happening. What he didn't understand was why the abominations weren't reacting. They seemed just as shocked as the researchers were.

Reynolds saw an opening and took it. Reaching over to his right, he hit a switch that would set off an alarm at the main headquarters installation. His movement seemed to break whatever trance had come over everyone else. The researchers all began screaming and scrambling for weapons, while the abominations' movements became a blur that he couldn't follow. The air was suddenly filled with thrown objects, and Reynolds knew that death would be quick and soon. As the blade meant for him pierced his throat, he gained satisfaction from knowing that the abominations would never make it out.

* * *

"JOHN, YOU'RE NOT going to believe this." Danielle called over to him as she continued reading.

"Try me." He moved toward the station where his wife was working.

"Looking around this chamber, you'd think we scored big, wouldn't you?"

"Well, normally I would say yes, but since you're asking me that question, I'm guessing the answer is no." She nodded slightly, never once taking her eyes from the screen.

"We did score big in the sense that we hit an information jackpot, but if you think that finding this place actually hurt these people as an organization, you'd be dead wrong, no pun intended. I haven't found much in the way of specifics yet, but we've stumbled onto something huge here. I'm talking worldwide. This chamber is nothing to them. At best, this place might be a listening post." John was barely able to contain his shock.

"We did get some good info though, right?"

"I won't be sure until we have a chance to sort through all the info the ghouls are collecting. One thing is certain. We are definitely getting a lot of information. It's tempting to stay here as long as possible, but I suggest we get the hell out of here quickly."

"Why?"

"Because I'm seeing a level of organization here that is far more complex than anything I expected. How long have we been here?" John glanced at his watch.

"We entered this chamber about six and a half minutes ago."

"If they did manage to get an alarm off, then whatever passes for a quick response team for these people is already on the way. Since they'll obviously assume that we are the source of the alarm, you can also assume that a serious amount of reinforcements are also on the way here." John couldn't fault her logic. It was definitely time to leave.

"I'll go along with that. Sam, we're done. I want you in constant contact with our teams outside. Tell them to converge on the back door and expect company." Sam nodded, pulled his disk out of the computer, and started calling for reports through his earpiece. "The rest of you have two minutes to finish, and then destroy everything." This equipment might not be that important to their enemy, but that didn't mean they were going to give it back.

John watched as his ghouls hurried to get as much last minute info as they could. At the same time, he saw Danielle leave her station and walk toward the chamber's armory. He was about to ask what she was looking for when he noticed the concerned look on Sam's face. Since he hadn't been paying attention, John tuned his earpiece over to the frequency the ghouls were using. Sam had a right to be concerned, and when he started his report, John already knew what he was going to say.

"Sir, teams one and three acknowledge and are moving into position now."

"What about team two?"

Sam's pause was brief but evident.

"There's no response."

* * *

JENKINS HAD NO explanation for the negative feeling he'd been experiencing all night. Thomas had been doing an excellent job getting the various necessary investigations underway. The extra men and supplies he had requested were on the way, and his superiors had not been angry about his recent losses. All in all, things were progressing as well as could be expected.

He had learned long ago to trust his instincts, however, and his instincts were telling him something was wrong. The night before, the team that was tracking the abominations reported suddenly losing all trace of them. There was a list of possible explanations that were much more plausible than the vampires discovering that they were being tracked. The team's leader was a trained warrior, and he hadn't been overly concerned about the sudden disappearances.

Jenkins's training was in the realm of the soul, not the physical. Who was he to argue with the instincts of a trained warrior? Try as he might, however, he couldn't stop thinking about what Thomas had said about the abominations. *They now know they are being hunted, and they will begin hunting us in return. We must destroy them quickly now, not only for God, but to ensure our own survival as well.*

The archbishop found a chair and tried not to look too tired as he sat down. Lately he had been spending most of his time at the headquarters installation for the city. He tried to constantly encourage his men by any means possible. Most of the men were far too busy to attend regular religious services, so he attended to them as they worked.

The recent losses had shocked many of the older members, and they had outright frightened most of the youngest recruits. He did his best to explain God's will, but how did one do that when he was afraid that he no longer knew it himself? *No!* He had to stop thinking like that. No one ever claimed it would be easy to understand or to do God's will, but it *must* be done. Even if all he could do was lend spiritual support. His men would get the job done, and he would provide them with the strength to do so.

With that in mind, Jenkins rose, a look of pure resolve on his face. He was determined to learn as much as he could so that he could take a more active role in the coming battles. Moving toward the nearest initiate, Jenkins decided that he would start by learning how his men accomplished their various tasks.

Seeing the archbishop approach, however, the initiate jumped to attention. With a silent sigh of annoyance, Jenkins quickly waved him back down. Over and over he had told these men to simply ignore his presence and continue with their work, but they acted as if he were God himself.

"Please continue your work, my son. I merely wish to ask you a few questions."

"Of course, Excellency." The initiate bowed, sat back at his station, and resumed his work. "How may I help you?"

"What is it that you are doing?"

"Well, Excellency, I'm part of the main investigative team responsible for finding the fiends' blood bank." Jenkins nodded his understanding.

"I see. Is it possible for you to take a moment to explain to me how this is done? I am proficient in using all of our most updated software, but how do you perform your searches?" The initiate turned to face the archbishop and began to rise again, but Jenkins motioned for him to remain seated.

"First, we get a list of all the privately owned—" His explanation was cut short by an alarm that grabbed everyone's attention.

"What is that?" Before the initiate could answer, a new voice cut in.

"That is a general alarm coming in from one of our outposts, sir." Jenkins turned to see Thomas coming toward him. He almost corrected his use of "sir," rather than "Excellency," since they were in front of others, but he decided against it. Thomas was a soldier, in what appeared to be a combat situation. Under the circumstances, "sir" would do just fine.

Thomas had discussed his new position with Jenkins in more depth a few days before. Rather than simply heading up their investigations, he wanted to command their combative forces as well. It made more sense to have a soldier with combat experience coordinate their efforts, instead of having a spiritual guide in charge. Jenkins was still in charge, and was responsible for all that happened, but he agreed to give Thomas's idea a chance. The way he was handling the current situation was evidence that he had made the right decision.

"Where's it coming from?"

"Outpost five, sir."

"Someone get an explanation from them and shut that alarm off." The alarm was silent in seconds.

"Sir, their phones are down."

"Only five of their workstations are active. The rest are either idle or off."

"How many were active?"

"As of a few minutes ago, thirteen."

"So, either eight people had to use the restroom at once or we have a problem. Alert the quick response force, and have them check it out. Get the ready force awake and suited up, in case they're needed."

"Done, sir. QRF reports ETA in seven minutes." Jenkins was stunned by the speed at which everything was happening, and he struggled to keep up with what was going on.

"Good. I want the situation monitored in detail. The rest of you, get back to work." His final order given, Thomas turned back to the archbishop to make his report.

"Sir, we've lost contact with one of our outposts. Some of their workstations are being actively used, but most aren't. It is my opinion that the abominations have raided it and are now using the workstations to garner information about us. The QRF will be on-site momentarily, and the ready force is approximately twenty minutes behind them."

Jenkins merely nodded. Something was nagging at the back of his mind.

"Outpost five? That's Lori's Bed and Breakfast. Isn't that where Templar Stevens's team operates from?"

"Yes, sir. Why do you ask?"

"Don't you remember Daniel's report about last night's tracking mission? He said they were tracking them normally until they simply vanished. Now, one night later, the outpost his team operates from gets attacked. It can't be a coincidence."

Thomas looked thoughtful for a moment. "He also said that they didn't return to base until nearly noon."

"Ghouls are not hampered by daylight."

Thomas's eyes went wide, as if he had just put together the pieces of an unseen puzzle.

"My God, they knew we were tracking them. The abominations set a trap for us. Thank you, sir, I hadn't noticed the connection. At least now we can prevent the same mistake from happening again."

Jenkins was not pleased with the situation, although he was very pleased that not only was he able to keep up with what was going on, but he had offered new insight that would save lives in the future.

"Sir, QRF reports contact with target. It's them, sir. Ready team acknowledges they need five more minutes to gather and arm, and fifteen minutes after that to get on target." Thomas faced the initiate and nodded his approval before turning back to the archbishop.

"Sir, we've got them. The QRF will attempt to pin them down until more reinforcements arrive."

"I applaud your efficiency, Thomas, but isn't our QRF the same size as the force we used in the ambush attempt? How can they hold against both vampires and however many ghouls are present, especially without the element of surprise?"

Thomas smiled wolfishly.

"I must have forgotten to tell you, sir. One of the first things I did was quadruple the size of the QRF. It now consists of sixteen werewolves and fifty men. Four of the werewolves are elders from Clan Red Fang. I apologize for my oversight, sir."

Jenkins stood in shocked silence as he contemplated those numbers. That was nearly a quarter of the total forces he had in this area. Of course, their reinforcements would begin arriving soon to balance that out.

"That's fine, Thomas. I trust your judgment, but is it not unwise to have such a large percentage of our force at that level of readiness? I am not an expert on these matters, but when do the men have the opportunity to rest?"

"Sir, that is an excellent observation," Thomas sounded pleased that his religious superior had noticed such a thing. "You are completely correct; however, it is simple necessity. We need that firepower, and we need it ready at all times. The men can handle it over the short-term, and this is a short-term situation. Even if the abominations have not been destroyed within the next week or so, enough of our reinforcements will have arrived to allow more men to rest at any one time without reducing our readiness numbers.

"That was my thinking when I made the initial decision anyway. It is quite possibly a moot point since it is probable we are about to destroy them both now." Thomas completed his explanation and received a nod of understanding from the archbishop.

"Is there any way I can monitor the battle?"

"Do you wish to speak to the men?"

"Good heavens no! I wouldn't dream of distracting them. I just want to be able to listen to what is happening. I do not wish to be sheltered from the realities of what is going on." Thomas looked at the archbishop with renewed respect and then reached for a set of headphones.

"Here you go, sir. These headphones are tagged for repairs since the microphone doesn't work for some reason. You'll be able to speak without worrying about your words being transmitted. The earpieces still work fine, so they should fulfill your purposes. I keyed it into the frequency that is being used for the battle."

"Thank you, my son." Jenkins put them on and was immediately immersed in the horrific sounds of an unholy battle.

* * *

"WE'RE SURROUNDED, master. Team two is down, but we seem to be holding our own for now. We think they'll start pushing harder when they realize how few of us there are. We can keep the back door clear for at least a few more minutes, master, but we think several men have entered through the other doors."

"Understood." When combat became inevitable, John usually took direct control of the ghouls himself. "Just stay out there and wait. We're killing anything that moves, so don't come into the building. They're just mortals. No werewolf would come inside a building to attack a vampire."

"Yes, master. It seems all the werewolves are trying to keep us pinned down. We count at least a dozen of them so far, but we've put down three."

"Anything else?"

"We're going through our ammo too quickly, and the werewolves are from the Red Fang clan. We also believe they have many reinforcements on the way."

"Okay, we're on our way out now. Kill as many as you can."

"Yes, master." John could hear the ghoul start shouting to the others that were left as he turned off his headset.

"All right, that's it people. We're done. Form up on the doorway and get ready to move. Danielle, what the hell are you looking for?" She had been rummaging around in the chamber's armory without a word for nearly two minutes now.

"This." As she held up the crate, John knew exactly what she had in mind, and he bared his fangs in anticipation. She had found a crate of white phosphorous grenades. Known to soldiers as "Willy Petes," the grenades were mostly used to destroy equipment. It made sense that a group of vampire hunters would keep them around, but John didn't think they had intended for them to be acquired by the enemy.

"Excellent idea." He saw the ghouls were ready and waiting. "Okay, Sam, get us out of here. There is an unknown number of enemy soldiers inside the building, but there are *no* friendlies."

"Got it, sir. You heard the master. Move out!" These were among the best-trained ghouls that they had, and additional instructions weren't necessary. They simply charged down the hallway. John could hear explosions as they threw grenades around the twists and turns before going around themselves.

As the ghouls were clearing the hall, Danielle selected two grenades and pulled the pins on both. She put one back in the crate, which she had set down in the center of the computer stations. The second one was tossed neatly into the center of the armory. Satisfied with the damage her work would wreak, she met her husband at the door, and they both linked up with the ghouls in the basement of the main building.

John quickly threw the trapdoor shut and motioned for the others to wait. It had been approximately seven seconds since Danielle had pulled the pin on the first grenade. He was beginning to wonder what went wrong when he heard all hell break loose beneath them. There was significant pressure building against the trapdoor, but he easily held it in place.

"What the hell did you guys do?" Sam gasped as the ground stopped rumbling.

"Danielle found a crate of Willy Petes. I'm sure you can figure out the rest. On the other hand," John faced his wife, "phosphorous burns, it doesn't explode like that. What else was in that armory?"

"Why, whatever do you mean, sweetie? Do you actually think I bothered to look in every single crate?" There was a brief round of laughter as she batted her eyelashes. John didn't know if she thought the innocent schoolgirl look actually fooled anyone or if she just did it for laughs.

"This is why we can't have nice things," he mumbled to himself ensuring it was loud enough to be overheard. "Okay," John got everyone's attention focused on him as he became serious again, "we have to link up with the ghouls guarding the back door and get the hell out of here." Sam nodded and got the ghouls moving upstairs, and John and Danielle were forced to follow behind.

In this situation, their vampiric senses were working against them. There was too much confusion both inside and out, and their senses were picking up every detail in one big mess. It was very disorienting, and they both felt a little off balance. Once they finally got outside, however, everything would snap back into focus.

The run through the building was surprisingly uneventful. A handful of mortals were the only resistance, and they were easily dealt with. John exchanged a glance with both Sam and Danielle, and he could see they were thinking the same thing he was. The enemy wasn't trying to overrun their position; they were trying to keep them pinned down. That meant reinforcements were on the way.

It didn't change the situation. Everyone knew the battle plan. The vampires would charge in, while the ghouls stayed behind cover and picked off as many as they could. They would run as soon as they caused sufficient confusion to keep from being followed. John shook any distracting thoughts from his mind as the back door came into view. As they burst outside, he instantly realized that he had been wrong earlier. The explosion Danielle had caused wasn't hell breaking loose. Hell had already broken loose outside.

Everywhere he looked, John could see the devastation of battle. Phosphorous rounds had started small fires in several places, grenades had left small craters in walls and the ground, and debris was scattered everywhere. Many of the bodies that littered the ground were burning, and the smell of fresh blood and burning flesh was causing his beast to stir.

Not all of the corpses were mortals and ghouls. John was happy to see at least four werewolves had been brought down as well. Most people wouldn't have thought ghouls were capable of doing that, but these ghouls were. A ghoul's power was determined by the power of the blood they fed on to stay alive. Since these ghouls had been created by ancient vampires, they were far more powerful than normal ghouls would be. Unfortunately, John only saw five ghouls remaining from the original twelve they had left behind.

To make matters worse, he could sense twelve werewolves still in the struggle. If they really were from Clan Red Fang, that was bad news. Red Fang was one of the few werewolf clans that actively used weapons, and at least three of them would be elders.

All this ran through John's mind in an instant, and then he charged with Danielle into the center of the chaos. The rest of the entry team joined the remnants of the first squad, and there was a definite increase in the rate of gunfire as they got into fray. To the two vampires, however, the ghouls were no longer a factor. The only things that mattered to them were the enemy and each other.

They announced their presence with matching fireballs that sent enemy troops scattering for cover. Danielle vanished in a blur of motion as she charged a group of mortals. At the same time, a young werewolf leapt at John, who simply waited for it. As the beast came within arm's reach of his throat, John put one of his claws precisely between the wolf's eyes. The beast went limp instantly, two inches of John's claw protruding from the back of its head.

He withdrew his claw and dove for cover. With a small explosion, a crater was all that was left of the area he had been standing in. Thankfully, he had dodged most of the blast, and his armor deflected the few pieces of shrapnel that did find him. A well-placed blast from his shotgun dropped the thrower, but there were three more ready to take his place.

* * *

WHILE JOHN WAS busy dodging grenades, Danielle had gotten into a nice mess of her own. She was trying to finish off a werewolf, but there was an annoying group of mortals making it difficult for her. It would be easy to finish them all off, but she was trying to conserve her blood. There was no telling how long this battle would last.

The werewolf attacking her was young enough for her to hold back with a sword while she kept the mortals pinned with bursts of fire. It was working, but she noticed another pair of yellow eyes moving toward her. Calling upon a small amount of additional blood, she increased her speed enough to overwhelm the first werewolf.

With a final stroke, she decapitated the beast and then focused on the mortals. Fire had been keeping them pinned, but it wasn't enough to kill them. Reaching her decision, Danielle pointed to where they were regrouping and began to chant. A single bolt of lightning struck the area, flinging charred bodies in every direction.

Danielle grinned in satisfaction. Calling forth lightning when the sky was perfectly clear was difficult, and she had been right on target. Her victory was cut short as the second werewolf completed its charge, knocking her to the ground.

As she began shredding the beast with her claws, Danielle wondered if they'd be able to make it out in time. If the enemy's reinforcements got there before they could escape, their blood reserves wouldn't last. Of course, on the other hand, this was no trap or ambush that caught her by surprise. This was the battle she and her husband had wanted to happen. Even if they didn't make it out, she hadn't had this much fun in decades.

* * *

"IS THAT THEM?"

"The abominations have engaged!"

"First squad, keep those ghouls pinned! The rest of you, bring those monsters down!"

"Third squad, form on me and—"

"Douglas is down! Close it up, people!"

"Shit, did you see that? How do we fight against lightning?"

"With the power of God. Now stay off the net, unless you have something useful!"

"Got one! Another ghoul down!"

"Nice shooting, Steve. Now—"

Jenkins listened to the horrific sounds of battle. He didn't show it, but every voice that got cut off felt like losing one of his own limbs. Fortunately, the monsters were paying for the deaths they caused. Several ghouls had already been brought down. Jenkins knew those ghouls would be among the strongest they had and wouldn't be easy to replace.

It also seemed that the vampires weren't trying to escape. They had to know reinforcements were on the way. It could only mean that they refused to abandon their ghouls, which meant the ghouls must be carrying valuable stolen information. Thomas's grin showed that he had reached the same conclusion. It was a lose-lose situation for the monsters. Of course, they had already underestimated them twice before. Jenkins hoped this battle wouldn't prove to be a third.

* * *

JOHN DOVE FOR cover behind a crumbling section of wall. A few rounds hit him, but most went wide. As he loaded more rounds into his shotgun, he took quick stock of the situation.

They were down to nine ghouls total, including Sam. Several werewolves had been put down, but the elders had yet to show themselves. Danielle and he were still doing fine, but they couldn't keep this up forever.

He was starting to use his blades and shotgun more often, to conserve his blood. It seemed to be working, but the situation was still a mess. They had killed so many, yet they still seemed to be surrounded. John used a bit more blood to scatter a group of attackers with a fireball. He lined up his shotgun to bring down a few of the now exposed mortals, and John saw Danielle appear out of nowhere to decapitate a pair of them.

The instant she completed her attack, however, an enormous werewolf took her by surprise with a powerful backhand strike. The blow sent her hurtling through a nearby wall, which then proceeded to collapse on top of her. John winced reflexively, knowing the impact with the wall, not to mention being buried under hundreds of pounds of rubble, had to have caused her heavy damage.

She would recover easily, but it would be costly in blood. Unfortunately, the werewolf didn't seem to agree, as it charged for his buried wife. John would have been able to easily stop it in time if it had been a normal werewolf, but the several new pairs of glowing eyes in the darkness confirmed what he already knew. The elders had joined the battle.

* * *

"ONE OF THE ELDERS just nailed the female hard!"

"Damn, she's buried; I can't get a clear shot!"

"Forget her. All the elders are gathering for a major assault. All squads, concentrate fire on the ghouls. Keep'em pinned down."

Jenkins dared not get his hopes up, but he prayed for all he was worth. With what he had learned about these vampires' abilities, he had been thinking they were holding back. Perhaps this was what they were holding back for? Although, it did seem as if the elder wolves had caught them by surprise. The female was down, and Jenkins didn't see how the male could possible assist her in time.

The elders from Clan Red Fang were among the most powerful in the SOG arsenal. Most of the male's magic wouldn't be very effective against a target moving as fast as the elder could. In addition, Jenkins doubted that the male had any conventional weapons with him capable of stopping an elder. Hurt it maybe, but not stop it.

His only chance was to reach the female first, but he was much too far behind, and he had apparently noticed the other elders approaching him. Even with all the death and destruction, Jenkins had to admit he was curious. What would the abomination do? It was strange enough for a demon to have a mate, but would he risk himself? Would he turn his back on the other wolves simply for the slight chance of rescuing his mate?

Jenkins doubted it. Odds were the male would realize the battle was lost and run away to save himself. He would get away, but at the female's destruction. There was no chance a demon would face near certain destruction in a hopeless struggle. Jenkins just wished the coming victory didn't have to be so costly.

* * *

JOHN CHARGED THE ELDER, knowing he wouldn't make it. Danielle would most likely survive, but she was about to take a pounding. It became a moot point when he saw Sam leap at the beast from the other direction and pull something from his belt. John had no idea what Sam was thinking. He had to know that he couldn't possibly win against a werewolf of that power.

The elder opened its jaws to welcome the incoming prey that seemed so eager to sacrifice himself. Sam didn't disappoint. In fact, he rammed his arm down the beast's throat. The werewolf easily snapped his arm off with its powerful jaws and tossed him aside. It could have easily finished him off, but it wouldn't be swayed from its original target.

John suddenly realized he had wasted the few extra seconds Sam had bought for him. He had been too busy being shocked by Sam's audacity to realize he now had a chance. The werewolf seemed to know that nothing stood in its way, and it let out a monstrous growl in anticipation of its next meal.

The werewolf's growl quickly turned to a yelp of agony as the white phosphorous grenade Sam had been clutching in his hand finally went off. John put the puzzle together instantly. The grenade must have been what he had seen Sam pull from his belt. The elder swallowed it along with his arm, and it melted through the beast's insides. John couldn't see the damage, but he could smell the phosphorous, and he knew Sam's move had delivered a fatal blow.

Danielle would be fine digging herself out now, and they had killed one of the elders, but at what price? His wife was badly injured, Sam was lying dead or dying somewhere among the debris, and only a handful of their ghouls were still able to fight back. They needed a new plan, and John had just thought of one. He turned on the werewolves that were charging him, ready to cause the diversion he would need, but he never got the chance.

There was a large crash of debris behind him as Danielle literally launched herself out from underneath the collapsed wall. John grinned at the prospect of watching how the remaining wolves would deal with his wife now that she was thoroughly pissed off. He was about to use her as the distraction, rather than causing one himself, when he noticed that she hadn't come down. Danielle was simply hovering about twenty-five meters above the ground.

There was no time for confusion now; however, the wolves were advancing once again. John lined up his shotgun with the smallest wolf he could see. The instant he pulled the trigger, two things happened. His target's head exploded in a spray of burning gore, and a lightning bolt struck the ground between himself and the advancing wolves.

The force of the bolt knocked John back a few feet but didn't injure him. It was soon followed by half a dozen more bolts striking all across the enemy's side of the ad hoc battlefield in rapid succession. The lightning was then followed by several fireballs and a fiery rain that seemed to blanket the area. His wife was letting them have it with both barrels, and under normal circumstances, he would be scolding her careless disregard for her blood levels.

Of course, these weren't normal circumstances, and the chaos her attack was causing was just what he had been waiting for. John immediately ran to search for Sam's body. He found him barely alive, but alive nonetheless. Scooping him up, John then charged off to where the remaining ghouls were still trading fire with a small group of mortals.

John threw his last grenade in the general direction of the enemy's fire. Within three seconds of the grenade's detonation, he had placed a shotgun round in the heads of all four mortals that had tried to run. Satisfied that his wife and he had bought their ghouls a brief respite, John set his simple plan into motion.

"Who's in charge here?"

One of the ghouls motioned for his attention. "I am, master."

"Okay, Marcus. This is what you're going to do. Take Sam, and anyone else not dead yet, and get out of here."

"We will not leave you here, master."

"Yes you will. The information we gathered today is priceless. Get out of here now, while they're distracted. Danielle and I will be fine. Meet us back at the haven one hour before sunrise."

"Yes, master." John could tell the ghoul wasn't happy, but he would do as instructed.

Marcus began shouting out orders, and the rest of the ghouls rushed to obey. Within twenty seconds, they were all out of sight. Pleased that at least most of the information they had stolen would be safe, he turned his attention back to assisting his wife.

John quickly made his way back to where Danielle was still causing a large amount of carnage. Adding his own blasts of fire to hers, they burned another werewolf to ash before increasing gunfire caused John to reflexively dive for cover. Unfortunately the shots weren't aimed at him. Danielle had been so intent on dishing out destruction that she hadn't realized how exposed she was.

At least seven phosphorous rounds had hit her, and while it wasn't enough to destroy her, it broke whatever spell she was using to stay in the air. She plummeted twenty-five meters straight down, causing a decent-sized impact crater. John was there to help her in time to see her wounds begin to close. By now most of her armor had been torn off or burned away, but she still seemed okay.

"You really need to stop crashing into things, sweetheart. It's bad for the bones." She grinned as her ribcage slowly expanded back out to its appropriate size. John quickly helped her out, and they stood side by side, ready to end this battle once and for all. Their unspoken challenge didn't go unanswered.

The three elder werewolves, along with four others, were grouped directly in front of them, barely ten meters away. Nearly all of them bore burn marks and singed hair, the result of Danielle's previous attack, and all were brandishing wicked-looking swords and axes in each clawed hand. They didn't seem very happy to see them, but they were obviously anticipating fresh kills.

All in all, it was a very frightening sight—or rather it would have been if either John or Danielle had cared. Taking on this many wolves would be no easy task, but it was their only option if they were to escape before enemy reinforcements arrived.

"What's the plan, love?" Danielle asked as she morphed her hands to claws and assumed a defensive stance.

"I'm tired of fucking around. We end this now!" They both sprang into action, instantly charging in different directions. The werewolves charged as well, trying to surround the vampires, and all nine combatants were suddenly moving at inhuman speeds.

John fired the rest of his ammo at any target he could see, but none of them dropped. The weaker wolves must have already been destroyed. He tried a few bursts of fire but couldn't be sure if he had hit any of them. There were simply too many wolves, and they were moving too fast. It was nearly impossible for him to track an individual target while, at the same time, preventing himself from being surrounded.

Danielle had opted for a different strategy. Rather than trying to track the wolves, she simply blanketed the area in front of her with fire. When she heard a yelp of pain, Danielle sent a directed blast toward the stunned wolf, reducing it to ash. The attack was much more successful than John's, but far more costly in blood. With the way his wife had been fighting throughout the entire battle, her blood levels had to be dangerously low by now.

Up to this point, John and Danielle had been exploiting the werewolves' one major disadvantage. The beasts weren't very intelligent. There was something about the change that caused a werewolf to lose much of its human intellect in "beast form." They hated vampires but knew to be cautious around them. That same caution was keeping them back and allowing the two vampires to pick them off. Unfortunately, it didn't last much longer. Eventually, the wolves noticed that they outnumbered their prey significantly. Realizing this, they adopted the best strategy they could. They charged. It was the most predictable thing they could have done, but it was also the only thing the two vampires were hoping wouldn't happen.

John and Danielle stood back to back as the wolves charged. They might be able to survive the attack if the wolves couldn't separate them. With no time to discuss strategy and little other defensive choice, the vampires drew their best swords and morphed their free hands into claws twice as long as they normally would. They would attempt to use their swords to deflect the enemy attacks, while using their claws to tear the beasts apart.

No mortal eye could have followed the ensuing struggle. Moonlight glinted off the combatants' weapons as the five remaining wolves surrounded their prey. The vampires swords flashed with as much speed as they could force, deflecting attack after attack. They were holding their own, but only barely.

"This isn't working!" Even as John successfully deflected a trio of attacks, he felt a sword bite into his right leg and an ax catch in his ribs. Instinctively, his claws shot upward, and he was rewarded with seeing a wolf fall back, clutching the stub where its right hand had been. There was no time for him to enjoy the small victory. As soon as the wolf had fallen back, an elder moved up to take its place.

"I've got an idea!" His wife's voice was strained, and he could hear the wolves on her side scoring successful attacks against her.

"I'm game. What's the plan?"

"On my signal, hit them with everything you've got, all at once."

Both knew it was risky. If they used all they had left, they would be hard pressed to survive any counterattacks. But with the way things were shaping up, they had to take the chance.

"Agreed!" John had already decided what form his attack would take.

"Now!"

Just as the elder reared back to strike, John sent a burst of fire directly into the beast's face. At the same time, he threw a ring of fire around himself and Danielle, to hold the wolves back while he concentrated on his attack. Danielle's attack took the form of several well-placed lightning strikes that were far more controlled than her previous ones. The sudden assault killed two more wolves and forced the survivors back to regroup.

"Quickly, mist now."

"Wait, I'm not as good at that as you are."

"Just do it!" Without waiting for a response, Danielle's form melted away as a cloud of mist took her place. Seeing no other choice, John followed suit. It was fortunate that he hadn't delayed any longer, or the rocket that impacted on his clothing may have destroyed him. The enemy reinforcements had arrived.

John had not even heard the rocket being fired. He hadn't expected to face weaponry that heavy. The weapon, which had been expertly aimed, had impacted on what was left of his armored jacket. Since his clothing was much heavier and thicker than normal, it was enough for the rocket to detonate, even though there was no longer any solid mass inside of it. John knew that if he had been even a second slower, he would have been gravely injured or worse. As it was, the explosion completely overwhelmed his senses and left him blind for a short time.

When his senses returned, John saw that any sanity the confrontation had retained up to this point had completely vanished. The warhead had been some kind of high-explosive phosphorous round, and while he and Danielle had escaped injury, the wolves had not been so lucky. The explosion had killed all of the remaining wolves except for a single elder. John watched as the elder, pure rage evident in its eyes, charged in the direction of the reinforcements, killing everything in its path.

Any other time and John would have found the situation comical, but at the moment, he was too busy trying to take advantage of it. He looked around until he saw where Danielle was going and did his best to follow her. Concentrating, John spread himself out as thin as possible. It wouldn't do to have gone through all this trouble just to have the enemy track the giant, thick cloud all the way back to its haven.

In their present forms, neither vampire could be injured by conventional means. They were also able to move in any direction they chose. Danielle slowly glided about half a mile from the battle, John keeping pace about ten meters behind her. When she started sliding up the side of a nearby building, he became concerned that he wouldn't be able to hold his form. He was expending blood at a much higher rate than his wife was, due to his lack of proficiency using this form.

It was difficult to tell how much farther he had to go, but it couldn't be much. He saw Danielle disappear and assumed the roof was close by. A moment later he could see the edge of the roof just out of reach. Just as it seemed he was in the clear, his concentration lapsed and his form failed. Something grabbed him as he reverted back to normal, and pulled him over the side before he could tumble three stories to the pavement below.

As he lay on the rooftop, naked and covered with blood-sweat, it was difficult for John to not feel annoyed with his wife. She was just standing there staring at him with a stupid-looking grin plastered on her face. True, her plan had worked and she had saved him from falling, but she didn't have to be so smug about it.

"Practice makes perfect, eh love?"

"Hush."

She winked and turned to peer back over the side. John decided she was checking to ensure they hadn't been followed. He could still hear the sounds of the elder werewolf wreaking havoc among the enemy reinforcements, but they could never be too careful. She turned back toward John, apparently satisfied that they were safe for the moment.

"Here, put these on." She handed him an armored jacket and a pair of pants. "As we left the battle, I passed one of our downed ghouls. I remembered that you wouldn't be able to take your clothes with you, so I grabbed his." They were covered with bullet holes, burn marks, and blood, but they were better than nothing.

"Thanks." He began to dress and then suddenly looked up again. "Wait, you were able to collect new objects while you were mist, and turn them to mist as well?"

"Aye, love. It's difficult, but we can't have you running around the city naked now, can we?"

"Damn, I really need to learn that," he mumbled as he finished dressing. Once finished, John joined his wife at the edge of the roof. "You hear that?"

"Yeah, sounds like the elder's really tearing into them."

"Apparently these mortals and wolves don't have as strong an alliance as we thought."

"It could just be because that rocket killed his clanmates, but we should hold off on making any assumptions until we review all the data we got."

"You're right, but I will admit to being very curious as to what headlines we'll see in the paper after all that obvious destruction."

They spent several minutes simply staring at one another. It had been centuries since they'd come so close to losing each other, and it had happened more than once in the last couple of weeks. Never had they faced an enemy with such overwhelming power and resources.

If the information they recovered didn't reveal any weaknesses, John didn't know what they would do. If they ran, eventually they would be found again. If they continued fighting, eventually they would be overwhelmed. The same thoughts seemed to be running through Danielle's mind. John could see the look of love, concern, and even a bit of fear in her eyes.

"Love?"

"I know."

"Me too." What else needed to be said?

"Well, we should really get moving."

"Haven?"

"No. I didn't realize how early it still was. Screw waiting for dawn. We'll link up with the ghouls now and head home together. If Sam is still alive, we need to get him home as soon as possible to make sure he stays that way. Do you still have your earpiece?" John's was lying in the pile of clothing and weapons he left behind when he turned to mist. That is, if anything in the pile was left after the rocket attack.

"Afraid not. It got smashed by one of the walls I crashed through."

"All right, we'll just find them the old-fashioned way. It won't be difficult to track down our own ghouls." Danielle nodded and handed him one of her remaining swords.

"Here, you may need it."

"Thanks, love. Any idea where to start?"

"Underground. They most likely went down into the sewers as soon as they were sure nothing was following them." John nodded and started scanning the streets. Seeing a manhole cover about a quarter of a mile away from them, he pointed it out to his wife.

"Let's go. It sounds like the battle is over, one way or the other. If there're any survivors, they'll be searching for us soon." Both vampires leapt from the rooftop and landed without a sound. A quick check showed that there was no one around, and they sped toward the cover, disappearing through it without a trace.

Chapter 9

"SO, HOW IS HE?" John turned to his wife but didn't return her smile. They had scoured the sewers for nearly an hour before finally finding their remaining ghouls. As annoying as it had been, John was forced to congratulate them on the excellent job of concealing themselves. Unfortunately, none of the ghouls with medical experience had survived. Aside from simple first aid, they hadn't been able to do much about Sam's wounds.

John had immediately grabbed him and sped off toward the haven. Danielle chose to stay behind and lead the ghouls in at their best pace. Using a borrowed earpiece, John had called ahead and made sure their doctor was standing by. Upon reaching the haven, he handed Sam over to the doctor, who took him into a back room to see what, if anything, could be done.

"I don't know. The doc's been with him since I got back and hasn't come out yet. I know better than to disturb him while he's working, but if it's taking this long, it can't be good." As if on cue, John heard the door opening. Any hope he had been harboring about Sam's condition was instantly dashed by the look on Dr. Peterson's face.

"Okay, Pete, let's have it."

"I tried my best, master, but the damage was simply too extensive. He lost too much blood, and it's too late to solve the problem by simply pouring more blood into him.

"He's dead?"

"Not yet, but he will be soon. Most of his organs have either shut down or been badly damaged. I believe that the only reason he's still alive is because he's a ghoul, although it won't be more than another ten minutes or so now. There's nothing I can do." To John, Sam dying was not an option.

"I can save him."

It didn't take long for Peterson to realize what John had in mind.

"Um, master, I must disagree with what you are planning."

"Explain yourself." It had been far too long a night for him to be getting questioned by a ghoul.

"Master, I have known Sam for a long time and consider him to be a close friend. He has always wished to someday be turned by you, but he wanted to earn it. I believe that he would be offended if you were to turn him simply to save his life, although—"

"Enough!" John interrupted, the beginnings of anger toughing his voice. "Sam has earned it more times over than I can remember. His recent injuries were inflicted by an elder werewolf as he brought it down, possibly saving my wife in the process. If you ever question me again, doctor, I'll rip out your throat and eat your heart." John felt his wife's hand on his shoulder, and his demeanor instantly softened.

"Are we too late for that to work?" Danielle asked the question as softly as she could, hoping to calm the other ghoul. It still took Peterson a moment to get over the terror he felt when faced with his master's anger.

"I don't think so. From what I understand, master, a person can be turned up to their moment of death. Unfortunately, I don't know if it works the same way for ghouls." John nodded, and waved the doctor away. Peterson, for his part, seemed to be relieved to be leaving with his head still attached to his shoulders. Danielle merely raised an eyebrow.

"It wouldn't hurt for you to watch your temper, love."

John sighed. "I'll worry about that later. Right now, we have to save Sam."

* * *

SAM HADN'T thought it possible to be in this much pain. He could no longer tell if he was breathing or even if his heart was still beating. Pain was all he could feel, pain and a desperate unwillingness to die.

The door to his room opened, but he was unable to move to see who had entered. A moment later both John and Danielle moved into his field of vision. He smiled, relieved to see that his masters had both survived the battle. What more could he have hoped for?

John was saying something, but Sam couldn't hear him. It didn't matter. He imagined that he was being praised for a job well done. The thought of death held no appeal for him, but he had to die sometime. At least he had accomplished his mission and would die in the company of friends.

Eventually, John must have realized that he couldn't hear him. Sam saw him look to Danielle, who nodded, and he wondered what was going on. Not that it made much of a difference. His vision was beginning to blur, and then it faded completely. The last thing he saw was John leaning in closer. He felt a small pinch at his neck, and instantly his pain dissipated. Sam's final thought as the darkness claimed him was that apparently death wasn't so bad after all.

* * *

UPON OPENING his eyes, Sam quickly noticed three things that were very wrong. First, he wasn't dead. Second, he felt great. Finally, there seemed to be a disgusting mess of meat and bone where his missing arm should have been. He was still lying on the table where the doctor had been examining him, but that much at least was to be expected.

Perhaps he had been dreaming for the last few hours. Of course, that didn't explain what he was doing on an examination table or what had happened to his arm. Unless he was still dreaming. He felt awake. Maybe he was dead after all? He didn't feel dead, but he had never been dead before, so how the hell should he know?

Turning his head, he saw that John and Danielle were still in the room, and they seemed happy about something. Maybe they could give him an explanation. Sam swung his legs over the side of the table and began to get up. John and Danielle both instantly went from looking happy to looking very concerned. John even looked as if he were about to jump up and start shouting.

As if Sam didn't have enough confusion at the moment, what the hell was wrong with them all the sudden? Not that he could do anything about it. At the moment Sam was only going to worry about one thing, and that was standing up, so he could join his masters on the other side of the room. He didn't even have time to notice that his legs couldn't support him before the back of his skull smashed against the table, knocking him unconscious for a second time.

* * *

WHEN SAM OPENED his eyes again, he was absolutely certain that he was alive and awake. It wasn't possible to be dead and still have your head hurt so damn much. Of course, to Sam, alive and in pain was far better than dead. Plus, he was much more comfortable than before.

John and Danielle must have carried him to the study while he had been unconscious. The soft leather couch on which he now lay was far more comfortable than the metal examination table had been. The vampires were both sitting near the couch, most likely to discourage him from trying to get up again. Not that he was likely to repeat his earlier blunder, but it was nice to know they cared.

"You think you can stay conscious for a few minutes this time?" Sam tried to answer but barely managed a few faint noises, which confused him even more. How could he feel great, aside from the pain in his head, but not be able to control his own body properly?

"Don't try to talk. Just listen and stay conscious." He managed a small nod. John spent the next few minutes relating to Sam the end of the battle, which he had been unconscious for. He was pleased to hear that his suicide attack on the elder werewolf had been successful, although it sounded as if their ghoul element had taken heavy casualties. Unfortunately, none of this answered any of his current questions. And to top it all off, he was suddenly very, very thirsty.

"I'll make the rest of this brief, since I know from experience what you're about to go through." This piqued Sam's interest. "You would have died from your injuries if we hadn't acted quickly. As reward for over a century of loyal service, and for sacrificing yourself to save my wife, you have been turned. Congratulations, my friend. You're finally a vampire."

Sam didn't know what to say—not that it really mattered, since he was unable to speak. His thirst was rapidly growing worse, and his throat felt completely constricted. The only thing he could think to do was point at his neck and hope John would know what he meant.

"Oh, sorry about that, Sam." He motioned to someone outside of Sam's field of vision. "Don't worry; we'll fix that in a sec. You can't move or speak very well right now because you've been a vampire for nearly twenty-four hours and have yet to feed." John realized that Sam most likely had no idea what day it was. "The battle was last night. You were turned a few hours before dawn, and you regained consciousness about two hours ago. Then, after knocking yourself back out, you just woke back up, and here we are.

"Your arm is a mess because you've yet to learn how to control your powers. Your injury started to heal the instant I turned you. Unfortunately, you're a fledgling—being unconscious didn't help either—so your arm began healing more randomly than normal. It's also adding to your body's desperate need for blood, which is the reason behind your weakness." Sam heard a door open and close, and footsteps approached them.

"Thankfully, your situation is easily remedied." A ghoul appeared with a large tray holding three glasses and three pitchers. The pitchers looked to be about two-gallon size, and they were filled to the brim with blood. "The first few days for a new vampire are extremely dangerous, so listen to me very carefully." As he spoke, John began to fill one of the glasses.

"You're about to experience many things at once. I realize that you can't move or speak, but that will change very soon. Until I instruct you to, however, do not move or speak. Do whatever I tell you to, whenever I tell you to do it. No more, and no less. Is that understood?"

Sam's confusion came back in full force. John was treating Sam as if he had never drank blood before. He had been living off John's blood for the last hundred years, so what was the big deal? He would, of course, do exactly as he was instructed. There was no doubting or arguing with the seriousness evident in John's eyes, so he managed a small nod of assent.

"Good." John put a straw in the glass and moved closer to him. Slowly Sam became aware of a smell that was steadily increasing in its intensity. He decided that it must be coming from the glass, but that didn't make any sense. He knew what blood smelled like, and this wasn't it. This was a far more intoxicating aroma than what he was used to, and it took all of his willpower to remain still and await instructions.

"Now, sip slowly." Sam eagerly accepted the offered straw and began to sip. It was more work than he had expected, since blood was so thick, but he wouldn't be swayed so easily. The straw had been John's idea, as a way to prevent him from drinking too much, too quickly. Sam didn't know this, and he didn't care. As he swallowed that first hard-won mouthful of blood, his mind exploded into clarity.

Every time he had consumed blood in the past, it had been merely to sustain himself. Never had he experienced such pure power and ecstasy, and it happened instantly. His senses seemed to stretch outward almost indefinitely, and his mind began to work faster than he could comprehend. Sam knew that technically he was dead, but he had never felt so alive, so ... immortal.

Every now and then, Sam had been fortunate enough to be permitted to accompany his masters while they were hunting. He remembered never understanding the glazed look they always had in their eyes when they were feeding. Now, however, he understood perfectly. All he wanted, all he could think about at this moment, was blood. John seemed to know exactly what was running through his mind, and he nodded permission for Sam to continue.

A few more mouthfuls and Sam could no longer even describe what he was feeling. It was as if pleasure had taken tangible form and wrapped itself around him. The entire time Sam was feeling this, he had to remember not to move or speak. He still did not understand those instructions. His reaction to the blood had been a surprise, but it had been a positive one. Where was the harm?

Sam was mulling over that question between sips when an odd feeling came over him. A deep growling, that he felt more than heard, seemed to begin in his belly and spread throughout his body. It was filling him with the need to drink more. Sam had already wanted to do that, but this feeling was much more intense and primal.

He had been about to ask John to remove the straw so he might drink a bit faster, but now he was considering killing John and taking his blood instead. The blood of an ancient vampire would be so much sweeter than the weak mortal blood he was being fed. A look of concern crossed John's face, and it snapped Sam out of his train of thought. What had just happened? Had he really been about to attack his master?

"That was the beast, my friend. I could see from the look in your eye that it had nearly taken over you. Thankfully, it seems you have forced it back down."

"And if I hadn't?"

"Then you would have already been destroyed." Sam now understood the seriousness of the situation. He could still feel the urges and the pull of the beast, but now that he understood, it was easier to ignore it. He listened as John continued.

"The beast will be with you forever. You cannot get rid of it because it is the essence of what you have now become. We will show you ways to combat it, but the actual struggle will be yours alone to bear, as it is for us all." Sam nodded solemnly.

"Well, since you passed our little test, we don't have to destroy you," John's wink alleviated the seriousness Sam had thought was coming, "so sit up. We need to discuss what we learned." It took a moment, but Sam was able to use his good arm to force himself into a sitting position.

"What's up?"

"Let's fix that arm of yours first." John drank the remaining blood that had been in Sam's glass, slashed his arm, and filled the glass back up with his own blood. "Here, drink this." Sam accepted the offered drink with a raised eyebrow.

"All blood is not the same. What you're feeding on determines how powerful the blood is. Basically, it goes animals, mortals, and demons. That's weakest to strongest. Demons include werewolves, ghouls, vampires, and so on, and demonic blood's power is determined by the power of the demon. As ancient vampires, both Danielle's and my blood hold more power than anything you're likely to encounter. One glass of my blood is the equivalent of several dozen glasses of regular mortal blood, and is more than enough to finish healing your arm—although if you lose it again, it will take much more."

"Why?"

"Okay, this is complicated, and most of it is guesswork based on personal experience." Sam nodded for him to continue. "Firstly, for some reason it doesn't seem to matter what injuries you suffer as a mortal. Once you're turned, they all seem to heal at relatively the same rate, no matter how strong of a vampire you are personally. However, injuries you suffer as a vampire work differently.

"Essentially, the stronger you are, the more difficult it is to injure you. Observe." John pulled out a regular pocket knife and easily pricked one of Sam's fingers. He then attempted to jam the knife into his own arm, but the blade snapped without leaving so much as a scratch. "The downside is that the stronger you are, the more blood it takes to heal yourself if you are injured."

"Okay, I get that much, but what determines a vampire's strength? If I'm less than two days old, how strong could I possibly be?"

John smiled, as if expecting that question.

"Three main things contribute to your strength: the purity of your blood, your age, and your training. The purity of your blood is the most important, and yours is far more pure than normal for these times."

"You lost me."

John sighed but continued.

"Okay, look, vampires have to have come from somewhere. Think about how we multiply. We aren't born, we're turned. That means a different species couldn't have evolved into vampires, the way humans eventually evolved from apes. There had to be an original, a single vampire who began turning others, who in turn turned others, and so on. Who that original was, or where he or she came from, we have no idea, but such a creature had to exist. The purity of your blood depends on how far removed you are from that original." Sam nodded slowly.

"So you mean, for example, if the original vampire turned me, I would be stronger than if, say, the original turned someone else, and that someone else turned me? Kinda like if my mother is Italian, I'm half Italian, but if my grandmother is Italian, I'm only a quarter Italian." John smiled, which Sam took to mean he had the right idea. It was annoying to feel so lost and confused, but it couldn't be helped. He was a vampire now, and he was determined to learn all he could.

"That's the basic idea anyway." Danielle took up the explanation while John stopped for a blood break. "We think of it in terms of generations. Of course, vampires only have one 'parent,' whereas mortals have two. The thing is we don't know how many generations there are in total because we have no idea when the original existed. The only way we can gauge our power overall is by comparison to other vampires.

"In the last few centuries, vampires as a whole began turning more and more mortals. This trend has continued even to this day. The result has been a vast decrease in the amount of time before a new generation of vampires appears in enough numbers to make a difference. We don't know why any of this has happened, but we can hazard a few guesses, based on the information we do have.

"First of all, in our day, the average vampire was very old. Unfortunately, the Inquisition destroyed most of them. I doubt that there are very many vampires left in the world over five hundred years old, but the overall number of vampires has skyrocketed. So you basically have a bunch of children running around turning mortals left and right because it makes them feel powerful.

"Whatever generation is currently the newest, they are most likely somewhere between twenty and twenty-five generations further removed from the original source than John and myself. Honestly, it could even be more like thirty or forty considering how quickly these idiots are multiplying. We've also noticed that vampires from this newest generation are little more than animals. Their blood is so impure that it carries very little power with it. What makes it difficult is that, since we're immortal, you can't base our generation from our age.

"Take yourself, for example. You're less than two days old, but your blood is more pure than the vast majority of vampires still in existence today. In terms of strength, the purity of your blood determines your potential and the power you have access to. You simply have to learn to use it."

Sam nodded his understanding. It was difficult, but he was able to wrap his mind around what they were saying.

John signaled to Danielle that he was ready to take back over.

"The second most important thing is your age. It works hand in hand with your blood's purity to determine how much potential power you have at a given time. The older you get, the more powerful you become. Right now you're obviously not receiving any benefit from your age, but your blood purity balances it out.

"I'm going give you an example of how the two work in more practical terms. Keep in mind that I'm making up the numbers for the purposes of simplicity." Sam nodded; interested in hearing it laid out for him.

"Let's say a brand new vampire of the twentieth generation is capable of retaining one gallon of blood in his system. When that vampire is fifty years old, he may be able to retain five gallons of blood. At two hundred years, maybe fifteen or twenty gallons. Age pretty much has that same effect on us all.

"Now, let's say that vampire was generation ten. In that case he might be able to retain as much as two or three gallons of blood when first turned. By age two hundred, maybe as much as thirty to forty gallons."

"So you're saying that even though I'm new, my generation will put me on the same playing field as many older vampires of a lesser generation?"

"Exactly."

"Is that the only effect age has on us?"

John looked thoughtful for a moment. "No, but it's the major one. The rest depends on the vampire. Most of the little things don't apply to you, which is another reason you'll be more powerful than most. It takes time for a vampire to learn their new abilities and discover new magic. Simple experience is an enormous benefit in anything you do, including being a vampire. You have us to help you there.

"The one negative change you have to look forward to is that with age, your beast will also grow in power. The more time you spend as a vampire, the more difficult it will be to hold on to your humanity. Don't concern yourself with this too much, because we can help there as well. Plus, you have to live that long first." Sam looked solemn but nodded.

"The final element is your training, which also goes hand in hand with experience. All the power in the world is useless if you don't know how to use it. The fact that Danielle and I possessed such superior training is what allowed us to take our sire and his coterie by surprise and destroy them. Your training as my ghoul will go a long way toward ensuring your own survival while you grow accustomed to your new abilities.

"Also, we'll be working with you as often as possible to teach you what you're now capable of and whatnot." That was easy enough to understand, but it seemed to Sam that John was reluctant to continue.

"Is something wrong, sir?"

"There is something that you need to know and be clear on right now."

"What is it?"

"Now that you are a vampire, I am no longer your master. You are no longer limited to my blood for your survival. I am your sire, and as such, it is proper for me to ensure that you understand what has happened to you and how to deal with it. Once that is done, however, you are under no obligation to stay with us. You may leave at any time, if you so choose, with no fear of repercussions.

"If, on the other hand, you choose to stay with us, you must accept my leadership. I lead our coterie, but I'm not your master any longer. Do you understand this?"

"I do, and I choose to stay, sir. You guys are my family, and there is nowhere else I wish to be." The three shared a smile. "Now, earlier I believe you said you guys were able to learn something from the raid last night."

John was pleased to see that even with all that had happened to him, Sam was eager to get back to the current problem.

"The information we gathered last night turned out to be a gold mine. It'll take a few more days for our ghouls to go through it all, but what we've learned so far doesn't bode well for our future. This organization calls itself the Sword of God. Take a guess which major religion is responsible for its existence."

"Catholicism?"

John was visibly surprised. "How'd you know that?"

"All those people were wearing crucifixes, which narrows it down considerably. And while many religions are quite violent in doing what they call 'God's work,' Catholicism is the most secretive. Almost any other major religion I can think of not only wouldn't hide this organization but would hail its members as public heroes."

"I'm impressed. The good news is that once we organize this info, we'll have locations for numerous bases, outposts, and troop concentrations. The bad news is that they're huge. Even if we knew the location of every base they had around the world, I don't see how it would be possible for us to topple them."

Sam realized that he was being given a very brief version of what they had learned, but he fully understood the implications.

"What's the plan?"

John began refilling their glasses while Danielle answered his question.

"We have two ideas at the moment, both of which only have theoretical chances of success. First, we destroy every base we locate and kill as many of them as possible. We might not be able to topple the organization, but perhaps they'll choose to leave us be if we become enough of a nuisance." Sam started to shake his head. "What?"

"If we're dealing with religious fanatics here, they'll never leave us be. We could kill them all, and each one would fight us to their dying breath."

"We came to the same conclusion, but at least we'd be able to hurt them. Our other idea is to go see the head of the organization, and 'convince' him of the error of his ways." Sounded logical.

"I like that idea. Cut off the head of the snake, and the body withers and dies."

"If you're done with the clichés," John began, "would you mind drinking the blood I gave you earlier? No offense, but your arm is really disgusting." Danielle chuckled as Sam began to meekly sip from the glass John had filled with his own blood.

Sam tried to prepare himself for the effects drinking blood now had on him. Since he knew what to expect, he thought it wouldn't take him so off guard. He was wrong. The sensations and desires that now coursed through his body felt at least a hundredfold more powerful than before. He decided that it was evidence of what John had said about his blood being more powerful. Without even realizing it, Sam's weak sips became hungry gulps, and he emptied the glass in seconds.

In the midst of his pleasure, Sam noticed John holding up a finger in warning, and he snapped back to full attentiveness. John's warning was clear: the more powerful blood might intensify his pleasure, but it would most likely have the same effect on the beast. He prepped himself, determined not to disappoint his former masters.

When the beast finally made its presence known, it was indeed much more demanding than it had been before. Sam was surprised by both the beast's intensity and his own ability to deal with it. Years ago John had told him that the beast was very easy to keep at bay if a vampire simply remained vigilant. The beast only became difficult to control when there were other things occupying the vampire's attention, such as in the midst of battle.

"Good, you handled that very well. And take a look at your arm." Sam noticed a slight tingling sensation and glanced down to see what was happening. He was surprised to see his arm actually re growing before his eyes. In less than four minutes, it was as good as new. *I definitely need to learn more about this kind of thing,* he thought as he flexed his arm in amazement.

"Wow, that's amazing! Thank you." John merely grinned and motioned for him to refill his glass and drink. "Back to what we were saying," Sam continued as he refilled his glass, "I see only one problem. How do we find the head of the organization?" John seemed shocked, and Danielle simply laughed. "What? What's so funny?"

"Are you serious, Sam?"

"Yeah, I guess. What's wrong?"

"Nothing. Your question's just a bit odd is all."

"Why? You said you were going after the head person, but we can't do that until we know who he is and where to find him."

"Well, we, along with the rest of the world, already know all that."

"Okay."

"Oh my God, you're not joking, are you?"

"No, I'm not. What are you talking about?"

"Pope William Stevens III, and he usually stays over at the Vatican. Does that answer your questions?"

Now it was Sam's turn to look shocked.

"You can't be serious. The pope?"

"Why not? The Catholic Church is responsible for this organization, and the pope is the head of the Catholic Church. Seems perfectly logical to me."

"But ... but ... you're talking about the pope. I mean *the pope*. You can't just attack the pope."

"And why not?"

"Damn it, because he's the pope, that's why."

"If I remember correctly, they attacked us first." It seemed as if John was starting to get annoyed.

Danielle remained unchanged, although she had stopped laughing. "They knew we were vampires. If they weren't prepared to deal with the consequences of their actions, they should've left us alone. Besides, we're not going to hurt him if we can avoid it. We'll try negotiating something first."

"And if that doesn't work?"

"Then we'll kill him, burn the Vatican down, and raze that entire area. I'm sure that would put a few kinks in the SOG's plans."

John's steely gaze was enough to almost frighten even Sam. He obviously didn't mess around when his own life or the lives of those he cared about were threatened.

"Okay, I admit that I'm a bit shocked, but I can't argue with that logic. When do we leave?" The steely gaze changed to a large toothy grin, which did nothing to ease the dread Sam felt building within him.

"You're not going anywhere." John chose to add to the current suspense by refusing to elaborate.

"John and I will be leaving in two hours, but you're in no condition to come with us."

"I don't understand."

"The easiest way to put it is that even though you're a vampire now, your body hasn't completely adjusted yet. Actually, I'm surprised nothing has happened yet. It may be due to you having been a ghoul for so long first, or perhaps it's that your blood is so powerful, or even just that body has reflexively prioritized healing. Whatever the reason, you've just been lucky so far."

"So? I'll just deal with it."

John stopped Danielle from continuing. "Sam, listen to me." His grin was gone, but John was trying to keep his tone lighthearted. "You're about to go through something that happens to all vampires, and it's going to be very, very bad. The pain is going to be tremendous and constant. Not only can you not come with us, but you will have to be confined and restrained while we are gone." As if on cue, Danielle reached behind her chair and produced several lengths of chain. Sam started to laugh but stopped when no one else joined in.

"You guys aren't joking, are you?"

To his credit, Sam didn't panic at the sight of the chains.

"No we aren't. You have to understand that you're going to lose control, most likely several times. There's no way of knowing exactly what's going to happen in each case, so we can't do anything more to prepare you. All I can offer is this piece of advice. Don't fight it. Let it happen. The beast is going to overwhelm you anyway, so it's better to give in and save your strength.

"You must remember that you already passed the test. Anything that happens to you in the next couple of days is only temporary. Don't let your failure dishearten you; failure is inevitable." Sam mulled over the information for a few minutes before nodding his acceptance.

"Just one more question. If I'm as strong as you say I am, and I lose control, how are those chains going to stop me?"

"Normal chains wouldn't, but these have been enhanced by Danielle's strongest magic. You won't be able to break them. Ghouls will come by and roll thermoses of blood to you, but they've been instructed to stay out of arm's reach. You should still be able to open the thermoses without too much trouble.

"The ghouls have also been instructed to not unchain you, no matter the circumstances. There's no telling how long this will last for you, but we can't take any chances. You'll just have to wait for us to get back. Sorry about that, but you'll understand soon enough."

"Yeah, but I don't have to like it."

"No, but we do need to get moving. We still have a lot of things to cover before we leave. You sure you're still feeling okay?" John asked as he and Danielle stood up.

"I feel great, but I'll trust your decision." Sam stood up and started to follow them out of the room. He made it three steps before keeling over and vomiting all over a two hundred-year-old, handwoven Persian rug.

* * *

"I'M TELLING YOU, he did it on purpose. Payback for us chaining him up to a toilet." They had spent the last hour packing and finalizing their travel plans. Traveling by plane was dangerous for vampires. They had no choice but to travel as luggage if they were to avoid the sun's deadly rays. In addition, they had to be met by someone trustworthy, or they risked being exposed to sunlight when they were opened.

Many vampires chose to travel in coffins. It sounded a bit cliché, but it actually made perfect sense. They were the right size to be relatively comfortable, and if x-rayed, it would be normal to see a body inside. Of course, having an unbelievable amount of resources came in handy. John and Danielle didn't have to worry about any of the normal concerns, since they had their own plane, customized so that a vampire could travel in complete comfort.

"I doubt he did it on purpose, although that was my favorite rug," John finished in more of a mumble. "Wait a minute," he raised his voice back to normal levels, "did you enchant the toilet? What good are the chains if he breaks through that, and just runs around killing everyone?"

"I can't enchant a toilet, stupid," Danielle started to respond, then hesitated a moment to think. "Well, I probably could, but it just seems weird. Don't worry, I wrapped him in so many chains the most he would be able to do is just flop around on the bathroom floor until we get back."

"You're probably right, but I'm still not getting him a souvenir while we're there."

She suddenly spun around to face him.

"Holy shit, that reminds me. Wait here!" Without waiting for a response, she vanished from the room, leaving John thoroughly confused. In the midst of confusion, however, it was always good to fall back on one's training as a husband. Do what you're told. John zipped up their suitcase and sat quietly on the bed, waiting for his wife to return.

As it turned out, he didn't have to wait long. Danielle returned within five minutes carrying a wrapped bundle. John's curiosity was heightened by the excitement evident on her face. There weren't many things that excited a person after nine centuries.

"What's this?" he inquired, accepting the offered bundle.

"Unwrap it and see."

John shrugged and began carefully unwrapping the bundle. Upon first seeing the sword, he was unimpressed. It was only after he drew the sword from its scabbard and examined its craftsmanship that his eyes widened in surprise.

"This is beautiful, sweetheart. Where'd you get it? Wait, is this why you've been running off on your own for the last couple of weeks?" She nodded and gave him a brief description of the weapons shop, its owner, and the extra touches that he had added to the sword.

"Well, this is truly excellent work. It looks strong too. Thank you very much, love. It's a shame I can't use it against anything other than mortals. I'd hate to snap such a beautiful blade." His comments were answered by a large grin from Danielle.

"That's the second surprise. I think I found a way to enhance our regular weapons with magic, similar to the way I enhanced those chains. If it works, our normal swords will have the same effect as our claws and be a match for the strongest of opponents, mortal or otherwise."

"That's great! When can you do it?"

"Well, I'm still experimenting, so I don't know. I'll figure it out after we get back from the Vatican."

"Okay, in that case I'll leave it here. No sense in risking any unnecessary damage to it." She nodded in agreement.

"There is one other thing." A slight pause. "I was thinking that we could really use this weapons master's skills. With all the resources we have, we could use someone who's capable of producing all of our weaponry for us. It's better than having to find and purchase the stuff, especially at the speed we seem to go through them. We also have to consider the paper trail and records we leave behind every time we purchase weapons like this from normal channels."

"Are you saying that you want to ghoul him?"

"I think the idea has merit, yes."

"What makes you think he'd agree to it? You know we don't ghoul people against their will."

"I admit that I read his mind. He's old, he has no family, and he has cancer. The only thing he has that makes him happy is his work.

He seems the perfect candidate." John seemed unconvinced. "At least let me talk to him about it."

"I'll think about it. Right now we have to worry about the situation at hand. We'll come back to this when we get back."

"As you wish." Danielle was about to add something when a soft knock sounded at their door.

"Come in," John invited, hoping this meant everything was ready to go. One of their ghouls entered the room, head bowed. "Yes?"

"Your transportation is ready, and the team is already aboard, masters." John nodded and waved the ghoul away. The team included their pilot and three ghoul passengers. The passengers were there to maintain appearances and take care of their "luggage" in case the plane landed during daylight hours.

"Well," John started, "I suppose we should get going."

"Agreed." They grabbed their duffel bags, filled with weapons, and headed for the door. "John?" A hint of concern touched her voice.

"Yes?"

"We're not really going to kill the pope, are we?"

"If we have to."

Chapter 10

"HOW COULD THIS have happened?" Jenkins knew that he should be keeping better control of himself in front of Thomas, but he didn't care. The battle had been a terrible failure, and he had called Thomas into his office in the hopes the man's combat experience could help him to understand what had happened. Their QRF had been annihilated, and their reinforcements had taken losses to the rogue Red Fang elder. Unfortunately, their losses didn't stop there.

Lori's Bed and Breakfast lay in ruins, destroyed along with all of the SOG personnel stationed there. To top it all off, only God knew how much stolen information the demons had made off with. Jenkins didn't know how much more of this he could take.

"Please, Excellency, we cannot change what has already happened."

"I would be satisfied with merely understanding it. How is it possible for the abominations to be this powerful? Why is it we keep underestimating them? And why do they act the way they do?" The vampires actions had been the most confusing piece of information Jenkins had gotten from the battle.

Every time he assumed they would retreat, they stood their ground and fought. The ghouls sacrificing themselves made sense; they had no choice. However, it wasn't supposed to happen the other way around. Demons simply did not sacrifice themselves for others.

Jenkins might be able to be convinced that they would risk themselves for each other, but for their ghouls? Never. Ghouls were minions, nothing more. Yes, in this situation they had valuable information, but weighed against personal survival? The information wouldn't have done them any good had the vampires been destroyed trying to protect it.

This brought other points to mind. Ever since the SOG became aware of these particular vampires, they had been monitoring them closely. He had yet to see or hear a report that they had killed an innocent for any reason. In fact, every violent act they had committed thus far had been in self-defense.

Yes, they had attacked Lori's Bed and Breakfast. They killed everyone there in their sleep, plus the researchers working underground. However, had not the SOG attacked them first? Had they not, in no uncertain terms, declared themselves as the enemy? Every person killed had been SOG personnel.

There were six innocents renting rooms at Lori's, yet the vampires had let them live. They were found bound, gagged, and trapped in the ruins of the building, but physically they were unharmed. All of this begged the question, what were they really fighting?

Merely saying or believing something is a demon doesn't make it true. What if it didn't act like a demon? What if the creature in question displayed signs of concern, self-sacrifice, and even love? How could that creature be a demon?

Jenkins knew the thoughts he was beginning to harbor were dangerous, and he decided to keep them to himself for now. In the long run, it wouldn't matter anyway. Whatever these creatures really were, they were pissed. Demons or not, they were at war with them now. If Jenkins wanted to survive, he no longer had a choice but to help fight them.

"We've been underestimating them because this is a first for us. That battle was against both abominations, in addition to several of their ghouls. Given our inexperience, I think we did well."

"How can you say that?"

"The battle was a tactical victory for the vampires, but it was a strategic victory for us."

At that, Jenkins immediately leapt to his feet.

"What! We lost over a hundred men and wolves, and God only knows what intel they got! How can you possibly call that a victory?"

"Excellency, please remain calm and allow me to explain." Jenkins willed himself to calm down and retake his seat. It was his job to keep others confident and calm; it shouldn't be the other way around. Satisfied that he had regained his composure, Jenkins motioned for Thomas to continue.

"First let me explain the difference between the two. Tactics refer more to the current battle or operation. Strategy, on the other hand, refers more to the overall situation." Jenkins nodded slowly, hoping Thomas's explanation would make sense to him.

"The vampires won the battle. We have no way of knowing what information they gathered, but they had access to our databases for several minutes. In addition, they completely destroyed one of our outposts, and I don't need to reiterate the total casualty figures for our side. It was definitely a tactical victory for them.

"The abominations, however, didn't get away clean. We've confirmed the destruction of nine of their ghouls. We think we got more, but identification is proving difficult. I would say at least ten, and at most twelve. Plus, we can't ignore that we learn more about the abominations' abilities with every passing battle.

"This may seem trite in comparison to our own losses, but we must compare resources. This is turning into a war of attrition.

Looking at the big picture, that's a war we can't lose. We have hundreds of thousands of soldiers and thousands of werewolves worldwide.

"It may seem coldhearted, but we have to keep in mind how easy it will be to replace our own losses, compared to the difficulties the vampires will face. It's safe to assume that the ghouls they brought with them were among the best they had. It isn't simply a matter of training new soldiers for them. If they lose a fifty-year-old ghoul, it will take fifty years to replace it.

"Yes, they can replace their losses easily, but the new ghouls won't be as effective. That's why, looking at the big picture, their losses were strategically heavier than ours." Jenkins couldn't argue that Thomas's argument was logical and made sense, but he refused to look at his men as simple numbers.

Thomas also failed to mention that every new ghoul the vampires took was one more innocent life ended. In a way, by killing their ghouls and forcing the vampires to replenish their forces, the SOG was responsible for ending countless innocent lives. To Jenkins, any battle in which they failed to destroy the vampires themselves was a total loss, no matter how one looked at it.

Of course, that was the real reason he had agreed to place Thomas in command of their combat forces. He had the right frame of mind for the job. The vampires had to be stopped, no matter what. Naturally, that consideration brought another thought to mind. Stopped from what?

They hadn't been doing anything wrong when the SOG discovered them. They hadn't done anything wrong since either, except in self-defense. The only thing wrong was the fact that they were vampires, but was that enough? It used to be enough for Jenkins, but he wasn't so sure anymore.

He was tempted to bring his concerns to light, but he already knew what Thomas's response to them would be. No, until he had more time to think and pray about this, he would keep his doubts to himself. He'd been finding himself questioning God's will more and more frequently as of late.

He felt strongly that God supported any war or conflict as long as it was just in its nature. So the real question was whether or not what they were doing was just. On the surface it was, but was it really? Did God Himself condemn all vampires just because of what they were?

The correct answer was yes, but wasn't he taught that God also loved all creatures fully and completely and was capable of forgiving all things? A person merely had to have sorrow in his or her heart, and while that might not be enough for some men, it was enough for God.

According to all the text and written records about vampires, most were turned against their will. Should they be punished just because of their bad fortune? Jenkins had an idea of what the SOG's official answer to that question would be: Of course not. We are setting their souls free. Either that or they'd claim they were acting according to God's will in punishing the monsters for their acts of carnage committed after becoming vampires.

He was also always led to believe that the older the vampire, the more monstrous it was. The two vampires they were now at war with were obviously very old, but they had yet to do anything Jenkins could consider monstrous. In Jenkins's humble opinion, they hadn't been acting like monsters at all. They'd been acting more like a husband and wife who were fighting for their lives against a far superior attacking army.

What would happen if a mortal was turned into a vampire but refused to be controlled by whatever demon was responsible for the change? Jenkins wondered what he would do if he were turned. He would never allow his life to be ruled by a demon. Most likely he would meet the sun on the following day and pray that God would have mercy.

Unfortunately, that further strengthened Thomas's argument. Any God-loving individual would just kill themselves. It wouldn't be suicide, since they were already dead, and it would defeat the demon within. Obviously, these vampires had no intention of destroying themselves. So was there any legitimate reason why a good God-loving person would choose to remain a vampire? The question reminded Jenkins of something he'd thought of earlier. *Of course!*

He already thought they were acting like husband and wife. Perhaps it wasn't an act. Was it possible they really were married? It was impossible to determine their respective ages, but they seemed equally powerful. What if they were married as mortals and turned at the same time? Such a thing had never been recorded, but what if that was the case?

Marriage was a sacred vow, one to be honored until death. It could be argued that, since they were dead, their marriage was void, but it wasn't that simple. Void or not, the love between a husband and wife was supposed to be absolute. Was it possible that they refused to be destroyed because they couldn't bear to lose each other? Love tends to grow stronger with age, so could their love have remained stronger than the demons inside them? More importantly, could a pure emotion such as love even survive the transformation into a vampire?

Jenkins didn't have any answers, only questions, but what if this was true? If so, it was perhaps the most legitimate reason to do anything in life. Love. If it was true, technically these "demons" would in fact be the best example of an enduring marriage in history. How could God condemn them? And if God didn't condemn them, then that made the SOG—not the vampires—the enemy.

With that troubling thought, Jenkins immediately halted his mental argument. His mind was wandering into dangerous territory. It was ludicrous to think vampires could be capable of such things as love, and yet something deep in his heart hinted that he was closer than ever to the answers he sought.

He noticed Thomas looking at him with no small amount of concern. He would be expecting some sort of opinion on the explanation he gave. Unless Jenkins wanted to voice his actual thoughts, he'd better start concentrating on the conversation at hand.

"I understand what you're saying, and I admit that it makes sense. It seems that I just don't have as strong a stomach for this sort of thing as I thought I had." Thomas smiled.

"You don't have to, Excellency. That's why you have you me."

Truth be told, Thomas seemed to be growing colder than Jenkins would have liked. Glancing at his prosthesis, he reminded himself that Thomas had a personal reason to hate these vampires in particular. Unfortunately, hate was a very dangerous emotion, and it clouded one's vision.

"I would still like to know how—"

The door to Thomas's office burst open, interrupting Jenkins's question. They both turned to face the intruder and saw that it was Senior Initiate Joseph, who had a huge grin plastered on his face. Jenkins was surprised that a mere senior initiate would dare burst in to his office, but he wasted no time in reminding Joseph of his inappropriateness.

"How dare you interrupt this meeting! This had better be important, Joseph." Joseph's grin was immediately replaced with a look of concern. Jenkins decided that he was rethinking his enthusiasm, and was regretting coming down on him so hard.

"I'm very sorry, sir, Excellency," Joseph bowed deeply, "but you asked to be informed immediately if we found anything." It was then that Jenkins noticed the stripes on the sleeves of Joseph's robe, identifying him as a researcher, and saw the look of hope in Thomas's eyes.

"You found something?" When Joseph realized that Jenkins wasn't going to throw him out, some of the researcher's earlier excitement returned.

"Yes, sir, we did. Unfortunately we have yet to find the abominations' main haven, but what we found is almost as important."

"Don't keep us in suspense, man! What did you find?" It wasn't intended to sound angry, and Thomas hoped Joseph could tell.

"We found their blood blank, sir." Thomas and Jenkins's eyes went wide.

"You did? You're sure?"

"Yes, sir. Actually, we found it about twenty minutes ago. I wanted to make sure I had all the necessary information to make a report and answer any questions you might have before I came to see you." Thomas nodded in approval.

"You exercised excellent judgment, Joseph. Now, please make your report."

"Yes, sir. Their blood bank is Alpha Blood Donations, in the city's main business district. As we expected, it's listed as a privately owned establishment. Officially, the blood is used for medical testing and experimentation. It's basically run the same as a normal blood bank. The only difference is the donors are paid twenty dollars each for their donation. The explanation is that since the blood isn't going to actual patients, the company feels that they should be compensated for their donation." Thomas looked over at Jenkins. Jenkins nodded and motioned that Thomas should be the one to fully debrief the researcher.

"Okay, that sounds pretty legitimate. How'd you figure out it belonged to them?"

"I admit it was very difficult, sir. In fact, if we hadn't been specifically looking for it, we would never have found it. The thing that caught our attention was that the blood wasn't being sent to any actual hospitals. Of course, that's not too uncommon by itself. Once we really started looking into it, however, we couldn't find out where the blood went at all.

"We expected to see a list of companies that were supposedly doing the testing and experimentation, but there was nothing that we could find. At first we were confused but then realized how ingenious it was. If they had listed a dummy company, it would've given them away immediately once it was checked into. This way any investigator is simply kept confused, and would probably just move on. Unless, of course, it's an investigator looking specifically for anything wrong, no matter what form that anything might take.

"Then we started checking into the employees. What we found was normal enough. Since we had already found one oddity about the place, however, we thoroughly checked each file we could find."

"What did you find?"

"Simply put, sir, that many of them were fakes. It took us several hours, but we were finally able to separate the legitimate records from the fakes. There have been no new hires, and no one has left the employ of that blood bank, in over ten years. It's impossible to say for certain, sir, but we believe that every last employee they have there is a ghoul."

"Is that all?"

"Yes, sir. This report contains more detail, but those are the basics."

"Excellent work. See that copies of your report are sent to all of our team leaders. Once you've done that, reassign your research team to assist in the search for the beasts' haven."

"Yes, sir, Excellency." With a pair of deep bows, the researcher left the office. Once the door was shut behind him, Thomas turned to face Jenkins. The feral gleam in his eye was almost frightening.

"This is perfect, sir. It's just the break we needed. We take out their blood bank, and we'll force them into the open. They'll be forced to either hunt far more often or steal blood from other banks or hospitals." He was right, but it sounded to Jenkins that it would just put even more innocent lives in danger.

"How do you suggest we proceed with the attack?"

Thomas looked thoughtful for a moment. "Well, we obviously want to do it during the day, and I'd prefer to not use werewolves. It'll be more difficult, but there will be innocents in the bank. Wolves are too difficult to control and may cause unnecessary casualties." Jenkins was relieved to hear him say that. He was afraid that Thomas would suggest overrunning the entire blood bank with werewolves.

"Let's see what other information Joseph has here." Thomas spent the next few minutes scanning the researcher's report. Jenkins, for his part, waited patiently for him to finish formulating his strategy.

"It says the blood bank has a total of fifteen employees, all of which are ghouls. These ghouls won't be as well-trained as the ones we would normally face in combat, but they will have had some training. In addition, we don't know if there are any actual combat ghouls stationed there to defend the building. It'll be difficult, sir, but I think I have an idea."

"Yes?"

"We send a dozen of our best men in to donate blood. When all are ready, they can take the nearby ghouls by complete surprise. At the same time, we have two dozen more men stationed right outside, ready to move in at the first sign of battle.

"That should be enough to handle the defending ghouls, but only if everything goes well and surprise is maintained until the last possible moment. We should have a few extra squads ready to move in to support the attack if needed. The more men we send in, the better the chances of innocent casualties. On the other hand, if we don't win and completely destroy the blood bank, we'll have tipped our knowledge of its existence."

Jenkins decided that Thomas's plan had a good chance of success. More importantly, he had factored in the risk to innocents. It didn't bother him that so far none of Thomas's plans had met with complete success. All of their failures so far were due to them underestimating the vampires' powers, and by attacking the bank during the day, they would effectively remove the vampires as a factor in the ensuing battle.

"It sounds like a good plan to me. I appreciate your attempt to minimize innocent casualties, despite how important victory is to us. The only question I can think of is how do our men get weapons inside the bank undetected? They must have something set up to prevent such an occurrence."

"Maybe, maybe not. It depends what's more important to them, secrecy or defense. They might be concerned that anyone noticing such detection methods would get suspicious and begin asking questions. If you'll notice, this blood bank is located in a very nice area. Things like metal detectors would draw unwanted attention.

"Of course, I would never make plans that relied on mere assumptions for success. The dozen men we send inside will carry weapons specifically designed to avoid detection." Jenkins nodded and thought of another suggestion.

"Also, we should make sure those twelve men are fairly large."

"Why?"

"I have donated blood a few times myself. Twelve men can't just walk in and all be seen at the same time, at least not at a facility this small. In order to maintain secrecy, they'll be forced to go through as much of the process as necessary. By the time the last of our men is in position, the first few will undoubtedly have started, or even finished, their donation.

"A standard blood donation is one pint. The larger the man, the easier it will be for him to deal with the blood loss. We can't afford to start the attack and then have our infiltration team passing out from the exertion."

"Of course, sir. I hadn't thought of that." Thomas jotted some notes on the back of Joseph's report.

"Oh, and please make sure they keep their crucifixes hidden." Jenkins held up a hand to forestall the coming protest. "I realize they see them as a badge of honor, but the vampires know we wear them. As you said, surprise needs to be maintained until the last possible moment. We can't afford something small like that giving us away. They can wear them, just keep them hidden."

Thomas grudgingly agreed and jotted down more notes.

"Is that all, sir?"

"Yes, as I said earlier, it's a good plan. Let us hope God agrees with us, and chooses to light our path."

Sensing that as a dismissal, Thomas bowed and left the office.

Once he was alone, Jenkins let his head drop into his hands. *What do I do? This all feels so wrong.* He didn't know if his doubts meant that he was losing faith—or perhaps that he was finally finding it. News of their discovery and the upcoming battle had done nothing to ease his thoughts. If anything, it had worsened them. *More death.*

The most important thing for him right now, he decided, was to act normally. No one else could be allowed to suspect that he was being plagued by these doubts. He would do the only thing he knew how to do. He would pray. If, after he had finished, he still felt the same, he would then take action.

Chapter 11

THE TRIP TO Rome turned out to be thankfully uneventful. Their pilot was able to land at the Rome Leonardo da Vinci Airport and secure permission to store the plane in one of the airport's small hangars for a period of twenty-four hours. John and Danielle continued to rest, safe and undisturbed, until a ghoul roused them at nightfall. The vampires spent a few minutes checking their weapons and left in search of the pope.

They had already known that the Pope was not to be found within the Vatican, but rather in his summer residence, Castle Gandolfo, which was located on the edge of Lake Albano, in the Alban Hills. The castle included a small village with a population of nearly seven thousand, but that would pose little difficulty to vampires accustomed to traveling crowded city streets unseen. Having been named after a castle belonging to the ducal Gandolfi family in the twelfth century, the vampires remembered Castel Gandolfo becoming the domain of the Holy See in 1608. Within a few decades, the Papal Palace was constructed, and it became the summer residence of the pope.

They were able to cover the short distance south to the castle quickly, and once there it was easy enough to confirm that the pope was in residence. Most mortals felt the same to the senses of vampires, but there were certain things that could set them apart. Faith was at the top of that list. Mortals possessing enough pure faith gave off a presence that was easily detectable by vampires that were strong enough to sense it. Within fifteen miles of the castle, they could tell that they were on the right track. The only question left was how exactly to introduce themselves.

* * *

"HOW DO YOU want to play this, love?" They were both clinging to opposite sides of the window to the pope's bedchamber. They had been hoping he would be asleep when they arrived. Unfortunately, the pope was sitting in an old-fashioned rocking chair, reading from a Bible. There was a cup of steaming liquid on an end table next to him, and he didn't appear to be the least bit tired.

The light being on didn't bother either one of them. That was of no consequence to ancient vampires. What they didn't know was if they could enter the room undetected. The pope was one of the most powerful mortals in the world, from a vampire's perspective, and he was wide awake. It was possible that he would be able to sense them, no matter how they tried to mask themselves.

In the end it wouldn't matter, but they didn't want to give him a chance to cause a scene. It was vitally important that they get a chance to speak with him before any violence broke out. Depending how their conversation went, there might not be a need for violence at all. It all depended on the next few moments.

"I have no idea. You think you can mist through this window and restrain him before he notices you? Then, you could just let me in, and we can work on getting him calmed down." John glanced over to his wife as she considered the question.

"I should be able to. Wait a second, he's moving." John looked back in time to see the pope set his Bible on the end table and get up. *Hopefully he's going to bed.* Even as he thought it, however, John could see him moving straight toward the window. *Damn it! Hell of a time for a breath of fresh air.*

John quickly crawled a few feet from the edge of the window. He didn't need to look to see that Danielle was doing the same thing. Better safe than sorry, after all. As the window slid open and John was contemplating his next move, the pope did the last thing either vampire expected.

"You two may come in whenever you wish. It is too cold a night to keep visitors waiting outside." His voice was soft and raspy with age, but it held all of the confidence of someone who knew exactly what he was doing.

W*hat! How?* Among the hundreds of things suddenly running through John's mind, these two questions were by far the most pressing.

How did the pope know they were there? Had he been expecting them? As John was turning these thoughts over in his mind, he noticed something about the way the pope was leaning out of the window.

He was just standing there, looking out into the darkness. Anyone seeing him would just think he was calmly admiring the scenery. What bothered John about it was that Danielle and he were clinging to either side of the window.

It was obvious that the pope knew they were there; however, he seemed unable to either see or otherwise detect exactly where they were. The implications of that revelation simply raised more questions. How could he detect them confidently enough to speak to them yet not realize they were clinging to a wall to either side of him?

Normally, they would have already fled the area, fearing a trap, but John didn't feel even the least bit threatened. Confused, definitely, but not threatened. He threw a questioning look at his wife, and received a shrug and small nod in answer. Her meaning was clear. *I'm as confused as you are but ready to follow your lead.*

In the end, John decided to just go with the original plan. There was no threat to them that he could detect, and the pope's awareness of them may actually make this go more easily. He slowly crept back to the window, jumped through, and ceased shrouding himself. Sure enough, Danielle was right behind him.

The instant their shrouds were down, the pope turned to face them. Oddly enough, he was smiling happily. It was almost as if he were about to welcome home a pair of old friends. John was about to ask just what in the hell was going on when the pope stopped him with a raised hand.

He thinks a mortal can prevent me from speaking whenever I choose? John thought to himself, shocked at the audacity. The odd thing was it was working. John could tell that the pope didn't have any actual control over him; however, he had such a strong presence that John simply couldn't bring himself to overrule him. At least, not until he felt threatened.

Danielle was obviously attempting to use her mind control abilities to take back control of the situation. John could tell by the look on her face, and he motioned for her to stop trying. Even if she might have been successful, John preferred to handle the situation honestly. So far, the pope hadn't done anything detrimental to them, and, for the moment, John was content to return the favor.

"Allow me to welcome you both. Please, make yourselves comfortable." He indicated a trio of chairs, arranged around a small coffee table. John and Danielle exchanged a small shrug and took seats at the table.

"I hope you don't mind if I fetch myself a fresh cup of tea." Without waiting for an answer, he took his teacup and walked over to a set of cabinets. John wished he could take the time to discuss what was happening with his wife. Unfortunately, he had no idea if they would be overheard, and he didn't want their unease to show.

The pope returned a moment later, and John took the opportunity to assess him. To say the man was frail would be a heavy understatement. Everything about him gave the appearance that his body might crumble away at any moment. That is, everything except his face, which held a certain youthful energy that belied his years. His facial features carried the signs of someone accustomed to frequent smiles. This old, frail, but happy man was the head of a major religion, and he had successfully subdued two ancient vampires with but a single smile and a gesture.

John was still studying him as the pope set a tray of three teacups and a pot on the table and took a seat in the remaining chair. John realized that he must expect the two of them to join him in a drink. They seem to have been expected, but apparently the pope didn't realize he was dealing with two vampires. John was about to pass on the coming offer for tea when he felt Danielle tense beside him.

Looking over at his wife, John followed her gaze to exactly what was in two of the cups, and his own eyes bulged with surprise. Blood. He sniffed the air carefully. It was fresh. There was also a small, fresh bandage on the pope's right wrist. *He's offering each of us a cup of his own blood!*

There was a time, long ago, that many vampires chose to live peacefully among mortals. Mortals began to offer cups of their own blood to vampires as a show of friendship. It was a gesture of the utmost respect, without any admission of inferiority. Not only did the pope know they were vampires, but he knew their customs, which was something that, sadly, many modern-day vampires didn't even know. John couldn't stay silent any longer.

"What is going on here?" The pope had been reaching for his teacup, but he stopped and looked up.

"What do you mean? Have I done something wrong?" There was a confused look on his face.

"No, actually you've done everything exactly right. But how did you know?"

At that he merely smiled and gestured upward. "The Lord works in mysterious ways, my son, and I live to carry out His will." That wasn't good enough for John.

"How did you know we were coming, or what we are?"

"The Lord speaks to us all every day. We have but to listen for His voice."

"What's that supposed to mean?"

The pope sighed but continued smiling.

"I know things that I shouldn't have known. I know that the Lord is the reason for this knowledge, so I go wherever it takes me."

"And where does this knowledge take you tonight?"

"I knew that I would meet two vampires this night and that they would mean me no harm. I feel that I must cooperate with whatever you want, because I stand to learn as much from you as you will learn from me. That's the limit of my knowledge on the events that will transpire tonight. Now, please drink, before your refreshment gets cold."

"How did you know about the offering ceremony?" Danielle asked with a hint of accusation.

"That was simple research on my part. I wanted you both to feel welcome, and to know I will help you to the best of my ability. Please, enjoy it, but do so sparingly. I'm too old to spare enough for a second cup." Danielle seemed satisfied, but she was still hesitant.

John picked up his cup and sniffed its contents. He detected no impurities, so, with a shrug, he took a small sip. He was quickly satisfied that the pope was being truthful. Taking her cue, Danielle followed his example and was equally pleased.

"Kind sir, your offer of friendship is accepted. By my own blood, I swear you have nothing to fear from me or my kin." With those words, both vampires formally fulfilled their parts in the ceremony.

"Thank you very much. Now, I'm very curious as to why you're both here. As I said earlier, I knew you were coming, but not the reason for your visit." Both vampires nodded. They had decided earlier that John would do most of the talking. Danielle was too uncomfortable, being this far out of her element. John wouldn't allow her to use any mind control, and her physical seduction techniques would probably create more awkwardness than success.

"Well, I have to admit that we came here for a single reason, but after seeing how friendly you are toward us, other questions are burning in my mind."

"Please, my son, what are these questions?"

John fidgeted slightly. He was about to hit on a sensitive topic for both of them.

"Do you know what we are or where we came from?"

The pope understood that he wasn't just asking if he knew that they were vampires.

"When I heard you both were coming, I thought that you might have questions along those lines. I am sorry to say that the Catholic Church was never able to determine the origins of vampires, nor do we know exactly what you are. I can, however, offer you these." He pulled a pair of discs out of his pocket and set them on the table.

"These discs contain all of the information the Church has gathered on vampires over the centuries. None of it is speculation. It's all facts discovered either by direct observation or research. Most of it was gathered by an organization known as the Sword of God.

"They were an offshoot of the Catholic Church that used to do battle with vampires, and all other creatures that the Church named as 'demons.' Of course, the organization was disbanded long ago, when we realized our mistake. It was—" The pope suddenly noticed both vampires were frozen in shock. "Is something wrong?"

"That was the original reason we came here tonight. We have been attacked more than once lately by a group of vampire hunters. They were very professional, well-equipped, and working with werewolves. We fought back, destroying one of their observation posts. In the raid we were able to steal a large amount of information.

"Once we learned that the Sword of God was part of the Catholic Church, we decided to come here to see you. Our plan was to get you to make them leave us alone. If you refused, we were going to kill you and destroy the Vatican." John looked a bit embarrassed at his declaration, but the pope barely noticed. All the color had drained from his features, and his expression was one of complete shock.

John exchanged a confused glance with his wife. They had discussed several possible reactions that they might face, but this wasn't one of them. Nothing about this meeting had made any sense. They had been welcomed as friends and offered all the information the Catholic Church had accumulated on vampires. The pope even told them the SOG was who gathered the information. He told them freely, as if he expected them to have never heard of such an organization. Then, he said they had been disbanded. It could have all been a lie, but he doubted it.

It was fairly easy to tell if a mortal was being truthful. He also doubted that a mortal as learned as the pope would dare lie to a pair of vampires. They didn't know how to proceed. John could only think to allow the pope a moment to recover from his shock before questioning him further. It didn't take long.

"Are you certain, my son?" He took a long sip from his tea.

"The information we gathered was quite specific. We took the liberty of copying most of it down for you here." John set his own disc on the table. "Originally we did so in case you tried to deny its existence for your own protection." The pope slowly refilled his teacup and let out a long, slow sigh before speaking again.

"The Sword of God was disbanded centuries ago by the pope of the time. They wanted to enlist the aid of werewolves to assist them in the destruction of vampires, since they considered them to be the bigger threat. The Catholic Church decided that using one demon to kill another made us just as bad as the enemy. In planning to join forces with evil, the SOG had gone too far and was subsequently ordered to disband. It would seem, however, that events didn't unfold according to the Church's plan."

"No, they didn't. So you're telling us that these guys have existed in secret ever since? Not only that, but they've followed through with recruiting werewolves, grown immensely in numbers, and established outposts around the globe?"

The pope's expression was one of frustration.

"I honestly don't know. My knowledge of the SOG only extends to when they were ordered disbanded. This is the first I've heard of their existence since then. You've demonstrated enough knowledge about them, however, that I'm inclined to accept whatever you say you've learned." Both vampires' hopes plummeted.

The last thing either of them had expected, and the only thing they hadn't prepared for, was for the pope to be completely clueless about the current situation. Was it possible that he was holding something back? John didn't think so, but could he afford to take that chance? Unfortunately, no, he couldn't.

"I'm almost ashamed to say this, but that's not good enough. My companion here has several mind control abilities. It would be a simple task for her to determine whether or not you are telling us the truth.

"You've been very kind and open with us, and I mean no disrespect. Unfortunately, this matter is far too important for us to take any chances."

The pope nodded, understanding what John was getting at. "You'd like my permission for her to confirm my integrity?"

John nodded.

"Of course. I understand completely and have nothing to hide."

John motioned for Danielle to begin.

The only outward sign of any change in Danielle's actions was a slight tightening of her eyes. The pope met her stare unflinchingly as she looked deep into his mind. This went on for nearly a full minute before she was satisfied.

"He is telling the truth. A bit confused perhaps, but honest," she declared, sounding very frustrated. If the pope had been lying, at least they would have known what to do next.

"I'm sorry, my child, but I don't know any more than either of you about the current state of the SOG." He looked honestly saddened by his inability to help. John was trying to decide what to do about this odd turn of events when Danielle made up her mind.

"Unsatisfactory," she whispered quietly. One instant she was sitting calmly in her chair. The next, she was standing, fangs and claws bared, mere inches from the pope. The temperature in the room dropped several degrees, and a slight wind was circling her, tossing her hair and causing her trench coat to billow out behind her. The pope's friendly demeanor was suddenly replaced by a look of pure fright. Seeing one of your guests go from a calm, beautiful woman to a rage of demonic fury, and in less time than it took you to blink, was bound to have that effect. "What do you suppose we do now?" she hissed through bared fangs.

"Danielle, that is enough." John spoke the words calmly, but it was enough to get his wife's attention. The wind stopped, and the room's temperature returned to normal. The pope watched in frightened awe as she morphed her hand back to normal and retracted her fangs. Giving a small nod, she returned to her seat. Knowing that she would give no apology, John turned his attention back to the pope, who was starting to calm down.

"You'll have to forgive her. One of the SOG attacks was an ambush that nearly destroyed her. Understandably, she's a bit anxious to plan our next move, and you were *supposed* to be instrumental in that planning." The pope nodded slowly, and, after another long sip of his tea, his smile returned.

"I still can be."

John eyed him skeptically.

"How?" Danielle asked, reading John's mind.

"I understand now the purpose of this meeting." The vampires waited for him to elaborate. "I knew that I was to cooperate with you because there was something I needed from you as well. Until now, I didn't realize what that might be." He paused, hoping they would pick up on where he was leading them.

"The SOG?"

"Exactly," he exclaimed happily. "If not for you, their continued existence would have stayed a secret for who knows how much longer.

The Catholic Church is responsible for their creation, and we are responsible for their actions today. I believe that this makes it my duty to assist you in any way necessary in removing the SOG as an organization." This didn't do much to raise the spirit of either vampire, but a glimmer of hope was better than none at all.

"How can you help us?"

"I have several ideas, but you must do something for me first."

"What did you have in mind?" John asked cautiously.

"I need you to capture one of their leaders and bring him to me."

"What good will that do?" Danielle demanded.

"I need to question one of their leaders to fill in some of the gaps in the information we have on them. There are several possible ways to handle this situation, and it all depends on what we learn from someone in charge." The vampires exchanged a glance that made it clear they were unconvinced.

"Why should we do this? In fact, why should we work with you at all?"

The pope had been expecting these questions.

"You have no logical alternative. Randomly attacking them may help you in the short term, but in the long run they'll just commit more and more resources to destroying you both. You don't want to seriously hurt the SOG if it means you die in the process, do you? You want to topple them completely, without sacrificing yourselves, correct?" They both nodded. "Well, that's where I come in.

"It is my responsibility to stop them, and with your help I can do just that. You both stand a far better chance of surviving if you work with me on this. Isn't it much easier to have a specific objective to accomplish?"

They both nodded once again, albeit reluctantly.

"Good, because I have one last thing to add, and I doubt either of you are going to like it very much. I understand the need for you both to kill SOG soldiers in self-defense, but please show some restraint."

"You're joking, right?" Danielle's tone made it clear that if he wasn't, he'd better have a damn good reason.

"No, I'm not. Please try to understand. These men all believe that they are doing God's will. They believe it with their whole hearts and souls. That's why I need to speak with one of their leaders. Someone in the SOG chain of command has to know that they are operating without the consent of the Catholic Church.

"These people, whoever they are, are responsible for keeping this information from the rest of the SOG. These are the people we need to stop. The rest of the SOG not only believes that they are doing the right thing, but that they have the full support of the Catholic Church as well." John thought about it for a moment.

"Okay, we'll bring you one of their leaders, and we won't initiate any random attacks. We will, however, show no mercy against those who attack us, and their werewolves are free game for us to hunt down however we wish."

"Agreed. I can rearrange my schedule to allow me to stay free for two more weeks. Will that be enough time for you to return with a captive?"

"Yes," they both answered in unison.

"Excellent. Now that we've decided on the next step of our plan, may I ask you both a few personal questions?" John looked to his wife, who nodded that it was okay with her, before giving the pope permission to ask his questions.

"First, I'm very curious to know how old you both are."

"We were both turned in the late eleventh century. We've been vampires for over nine hundred years." The pope's eyes widened with amazement.

"Oh my, to live that long! I can hardly imagine the wonders you must have seen."

"Is that an offer?" John was about to once again stop his wife from threatening their host when he saw her playful grin and realized it was only meant as a joke.

"Um, no. Thank you for the offer, but I have no wish to live forever," the pope responded with his own grin. "My next question is a bit more personal, but I have to ask."

"Go ahead."

"Well, I noticed you were both wearing wedding rings." He let the statement hang, allowing the vampires, who both reflexively twitched their ring fingers, to respond as they saw fit.

"Yes, your Excellency, this is my wife." At the time it didn't occur to anyone that John had addressed the pope properly for the first time since they arrived.

"Interesting. I wasn't aware that vampires, well, you know, had relationships."

"They don't, but we do."

"I'm afraid I don't understand."

"Truth be told, Excellency, neither do we. We believe it has to do with the way we were turned." The pope leaned back in his chair.

"Please, you don't need to call me that. It feels wrong for someone several centuries older than I am to refer to me in such a way. Please elaborate though; I only thought a vampire could be made in one way."

"That is correct, but I was referring to the circumstances that surrounded the event." John spent the next ten minutes telling the pope about their lives before they became vampires and the events that transpired on their wedding night. When he finished, Danielle continued the story up to the point that they turned on the coterie, destroyed them, and were left alone. By the time they finished, they were both surprised to see several tears rolling down the pope's old, friendly face.

"Oh my, I'm so sorry that you had to endure such a thing."

"Don't be. It was hard at first, but after the first few decades, we grew to enjoy our new lives together. The day we were married, I had only one wish. That was to spend the rest of my life with my beautiful and loving wife. Never in my wildest dreams did I imagine how long that would be." Both vampires were staring lovingly into each other's eyes, the pope momentarily forgotten.

"If it is your wish, then, I shall be happy for you instead," the pope interjected, brushing away a final tear.

"Please do. I don't relish the idea of being a demon, but it's a small price to pay to spend immortality together." The pope cocked his head to one side, slightly confused.

"I don't understand what you mean. Neither of you are demons." The pope suddenly had two pairs of eyes locked on to his own.

"What did you say?"

"You're not demons." He had the same expression one would expect of a teacher whose prize pupil had suddenly gone completely brain-dead.

"If this is some kind of joke, I'm warning you that we don't appreciate your sense of humor."

The pope raised both his hands in a disarming gesture. "Wait, wait, it seems we have a misunderstanding. You both honestly believe that you are demons?"

"Yes, of course we do."

"Why?"

"We're vampires. Everyone knows that vampires are demons."

The pope had a bemused look on his face.

"Really? I was under the impression that no one knew what vampires were. Wasn't that the reason for the very first question you asked me? You are unsure of your origins?"

"Well, yes, we are, but we always knew that we were demons. We simply had to accept that fact, and we have."

"I'm sorry, but you're both wrong."

"What makes you say that?"

"I want to make it clear that I don't have all the answers, but I think it's quite clear that you aren't demons. The rings on your fingers are proof enough for me. You were married by a Catholic priest and have remained true to your vows ever since. How can you possibly be demons?"

John became thoughtful. "I don't know how, but I just know that we are."

The pope shook his head slightly. "Okay, wait a moment." He got up and shuffled over to the small bathroom in the corner of his bedchamber. A moment later, he returned with a small basin of water. What neither vampire knew was that he had quickly blessed the water.

"I would like you both to place a hand in this basin." The two vampires shrugged and then did as requested. A full minute passed with nothing happening. Finally, Danielle began to grow impatient.

"Excuse me, but what's the point of this?" The pope leaned back in his chair once again and grinned widely.

"That basin is filled with holy water, blessed by me personally."

"What?" Instantly, both vampires' hands began to smolder inside the basin. They rapidly withdrew their hands, clutched them to their chests, and glared at the pope in anger. The pope, for his part, simply looked amused.

"I'm sorry about that, but I was trying to make a point."

"And what might that be," Danielle hissed.

"Did you happen to notice that the water didn't bother you until after I told you it was blessed? Holy water is holy water. What difference does it make whether you know if it's blessed or not?"

Their angry expressions were slowly replaced by looks of confusion.

"I don't know. It should have burned us immediately."

"Wrong again. It shouldn't have burned you at all. Blessed objects are only a threat to demons, something you both are obviously not."

"Then why did it burn us after we knew it was blessed?"

It was the pope's turn to look thoughtful.

"That I'm not too sure about, but I have a theory." John motioned for him to continue. "I know that the mind is a very powerful thing. If a person believes something strongly enough, it often comes true. Since you're vampires, your minds are far more powerful, so I would guess this is even truer for your kind.

"You both lived in very superstitious times. People of those times, and for several centuries after that, simply didn't know the things that we know today. They considered vampires demons because there was no other explanation that made sense to them. You've spent the last nine hundred years or so believing with every fiber of your being that you were both demons, and that your bodies should react to things as demons should.

"I believe you've actually trained your bodies to react that way. That's why the holy water burned you, but not until after I told you it wasn't regular water." It was clear that both vampires were thinking hard about what he was saying. The pope decided it was time to press his attack.

"I understand that you hunt mortals for their blood. How many people do you kill on an average night of hunting?" By their expressions, it looked as if they had both been deeply offended.

"We take great pride in not killing those we hunt. We have made mistakes in the past, of course, but ever since we learned to properly control ourselves, we've yet to take an innocent life. Actually, our victims don't feel any pain, and never remember the experience."

The pope nodded in what seemed to be satisfaction and then continued. "That doesn't sound like a very demonic thing to me. Do you both know the difference between right and wrong?"

"Yes," came both replies.

"How often do you choose wrong over right?"

"Excuse me, we might no longer have our mortal lives, but we still have our honor. We have never knowingly chosen wrong over right. We have killed many, but only those who threaten us."

"I wouldn't think a demon would care about honor, or about doing the right thing. Honestly, neither of you are making a very good case to convince me that you're either demons or even evil in the slightest. I understand that neither of you are regular church goers, but you're also probably the best example of a successful and faithful marriage in the history of mankind." The pope was getting ready to list several other points when Danielle motioned for him to stop.

"Please, you've made you point, but try to look at it from our point of view. You've made a very convincing argument, but we've had these beliefs for over nine centuries. One conversation isn't going to immediately change our minds, no matter how right you are. We need time to think about what you've said, and right now the SOG presents a much more pressing problem than our beliefs." The pope bowed his head slightly.

"You are correct, my child, but don't underestimate the importance of belief. I urge you to think hard about what I've said." She nodded, and he looked back to the male, who had done most of the speaking. He was being oddly unresponsive and had his eyes downcast. "Is something troubling you, my son?"

"Well, yes. The crucifixes worn by the SOG did not burn us and we found that to be very strange, but now it sounds as if that is the way it should be? Another example of what you are saying to be true?"

"Perhaps, my son. It is very possible you were both simply too distracted for your bodies to 'remember' to react properly. Based on how you described the situation to me, once that happened you quickly came up with your own possible explanations so it would make sense that you never considered the truth. Who knows what happened and why? I can only tell you the truth as I see it."

"Ok, but there is one other thing. Something I've purposefully not thought about in a very long time. The reason we accepted what we have become, and why we fight so hard against anything that threatens us, is that we have always believed that this present existence is all we have left. When we are finally destroyed, we have always believed that we will burn for eternity in the deepest pits of hell for what we have become ... alone, never to see one another again.

"Neither of us could bear for that to happen, so we cling to our immortality with every drop of blood in our bodies. But these things you're saying ... they make sense. If they are true, and we are not truly demons, then does that mean we have a chance for ..." John paused, a single tear of blood streaking the side of his face with red. He had never dared to hope what he was now hoping. He had made a pact with his wife over five hundred years ago to never even speak of it again. He was afraid to continue, as if by speaking the word aloud his new hope would be stolen away.

"Go on," the pope urged gently, intrigued by the actions of the two vampires. The male seemed about to crumble, and the female appeared to be petrified with fright.

"... redemption?" As he spoke the final word, he raised his eyes back to the pope's face. The female's jaw dropped open, as if she couldn't believe that he would ask such a thing. The pope understood immediately and wanted badly to weep out of both joy and sadness.

These two powerful creatures were likely capable of doing anything they wanted, but they only seemed to truly want one thing. Forgiveness. They wanted it so badly, but were so completely convinced that they weren't allowed to have it that they were *afraid* to ask.

The pope silently cursed the monster that had done this to them both, for he truly was a demon. These two, however, had done nothing to deserve the way they thought about themselves. Silly superstitions and fear were responsible for over nine hundred years of repressed sadness and agony.

"Of course there is," the pope said as gently as he could. He reached across the table and placed a hand on the male's head. "Why wouldn't there be?" With that, he gently patted the vampire's non-bloodied cheek.

"You are both so old, and yet you think like children. I wish that we had the time for you to spend several nights here. I would like nothing more than to remove the suffering that you have both carried for all these centuries. Such an unnecessary burden." He shook his head in a gesture of sadness. "But I'm afraid that our duty calls the three of us to right the current situation with the SOG first. For now, I want you both to look me in the eye and gauge the truth of my next words." He waited for both vampires to lock eyes with him before continuing.

"Complete redemption is not something to be taken lightly or given easily. However, I don't know if I've ever met a pair more deserving than you. I feel it in my heart and soul, and I believe the Lord will find you just as deserving as I. After all, He forgives all things, and gives the shepherds of His flock the same power." Both vampires were weeping freely now. Nine centuries of hidden sadness and fear poured out in bloody tears.

"If you both follow my instructions in dealing with the SOG, I promise to personally help you see yourselves in the way that the Lord sees you." He gave them time to compose themselves, after which they both agreed to his deal. He was about to bless them when a sudden thought occurred to him and caused him to chuckle.

"Did we miss something?" John asked curiously.

"No, no, my son. I just realized that in this entire conversation, I never learned your names." The vampires smiled back, sharing the brief humor.

"Forgive me, please. My name is John Wolf, and this is my wife, Danielle." They both stood and offered their hands to the pope, who shook them both in turn. When they returned to their chairs, John glanced at his watch and sighed. "It has been truly wonderful talking to you, but we must be going."

"Of course. One moment please." The pope rose and moved closer to where John was sitting. Once within arm's reach, he placed his left hand on John's head. "I bless you, John, in the name of the Father, the Son, and the Holy Spirit, amen." He moved over to Danielle and gave her a similar blessing.

The vampires rose, bid their farewells, and vanished. They never seemed to realize that they had just received a blessing from the most prominent religious leader on the planet and it hadn't hurt them a bit. Watching them leave, the pope mumbled a short prayer.

"Watch over them, Lord, and protect them. They've already earned their redemption. Please keep them alive long enough for me to prove it to them."

Chapter 12

"THANK YOU FOR your donation, sir. Have a nice day, and remember, you have to wait at least eight weeks before you can donate again." The donor nodded politely as he turned to leave the bank.

Maxwell watched him leave, wondering why it had turned out to be such a slow afternoon. Weekday afternoons were always the slowest part of the day for a blood bank, but they usually weren't this slow. Looking around, he saw that there were only six donors waiting, one of which was still filling out paperwork.

It didn't matter much in the long run. His masters were very kind and wouldn't hold the day's low yield against him. Besides, they had huge stockpiles of blood hidden away, just in case. In the end, Maxwell just shrugged his shoulders and went back to work. He never noticed that someone had hung the blood bank's "Closed" sign in the front window.

* * *

RECENTLY PROMOTED senior Templar Daniel Stevens was pretending to think over a confusing question on his paperwork as he watched the last innocent donor leave. Arch-Templar Andrews's new ways of organizing their military structure had left room for many promotions, and the archbishop had approved them all. Their numerous casualties in the past few weeks had also attributed to the holes in their rank structure, but Stevens tried to not dwell on that.

This was his first assignment as a senior Templar, and it was a very prestigious one. He was leading the six-man infiltration team that was responsible for creating havoc inside the blood bank before their main assault element arrived. Originally, it was supposed to be a ten-man team, but it was decided that would have been too many men to get into position without one of the ghouls noticing that something was wrong.

The five other members of his team were the largest soldiers the SOG had in the area. At least four of them would be actually donating when the attack began. They would have to rip out their own needles and jump into action instantly, without fainting or stumbling.

They had been given new weapons for this attack as well. It was a foregone conclusion that there would be extensive security within the building, so normal weapons would be detected. Instead, they had all been given small plastic blowguns, which were accurate up to barely twelve feet.

They were each given a dozen darts to go with their new guns. The darts were solid plastic, razor sharp, and coated with a powerful neurotoxin. Each man had spent several hours practicing before the mission, and they were all deadly accurate with the new guns. The fact that they would be fighting in very close quarters also meant that the guns' short range wouldn't be much of a problem. Unfortunately, there were two other problems that would come into play in the coming battle.

The first was that the darts were plastic. It was necessary to avoid detection, but they couldn't be counted on to penetrate clothing. There were other stronger materials that could have been used, but there simply hadn't been time. This severely limited the areas of their enemies' bodies that were vulnerable to attack. Stevens wasn't too worried about this, however, since they were all excellent shots.

The second and worse problem was in the neurotoxin that they were using. It was very potent and could kill a man in seconds, but it had never been tested on ghouls. There was constant debate within the SOG as to whether ghouls were even living creatures. Everyone was convinced that the toxin would work, but no one had a clue how long it would take.

Ghouls drew their strength from the blood of their masters, but the toxin attacked the brain. The SOG knew that ghouls were not as dependent on their brains functioning properly as mortals were. On the other hand, it was the SOG's general consensus that they did still need them to live, but that didn't mean it was true. How long could a ghoul continue to fight once its brain shut down? Would it even notice?

These questions did bother Stevens. It was already likely that most of the infiltration team would die, but if the toxin didn't work, they would all die for nothing. He took grim satisfaction from knowing that if the toxin did fail completely, the SOG would at least learn the answers to some of their questions about a ghoul's capabilities.

Stevens took a final discreet look around. After ensuring that there were no more innocents present, he took out his cell phone.

It was decided that cell phones would be the best way to contact the assault team. They weren't suspicious, so he could carry it openly. All he had to do was call Templar Scott Bryant, who was leading the assault element, let it ring twice, and hang up. Once Bryant confirmed the number that had just called him, he would wait exactly ninety seconds and then storm the building. Stevens checked his watch and then carefully dialed his number.

"Excuse me, sir, but you can't use that in here." The ghoul behind the desk had seen him, but Stevens could use that to his advantage. His call connected and rang once.

"Oh, I'm sorry." It rang a second time, and he hung up. "It's my first time. I didn't realize that cell phones were not allowed." He spoke loudly so that the rest of his team would hear him. It seemed a good way to signal them that the attack was about to begin.

"It's no problem, sir. Thank you." The ghoul turned away and walked over to a filing cabinet.

It had been nearly half a minute since he had hung up. Stevens got the attention of the only member of his team that he could see and waited ten more seconds. Then, in one swift motion, he stood up, pulled out his gun, and sent a dart into the back of the ghoul's neck.

* * *

MORTALS CAN BE so stupid, Maxwell thought as he rummaged through the filing cabinet. First visit or not, there were signs everywhere prohibiting the use of cell phones inside the building. Only an idiot could miss the warnings, but he was supposed to be polite, no matter what, since repeat business was very important to his masters. He merely sighed and continued his search.

Finding the file he was looking for, Maxwell was about to turn back around when he felt a sudden sharp pinch on the back of his neck. *There shouldn't be any insects in here*, he thought as he reflexively probed the area with his free hand. He felt a small object sticking to his neck. Quickly he pulled it out and began to examine it.

When a second pinch followed in the same area, he realized something was wrong. Turning around, Maxwell saw that the man who had been using the cell phone was now standing and pointing what looked like a small straw at him. He realized he was being attacked, but he couldn't decide what to do about it. *What's wrong with me?*

The man was simply standing there, as if unsure what would happen next. Maxwell's sensitive hearing began to pick up unusual sounds throughout the building, but his brain didn't seem able to process them. He knew the situation was wrong, but he couldn't focus.

I'm dying. Under attack. Must protect. Complicated thoughts were becoming impossible for him, but he knew he had to do something. Maxwell nervously looked around for something that could help. Finally, he saw something that set off a light in what was left of his mind. *That button, have to push it.* He no longer knew why or how, but somehow the button he was looking at would solve the problem.

Maxwell began stumbling toward it, his movements becoming increasingly hampered. His mind seemed to be completely caving in on itself. Soon, Maxwell knew, he would be dead, but if he focused simply on pushing the button, maybe he'd be able to do it.

The man, seeing what was happening, suddenly rushed toward him. An instant before Maxwell could push the button, his body simply stopped working, and he collapsed in a useless heap. He never heard the man's curse, as his now lifeless body fell onto the building's silent alarm.

* * *

DAMN! The toxin had worked, but Stevens had been so intent on watching its effects that he hadn't noticed what the ghoul was trying to do until it was too late. He didn't hear any noise, but the button had to be some kind of alarm. Placing another dart in his gun, he ran to the donation area, where the battle was just beginning.

What he saw, upon linking up with his team, would have been fascinating under other circumstances. There were very few bodies on the ground, but there were several ghouls wandering aimlessly around the room. The toxin seemed to be working, but why weren't they dying? His target had collapsed in less than fifteen seconds.

That was when he remembered that he had shot his target twice. There were many more ghouls in this area, and his teammates were most likely only sparing a single shot per target. Each dart appeared to be capable of removing a ghoul as a threat; it just took a longer time to finish it off.

Unfortunately, the ghouls that had not been targeted first reacted quicker than expected. They were also far more intelligent than the SOG ever said ghouls could be. They had quickly determined what types of weapons were being used and that if they kept their heads down they were safe.

His men, on the other hand, were being counterattacked by handguns, and their makeshift barricade wasn't holding up very well. One of his men, Reynolds, took a chance at a risky shot and fell back screaming, a throwing knife stuck in his arm. To make matters worse, there was a loud crash behind the surviving ghouls, followed by several voices shouting orders.

Stevens didn't have to look to know that the security ghouls they expected had joined the fight. Apparently needing to see for himself, one of his men tried to steal a quick peek above their barricade. His head was almost instantly disintegrated by a shotgun blast. From the look on the faces of his other four teammates, Stevens knew that they had reached the same conclusion as he.

The small barricade they had made would be worthless against the firepower the security ghouls had surely brought with them. Any momentary confusion brought on by seeing some of their fellow ghouls wandering into walls had surely passed. Bryant's assault element would have an excellent chance of victory, but they wouldn't be here in time to save Stevens and his team.

They all loaded fresh darts and got ready. Perhaps if they all attacked at once, one of them would be able to get a good shot off before being killed. There were worse ways to die than in the service of the Lord.

* * *

BRYANT MOTIONED for his men to get ready. All eighteen soldiers of his reinforced squad quickly checked their weapons and prepared to move. It was obvious that they were nervous, but also confident. Their mission was very straightforward and simple.

Charge in, kill anything that threatens them, and protect any survivors of the infiltration team. His men were all armed with a variety of heavy weaponry—shotguns, grenades, heavy caliber handguns, and a few fully automatic assault rifles—and all of their ammo was phosphorous, just to be safe. Each member of his squad also carried a spare weapon. It was decided that anyone finding himself close to a survivor from the infiltration team would throw him a weapon, so he could protect himself. While his team was all wearing the heaviest body armor they could find, Bryant knew that the infiltration team had nothing but regular clothing and plastic blowguns.

All in all, there was no reason to expect anything other than complete success. However, it was hard to forget what had happened every other time they had engaged the abominations or their minions. It was understandable that there was a healthy amount of tension in the air.

Bryant checked his watch for what seemed to be the hundredth time and saw there was still over half a minute left before he was supposed to attack. *I don't know if I can wait that much longer.* It was very hard to sit back and wait when his fellow soldiers were right now fighting an enemy that was stronger, more numerous, and better armed than they were. Plus, Stevens was his friend and a very good man.

The rest of the squad looked just as restless as he felt, and he was about to say something to them when he suddenly heard gunfire. A lot of gunfire, punctuated with the booming reports of shotguns. There was still twenty-five seconds to go. *It's too soon. Something's wrong.* The ghouls' security forces weren't supposed to be able to respond that quickly.

If they waited any longer, the infiltration team would be wiped out. *Plans change.* His squad had all heard the gunfire and reached the same conclusions as he. He felt all eyes on him, awaiting his orders.

"We're moving early. You all know the plan, so God bless and let's go." He led the charge across the street and into the battle that awaited them inside the blood bank.

* * *

THE MEMBERS of the infiltration team were about to execute their final, futile attack when they heard the front doors smash open. Bryant had apparently gotten tired of waiting, but Stevens doubted any of his men would complain about his violation. They quickly backed down, dragging their wounded, and gave the fresh squad space to fight.

The ghouls reacted to the fresh troops immediately and met them with a hail of gunfire. Five soldiers fell screaming, their body armor unable to stand up to the vicious assault. The ghouls' attack was met by nearly a dozen fragmentation grenades, which killed most of them instantly.

The assault team charged the ghouls' position immediately after the grenades exploded. It was a simple task for them to put a phosphorous round into the head of every surviving ghoul. Less than three minutes had passed from when Stevens placed his call to begin the attack.

“I hope you don’t mind that we decided to move early,” Bryant said as he helped Stevens to his feet.

“Not at all, my friend. Thank the Lord you did.” Six men began searching the building for anything useful, while six others began carefully placing explosives. Stevens looked on as two medics came over to tend to the wounded.

While almost everyone in Stevens’s team had suffered a variety of injuries, thankfully there had been no further deaths on his side. Although the total loss of six men weighed heavily on him, he said a silent prayer of thanks that it hadn’t been worse.

The search parties returned a moment later, having come up empty-handed. Bryant double checked the explosives, ensuring that they wouldn’t damage the neighboring buildings too badly, and signaled that it was time to go. There was already a crowd gathering outside, curious to see what was going on.

Stevens agreed and had the survivors gather to make sure everyone was accounted for. Satisfied, they set the explosives for five minutes, gathered their dead, and left the building. The soldiers headed for the closest manhole cover and disappeared into the sewer, while Bryant stayed behind a moment longer to pass a warning on to the crowd about the coming explosion.

* * *

ARCHBISHOP JENKINS was quietly praying in his office when there was an excited knock at his door. Expecting that it would be Arch-Templar Andrews, coming with news of the strike against the vampires’ blood bank, he quickly took a seat behind his desk.

“Enter.” Andrews entered quickly and gently closed the door behind him. Jenkins invited him to take a seat in front of his desk and awaited his report with mixed emotions.

"I just finished personally debriefing Senior Templar Stevens and Templar First Class Bryant," Andrews began once he sat down.

"Judging from your expression, Thomas, am I to assume all is well?" Even asking the question, Jenkins had no idea what he wanted to hear.

"Better than that. Please excuse my slight bit of unprofessionalism, but the news has been spreading quickly through our ranks, and I admit to getting a bit caught up in the excitement." Jenkins smiled for his benefit and shook his head slightly.

"Thomas, please, I've been praying for hours and have not heard anything yet. What's the cause of all the excitement?"

Andrews smiled broadly. "Complete and total victory for us."

"Meaning?"

"Not only were our objectives accomplished completely, but there wasn't a single innocent casualty. Not even an injury. Plus, the property damage to the surrounding buildings was very slight, and all of our wounded will make full recoveries."

Jenkins's smile became genuine. This was truly excellent news. He had feared that there would be unnecessary deaths involved.

"What about our own losses?"

Andrews sobered slightly. "Unfortunately, we did lose six men, one from the infiltration team and five from the assault squad. There were also nine more injured, but as I said before, they will all make full recoveries."

Jenkins's smile faded.

Six more souls lost. The question was, were their deaths necessary? Jenkins didn't know anymore.

Andrews noticed the archbishop's sudden change in demeanor.

"It was still a complete victory, and the men are thrilled. Morale is higher than it's been since this war began."

Jenkins had noticed that Andrews had begun referring to the current situation as a war, but he chose to not make this the time to comment on it.

"The men are not saddened by our own losses?"

"Of course they are, but their reactions are understandable. We've had three major engagements with the abominations and their minions. In the first two, our forces suffered near total losses. This time our losses were only about 25 percent.

"Of course, 25 percent is still high from a military standpoint, but it's far better than 100 percent. The men see this victory as proof that God is on our side, and they're heartened by the lack of innocent casualties. They understand that doing God's will requires sacrifices. They are saddened by the deaths of our men, but happy that their sacrifice was not in vain."

Jenkins noticed how easily Andrews put a positive light on everything.

"So, what's next?"

"We wait for them to make the next move. This was a serious blow, both to their minions and to their resources. They'll have no choice but to operate more openly, and when they do, we'll be waiting for them."

Jenkins managed a weak smile. "Sounds like you have the situation well in hand, Thomas. You have a lot of work to do I assume?"

Andrews properly interpreted this as his dismissal and, with a small bow, left the office.

As soon as the door closed, Jenkins's head fell into his hands. *This is all wrong.* He had been meditating all day and was still no closer to the answers he sought. If anything, he had even more doubts than before. To make matters worse, Andrews seemed to be growing more coldhearted with each passing day.

The vampires were sure to respond to this last attack most violently, and could they be blamed? The SOG had started this violence, and now they had destroyed their main source of food. Of course they would respond strongly.

This is all wrong, he thought again. *I'm supposed to be preventing atrocities, not triggering them.* His superiors were constantly encouraging him and sending reinforcements, but it did nothing to soothe his doubts. Lately, Jenkins had felt as if he were trapped in the proverbial lion's den, rather than surrounded by compatriots.

He looked to the large crucifix that adorned the corner of his desk with pleading eyes.

"What am I supposed to do? All this death *can't* be Your will." Several minutes passed, but there was no answer.

Chapter 13

"WHAT!" Their first order of business upon returning home would have been to release Sam and see how he was coping. Instead, the instant they returned to the haven, they were met by Marcus, who informed them of the successful attack on their blood bank by the SOG.

To Marcus's credit, he was standing straight and tall. None of the terror he had to be feeling upon delivering this news was showing on his features. A detached portion of John's mind noticed this with approval. Marcus had definitely been the right choice to replace Sam as their head ghoul. The rest of John's mind, however, was overwhelmed with fury.

"How did they find it? How did they succeed? Do they really think we're just going to give up now?" He was pacing back and forth in their hotel's lobby, shouting to no one in particular. This continued for a moment, followed by a howl of rage. "Those goddamn mother-*fuckers*! I'm going to *fucking* slaughter every last *fucking* one of them! Then, I'll put all their hearts in the same crate and mail it to whoever's in fucking charge of these *bastards*!"

It was very rare for John to lose his temper. Even when he did, he normally swore in the dialect he grew up speaking. In fact, he'd probably uttered more modern curses in the last few moments than he had in the last few years.

As John stormed around the lobby muttering and breaking things, Marcus cast Danielle a hopeful look. He was quite dismayed to see that even she had taken a few tentative steps back.

Once she noticed Marcus looking at her, Danielle sighed in acceptance. She really did not want to approach her husband right now. In over nine hundred years, she had rarely seen him descend this far into raging madness. In the end, however, she had no choice, and it wasn't just because of love. It was practicality. She was the only one who could interrupt him right now and live, at least in theory. Probably.

When he began storming back toward them, Danielle took a few steps forward and threw up a barrier in front of him. It was nothing strong enough to stop him—she didn't want his anger transferred to her—but just enough for him to feel it and acknowledge her. When she was sure that she had at least most of his attention, she risked speaking.

"My love," she began, turning her seduction on full force, "you are tired, worn, and angry. Please, drink me." With that, she seductively sliced open her neck with a fingernail and offered it to him.

When a vampire allowed another to drink his or her blood freely, the feeling was similar to what he felt himself when feeding. If the vampire who first offered then began to feed from the other vampire as well, the shared feeling of ecstasy was immensely gratifying for both.

In fact, two vampires feeding from each other willingly and simultaneously was the vampiric equivalent to mortal men and women making love. Unfortunately, since most vampires were animals who only cared about themselves, this was a very dangerous prospect. Usually, while the act may have begun innocently enough, it ended with one vampire refusing to stop and eventually killing the other.

In John and Danielle's case, they received the same gratification from either the mortal or the vampire form of lovemaking. They vastly preferred the mortal methods, since there was no place at all for love in the vampiric ones. While the pleasure may be the same, they both preferred to practice their lovemaking with real love, rather than lust. Danielle simply guessed that, at the moment, it would be easier to appeal to John's vampiric lust than his human love.

The instant his mouth closed over her self-inflicted wound and his teeth pierced her neck, she knew it had worked. There was no anger or rage coming from her husband now. With tremendous lust and desire, he drank hungrily from her. She fought to maintain her own control, wary of Marcus's presence, as the waves of pleasure flowed through her.

Her knees began to grow weak, and Danielle knew she would need to break the moment so they could get to work. As her husband's fingers slid underneath her armored clothing and his claws bit into the skin of her back, she knew she was fighting a losing battle. *Oh, to hell with it. A girl can only take so much.* Finally giving in, she sank her own fangs into John's neck.

Seeing his masters engaged in their dark embrace, Marcus immediately turned around and wished he could be anywhere else. The polite thing to do would be for him to just leave, but he couldn't. They had much to do, and while Danielle had succeeded in calming John down, now they were both hopelessly distracted. More importantly, what happened if one of the hotel's mortal guests were to see them?

Having mortals as guests was an excellent cover, but it would backfire severely if they weren't cautious. Marcus didn't possess nine centuries worth of wisdom, but even he could see the obvious disaster waiting to happen.

Wondering how to break them up, he turned to face his masters just in time to see them carefully lick each other's wounds closed,

John rested his head on his wife's shoulder, his own shoulders trembling. With curiosity building, Marcus crept close enough to hear the ends of his mumbling.

"How could we let this happen, love? Seventeen of them, just gone." Marcus knew at once what was happening and felt a surge of pride.

There had been seventeen ghouls working at the blood bank when it was attacked. Nine workers and a security force of eight. All of them had been killed in the attack, and his masters were both fighting back tears over the loss.

It was said that vampires were demons at worst and animals at best. He knew that his masters were ancients, yet *they* were close to weeping over the loss of life among their ghouls. It wasn't anger at the difficulty needed to replace a valuable resource, but the sadness of suddenly hearing you've unexpectedly lost several close friends. When he saw their reactions, Marcus was reminded, once again, why he served them so fiercely.

Regaining his composure, John turned to glance at Marcus, who suddenly found the floor very interesting.

"I apologize for my outburst. Let the staff know that if they receive any complaints about the noise, the guests are to be given whatever they can reasonably ask for."

"Yes, master."

John grinned at his formal tone. It had taken Sam a long time to get over that. He wondered how long it would take Marcus.

"Okay, now what do we do about the—what?" Danielle interrupted his question with a devilish grin.

"I have an idea," she said in a sultry voice.

"Um, we don't really have time for that right now, dear. Maybe later, once we—"

She playfully slapped him. "What is it with you men? Is that all you can think about? I meant I have an idea about what to do next about the SOG. Follow me." Without waiting for a response, she started walking toward the elevators. John looked back over at Marcus, who was still studying the floor, slightly confused.

"Women," he muttered before following his wife.

Marcus hesitated a moment before following. It wasn't out of deference to his masters. He simply didn't want them to see the smirk that he couldn't seem to wipe from his lips.

* * *

DANIELLE LED THEM to one of their main offices, where half a dozen of her ghouls were working at the computer stations the room contained. John wasn't surprised to see that none of his ghouls were present, save for Marcus, who had just followed them in.

Technically, they treated all their ghouls the same, with one notable difference. Their training. A ghoul gained its abilities from the powers passed on by its master. Unfortunately, they discovered centuries ago that ghouls had no capability whatsoever for mind control or powerful magic, which meant that it was impossible for Danielle to train her ghouls in the use of her main abilities.

John's ghouls, on the other hand, were easily able to benefit from his main abilities, since they were mostly physical in nature. The decision they reached was a simple one. Warriors were not the only thing that would be of assistance to two ancient vampires. They would need workers of many different types, especially in this new computer age that they found themselves in.

They decided that every ghoul that John made would be trained in combat. Danielle's ghouls, however, were trained as hotel staff, medical specialists for the blood bank, computer specialists, and more.

They both found that things worked more smoothly that way, since the ghouls' training reflected on the abilities they had already gained.

A side effect was that Danielle had over three times as many ghouls as John did, but it didn't really matter, since all their ghouls were ordered to treat them both equally as their masters. Usually, the ghouls just took orders from whatever ghoul they placed in charge of them all, but occasionally a ghoul would show favoritism to their specific master in some negative way. These ghouls were always immediately destroyed, something that hadn't happened in decades. All in all, the vampires had set up their infrastructure very well.

"So what's your idea?"

Danielle motioned to the working ghouls. "Before we left for the Vatican, I had these six start organizing the information we got in the raid. I'm hoping that they've come across something useful."

John nodded, noticing stacks of paperwork and discs next to each working ghoul.

"Hey, Jasmine, how's it going?" Danielle asked the ghoul John took to be the head of the small group.

"Very well, mistress. We still have much to do, but we believe we have created all of the necessary files. All we're doing now is adding to those files as we find the information. I also had someone place desktop icons on the computer in your bedroom that will correspond with every new file we have. It's all on the local secure network so you should be able to access anything we organize with no problem."

"Good. Can you bring up a map showing the locations of any SOG strongholds around the city?"

"Of course, mistress," Jasmine answered as she turned back to her computer.

It appeared that each of the six ghouls was working on separate types of data, but John knew that all the computers were on the same network. It would be possible for any ghoul to access everything they had from any computer.

"This is what we have so far, mistress." Jasmine turned the screen to give Danielle a better look. "We believe it is complete, since one of the files you stole contained a map of every SOG facility in the world."

Danielle smiled. "Excellent."

Jasmine offered her chair to Danielle and went to check on the work the rest of her team was doing. Danielle spent a moment orienting herself to the map, while John and Marcus both looked over her shoulder.

"Okay, I say we strike back by destroying their facilities. We promised to be careful with the lives of their men, but nothing was said about their structures. It looks like they have seven facilities left in the city, since we destroyed that one." She tapped the red dot that indicated Lori's Bed and Breakfast.

"The problem is, I don't know what these different symbols mean, and there's no map legend or anything. I'm guessing that they're all simply supposed to know already."

John could see the problem. It would be a disaster if they planned on attacking an outpost, and it turned out to be a heavily defended headquarters building.

"Well, we know that Lori's was an outpost, so the symbol that indicates Lori's should be the symbol that indicates their outposts."

Danielle nodded slowly and counted how many symbols of that type were shown on the map.

"If you're right, that would make four more outposts. I suppose that makes sense, since an organization like the SOG would need outposts more than anything. Plus, if Lori's is any indication, their outposts also double as barracks facilities. So, what do you make of these other symbols then?"

"One problem at a time, dear."

Danielle bared her fangs in a toothy smile. "Fine. As I was saying, let's destroy all of their outposts. Nothing fancy, just a group of ghouls going in during the day and planting enough explosives to blow the buildings. We can even call in a bomb threat ten minutes before detonation, so they can evacuate."

John laid a hand on her shoulder. "I like it. I don't think we have the manpower left to handle all four of them at once so we should target the two outposts that look to be in the center."

"Any particular reason?"

"We have to assume that they've been looking for our main haven since this nonsense began. They know we stole information from them, but not what that information is. When we suddenly destroy a pair of their outposts, they'll figure we know where they all are."

"And they'll probably guess we simply started with the ones closest to our haven." Danielle finished the thought for him.

"Exactly, but if we destroy the two in the center, it'll leave the other two separated to either side. They'll guess that either our haven is in that area or we're smarter than they thought. At best we'll send them on a wild goose chase for the haven; at worst we won't have given them any inadvertent help."

"Okay, so we're agreed. We destroy both of these outposts. Send in the ghouls with explosives, and give time and warning for the buildings to be evacuated." She waited for him to agree.

"Sounds good, unless you have anything to add, Marcus." Marcus seemed lost in his own thoughts and started slightly when asked the question.

"Um, actually I do, master."

"Well, out with it then."

He nodded obediently. "The ghouls need to be told that the target for their explosions should be the bottom floor of the building, not the building itself."

A light went on in both vampires' heads.

"Of course! In Lori's, all the important stuff was underground. Will that be a problem, Marcus?" Marcus had been a demolitions expert before joining the vampires' ranks.

He considered the question for a few minutes before responding. "It shouldn't be. Does that map thing show you if all the outposts are laid out the same way as Lori's, mistress?" Danielle rapidly tapped several keys, which showed them a close-up blueprint of each outpost.

"It looks like they are. At least the position of the rooms seems to be the same."

Marcus nodded thoughtfully. "Thank you, mistress. That's all that matters. Since the SOG facilities are more or less underneath the main buildings, we just need to destroy the ground separating them."

John could tell that Marcus was in his element. "What's your plan, Marcus?"

"Well, master, if we place enough explosives in the right areas, we can basically remove the ground separating the SOG chambers from the rest of the building. If we make sure to destroy the building's remaining supports as well, it'll just collapse into the chambers below."

"And that will destroy both." Marcus nodded. "But how can you remove that ground? It's nearly fifteen meters thick, and mostly concrete."

Marcus just smiled.

"Master, if you give me enough explosives, I'll move Mount Everest out of your way. It's really just a matter of shaping the charges in such a way that most of the explosive force goes down, rather than all over. The only difficulty I can see is the tunnel that each outpost has leading down to the SOG portion. That tunnel winds around a lot between them both, so it'll be more difficult than just destroying solid ground. Also, we aren't technically destroying the ground as much as we want to break it up and blast through so that it caves into the subterranean chambers."

"What will you need?"

"I need to study these blueprints first, master."

"Okay. Let us know when you're finished." John and Danielle turned to leave, but Marcus motioned for them to wait.

"I'm sorry, master, I almost forgot. Sam wants to speak with you both at your earliest convenience."

Both vampires' eyes went wide.

"Oh shit, we forgot all about him," John said as Danielle began to laugh.

"Think he'll be pissed, love?" she asked.

"What do you think? We left him chained to a toilet. We better go let him out before he tries to chew his arms off or something." Seeing that Marcus had already begun to examine the blueprints, John led the way out of the office, followed by his wife, who was still trying to control her laughter.

* * *

"WHAT THE HELL took you so long?" Sam was understandably a bit annoyed with them. "I know you've been back for a while. What the hell were you doing?"

John was about to answer before he realized that Sam must not know about their blood bank's destruction yet.

"Sorry about that, Sam. Things have started to heat up around here." Danielle moved closer and removed her enchantments from the chains.

"Why? Has something happened?"

"One thing at a time. First, how do you feel?"

"Much better now," Sam said wryly as he broke the now unenchanted chains and stood up. "Although, I now understand what you meant and why you insisted on this. The last day has been ... unpleasant." John nodded knowingly.

"Just be thankful you spent so much time as a ghoul. The change your body just went through wasn't as drastic as it is for normal mortals who are turned." Sam shuddered at the thought. "Just remember that it's over. Nothing that happened during that time makes you any weaker or any closer to being a monster."

"Okay, so what's going on?"

"Later. First we need to give you your first lesson."

"Well, I definitely want to learn all I can, so let's get started. What do I learn first?"

John looked to his wife and shrugged. She thought for a moment and then her eyes lit up.

"Let's go hunting." It was the perfect suggestion and just the thing to take their minds off the current situation.

"Sounds good, but isn't that dangerous, what with the SOG all over the place and me not knowing what I'm doing?"

"Don't worry, Sam. This is your first lesson, so we're going to do all the work. You're not actually going to be hunting. Just follow us and do what we tell you. Mainly you're just going to work on getting the hang of controlling your new senses and controlling yourself while you feed." The trio walked into the kitchen and sat down. Almost immediately a ghoul entered and set three pitchers of blood before them.

"May I ask some questions before we start?"

"Of course."

"Okay, I thought we were hunting? Why then are we all sitting in the kitchen drinking blood?"

"One reason and this is very important," John spoke up. "We do not hunt out of necessity. We hunt for pleasure and to practice our skills. As young as you are, you could survive just from hunting, but it isn't practical for us. Also, the more often you hunt, the greater the risk of discovery. We play things safe.

"As you will soon see, drinking fresh blood from your prey is one of the single most pleasurable experiences you will ever have from now on. I can't even describe the sensation. You'll just have to wait and see. The downside is that you won't want to stop.

"You'll soon notice that no matter how much blood you drink, you will always be thirsty for more when it is offered to you. Eventually, through trial and error, you'll get an idea of how much blood your body can store. As time goes on, you'll also learn how to ignore the thirst. So long as you don't let yourself get too low on blood, the thirst is easily ignored.

"Unfortunately, one of the times that the thirst is the most difficult to ignore is when you're feeding from live prey. The urge to drink it all and kill your prey is very strong. Drinking large quantities of blood right before we hunt is one way to help keep the thirst at bay. It doesn't help much, but you'll soon be grateful for every bit of help you can get." John paused and drained half his pitcher.

"A second reason is because of how dangerous times have become for us. You must always remember that you're now totally dependent on blood. If your body runs dry of blood you'll die. As you get older, running out of blood won't kill you, but it'll still make you helpless until something else does. We treat ourselves to a fresh hunt so rarely that we want to make sure we're prepared for anything when we do."

"Okay, I understand, except for one thing. You keep saying 'the thirst.' What the hell is that? I thought I only had to worry about the beast." That was something John had forgotten about.

On their way back to the airport from Castel Gandolfo, they had briefly discussed what the pope had told them about not being demons. They agreed not to worry too much about it, one way or the other, until the SOG was dealt with. They couldn't afford to get their hopes up now, but they did make one agreement.

They agreed to stop referring to themselves as demons, or with demonic references. The beast, for example, was the essence of the demon within every vampire. Or so they had thought. Now they weren't sure about things like that. They agreed to refer to 'the beast' as 'the thirst' from now on. At least until they had the chance to discuss that matter with the pope.

It was surprising how much better that one small change made them both feel. The more they thought about it, the more sense it made. The beast was generally its worst when blood was involved. Maybe they didn't have demons inside them. Maybe they were just very thirsty all the time?

They had just realized that they hadn't discussed any of this with anyone else yet. It was understandable that Sam was confused, since the first thing John had done when he was turned was lecture him about the beast. But he just didn't want to get into that discussion with him yet.

"Oh, I'll explain that later. Any more questions about hunting?"

"Several, actually, but I suppose I can make them all into one general question. How do I control all this stuff? My senses are going crazy." John smiled while Danielle started to answer.

"Practice is the only way really. Concentrate on one sense—hearing for example. Close your eyes and just listen to everything you can. Try to judge how far away things are by how they sound, how to ignore sounds that aren't important, and how to focus on the ones that are.

"It takes a lot of practice, but you'll get the hang of it." Sam nodded, but it wasn't the easy answer he was obviously looking for.

"My wife raises an interesting point," John started, taking the lead in the discussion again. "Much of your time now must be spent in practicing your new abilities. All of the duties you had when you were a ghoul are no longer yours. For the time being, you are not to worry about or do anything unless we tell you to.

"When you were a ghoul, you were excellent at your job ... the best fighter we had. You were such a huge asset to us that we delayed turning you into a vampire for as long as possible. However, now that you are a vampire, you are weak, inexperienced, and generally a liability to us. If you were to be involved in a battle, odds are your senses would quickly be overwhelmed and you'd lose control. God knows what would happen next.

"Once you learn, on the other hand, you'll be more of an asset to us as a vampire than you ever were before. We'll take things one step at a time. Compared to us, you know nothing and are worthless, but we're going to teach you all kinds of things. Before we do that, though, we have to help you discover what you already know and are capable of." Sam was listening intently.

"Take your physical abilities. As a ghoul you were stronger and faster than any mortal, but you couldn't control it. I gave you blood, and the blood gave you power, and that's just the way it was. As a vampire, your blood controls everything you do, but you have to control your blood.

"This is kind of tricky at first, but once you learn, it's the same as breathing for a mortal. You have to force your blood to go where you need it. If you want to run fast, for example, you need to force blood into your legs to power you.

"Once the blood is there, the rest happens on its own. The same goes for your strength. You want to punch through a wall? Force blood into your fist and arm. Physical things like strength and running don't require you to actually learn anything. You can do it all right now. It just takes practice to learn how much blood you need to do this or that or whatever. The goal is to accomplish your task using as little blood as possible. Just be careful when you do practice, because your blood is very strong, and we don't want you destroying the city." Sam grinned but saw that John was only half-joking.

"Okay, I understand that, and I think I know how to force blood throughout my body. I don't know how I know or how I'm doing it; it just sort of happens when I want it to."

"Exactly. Don't worry about it. All you really have to do is think about what you want."

"Okay, so what about fighting?"

"Well, when it comes to physical combat, it'll take some getting used to. All the moves and techniques you know are good. It's just that now you'll be doing them much faster and carrying much more force with your blows." John paused for moment trying to think of a good example.

"Let's say you are in a situation where you want to leap towards your opponent. Nothing fancy, and something you have done countless times before without thinking. If you were to do that right now, odds are you would end up jumping over a building. You would reflexively use your body to its max potential just as you have always done, but that potential is far higher now. As you grow accustomed to the changes, you'll be capable of using the necessary control to meet each situation with the appropriate amount of force. So, again, you aren't really learning anything new, just practicing all the old stuff in a different way.

"As for all other types of combat, we'll teach you once you learn the basics."

Sam almost looked disappointed. "I really want to learn how to do some of those amazing things I've seen you both do, but I understand."

Danielle flashed a questioning look at her husband, who nodded in agreement.

"We will show you one thing. This is very simple to do, but it's extremely useful in combat. It's perfect for someone like you because it doesn't take much blood." She placed her hand on the table and morphed it into claws.

"Put your hand on the table." He did so. "Now concentrate. Think about the claws of an animal. Think about them ripping apart the animal's prey. Now concentrate hard on how you could tear apart your own enemies if you had claws like that. If it helps, look at my claws while you are doing it." Sam closed his eyes and tried to follow the instructions.

He opened his eyes a moment later, but his hand remained unchanged. Frowning, he tried again, but this time took Danielle's advice and focused on her claws. Finally, his fingers began to stretch and change. He watched in amazement as his own hand morphed into a set of wicked-looking claws.

"Wow, that's ... cool. Now what?"

"This is the easy part. Just picture your hand the way it was." Sam did so, and his hand immediately began to change back. Within seconds, it was as if nothing had happened at all. "Very good. Now every time you want claws, just picture your hand the way it just was. The first time you do something new as a vampire, it's always hard. After your first success, however, all you need to do is think about it, and it happens.

"Those claws will cut through anything, from body armor to the strongest werewolf hide. They will also stay claws for as long as you want. The best part of it is that the claws will not drain any additional blood from you until you choose to change them back to normal. So you essentially have a low-cost, but extremely powerful, weapon. Just don't forget to change them back after the fight, otherwise people will definitely notice the difference in your appearance."

"I won't. Thank you." Sam spent the next few minutes morphing his hand into claws and back to normal several times.

"Okay, that's enough. Let's move on."

Sam smiled sheepishly and started paying attention again.

"All right, when we start hunting, I don't want you to do anything but follow us. We'll shroud you, and we'll find your prey.

"As you follow us, just work on understanding your new senses without getting overwhelmed."

"Got it. When do we leave?"

"As soon as we finish our pitchers." The three vampires toasted their remaining blood and tossed it back.

* * *

THE VAMPIRES WERE concealed in an alley a few miles from the haven. Sam was still amazed by how fast he was now able to travel. It was difficult at first, but after a few minutes of confusion, he was able to keep up with the two ancients. He suspected that they were holding back to allow him to keep up, but they still covered the distance in under two minutes.

It was obvious to him now why the ancients didn't want him to bother with the actual hunting. He could barely keep from being overwhelmed by all the new sensations his heightened senses were opening up to him. He could hear the insects crawling, hopping, and flying through the night. He could smell the pizza being served at a corner restaurant two miles down the road. He could taste the air, and knew that it would rain in the morning. How was he ever going to learn to keep things straight?

He had been instructed to just sit back and wait. The plan was for Danielle to use her considerable mind control abilities to lure a random mortal into the alley where they lay waiting, and then he would be instructed on how to proceed. Sam tried to wait patiently, shaking his head in an attempt to clear his beleaguered senses.

Finally, John signaled to him and pointed. Following his gesture, Sam saw a figure turn the corner and begin wandering down the alley. With his vampiric sight, he could easily see the large grin on the man's face, and he shuddered involuntarily at the thought of how much power Danielle possessed.

Not yet receiving any further instruction, Sam waited and watched as the man drew closer. When he came within arm's reach of Danielle's position, she stepped forward and simply waved a hand in front of his face; as if on cue, the man simply collapsed where he stood. Danielle caught the body and carefully carried it to where John and he were waiting.

Nodding to his wife, John began to stare down the alleyway. Sam could actually feel his former master's senses penetrating the night. He had always known that the ancients were powerful, but until now he hadn't realized just *how* powerful. Now that he was a vampire himself, he could feel power simply radiating from both of them, and it filled him with a mingled sense of fear and excitement.

"Come closer, Sam," John said after satisfying himself that all was well. His voice so suddenly cut through Sam's thoughts that he nearly stumbled in the dark. Recovering quickly, Sam moved next to Danielle, who was still gently cradling their unconscious prey.

"We usually don't do this, but since we're taking our time, it seemed safer to just render him unconscious." Sam nodded, one of his unspoken questions having been answered. "You might not have noticed it before, due to your senses going crazy, but you should be able to detect the strong smell of fresh blood by now." Sniffing the air, Sam was surprised that he hadn't noticed it before. John had a point about his senses going crazy, but the scent was so powerful!

"Feel free to enjoy everything that is happening, or is about to happen, my friend; just take care not to allow it to take control over you." Sam agreed solemnly, remembering the experiences of the previous twenty-four hours.

"Um, what do I do?"

John smiled, pleased that Sam hadn't made a move to simply dig in.

"First, remember that every drop of blood is precious to us. Also, despite the pleasure, speed is always of the essence when feeding. The ecstasy that will overcome you, while amazing, will prevent you from shrouding yourself while you feed. No matter how strong we are, it's simply a limitation we have to deal with.

"This is why you always feed from your prey's neck, right here." He indicated the man's carotid artery. "The blood will flow into you very quickly and easily. You will have a natural reaction to suck on the wound, but you must ignore it. It'll make the blood flow too quickly, which will vastly increase the chance that your prey will die. Also, the pressure on the wound from you sucking will cause much more damage to the neck.

"It is very difficult for us to heal the wounds of a mortal. If you feed properly, however, all will be well. The body's heart will do all the work, pumping the blood directly into you, and you'll leave behind two simple holes from your fangs. Those you can simply lick a few times and then they'll heal on their own. The person will wake up in the morning a bit dazed and light-headed, but no worse for wear." Sam was listening to this intently, his excitement mounting by the second.

"Oh yeah, I almost forgot. We never really talked to you about how we drink blood from mortals. Odds are, even being a vampire now yourself, you believe what most mortals read in their books of legends." Curiosity temporarily overrode Sam's excitement.

"What is it?"

"Our fangs are not hollow."

"Really?" Sam unconsciously ran his tongue over his fangs. "So how do we suck blood?"

John laughed softly.

"Aren't you listening, stupid? We don't suck blood at all; we drink it." John's obvious amusement kept Sam from thinking he was being rebuked. Use your fangs to pierce deep into the artery. Then withdraw them and cover the wound with your mouth. The holes will be deep and fairly large, allowing the blood to flow quickly if you just let the heart do the work for you. If you leave your fangs in and try to suck through them, all you'll end up with is a mess."

The more Sam thought about it, the more sense it made. *Hollow fangs? What idiot mortal made that up?* "Is that everything?"

John nodded, but now it was Danielle's turn to speak.

"I want to add something." Sam regarded her, a touch of impatience evident on his face. "Relax, will you. There's no rush here. Anyway, there's a trick you can try while you're feeding. Once the blood starts to pump down your throat, try to elongate you lips and widen your tongue. It'll feel strange at first, especially once the ecstasy takes over, but it'll keep you from spilling any. As John said, every drop is precious." Sam considered this and nodded.

"Without further ado then, Sammy, my boy, he's all yours. Take it nice and easy, and enjoy yourself. We'll stop you before you kill him, so no worries there. He's all yours." With that, John took a step back, and Danielle, after handing the body over to Sam, joined him. They would step forward when the time came to stop him, but this was a very private moment for a vampire.

Due to the ecstasy, and the accompanying vulnerability, of feeding, most vampires took personal offense, usually in a very violent manner, at being interrupted during the act. To this end, both John and Danielle wanted to give Sam at least some semblance of privacy. Of course, they were both also ready to leap into action if the thirst overcame their young friend.

Sam, for his part, was no longer even aware of the presence of the other two vampires. His focus was placed wholly on the body in his arms and the strong pulse in that body's neck. Taking a moment to attempt to gain control over his own excitement, Sam quickly gave up and proceeded to feed.

The instant his fangs pierced the man's skin, a wave of pleasure swept over him. It was more instinct than conscious thought that caused Sam to pierce the artery and withdraw his fangs. Even the pleasure that was currently washing over him couldn't have prepared Sam for that first rush of fresh blood.

He was immediately enthralled by the feeling, thc taste, everything about the moment grasping him and refusing to let go. The only thing that broke the spell of ecstasy was the sudden horror that some of the blood was escaping his grasp. It was spurting from the wound faster than he could drink it, and the extra was forcing its way through the seal he had made with his mouth.

Shocked at the horrible injustice of even a drop of his sweet blood escaping him, Sam forced himself to relax and remember what Danielle had said. He focused on forcing his tongue to flatten out and widen, and was almost shocked to see how much easier it was to swallow the blood. Within seconds he was able to keep pace with the man's heart. Every beat would send a fresh flow of blood into his mouth, and with Danielle's trick, he was able to swallow every drop easily.

Soon Sam felt the man's heartbeat begin to weaken and then slow, but he didn't care. Some part of his new senses told him that the man was rapidly approaching the point of death, but he ignored it and kept drinking. There was nothing more important to him than draining the body of every last drop of delicious blood.

Suddenly, Sam felt a strong grip on his shoulder. It was beginning to push him back, away from his blood, and something inside him began to panic. He began to growl a warning to the offending party, and the next thing he knew, he was being held against the back wall of the alley by a force he couldn't even struggle against.

"Take it easy, Sam. Just calm down," said a soft, familiar voice. Slowly, he began to regain control over himself, and he recognized the figure standing before him as a friend.

"Danielle, I'm ... I'm sorry. What happened?"

"You lost yourself too deeply in the feeding and nearly killed that man. When John tried to stop you, you grew violent, so I restrained you."

"I'm sorry. I don't know what happened." Even as he said it, Sam knew it wasn't exactly true. The pleasure might be ebbing, but he could still feel it inside him. Now, the remnants of that pleasure warred with the sickening feeling that he had almost taken an innocent life.

"Yes you do, Sam. I don't need to use my abilities to be able to see the turmoil within you now. Take my word for it, it'll get easier in time, but you can never drop your guard. Eternal vigilance is far easier to handle than the knowledge of having taken an innocent life." She held his gaze until he nodded his understanding. Satisfied, she waved her hand, releasing him from the invisible bonds she had placed him in.

"Is he okay?" John had moved up to stand beside his wife.

"I'm fine," Sam answered for himself, "but is he okay?" He gestured toward the man he nearly killed.

"Don't worry about him, Sam. I closed his wounds, and he's sleeping quite deeply at the moment. He'll be fine by morning." Sam was noticeably relieved. "So, how was it?" The ancients' expressions went suddenly from serious to friendly.

"It was ... it was ... I don't know how to explain it." The ancients' grins broadened. They both remembered what it was like to have that first taste of warm, fresh mortal blood. Sam returned their grins, and the three simply relaxed with their memories for a time.

"Sorry to break the mood, boys, but we still have a lot to cover tonight." Danielle was the first to speak up, but John knew she was right.

"Does this mean you two are finally going to tell me what's going on?" Sam asked in earnest.

"Yes, but not here. You know your way back to the haven?"

"Yeah, why?"

"Good, because I doubt you could keep up with us." Sam nodded, accepting the unspoken challenge; however, both ancients had already vanished and were halfway back to their haven. Shaking his head again at their unbelievable power, Sam did his best to not run into any solid objects.

* * *

"WOW," SAM MUMBLED, still shaking his head slowly. John and Danielle had just spent the better part of an hour briefly going over everything that had happened since they left for the Vatican the previous night. They decided for now to keep quiet about the portion of their discussion with that pope that centered on whether or not they were demons, but it was still a lot of information. Unfortunately, once they informed Sam of their blood bank's destruction, he couldn't seem to focus on anything else.

It was understandable that he would react even more strongly than either of them had. Every one of their ghouls was very important to them, and both ancients treated them all very well. However, no matter what they did, there would always be that invisible line separating master and servant. Sam, on the other hand, had been a ghoul himself for a very long time. Every ghoul that had been killed by the SOG had been a personal friend of his; moreover, the ghouls all looked up to him as their immediate superior. Suddenly finding out that he had lost seventeen more friends in the blink of an eye was bitter news to swallow.

They gave Sam a few more minutes to absorb the horrible news they'd just shared before signaling that they had to move on. Closing his eyes briefly, in a futile attempt to banish whatever demons were assaulting him, Sam nodded that he was ready to proceed. The ancients quickly began to lay out their planned counterstrike, and a grim smile started to form on Sam's lips. They decided it best to conceal the fact that they would be giving the SOG the chance to evacuate their doomed outposts in order to avoid unnecessary casualties.

"I am finished, master." Marcus stood in the doorway, and John motioned for him to join them in their brief war council. Sam covered his mouth quickly, as he lightly chuckled at the look in Marcus's eyes. He remembered what it was like when he was first appointed head ghoul. Most ghouls only spent time with their masters when they were being fed or when their masters needed something. It had been both frightening and exciting to constantly be asked to accompany the ancients on their various outings. For the entire first decade that he held the position, Sam's only thought had been to not make a mistake. He would have to remember to corner Marcus later and give him a few tips.

"So how's it look?"

Marcus leaned forward and handed John a sheet of paper. "This mission will be a simple matter, master. If you will allow me to use the supplies I have listed, then I can begin preparing my team." John was pleased with the report but knew Marcus was missing some of the points of his new job. It wasn't his fault. There hadn't been time to really explain what was expected of him yet, and John made a mental note to correct that.

"Good work. Use anything you need, but we need you in here first."

"Yes, master."

"All right, now that our counterattack is well in hand, let's assess the damage we've sustained so far. We know that we've lost the blood bank, and that's only slightly better than losing our actual haven. How much blood do we have on hand?"

Danielle was about to speak up, but Marcus beat her to it.

"I have that information, master." John nodded for him to continue. "When we first learned of the strike, I told some of the other ghouls to figure that out. Our stockpiles our quite large, but after a month, the blood goes bad anyway, at least for your purposes. No matter how much you can cut back, there's nothing that will extend our supplies beyond that one-month limit, short of obtaining more."

"Will it last the entire month?" The question came from Danielle.

"If we use care, mistress, it will. According to your increased blood usage this situation has caused, it'll only last three weeks, max. We decided that was unacceptable, and tried to consider ways to stretch it out, especially since there are three of you now. We know that the two largest drains on your blood are combat and feeding us ghouls. Obviously, you can't cut back on what you expend in combat. That would be foolish and dangerous, so—"

"If you think we'll sacrifice any of you to save our own blood, you can forget it," John interrupted, leaning forward slightly.

"Please, master, hear me out." Reluctantly, John settled back in his chair and nodded. "We took into consideration the extra blood that Sam will now consume and the recent casualties we've taken. The two come close to canceling each other out, and the other ghouls and I have reached an agreement.

"We realize that we all must make sacrifices, and that the SOG is a threat to us all. All of the noncombative ghouls have agreed to accept less blood to help the supply last longer. They realize it will impair them, but they'll still be able to perform their tasks. The combative ghouls obviously cannot afford to do this, but since the noncombatants outnumber us by so much, it will be more than enough." He paused, awaiting his master's decision.

"They have all agreed to this?" A ghoul that did not receive enough blood was not a pretty sight to look at. It was also quite painful to the ghoul in question.

"Yes, master."

John sighed, seeing no easy alternative.

"Okay, so we have one month to figure something out. Obviously, we could steal large quantities of blood from hospitals, but that would end up hurting us in the long run. If anyone thinks of something that might work, speak up. My next question is easier. What do we have left in the way of numbers?" Marcus was able to answer that question as well.

"We have a total of fifty-two noncombative ghouls and thirty-four combative ones, including myself. I organized the other thirty-three soldiers into three reinforced squads of eleven and stationed them throughout the haven. With the loss of the blood bank, this is the only real structure we have to defend." John nodded solemnly. They had started with over one hundred and twenty ghouls, and now they were down to only eighty-six. It was plenty with which to defend the haven, but not much to face the SOG.

John's thoughts were reflected in the eyes of the other three.

"We need help, don't we?"

"We need a plan first," Danielle answered.

"Simple. Find which base is their headquarters for the city, assault it, and capture their leader. That's the easy part, but we just don't have the strength to do that and defend the haven. In other words, we need help."

"Agreed, but who's going to help us?" John thought about it for a moment and then came up with the perfect solution.

"I can think of two elders that'd be willing to help out, especially when we tell them there'll be werewolves to kill." Danielle and Sam both immediately knew who he was talking about.

"Jose and Chris?"

"Yep."

"Why didn't we think of calling on them sooner?" It was a rhetorical question, so John bit back his initial response.

"You think forty-eight hours is enough time for them to get here?"

"Sure, provided they agree to come at all."

"They will."

Sam listened to the interchange between the two ancients before finally venturing a question of his own.

"How are we going to contact them?"

"Leave that to us, Sam." The ancients rose. "You stay here and brief Marcus about his new job."

"You got it, boss." Sam threw a mock salute as John and Danielle left the room, and then he turned to face Marcus. "I suppose I should congratulate you on the promotion." Marcus quickly stood and bowed.

"No, sir, it is I who should congratulate you on becoming one of the masters." Sighing, Sam realized he had his work cut out for him.

"Okay, first of all, sit down, and cut that crap out. Secondly, they hate it when you call them 'master.' What you really need to be doing is this......."

Chapter 14

1652 AD, San Blas (now known as Coamo), Puerto Rico

"SO, HUSBAND, what do you think?" Growing bored with Europe, John and Danielle had decided to visit Puerto Rico in hopes of finding something to capture their interest for a few years or so.

"I have to admit that this was a good idea, and the Spaniards definitely know how to throw a party." Danielle smiled, happy that her husband was pleased. They had enjoyed visiting Spain on several occasions, but they were not fond of the country itself. Danielle had suggested Puerto Rico as a possible compromise.

The Spaniards had colonized the island over a century ago, and it was rife with their culture, which both vampires enjoyed thoroughly. Even better, it was a small island, rather than a large country. This significantly reduced the chance of them running into problems with either the church or their own kind.

Having just arrived in San Blas early that evening, they quickly noticed the city in the midst of celebration. Festive banners were hanging from several of the surrounding buildings, and the cobblestone streets were lined in places with candles. They seemed to have arrived in the middle of a holiday that John knew nothing about.

"What are they celebrating? It doesn't seem like a normal Christmas celebration, and it's a bit early for that anyway," John remarked as they passed a small stand selling religious paraphernalia.

"The Festival of the Three Kings, which is their version of Christmas. They celebrate for almost all of December and up to the sixth of January. Children place straw or hay in boxes under their beds for the Kings' camels. In return, the Kings leave presents when their camels are finished."

"How do you know all that?" His wife simply pointed at a gentleman who stunk of alcohol.

"He knows, so now I do too." John just shook his head. His wife's mind control abilities seemed to be growing noticeably stronger every day. Unlike his more physical abilities, she was able to practice her mind control whenever she chose, without endangering herself or others.

"Impressive, as always. Let's find somewhere to stay, and then we can explore the festivities. How long has it been since I took you dancing?" Eyes lighting at the implied suggestion, Danielle gave her husband a quick kiss.

"Far too long, love, but I suppose I'll forgive you if we go tonight." Actually, it had been quite recently, but their surroundings were putting her in a more playful mood. Of course, she knew that the first priority for them in any new area was to find a safe haven. Neither of them would ever forget nor argue that.

Simply purchasing a room at a random inn wasn't very safe without spending more time getting to know the city's inhabitants. It was usually safer to find a neglected building with a deep cellar, but even that was risky. The two vampires continued strolling through the city, quietly discussing their options, when John suddenly froze.

"What's wrong?" Danielle asked, recognizing the look on his face as one of caution.

"Can't you feel that?" Danielle shrugged and concentrated, and suddenly she knew what was wrong. They had sensed the presence of another vampire, and it was close.

They had run into other vampires on numerous occasions, and the results were almost always violent. Most vampires were very territorial. They had to be. If there were too many vampires hunting in the same area, the risk of discovery was far greater. At first they had both agreed to simply avoid other vampires if they wandered into their territory by mistake, but that didn't last.

They both soon discovered that most vampires were nothing more than animals and would treat mortals as mere food. Neither of them cared what other vampires did, so long as they didn't randomly kill people, which was unfortunately true for most of them. After witnessing a particularly violent vampire in action, they made a pact to destroy any vampire not meeting their standards.

In John and Danielle's minds, they had a duty to protect mortals, since they provided them with the blood they needed to survive. Plus, it just seemed to be the right thing to do. If his wife and he were able to feed from mortals without killing them, then there was no excuse to kill a mortal unless they posed a threat.

All thoughts of finding a safe haven were temporarily banished once Danielle's senses confirmed his. They quickly turned a corner, shrouded themselves, and began to track their target. They were not overly concerned—the presence hadn't felt particularly strong—but it never hurt to be cautious.

It didn't take them long to track the other vampire to a small house on the outskirts of the city. Reaching out with his senses, John confirmed that there was only a single vampire in residence there, although he also felt the presence of a mortal. Deciding that quick action was needed to save the life of the mortal, the two vampires approached the house's front door.

The belief that vampires cannot enter a house or room uninvited, along with so many other common beliefs, was born of legend rather than reality. It was something told to frightened children or superstitious adults to make them feel safe once night closed in over their heads. In reality, a vampire could go wherever he or she chose, and at the moment, John and Danielle both chose to interrupt their target vampire's nightly feeding.

Once they entered the building, they quickly checked the various rooms that they came across. In moments, they found what they were looking for in the master bedroom. Thankfully, it wasn't yet the bloody massacre that most vampires left in their wake.

There were two people in the bedroom—a young-looking man that they knew to be the vampire and a scantily clad young woman. As of yet, the woman didn't seem to know that she was about to become a midnight snack, otherwise she wouldn't be enjoying herself quite as much.

John and Danielle had also both heard the legend that vampires preferred the blood of young women, especially if they were virgins. Something about the blood being pure. That was laughable, since all mortal blood tasted the same to them.

While male vampires did tend to hunt women far more often than men, it had nothing to do with their blood being different. It was simply easier to seduce a young woman, not to mention safer, than it was to hunt a male. A male could turn out to be a member of the church, which was very bad if you hadn't planned on killing them afterward. All a good vampire really had to do was wink, and any woman they wanted would easily follow them home. The vampire could feed at his leisure, and the woman in question would wake the next morning, simply thinking she had had a particularly rough night. An added bonus was that if a vampire was careful, and feigned enough sexual or romantic interest, the woman could be counted on to return again and again, never realizing that she was being fed off of by a demon.

Immediately after visually identifying their target, John and Danielle dropped their shrouds and waited to be noticed. Their target's demeanor instantly changed from one of playfulness to one of caution, as he felt their presence. Looking around his room, his caution turned to fear when he saw they were actually inside his haven.

"Maria, why don't you go to the kitchen and get us some drinks." Their target seemed to gain control of his fear and was facing them head-on.

"But we were having—" She stopped short when she noticed they were no longer alone. "I'm sorry; I didn't know you had visitors." She blushed deeply, having been caught in a very uncompromising position for one of her young age.

"Simply two old friends, my dear. I just didn't expect them so early. I shall join you in a moment." John was allowing this interlude to continue simply because it appeared that their target wanted the mortal to leave as much as they did.

"They seem so strange," she mumbled, looking John in the eye.

"Leave," Danielle hissed, having far less patience for mortal women than John. The woman visibly paled, gathered her few discarded articles of clothing, and hurried out the door. They waited until the sound of the front door opening and closing signaled that she was safely gone.

"What do you two want?"

"Isn't it obvious? We're here to destroy you."

"For what reason!" The other vampire's fear was starting to return.

"Because you are too dangerous to be allowed to prey upon the weak of this island."

"But I don't understand! You're both vampires. Why attack your own kind?" He took a step backward.

"We find that most of our own kind are deserving of destruction. Fortunately, we arrived in time to save the young woman."

"Save her from what?"

"From you slaughtering her, fledgling." John was simply stalling for time. Despite his tough talk, he would never randomly kill or destroy anything. While he was keeping the vampire's attention, Danielle was using her abilities to see what kind of vampire he was. He was waiting for her opinion as to whether or not it was necessary to destroy him.

"I don't slaughter innocents!" The vampire's fear was changing to anger. "I've lived on this island for nearly a century. Do you think I'd still be here if I killed everyone that I fed on?"

"Where is your sire?"

"How the hell should I know? He left for Europe about fifty years ago. Said this place was too boring for him. But I wanted to stay here. It's nice and quiet, just the way I like it. That is, until just now. How about telling me just who in the hell you are!" John ignored the question, turning to his wife.

"Well?"

Danielle smiled genuinely. "It's okay. He's confused, annoyed, and more than just a bit scared, but I don't sense any real evil intentions from him. I gather that he probably enjoys playing with his food, but he never intends undo harm to those from whom he feeds."

Surprise registered on the other vampire's face, as he hadn't realized yet that she possessed the ability to read his mind. Once Danielle's words sank in, however, he seemed to relax slightly. Whatever her methods for obtaining the information, it didn't sound too bad, and it seemed as if they were going to spare him after all.

"What is your name, fledgling?" John's harsh tone made it clear that the young vampire wasn't out of the woods just yet.

"My name is Jose," he answered, trying to retain a shred of his dignity.

"Well, Jose, you may have a chance to see another night. According to my wife here, you don't kill needlessly, and you haven't foolishly attacked us yet. Both are high marks in your favor. How old are you?"

Jose couldn't hide his sudden curiosity at the brief mention that these two vampires were married, but first things first.

"I was twenty-six when I was turned, and I've been a vampire for eighty-four years."

John nodded. "When your sire left, did he tell you how to react to your own kind?"

Jose's eyes narrowed in thought.

"He told me to be wary of vampires my own age or younger, that there was a good chance they would attack me at their first opportunity. On the other hand, he told me to be very respectful toward elders, should I ever encounter any. He said if an elder wanted me destroyed, there was nothing I could do about it, so my best chance would be to mind my manners as it were. May I ask where this is going?" Jose allowed his annoyance to win out over fear for a moment.

"I suppose it is only fair to introduce ourselves. My name is John Wolf, and this is my wife, Danielle. As for our age, we are both approaching our sixth century," he finished with an arched eyebrow.

Jose's demeanor changed the instant he heard John's final words and saw Danielle's nodded agreement.

They watched in amusement as shock and disbelief swept over him. It would be easy enough, however, for even a vampire of his young age to sense the overwhelming power coming from the elders. A moment later they saw what appeared to be realization dawn in Jose's eyes, as he finally understood what they were doing to him. This was all merely a test by two elders to see if he was worthy to be counted among them. It was close enough to the truth that they decided not to correct the slight inaccuracy. If nothing else, having a clear understanding of where he stood seemed to put Jose at ease.

"Please, forgive me, honored elders. Your appearance was too sudden and frightening for me to realize to whom I was speaking." He bowed down low before adding, "What is it you require of me?"

John sighed, while Danielle coughed to cover her own laughter. This hadn't been quite what they were expecting. If Jose thought it odd for a vampire, who didn't require oxygen, to be coughing, he wisely didn't mention it.

"First, we require you to cut that nonsense out. We are far older and more powerful than you, but that doesn't make us any better, so stop bowing and sit down." Jose did as instructed, and the other two settled into a pair of wooden chairs.

"We came to visit this island because we'd grown bored with Europe. When we sensed your presence, we decided to investigate. It is our experience that most vampires, due to their demonic actions, do not deserve to exist, and we've made it our habit to rid the world of as many of these demons as possible." Seeing a look of fear crawl back into Jose's eyes, John was quick to add, "You have nothing to fear, at least not from us." Jose relaxed once more and continued to listen.

"My wife has the ability to read your mind, and she determined that you are honorable enough to deserve a chance at unlife." Jose nodded to Danielle.

"I'm honored. Thank you." Danielle returned his polite nod, a smirk playing across her face. "So, since you've both decided not to kill me, what do you want? And how do you speak such flawless Spanish? And how do vampires get married?" Jose stopped himself when he realized he was beginning to sound like an excited child. This time neither of the elders made an attempt to hide their laughter, and he lowered his eyes in embarrassment.

"Slow down, fledgling. First, we can't speak Spanish. You hear us in your own language because we are all vampires. As for what we want, we want to make a deal. Since we've decided you're fairly honorable, there's a way we can help each other out." Jose leaned forward, growing more interested in the current turn of conversation.

"As we said, we're new to this area. We've yet to find a haven, and we know nothing about this island. Act as our guide for as long as we wish, and we'll teach and train you while we're here."

"You are more than welcome to share my haven. In fact, I insist. As for my training, my sire trained me very well already." He swelled with pride at his final statement, to which the elders merely smiled.

With a few spoken words, four-inch flames shot from the fingertips of John's right hand. Danielle sent a sudden, severe gust of wind to extinguish the candles throughout the room, although it did nothing to put out the flames John was creating, which now illuminated his face with an eerie light. Jose observed the sudden acts with shock and disbelief.

"Oh, I don't know." Flames danced in John's eyes. Whether they had a life of their own or were a simple reflection of the ones on his fingertips was anyone's guess. "I'm sure we can teach you a thing or two."

1741 AD, Philadelphia, Pennsylvania

"ALL IN ALL, I expected it to be a bit more exciting here."

John grunted his agreement. "Perhaps we should've waited another decade or two," he added. They had enjoyed their stay in Puerto Rico immensely. The island was simply beautiful. The people were friendly, and they didn't encounter a single problem in the eighty-nine years that they spent there with Jose. They had taken the time to teach Jose more advanced vampiric abilities as well as all the magic he could learn. He didn't have the same capacity for mind control that Danielle did, but she was still able to teach him to at least be more suggestive to mortals, which assisted greatly in his hunting. In the end, however, the island's lack of excitement, which so appealed to Jose, had led them to seek out a new adventure.

In the last few years they'd been hearing rumors about tension rising between Great Britain and some of her colonies. As the rumors grew more frequent, they decided perhaps this new America was the place to go for some much-needed excitement. Jose had chosen to remain on the island, so they bid a friendly farewell, found a boat that fit their special needs, and set out to see what all the rumors were about.

The decision to go to Philadelphia was a simple one. It was the largest major city in all of the colonies; where else to find out if anything was going to happen? Unfortunately, it appeared that they were going to be disappointed.

Danielle was able to read the minds of passing mortals, and what she found wasn't too promising. She never pried into the private regions of a person's mind, unless that person was a threat. She would simply skim the surface of their minds to see what was uppermost in their thoughts. So far they had discovered that there was a basis for the rumors they'd been hearing, but it wasn't really serious.

The people appeared dissatisfied about a number of things, but all they were doing about it was grumbling. They both knew, due to their extensive life experience, that the grumbling would eventually turn to violence, but it probably wouldn't happen for at least another couple of decades. Which begged the question, should they stay here or find excitement somewhere else?

"A little dissatisfaction aside, these people seem perfectly content to just live out their lives in peace, at least for now. What do you want to do?"

Danielle shrugged at the question, her thoughts occupied elsewhere.

"You know we're being followed?"

John nodded. "Of course, at least four blocks now. We should've expected at least one vampire to take up residence in this city." In unspoken agreement, both vampires headed toward the darkest area they could see and turned around.

The vampire following them quickly realized he had been discovered and immediately attacked. John arched a brow at the blur closing rapidly on their position. Danielle waited for the attacker to close within ten feet before she simply pointed and froze him in place, just out of arm's reach.

The attacking vampire glared at them with surprise that quickly turned to rage. They could see him straining against the invisible bonds that Danielle had placed around him. Five minutes of wasted effort ended when their attacker gave up struggling and went back to staring at them in barely controlled rage.

"What do you want?"

The question caused confusion to eat at the edges of the rage in the attacker's eyes. "It is obvious. You have trespassed in *my* city.

This is a challenge against me. Therefore, to protect myself, I must destroy you."

Normally John or Danielle would have reduced him to ash simply because he attacked them. However, their trip to Puerto Rico had changed the way they looked at things.

Teaching and training Jose had been more than just a way to pass the time. It started as simply fulfilling their end of the agreement, but it had resulted in something they hadn't expected. It had given them a good feeling. They had helped someone in a predicament similar to their own, and that had been a remarkably enjoyable experience.

What if they could do the same thing here? What if, instead of killing every vampire they came across, they helped them accept what they were? If the vampire in question couldn't overcome his blood-lust, they could always choose to destroy him later. It was with this in mind that John decided to question their attacker first.

"We have no intention of challenging you. As you can see, we are far more powerful than you are, but we do not believe in wasted death." The other vampire laughed briefly.

"You are demons, just as I am. Death is what we do. Now, stop toying with me and fight!"

Danielle started to shake her head, but John wasn't willing to give up just yet.

"We may be demons, but we make our own choices, and we choose to not kill unless it's necessary. Acting with honor allows us to better control the beast that dwells within us all, and it has allowed us to survive for all these centuries."

"*Centuries?* How old are you?"

John grinned wolfishly. "We both celebrated our six hundred and fiftieth year as vampires not too long ago." If their attacker had been mortal, he would've immediately gone pale. As it was, John saw all the rage in his eyes turn quickly to fear, as he realized he had just attacked two elders.

"So much for fighting. Could you at least destroy me quickly? I never was a big fan of pain." John glanced at his wife in triumph, and the message was clear. *He's not very honorable, but he knows his place. There's still hope for him.*

Reluctantly, she nodded agreement.

"We never said anything about destroying you. So far we've only acted in our own self-defense. It was you who attacked us."

"So what do you want with me?" he demanded, fear turning to annoyance.

"Your name would be a good start."

"Chris."

"Well, Chris, we have a proposition for you. We are new here and could use a guide. We also need someplace to stay. In return, we'll teach you how to better control yourself, as well as train you in more powerful abilities."

"Can you let me go first? I realize that if I attack or run, I'll be destroyed." John considered it and then motioned toward Danielle. She waved a hand briefly in Chris's direction, and he stumbled to the ground. They gave him a few moments to regain his composure and consider their proposal.

"If I agree, then how will you know to trust me?"

"Simple. Until you prove yourself honorable, you will follow our instructions closely. And if you step out of line, we will destroy you. My wife has extensive mind reading and controlling abilities, as you've no doubt realized by now. You cannot attack or betray us without our knowledge." John could see that Chris still wasn't convinced, so he decided to hit on a soft spot for many younger vampires.

"Immortality is much better when it's not spent alone. To know that there are others like you out there, willing to help you, can mean the difference between tolerating your existence and meeting the sun with open arms." John's softened tone struck a chord with the young vampire, and he leaned against the side of a building in thought.

"Okay," Chris said finally, a hint of disbelief remaining. "Where do we start?"

Chapter 15

JOSE WANDERED through the city aimlessly, trying to decide why John had contacted him. It wasn't that he particularly cared; it was just a matter of curiosity for him. In the last few centuries, the three of them had gotten together many times for various reasons. Usually, Chris would come along as well.

He was looking forward to seeing his friends again, but something wasn't sitting right with him. When John had contacted him, he said that Jose needed to get to the city within forty-eight hours. In addition to that, John had also instructed him to bring a few of his best ghouls with him. He supposed it could mean almost anything, but it sounded like trouble.

Jose was more than happy to help both John and Danielle, no matter what they needed—he felt as much affection toward them as one vampire could normally feel toward another—but he'd be lying if he pretended to not be concerned about whatever was going on. If something was threatening them, it would have to be major for them to call for help. Even if it turned out to be something that major, what could he possibly do to help two immensely powerful ancients that they couldn't do themselves?

Whatever was going on, the first order of business was to find them. Jose had grown very powerful over the last three and a half centuries, but he was still nowhere near as strong as the ancients were. If they were in hiding, he'd have to search the entire city to find them.

That would take far too long, and there was still no guarantee that he'd be successful.

The beginnings of a plan had just started to form in Jose's mind when he realized he wasn't alone. Looking to either side, he saw John keeping step with him. Jose tried to not seem surprised that John had been walking with him and he hadn't noticed until just now.

"How long have you been there?"

"About the last twenty minutes or so. How many ghouls do you have following you?"

"Three."

"Good. I just needed to ensure that no one else was following you before I led you to the haven."

Jose didn't like the sound of that. "So you guys are in trouble?"

"Actually, *we* are in trouble."

Jose stopped walking and turned to face John. "What's that supposed to mean?"

John shook his head and kept walking. "It's not safe here. Just follow me. Once we get to the haven, I'll explain everything."

Jose knew that arguing would be useless, so he just did as he was told. "So long as we move slow enough for my ghouls to keep up."

"Of course."

* * *

THIRTY MINUTES LATER Jose followed John into the haven's main lounge room and looked around. There was a scattering of rare collectibles that John and Danielle had acquired over the centuries, but nothing that stood out. They also had an extensive entertainment center, complete with several very comfortable-looking overstuffed chairs. Jose was admiring one of the several seventy-two-inch high-definition LED televisions which dotted the room when he noticed who else was there.

"Chris? Where've you been hiding for the last decade?" The fact that Chris's presence meant the situation was more desperate than he thought didn't register to Jose, who simply moved to greet his friend.

"I've been bouncing around California for a while. What about you?" he asked, shaking Jose's hand.

"Argentina mostly."

Chris blinked in interest. "Really? Why Argentina?"

Jose shrugged weakly. "I'd never been there before."

Chris accepted the answer with a nod. When you were immortal, that was the only real reason you needed to go anywhere.

"It's good to see you again, Jose." He turned toward the familiar voice and smiled broadly.

"Milady, I see you're looking even more ravishing than the last time I was graced with your presence." He took her hand and touched it gently to his lips. Chris rolled his eyes at the spectacle, while Danielle giggled girlishly.

"My, my, such a gentleman. How nice for a change," she responded, flashing John a mocking grin.

"Very funny, you two," he retorted. Looking at Chris and Jose now, John couldn't help but notice the changes in them. They had both been little more than wretched fledglings when he had first met them, but now they were powerful elders. Danielle and he had both enjoyed watching the changes take hold of them over the last few centuries, and he was grateful for their presence here now. He was also curious to see Jose's reaction to Sam, and vice versa.

Jose had known Sam for decades, and they got along remarkably well. Sam had no reason to even be polite to any vampire other than

John and Danielle, but he always was. He had insisted on referring to both Chris and Jose as "sir," and had treated them both as if they were simply one step away from being his actual masters. Unfortunately, Jose had the habit of teasing him constantly. Now that Sam was a vampire himself, it would be interesting to see how he would respond to Jose's annoying habit.

"Nice to see your advanced years haven't affected your maturity level, Jose." Jose reluctantly released Danielle's hand, turned, and froze in shock when he saw Sam smiling at him. That playful little insult was extremely out of character for Sam, but Jose wouldn't be outdone by a mere ghoul.

"Well, well, look who's finally learned to loosen up. Put 'er there, Sammy, my boy." Jose stuck his hand out and grinned mischievously. A quick demonstration of his vampiric strength would be a nice response to Sam's wisecrack.

"Don't mind if I do." Sam gripped Jose's hand and instantly squeezed as hard as he could. There were a few loud cracks, and Jose yanked his hand back, yelping in sudden pain.

It had been a risky ploy, but Sam was gambling on taking Jose by complete surprise. The instant before he gripped Jose's hand, Sam had forced as much blood as he could into his own. The added power allowed him to crush Jose's hand as if it were in a vice. Although Jose had far more power than he, the older vampire didn't have a chance to use it.

"What the hell?" Jose began, staring at his broken hand in total shock. He spent a moment healing the damage and then began to sniff the air carefully. His shocked expression slowly turned to one of joy. "By God, you're a vampire now."

"Damn right I am, and it's about time I finally gave you some payback."

Jose laughed heartily and pounded Sam on the back. "Congratulations on the promotion, my boy!" They shook hands again, however this time it was simply a friendly action.

"Thank you, Jose. That means a lot coming from you." Jose eyed him for a moment, no doubt scanning his words for sarcasm. Finding none, he became a bit more serious.

"No thanks necessary. From the time I've spent with you, I know that you deserve it." Jose sat back down and faced John and Danielle. "Sam's the first person either of you have ever turned, isn't he?"

"Yes," they both answered.

"Well then," Jose grinned, "I suppose congratulations are in order for you both. It's a boy!"

Danielle's eyes clouded over in sudden sadness, while John flashed Jose a look of anger. Jose glanced around in confusion, and when he saw Chris gaping in astonishment, he realized what he had just said.

He knew the story of John and Danielle's unlife as well as anyone. He knew how close they had come to destroying themselves only to decide to endure immortality so that they could be together. He also knew that there was one thing they could never have, but had always wanted—a child of their own.

They hadn't been given the chance in their mortal lives to produce a child, and no matter how powerful they became in their immortal lives, they'd still never be able to have one. It didn't matter how much John loved his wife; he would never be able to give her a child. Walking corpses tended to be completely sterile. There were other methods of obtaining children, but they would never have one of their own.

It was something that had caused them centuries of sadness. Both of them had tried finding ways around the problem with magic, but to no avail. Eventually, they'd had no choice but to face reality and deal with it. They never even thought about it anymore, having learned to not worry about things they can't change long ago. *Unless, of course, some insensitive prick like me brings it up,* Jose scolded himself.

"Shit," Jose muttered, raising his hands in a disarming gesture. "Dani, I'm sorry. I didn't realize what I was saying." He met John's angry gaze and stammered, "It was just supposed to be a joke." John cut off anything else he might've added with a wave of his hand.

"It's all right, Jose. We know you didn't mean any offense." Danielle nodded meekly. "Now, if you could all get settled, it's about time we began." A trio of ghouls entered, spread a tablecloth over the large antique coffee table in the center of the room, and placed five heavy pitchers of blood on it. Once the ghouls departed, the vampires began moving their chairs closer to the table, and Chris took the opportunity to whisper something to Jose.

"Upsetting someone who can reduce you to ash with a wave of her hand isn't the best way to live long enough to become an ancient, you idiot." He finished by smacking Jose in the back of his head and hoping he'd think before opening his big mouth anymore this evening. What neither of them realized yet was that the news they were about to hear would push all memories of Jose's foolish comment right out the window.

John waited for everyone to rearrange themselves behind their pitchers and sighed inwardly at Jose's constant childishness. *As if we didn't have enough problems already, he had to bring that up again.* He could tell from the haunted look in her eye that his wife was reliving some painful memory that he could only guess at. Knowing that the moment would pass soon, but hating that it had to come at all, John decided to get started.

"By now you both have probably guessed that we called you for help. Whatever either of you are thinking the problem is, it's far worse." John paused to ensure he had their full attention. The ghouls were too busy warily eyeing each other to pay much attention, but he supposed that didn't make much of a difference.

"I want to first give you an idea of how desperate the situation is, and then we'll fill you in on all details." Neither elder looked too concerned yet, but John suspected that was because they both expected him to start out this way. *That won't last much longer*, he guessed.

"Recently, a very old and very powerful organization of vampire hunters became aware of our presence in this city. Their forces and ours have clashed several times in the last couple of weeks, but we'll go into detail about that later. You should know, however, that Danielle was ambushed by them, and they nearly destroyed her." Jose gasped, and Chris choked on the blood he had been swallowing.

"But how is that possible?" Chris managed to ask, wiping spilled blood off his lips. It was basically the reaction John had expected, and he knew it was time to fill them in completely.

John and Danielle spent the next two hours going over everything they knew about the SOG with Chris and Jose. They went over the recent attacks by both sides, including the loss of their blood bank. Finally, they discussed their recent meeting with the pope, although they left out all mention of redemption for the time being.

Once they finished explaining the situation, John waited for Jose and Chris to come to terms with everything they had just heard. He had to admit that it was a lot to swallow all at once, but giving them all the information up front seemed to be the right thing to do. The elders' ghouls began shifting around nervously in response to their masters' somber moods. After several tense minutes, Chris finally spoke up.

"My God, you two have been having all this fun, and you didn't call us sooner?" His attempt to lighten the mood was answered with brief, uneasy laughter. "Seriously though, you met with the pope about this?"

"Yes. As I said, we thought he was in charge of the SOG."

"But now you really think he's willing to help? Isn't the Catholic Church one of our oldest enemies? I mean, why would he even want to help a pair of vampires?" John understood the wariness that both Chris and Jose were obviously feeling.

"We didn't spend a lot of time debating the Catholic Church's current stance on vampires. Actually, they seem quite content just letting people assume that we don't exist. Personally, the pope didn't seem to care that we were vampires. He just cared that we hadn't done anything wrong but were being hunted down by an organization that the Catholic Church created. When he learned the SOG never disbanded, he decided it was his responsibility to bring them down. Actually, in his mind, we're assisting him, not the other way around."

"And you think this idea of his has merit?"

"It's better than randomly attacking them until they finally gather enough forces to destroy us." Chris looked to Jose, and the two seemed to come to a decision.

"Of course we'll help you, but what specifically do you need from us?"

John restrained the urge to sigh in relief. Even though he'd had every confidence that they were going to help, it felt much better to hear them actually say it.

"Nothing really specific, just extra muscle mainly. We know that the SOG possesses an unbelievable number of soldiers and werewolves. It stands to reason that they're going to be calling in massive reinforcements, if they haven't done so already, to destroy us. We also don't know how long it will take for the pope's plan, whatever it is, to work. We just need the strength to hold on until we figure out what we're going to do."

"Plus your ghouls could go a long way toward replacing our losses," Danielle added.

"Okay, I admit this is all pretty overwhelming, but I agree with Chris. Have you planned out our next move yet?"

"We just told you, Jose. We have to capture a member of their leadership."

"I meant have you decided just how we're going to do that yet?"

John was grateful that both elders seemed anxious to get right down to business.

"Well, the best idea we have so far is to just storm their headquarters here in the city and nab whoever's in charge. The only major flaw in our plans, which we can't correct, is we have no idea how high up their chain of command we need to go to get the real information we need. We have to just use trial and error. If their local commander isn't high enough, at least he'll be able to point us in the right direction."

"Do we know where?"

"Yes and no, actually. We know the locations of every base they have in the city. Unfortunately, we don't know which is which yet. We're planning on giving our ghouls another day or so to figure it out. If they can't, we'll just have to storm them all."

"Why not let us have a look at these maps you have? Maybe we can help figure it out."

John wished that things were that simple. "I'm afraid that isn't very important right now."

"But you just said—"

"We still have about a week and a half to do this," John said, cutting Chris off before he could finish. "That's plenty of time. We've got more important things to figure out first."

Jose and Chris both seemed confused. They were no doubt trying to guess what could be more important than a worldwide organization of religious zealots trying to kill you.

"The way I see it, we actually have the upper hand right now. By now, the SOG has a good idea how powerful Danielle and I are, and they're no doubt going to be better prepared for us. Now, however, it's not just the two of us anymore.

"Your presence here gives us a major increase in power. Add to that Sam's change in status, and the SOG is suddenly facing five vampires instead of just two. Hopefully, they'll panic and take time to gather even more forces." This information didn't have a very calming effect on either elder.

"I didn't think we wanted that to happen."

John rolled his eyes. "Look, the pope knows that we can't possibly stand against the entire SOG. Whatever plan he has, it must take that into consideration. We just need to buy as much time as we can while he puts his plan into action, and in the meantime we can hit any targets of opportunity that present themselves." They at least seemed satisfied that he wasn't going insane.

"Okay then, what is it that's so important we have to take care of it first?" The question came from Jose, although John suspected both elders already knew what he was going to say.

"The blood problem needs to be fixed before we do anything else. Our current supplies will only last about seventeen days, since there are five of us now. Of course, if we don't do anything, it'll last longer, but we've got to fight eventually." The meaning was clear: fix the problem now before it became desperate. "Also, we could use more ghouls to help us, but that's a much lesser problem."

Jose and Chris nodded and began discussing different possibilities with each other. They both knew that the ancients had filled them in because they expected them to come up with their own ideas of how to help. It made perfect sense, since there was no way for either ancient to know the extent of Jose or Chris's infrastructure, or how it might be best used to assist them.

John shared a hopeful glance with his wife as Jose and Chris involved their ghouls in their discussion. The blood problem was the only thing that they hadn't been able to figure out on their own, and it was frustrating the hell out of them both. Normally blood was very easy to obtain in large quantities, with or without the blood bank. Unfortunately, with the SOG no doubt waiting for them to try something, it became far more difficult.

If John were in his enemy's position, he'd be monitoring every large source of blood in the city and all the surrounding areas. Any sudden purchases or thefts would be suspect. They needed to find something a bit more discreet, and he could only hope that either Jose or Chris were capable of such a thing. Meanwhile, Sam was just sitting quietly, knowing enough to just do as he was told.

"We think we've got something." John shook his head, clearing it of his reflections, and gave Chris his undivided attention. "The ghoul problem is an easy fix. Both of us can spare a dozen more combat ghouls without endangering anything back home. We'll bring more if we have to, but it would be difficult."

John's eyes widened in surprise. Twenty-four more soldiers, plus the five they'd already brought with them. It was more than he had dared hope for.

"That's great! Hopefully you've got an equally great solution to our blood dilemma." Chris shifted a bit in his seat, and John could feel his hopes starting to drop.

"We think so, but I need to ask a few questions first." John motioned for him to go ahead. "First, should I assume that you refuse to resort to stealing it?" John just nodded again, not needing to stress the importance of keeping a low profile with something this important. "I thought so." John saw him glare at Jose, who just shrugged. Apparently, theft had been his idea.

"Okay, here's my idea. Jose and I both have our own secure sources of blood back in our respective homes. What if we could arrange to have our own blood delivered here? We could do it very carefully and discreetly. Nothing more than, say, forty gallons a shipment, but the shipments would be constant. Are your ghouls capable of meeting the shipments and getting the blood here?" John liked the idea, and Danielle's eyes sparkled with renewed hope.

"Sam, Marcus, what do you think?" They both knew more about their ghouls' capabilities at the moment than he did. After thinking it over for a moment, Sam spoke up.

"It'll be tight with our recent losses and the need to maintain a workforce here at the hotel, but we shouldn't have a problem."

"Excellent. You all stay here and work out the details. We'll keep trying to pinpoint the SOG's headquarters, but we're not going to make any offensive moves against them until the shipments start arriving." He rose to leave.

"Where're you going?"

"Danielle and I have something we need to discuss. We'll be back in a few minutes." There was a round of various acknowledgments as the others got to work. Danielle arched an eyebrow in confusion but made no argument as she followed her husband out of the room.

* * *

"THINGS ARE FINALLY starting to go well," Danielle observed as she and John entered the privacy of their bedroom. When he didn't respond, she noticed her husband wasn't even looking at her. "What's wrong, husband?"

"Are you satisfied, Danielle?" The question took her completely off guard. As she was about to answer, John turned to face her. Suddenly, she suspected that there was more to his question than he was letting on.

"What is this all about?"

"I've been doing a lot of thinking about what's been going on."

"And?" Danielle prompted. John turned back around to face the wall again.

"How long have we lived in this city?"

"Seventeen years. Why?"

John ignored her question.

"How many of those years were spent trying to secure our presence?"

"About ten." It was true. While they had purchased the hotel and the blood bank fairly quickly, it had taken much longer to secure them. They couldn't get rid of all the mortal employees, without drawing unwanted attention. It had taken them years to slowly replace them all with ghouls.

"All that hard work, and you managed to ruin it with one bad decision." John faced her again, and he didn't look pleased. More importantly, whatever anger he was feeling was directed at her. *What the hell is he talking about?* Apparently sensing that his wife still didn't understand, John continued his line of questioning.

"What is my rule regarding mortals who threaten us?"

Suddenly Danielle knew what he was leading up to, but she also recognized the look in his eye. There would be no distracting her husband with love or lust this time. She would just have to let him have his say.

"We're supposed to kill them."

"Without exception?" he added.

"Without exception," she repeated.

"Is that so hard to understand? If you hadn't spared that soldier's life, none of this would be happening. Now, even if we're successful defeating the SOG, we'll still have to start over again somewhere else." Although she didn't want to, Danielle had to admit that her husband had a point. Of course, that didn't mean she wasn't going to defend herself.

"I spared him because he wasn't really a threat to me."

"Oh really. How about the ambush they set for you three nights later?" She shuddered at the reminder.

"How was I supposed to know who that guy was?"

"Let me think about this. Hmm, I don't know. Read his mind maybe. That *is* your specialty, isn't it? How about the fact that a mortal got the drop on you—a mortal armed with a shotgun loaded with phosphorous ammunition? Didn't any of that strike you as odd, or were you too busy trying to spare him?"

John might be making a good point, but she refused to be spoken to like a child.

"Look, I made a mistake, okay? I admit it. Now let's go back to the others and work on fixing it. We eventually would've had to face these guys anyway. Might as well do it now."

"Maybe, but mistakes aren't something we can afford to make anymore." There was something else that was bothering him, but

Danielle just couldn't put her finger on it. He just seemed more upset than he should be. What was at the root of his complaint?

"There's something else bothering you, love. What is it?" She could see him grinding his teeth together as he decided whether or not to answer her. Usually a person seeing this expression on his face was about to die, but she faced him unflinchingly. Finally, he reached a decision.

"You disobeyed me." The words were spoken with an anger that shocked her.

"That's it?" Danielle immediately regretted wording her response so callously.

"What do you mean, 'that's it?' You've never disobeyed me before." He seemed to be getting angrier, if that was even possible.

"You do realize, of course, that I'm an individual, capable of making my own decisions?"

"What you are is my *wife*! Don't ever disobey me."

Danielle's thoughts suddenly went back to the late eleventh century, to their wedding ceremony. *So that's what this is all about.*

In the days when they originally fell in love and were married, women were looked at differently than they were now. Husbands were expected to show their wives the utmost respect, but wives were expected to obey their husbands without question. Disobeying one's husband in those days was considered an almost-criminal act. She was surprised that he still thought that way, but it was the only thing that could explain his anger.

John did have one point. In over nine hundred years of marriage, she had never once disobeyed him. It was out of love that she obeyed him, however, not because she believed him to be superior to her. Danielle knew that she had to consider her next response very carefully.

Spending nearly a millennia married to him, Danielle knew that John didn't really consider himself to be her superior. He was just the type of person that was used to being obeyed and was shocked that his own wife would disobey him after all these years. With that in mind, she forced down the anger that was beginning to build within her and tried to respond as calmly as possible.

"Listen to me very carefully, husband. I obey you because I love you, but I'm capable of making my own decisions and changing my own mind. Yes, I should've killed him, but at the time I didn't think it was necessary. Yes, it was a mistake, but it was *my* mistake to make! You've known me for almost a thousand years. You should know that I *choose* to obey you, but I do not *have* to!" She was beginning to hiss in anger, despite her best efforts to control herself.

For a moment, John looked as though he was ready to respond in kind, but he instead chose to consider her words more carefully first. She could see the anger slowly releasing its hold on him until he finally just sat down, shoulders slumped, on the bed.

"I'm sorry, Dani. I don't know where that came from." She sat next to him, draping an arm around his shoulders.

"Yes you do, and so do I. This whole situation is insane, and it's making you angry. If you are able to place the blame somewhere, you'll be better able to focus your anger. Personally, I believe this would've happened eventually, regardless of what I did that night; however, I do accept responsibility for causing this to happen now."

"Yeah, but the whole thing about you disobeying me was uncalled for. I don't think you're required to obey me. It just feels odd to me because you always have."

"And because the first time I disobeyed you, all this happens. I understand your anger toward me, but in the future, just come out and tell me."

"Agreed. For the record, I know that I shouldn't be angry with you for that, but I just am. I'm sorry, love." At his soft tone, Danielle could feel the last remnants of her anger fade away. Danielle gently pulled her husband down and placed his head in her lap.

"I understand, love. You don't like to be disobeyed by anyone. You're a very proud man, but that's why I married you."

"As I recall, it was I who married you." Danielle smiled, caressed his cheek with one hand, and began toying with his hair with the other.

"Like I said before, I make my own decisions; although, if I remember correctly, your proposal did sound more like a command than a request." They shared a laugh at the memory, and the last remnants of tension evaporated.

Danielle leaned down and kissed his forehead gently. As she sat back up, their eyes locked, and she saw something in his gaze that she didn't like. It wasn't anger, but it bothered her just the same. He looked ... sad.

"What's wrong, my husband?" she asked as lovingly as she could.

"Nothing really, it's just—" As his voice trailed off, Danielle once again gently stroked his face and waited for him to continue. "You said I was a proud *man*, but I'm not even a man anymore."

She nodded knowingly, noting the sadness in his eyes. They were both prone to odd mood swings from time to time. They had decided some time ago that it must just be a side effect of having lived so long while retaining most of their humanity. Whatever the cause, it was a common problem for them both, and they were both experts in dealing with it.

"Whatever you are in reality, you will always be my man, as I will always be your woman." As expected, he took comfort in her words.

"You have always been my strength," he admitted, placing his hand over hers.

"I could say the same thing to you, John, but it's our love and devotion that strengthens us both. It was our love and devotion that kept us from embracing the sunrise centuries ago, and it's what will see us through this confrontation.

"There are many people and creatures out there that wish to destroy us, but there are also those who wish to help see us through. We owe it to them to get up and get back to work." As if on cue, there was a knock at their door.

"Enter," John spoke, a note of command and conviction back in his voice. As the door opened, he sat up straight but made no move to release his grip on his wife's hand. Seeing Marcus in the doorway made John suspect that everyone else had been too afraid to disturb them.

"Master, mistress, please forgive my intrusion."

"Don't worry about it. What is it?" Seeing Marcus visibly relax convinced John that he had guessed right.

"We have finished outlining a basic plan for handling the blood shipments and bringing in more ghouls. The others request that you come approve the plan, so we can begin working out the rest of the details." Danielle eyed her husband, making it clear that the decision to get back to work or not right now was his.

"Of course. Tell them we'll be there in a moment."

"Yes, master." Marcus turned and headed back toward the lounge room, leaving their bedroom door open. *No doubt his way of telling us that sooner is better than later*, John thought to himself as he started to get up. When Danielle rose to join him, he turned to kiss her.

"Thank you," he whispered to her, and Danielle gave him a wink. When he turned to lead her back to work, Danielle noticed that her husband made no move to let go of her hand.

Chapter 16

ARCH-TEMPLAR THOMAS Andrews reached down to scratch at his injured leg. Upon coming into contact with his artificial limb, however, the fingers drew back as if they had been burned. Thomas cursed the phantom pains that seemed to constantly plague his missing leg, as to him they were a sign of mortal weakness.

The doctors had told him the pains wouldn't go away for at least another month or two, but those same doctors had also told him he would have a bad limp for at least twelve weeks. He had proven them wrong once, and he would do so again. *Phantom pains*, he thought to himself in disgust. *If I'm not careful, I'll end up as weak as that fool archbishop*. He immediately crossed himself when he realized what he had just thought. *What am I thinking? I must remember to control my anger.*

Archbishop Jenkins, along with every other priest in the SOG, had the most difficult job there was. They had to ensure that soldiers like him never lost sight of why they did what they did. All Thomas had to do was destroy a few vampires. Jenkins, with the help of the priests under his command, had to keep the thousands of SOG souls that operated all along the East Coast pure.

Still, priests have no place on the battlefield. The SOG's policy of their priests being in direct command of everything was the only thing that Thomas disagreed with. Fortunately, the archbishop had seen the wisdom of his arguments when Thomas had been assigned his new duties; although, he was growing more and more concerned about the archbishop's health.

The longer this little war lasted, the worse he was likely to become. The high body count wasn't helping either. Thomas didn't like them, but he could accept casualties as a necessity of battle. The archbishop, on the other hand, seemed to age with every death. It was the main reason why he dreaded the report he was expected to make for the archbishop soon.

Word of the latest attacks against their outposts had already spread, and Thomas feared that the archbishop would be taking the news much harder than necessary. It was true that two of their remaining four outposts had been completely destroyed, but there had been no casualties reported at either site. Thomas had actually taken the news as a good sign.

Out of desperation, the abominations were beginning to trust their ghouls to carry out attacks for them. It seemed that both attacking groups had been spotted doing something suspicious, and both facilities had received warning from anonymous citizens. There hadn't been enough time to find the threat, but it gave them plenty of time to evacuate.

It was exactly what Thomas had predicted would begin to happen. The abominations were backed into a corner and beginning to make mistakes. It wouldn't be too much longer before their mistakes would increase in severity, and then the SOG would be able to move to destroy them. Thomas was certain of it.

All he had to do now was convince the archbishop that all was well. Jenkins would definitely be happy that there were no casualties, but he was sure to be disturbed by the loss of the outposts. He would see it as the abominations becoming even more dangerous, rather than the last strikes of a desperate opponent.

Thomas made a few last minute notes and then began to gather his paperwork. He couldn't put this off any longer. The archbishop had been working all night and would be leaving soon to get some rest.

Whispering a final short prayer for patience, Thomas went to deliver his report.

* * *

ARCHBISHOP JENKINS listened to Thomas's report with an expression of forced calm. It wasn't that the news bothered him. The fact that there were no casualties was a huge relief to the archbishop. Personally, he didn't care how many buildings got blown up, so long as there were no people inside when it happened.

All of the time Jenkins had spent in prayer or meditation since this confrontation had begun had gone unanswered. The uncertainty of it all was driving him mad, and it was all he could do to appear in control for the others. Every new report just caused more doubts, and every attack, on either side, more sadness.

Still, he listened to the arch-Templar, noticing the small discrepancies between his report and what really happened. Since the beginning of this confrontation, Jenkins had managed to get original copies of every report that had come through his headquarters. It required large amounts of his free time to read them all, but he had to know what was going on for himself.

It wasn't long before he noticed that Thomas adjusted some of the things in the reports he made to him. Jenkins never said anything about it because it was never anything too important. It only appeared that the arch-Templar was trying to shield him from certain things. At least, that's how it seemed at first. Now, however, it seemed that Thomas was trying to sway his opinion by slightly coloring the reports with too many of his own opinions.

"Thank you, Thomas. Your report was very thorough, as always," Jenkins said as Thomas finally finished the report.

"Would you like to suggest a course of action, sir?" Thomas seemed pleased that Jenkins didn't collapse in sorrow over the news of the destruction.

"I believe that I'll leave that in your own very capable hands. I'm exhausted, and I doubt any contribution I make now would even make any sense."

"You should go home and get some rest. I can have a plan of action ready for your approval when you return tonight." Jenkins smiled and nodded.

"I just have a few things to finish up here first. I should be leaving within the hour."

"As you wish. If you'll excuse me, I'll begin drafting our response immediately." Not needing to wait for a response, Thomas bowed and left. Once the door closed behind him, Jenkins stood up and turned to face the painting on the wall behind his desk.

The painting was one of his favorites. It was a large, colorful depiction of the archangel Michael standing over Lucifer, a fiery spear held against the demon's throat. Jenkins used to believe that it was the archangel's example that the SOG was following. Now he was no longer sure.

As he studied the painting, something about Thomas's report began to nag at him. Thomas had said that both of their outposts had received warnings of the attacks. He failed to mention that both warnings occurred at the same time, exactly ten minutes before the explosions that destroyed both SOG facilities had gone off. Thomas had interpreted the warnings as a sign that the vampires were growing weak and desperate, and were beginning to make mistakes. Jenkins was sure that there was more there than what Thomas believed.

It was easy to believe that the vampires were getting desperate, but desperation didn't always necessitate weakness. There were many words that Jenkins could think off to describe a vampire that was several centuries old, and weak was definitely not one of them, especially when there were two vampires involved, in addition to their supporting infrastructure. So what was he missing?

Both outposts were warned at the same time. There had to be something that he was missing. *Both outposts were warned at the same time.* The answer was at the edge of his awareness. Jenkins looked at the painted eyes of the archangel and begged for the answer to be revealed to him.

Both outposts were warned at the same *time. How could that happen, unless both attacking groups were discovered at the same time? Even if that did happen, the warnings were too late to stop the attacks.* He picked up a glass of water and took a small sip, forcing his mind to follow the trail of logic to its conclusion.

Both outposts received anonymous warnings at the same time, and too late to save the facilities. There had been just enough time to evacuate the buildings. It all seemed to be pointing to something obvious. Why couldn't he see it?

How could everything have worked out so perfectly? The answer came to Jenkins so suddenly that he nearly choked on his water. *My God in heaven!* They *were the ones to warn us!* It seemed both absurd and obvious at the same time.

Assuming that he was correct, there was only one logical reason for them to do such a thing: they didn't want to kill anyone. It was understandable that such a possibility would never even occur to Thomas, but the more Jenkins considered it, the more it made sense. Once he accepted his conclusion as fact, everything else fell into place quickly. He had finally made up his mind.

He had been wrong. The entire SOG was wrong. All this time he had spent distressed that he wasn't receiving a clear sign of God's will, and the answer had been right in front of him. All of the doubts he had been feeling, when viewed in retrospect, had been signs of perfect clarity. It had just taken time for his unworthy mortal mind to catch up to the final answer.

The vampires had been attacked by the SOG, not the other way around. He had yet to see a single report involving them taking an innocent life. In their attack on Lori's Bed and Breakfast, they hadn't harmed anyone not wearing the standard SOG crucifix. In their latest attacks, they had warned the SOG so that they could evacuate the doomed outposts.

Finally being sure of himself again gave Jenkins a peace of mind he hadn't known since this whole fiasco began. There was only one oddity in the facts. It was obvious that the vampires were trying to avoid spilling innocent blood, but they didn't seem to mind spilling SOG blood at every opportunity. So why warn the SOG about the bombings?

Both outposts combined only contained a small handful of innocents. Compared to the large number of SOG soldiers, militarily it seemed to be an excellent trade-off. If their situations had been reversed, Jenkins was certain that Thomas would have had no problems sacrificing a couple innocents to kill such a large number of ghouls. Considering the threat that the SOG posed to them, Jenkins would have thought the vampires would have made the same decision.

Unless they didn't want to spill SOG blood unnecessarily, he thought. Of course, the thought was ludicrous. Why wouldn't they? Jenkins was distressed at the thought of any bloodshed, but even he had to admit that the vampires had just cause.

Jenkins was by no means a military genius, but even he understood the basic progression of warfare. War was supposed to escalate to greater degrees of violence. When one side was clearly outmatched, it tended to forego basic morals, opting instead for basic survival. Jenkins had agreed with Thomas when he had advised that they be prepared for an extremely bloody retaliation for the destruction of their blood bank. So why did it seem that instead the vampires were growing less violent? He refused to believe it had anything to do with either weakness or surrender.

Whatever the answers to his new questions were, Jenkins needed to plan his next move. Improbable as his revelations may seem, he knew that he was right. He felt it with every fiber of his being. Ironically, he wasn't too surprised to realize that he was on the wrong side of this confrontation. Just knowing for sure was enough to calm him into quick, rational thought.

He needed to get out of here as soon as possible. These men believed they were doing the right thing, but Jenkins now realized they were the enemy. If he was going to help them see the truth, which he planned on doing, it couldn't be from here. The beginnings of a plan formed in his mind, and he almost cringed at the cruel irony. The plan was incredibly simple, but it depended on one crucial thing: him being correct about the vampires.

Jenkins would allow himself to be captured by them. It was reasonable to assume that they would have the ruins that used to be their blood bank under surveillance. If he just went there, his crucifix in plain sight, eventually a ghoul should approach him. He could easily tell a ghoul apart from a normal mortal. Once he was sure he was speaking to one, he would tell him or her what he wanted to do.

It was possible, of course, that he would be killed immediately. A single ghoul could easily kill him, and he might never see it coming. He was hoping that if he refrained from doing anything threatening, their curiosity would eventually encourage them to at least see what he was up to. His biggest concern was the rest of the SOG noticing that something was amiss.

It might take some time for him to draw the necessary attention, and sooner or later, SOG operatives would notice where he was. Odds were that he would be followed immediately after leaving the headquarters building. It was for his safety, of course, but it would complicate matters. He wasn't nearly skilled enough to lose his possible bodyguards, and trying would only alert their suspicions.

Jenkins sat back down and began drumming his fingers on his desk. He needed to get to what was left of the blood bank and stay there for an indeterminate amount of time, all without raising suspicions. How? Considering the problem for a few moments, Jenkins decided to stick to one of his favorite sayings: honesty is the best policy. Picking up his phone, he dialed the number to the cell phone Thomas carried at all times.

"Andrews," he answered after a single ring.

"Thomas, it's Jenkins. May I see you in my office at your earliest possible convenience?" It was the same way military commanders all over the world told their subordinates to report to them immediately without having to sound impolite. Very few people ever took the phrase at face value, and those who did learned the error of their ways quickly.

"Yes, of course, sir. I'm on my way."

Jenkins hung up his phone and began to quickly go over what he was going to say. Less than two minutes after his phone had reentered its cradle, there was a sharp knock at his door.

"Enter."

As Thomas entered the office and walked up to his desk, Jenkins noticed a slight limp to his step and resisted the urge to shake his head slightly. Thomas rarely limped anymore, so he must have rushed to answer the archbishop's call and, in doing so, overexerted himself. Jenkins knew how much he hated to be pitied, so he pretended not to notice.

"You asked to see me, sir." It was statement, not a question, which Jenkins acknowledged with a curt nod.

"I'm getting ready to go home as you suggested, but I need to make a stop along the way." He paused for a response, but Thomas was obviously awaiting more information first. "I want to stop by the remains of the vampires' blood bank. I wish to say a few prayers for the comrades we lost in the assault there.

"While I'm there, I can also cleanse the area of any lingering demon taint. Perhaps it'll make it safer for others to rebuild and turn the building into an honest business of some sort. I'm letting you know because I would like a few men to accompany me there. Even though it's still early in the day, I would feel safer with an escort."

There was a slight pause as Thomas no doubt tried to think of a way to talk him out of what he was planning to do. He obviously considered the idea an honorable one, but far too dangerous. That was why Jenkins had been careful not to ask his opinion, but to instead simply inform Thomas of his plans. An archbishop still outranked an arch-Templar by a large margin, and Jenkins could damn well do as he pleased. Thomas knew that as well and seemed to reluctantly accept the inevitable.

"I shall assign four of our best men to accompany you, sir."

"Have them report to my office as quickly as they can. I shall leave once they arrive."

"Understood."

"Thank you, Thomas, and don't worry. I shall be very careful." Thomas seemed to relax a bit, and then, with a bow, he left to round up his men.

Jenkins was surprised at how easy it had been to get his way without an argument. He often seemed to forget just how much authority he possessed. It was regrettable that if his plan worked, the four men assigned to guard him would almost certainly be killed, but he couldn't think of any way around it. Jenkins was certain that even had he not requested an escort, one would've been sent to follow him anyway; however, that knowledge didn't cause his regret to fade. If more lives must be lost, he swore he would make those deaths meaningful by doing everything he could to help end this conflict before it got any worse.

If only there were another way, Jenkins thought to himself. Unfortunately, he didn't need to pray to understand that there wasn't. Sighing in full acceptance of what he must now do, Jenkins gathered a few personal items and prepared to face the unknown.

* * *

"EXCUSE ME, commander, but could you come here for a moment?" All the other ghouls insisted on calling Marcus "commander." He didn't mind it too much, since he *was* their commander, and it helped to remind everyone of that fact. It did, however, get annoying from time to time. He suspected he was beginning to understand why "master" and "mistress" annoyed John and Danielle so much.

It was nearing noon on what was turning out to be a very beautiful day. He felt a pang of sorrow at the knowledge that his masters would never be able to enjoy it's like again, but this passed quickly. He had work to do.

While his masters spent the day in slumber, it was his job to make sure that everything ran smoothly and everyone remained safe. Ghouls required no sleep, so it was easy for him to keep an eye on everything all day and then work with his masters all night. He was also old and strong enough that stress wasn't really a factor for him, as it was with many younger ghouls. They were still human after all. Well, sort of.

Marcus had been making his usual rounds of the various duty stations throughout the haven when the young ghoul had called out to him. Nodding to the younger ghoul, Marcus turned and began to follow him back to his post. The trip was a short one, and Marcus had spent it trying to remember the younger ghoul's name, to no avail.

Sooner or later, I swear I'll be able to keep everybody straight. He might have no idea who the ghoul was, but the headset he was wearing gave away his duty. Every team of ghouls that was working, patrolling, or simply running errands outside of the haven had a ghoul assigned to keep track of them from within the haven.

The ability to stay in constant contact with the haven, no matter where a group of ghouls went, was necessary. Problems could arise at any moment, or necessary information could be discovered. This method of staying in contact ensured that no one was left in the dark as to what was happening. Having a separate ghoul assigned to monitor each external team helped to alleviate the confusion that was often the result of constant communication.

The monitoring room was really just a large conference room that had been divided into several small booths. Each monitoring ghoul had his own booth to work out of. Strictly speaking, the booths weren't really necessary; they just helped to keep each ghoul's conversations from interfering with those being conducted by the others.

Since the ghoul had left his post to track him down, Thomas assumed that there must be a problem with the team he was monitoring. Not that leaving his post really made any difference—the headsets allowed them to do their jobs from anywhere within the haven—it was just something that they rarely did. Hoping the problem was nothing major, Marcus seated himself next to the younger ghoul's workstation inside his booth.

"Before you start, I'm ashamed to say that I can't remember your name."

"It's Michael, sir."

"Okay, Michael, what's the problem, and how do we kill it?" Marcus was trying to keep the mood as light as possible. It would help to ensure that the younger ghoul spoke candidly, which was always preferable to him.

"Oh, it's nothing bad, sir. It's more something odd, and my team wants advice on how to proceed." Marcus was careful not to allow his immense relief to show.

"Which team are you monitoring?"

"The ones keeping watch at the blood bank, sir." Even though the blood bank had been completely destroyed, John had assigned a pair of ghouls to keep an eye on what was left. It was a long shot, but he thought the SOG might come back later to sift through the rubble for clues as to the location of their haven. If they tried anything like that, it would be a waste of time, but he still wanted to know about it.

"The SOG is actually trying to loot the place for information?"

"Not exactly, sir. At least we don't think so."

"Explain."

"Well, sir, according to the team in place, there are five SOG operatives on the property that they can identify. They've been there for nearly twenty minutes now, but they don't seem to be looking for anything."

"So what are they doing?" Michael checked some notes that he must have jotted down earlier.

"According to Theo," Marcus guessed that was the name of the senior ghoul of the pair on watch, "four of them appear to be looking just about everywhere except inside what's left of the building. He figures they must be bodyguards for the fifth man. Martin, the second member of our team, agrees with him."

"Interesting, but how do we know they're SOG?"

"Theo says each one is wearing a crucifix matching the description of those worn by all the SOG members we've encountered thus far." It was a good assessment, except for one thing.

"Why would SOG operatives wear their crosses in plain sight, knowing that we know what to look for now and will kill them on sight?" Michael repeated the question into his headset for Theo and then considered it himself.

"They are fanatics, sir. Perhaps they're too proud to hide them."

"The men who attacked the blood bank hid them. If they hadn't, our ghouls would've never been taken by surprise." Michael was forced to concede the point, and Marcus could hear a voice coming from the headset.

"Theo's guessing that it's because it's during the day. They know our masters can't get to them, and they simply aren't afraid of us. The only reason they hid them at all at the blood bank was to ensure surprise." Marcus nodded. He could accept that the SOG were arrogant enough not to fear ghouls.

"Okay, I agree that they're SOG then. What about the fifth person? If the other four are bodyguards, who're they guarding?" Marcus could feel a glimmer of excitement, at the thought of identifying a possible leader.

"We aren't really sure, sir. Theo and Martin think he's a priest."

"A priest?"

"Yes, sir. He's wearing normal clothing, but they've both caught glimpses of his white collar. Plus, he seems to have spent the whole time at the site praying. What we don't know is whether this is a good or a bad thing. He's being guarded, but it could just be because he's a priest. He might not really be anyone important." An interesting problem. Marcus knew that John and Danielle had discovered that the SOG really wasn't a part of the Catholic Church anymore, so what were they doing with a priest?

"Okay, we need more information, and I think I know where to get it. Tell them to keep an eye on them. If they move, follow them. Also, get our closest combat patrol on its way over there. If we have to fight, I want it to be quick and decisive. I'll be right back."

"Yes, sir." Michael began repeating his orders as Marcus left the room.

Marcus walked down the hallway to the closest hotel phone. The phones were spaced, a few on the wall, on every floor. They were unable to call outside of the building, but they were a quick, excellent method of reaching every room inside of the hotel. He quickly dialed the extension for the main computer office.

"Jasmine speaking." Marcus could hear the clicking of a computer keyboard in the background.

"Hi, Jasmine, it's Marcus." The clicking suddenly stopped.

"Hello, commander, what can I do for you?"

"Actually, I was on my way up there to check on you guys, but I got sidetracked." He quickly explained the situation.

"Sounds interesting, sir, but what do you need me for?"

"Since you're the one in charge of organizing all the data we stole, I was hoping you could answer a question for me."

"Of course, sir."

"Before I decide how to proceed with this, I need an idea of how important this priest is. We have no idea who he is, only that he's a priest. Think you can shed any light on this?" The line was silent for a moment.

"Without a name, sir, I can't tell you anything specific; however, they are religious fanatics. Like all groups of their kind, they're divided into two main castes: soldiers and priests. And guess who's in charge?"

"The priests?"

"That's right, sir. At worst, this guy's just a local leader. At best, he could be someone of major importance. The SOG has bishops and archbishops just like the Catholic Church does. Who knows how important this guy could be." Marcus nodded to himself, his decision made.

"Thanks, Jasmine. I'm going to be tied up for a while with this. You guys need anything?"

"No thanks, sir. We should be finished sorting through all this information by the end of the day. Then we can start trying to figure out what it all means. Although, if you could let us know how this situation turns out, we'd appreciate it. It gets pretty boring up here."

"No problem. Talk to you later, Jasmine."

"Good-bye, commander." As Marcus hung the phone back up, he could feel himself getting more excited. Trying to control himself, he quickly realized it was no use. If they were lucky, this priest might turn out to be someone of real importance. Then his masters wouldn't have to trouble themselves with capturing someone else.

Returning to the monitoring room, Marcus could hear Michael talking with Theo over his headset. He got Michael's attention and motioned for him to hand the set over to him. Taking a moment to readjust its size, Marcus asked for the status of the SOG group.

"They're still here, sir, and they don't show any signs of leaving soon. What are your orders?"

"Capture the priest alive, and bring him to the haven. He may be important."

"Understood, sir. What do we do with the bodyguards?"

"Take them out, of course, but if it's at all possible, don't kill them. The masters will be very pleased if we can capture the priest, but they'll be even more pleased if we can do so without bloodshed."

"Yes, sir. Jeremy's team will be here in a few minutes. We'll make our move once they arrive." Jeremy, Marcus knew, was senior to Theo.

"Okay, I'll have Jeremy's controller update him on the situation. Also, he'll be informed that since you're already on the scene, you'll be in charge of the operation. He'll understand and follow your orders once he arrives."

"Yes, sir. Thank you, sir."

"Don't let us down." Marcus gave the headset back to Michael and went to give Jeremy's controller his instructions.

His orders given, it was now up to Theo to accomplish the mission. Any more interference from Marcus would only serve to confuse the situation. There was simply nothing left for him to do, other than wait to see how it all played out.

* * *

JENKINS DISCREETLY checked his watch and began to doubt the brilliance of his plan. They'd been here for over twenty minutes, and nothing had happened yet. He knew that there were no guarantees, and God only knew how long they'd have to wait, but it was getting increasingly difficult to keep his bodyguards calm.

As an archbishop, he could always just inform them that they'd be here all day, and that would be that. Unfortunately, his plan depended on him acting normally. The SOG had to think he was captured. There could be no doubts that had not gone willingly.

"Excuse me, Excellency, but it is not safe here. We really should be taking you home now." It was starting already. Jenkins fixed the man who'd spoken with his best holier-than-thou look.

"My son, did you know any of the deceased among our men?" The question caught the man off guard.

"Of course, Excellency. We all knew them."

"Then you should appreciate what I'm doing right now. Our men deserve all the prayers we can give them."

"Yes, Excellency. Do you know how much longer you will be?"

"When I feel that the Lord has been satisfied, we will leave. Don't worry, my son, it will be long before sunset." The guard wasn't completely successful in hiding his relief.

Jenkins was telling the truth, sort of. He was spending his time praying for their lost men while he waited for something to happen. Since God was all-knowing and all-powerful, one could say that if something did happen, it would only be because He was satisfied. It was a huge stretch, Jenkins knew, but he couldn't bring himself to lie. It was only a matter of time before they started asking the wrong questions.

What's taking so long?

* * *

"THE COMMANDER said you're in charge, Theo. What's the plan?" Jeremy's team had just linked up with Theo and Martin, and they were all eager to get started.

"On my signal, we're all going to throw rocks at them." Jeremy waited for the punch line, but it never came.

"You're serious?"

"Sure am," Theo answered, gesturing to a pile of fist-sized rocks he had gathered. "Okay, look," he started, seeing that the others didn't appreciate his genius, "the masters don't want us killing people that aren't a threat. These guys aren't a threat; they're just in the way."

"Point taken, but throwing rocks? They're bound to be fairly well-armed, and I'm betting they're wearing some kind of body armor. I'd feel better if your plan was a bit more detailed than just throwing rocks." Theo shrugged and started to explain.

"There are six of us. We each grab two rocks, and pick our targets carefully. That gives us three rocks per target. Throw as hard as you can at the target's torso. Even if only two rocks hit each one, it'll stun and confuse them. Then we just charge and knock them out. With our superior strength and speed, this should work fine. If it doesn't, we can always shoot them later." Martin had already decided to go along with the idea. The members of Jeremy's team were looking to him. They would agree, so long as their leader did first.

"That's a really stupid plan," Jeremy started and then broke into a grin, "but I like it. You think we can hit them from here?" It was over twenty meters to the closest soldier.

"Probably, but when we're ready, I'd like to move closer. We need to make sure we hit them with enough force to stun them through their body armor."

"True, but what if they aren't wearing body armor at all? It'd be a shame to kill them all by mistake." Not that any of them really cared, but orders were orders.

"You think we should stay here then?" Jeremy shrugged.

"This is your show, Theo, but yeah, I think we should stay here. If our aim is good, and it damn well should be, we'll still hurt them from here. We should be able to cover the distance before they can draw any major weapons." Theo considered it, knowing the final decision was his to make.

"Sounds good. Okay, everyone pick out your rocks and get your targets straight." It wouldn't do to have all six of them aim at the same soldier.

As he waited a few moments for the other ghouls to get ready, he realized how comical the situation was. He was about to lead an attack against a small group of the most highly trained and well-armed vampire hunters in the world, and his men were throwing rocks. He allowed himself a brief smile at the thought and then banished all notions of comedy as he saw his ghouls ready to strike.

"Ready?" He was answered by five nods. "Take aim." Five arms drew back in preparation to throw. A couple who passed by their position eyed them warily, but Theo ignored them. It was now or never.

"Throw!"

* * *

THOUGH JENKINS knew he'd been in the blood bank for barely thirty-five minutes, it felt like an eternity. He could hear his bodyguards shuffling around nervously. They were professional soldiers, not real bodyguards. Standing in one place out in the open for this long obviously didn't sit well with them. Jenkins began to doubt his choice of action.

No, he scolded himself sharply; *the time for doubts is long past. I've chosen my path. Now, it's time to walk it.* Of course, that was easier said than done. He'd finished his prayers for the dead, so he began to say a new prayer for the four poor souls who'd accompanied him here.

Thwack. Thwack. Thwack. Thwack. Thwack. Thwack.

Startled by the sudden noise, Jenkins turned in time to see his four bodyguards staggering in confusion. They were all clutching their chests in what looked more like surprise than actual pain. What had just happened to them? Amid all the rubble, no one noticed the six rocks that hadn't been there before.

Thwack. Thwack. Thwack. Thwack. Thwack. Thwack.

The second wave of rocks served to dismiss all remaining confusion. The soldiers had no idea what had happened, but it was obvious they were under attack. All four began scanning the street while they drew their weapons. The soldier closest to Jenkins actually managed to get his finger on the trigger of his shotgun before he was rendered unconscious. Less than ten seconds after the first sounds of the attack, Jenkins found himself surrounded by six individuals he immediately sensed were ghouls.

I put my trust in you, oh Lord. Although he had been expecting an attack, its speed and efficiency still frightened him. He stood tall, folded his hands in front of him, and tried to look as helpless as possible. He doubted that the ghouls would be impressed by submission, so he made no attempt at a verbal surrender.

Jenkins watched as one of the ghouls pointed to two others and then toward him. He quickly found himself in grips that felt like pure steel, as the indicated ghouls took hold of him. Making no attempt to struggle, they led him to what used to be the rear of the building, where the other four ghouls were working quickly to clear away the rubble.

Fear gave way to curiosity as they lifted a portion of the floor away, revealing a secret exit. Jenkins wasn't surprised; if he knew he'd most likely be hunted someday, he'd have secret exits too. His captors carefully forced him down into the tunnel without releasing their grip on him.

It was obvious that they weren't going to kill him, but why were they being so careful with him? They could just as easily be shoving and kicking him around without actually endangering his life. Jenkins began to wonder if they'd been planning to capture him all along. If he was the day's prize, it'd make sense that his captors would want him undamaged to present before their masters. *An interesting development.*

Once the rest of the ghouls had entered the tunnel, a pair of them secured the trapdoor back into place. Jenkins was released, and, once again, all six ghouls surrounded him. They seemed to be studying him, as if they weren't sure what to do with him.

"What is your name, priest?" one of the ghouls demanded. Jenkins forced the remaining tendrils of fear from his mind.

"My name is Matthew Jenkins, and I'm an archbishop, not a priest." The ghouls seemed both surprised and excited by his answer. Apparently they hadn't expected him to be so cooperative, but they obviously understood his rank was a very high one. He decided to try to take the initiative with the conversation.

"What of my guards?"

The ghoul who had spoken earlier seemed shocked that he had talked out of turn, but apparently decided to humor him.

"You mean the four soldiers up there?"

"Yes. What did you do to them?" Jenkins knew they were dead, but he was curious as to what the ghouls used to start the attack. The few sounds that he had heard hadn't been enough to give any idea.

"Nothing much really." The ghoul grinned, amused at the memory no doubt. "We threw some rocks at them and then knocked 'em out before they could sort out what was happening." He seemed to be waiting for a response, but Jenkins was so taken aback, he didn't know how to respond.

"You ... threw rocks?" he managed to stammer out. It was absurd, yet the sounds he heard seemed to fit the claim. He noticed the ghouls taking no small measure of amusement at his shock. Ghouls surprising and immediately overwhelming their enemies by throwing rocks? He had to admit, if not for the four men who had died, it would've been an amusing thought even to him. Jenkins was considering what to say next when something else the ghoul had said finally registered in his mind.

"Hell yeah, we did ... no offense."

"You didn't kill my bodyguards?"

"Um, no. You want us to go back and finish them off?"

Joy mixed with confusion started to mount within him.

"No, of course not. Although, I must admit, I am a bit confused. Why did you spare them?" He could see several of the ghouls' expressions go hard, and he wondered if he'd crossed some imaginary boundary.

"Don't push us, priest." Apparently they liked the sound of "priest" better than "archbishop." Jenkins was disinclined to argue the point. "If we had our way, we'd gut every last one of you. Fortunately for you, however, our masters have instructed us to avoid bloodshed unless absolutely necessary." The ghoul looked about to say more but was cut off by one of his comrades.

"If you want to keep talking to him, that's fine, but tie him up first. We need to get moving." The ghoul who just spoke was obviously the one in charge, and Jenkins turned to face him.

"That's not really necessary. I come with you of my own free will." Jenkins didn't know what prompted the statement. Perhaps hearing that his men had been spared had further convinced him of his course of action. Whatever the cause, he couldn't very well take it back now. "There are things that I must discuss with your masters." The ghoul eyed him suspiciously.

"You're telling us that you allowed yourself to be captured?"

"Well, yes and no. I make no claims to have been able to stop you from capturing me, but yes, I did put myself in the position to be captured on purpose. I couldn't think of any way to get in touch with your masters that would be above suspicion, so I decided to try this."

"Why?"

Jenkins struggled to find a brief explanation that would satisfy the ghoul.

"Long story short, I've come to the conclusion that I'm on the wrong side of this conflict. I want to bring it to an end, and I think your masters are more interested in doing that than mine are." The ghoul seemed to mull this over for a moment. Meanwhile, the original ghoul that had spoken to him had fished a length of rope out of a small backpack and was now just waiting for their leader to make up his mind.

"Whether or not you're telling the truth doesn't matter to us in the long run, so here's the deal: we're in for a long hike back to the haven, and you're going to be blindfolded the entire time. However, if you promise to behave, we won't bind your hands."

Jenkins simply nodded his acceptance of their terms.

"I'm sure I don't need to inform you that allowing you to remain conscious is a courtesy easily revoked?"

"I give you my word that I won't cause any trouble."

"Good." The ghoul turned his attention back on his men. "All right, let's go. We've already been here way too long." Jenkins's arms were held in place as he was quickly blindfolded. As promised, however, his hands remained free. When the ghouls were ready to move, Jenkins felt one of them take his left arm.

"My name is Martin. My job is to keep you from walking into anything or otherwise injuring yourself." Not knowing whether he should speak or not, Jenkins just nodded. "I'll be leading you by the arm the whole way. Just walk straight. I'll let you know when to avoid an obstacle."

"I understand. Thank you, Martin." With a firm but not forceful tug on his arm from Martin, they started moving.

"Don't mention it, priest. You seem like a fairly decent guy. For what it's worth, I hope my masters decide against disemboweling you."

Indeed.

* * *

THOMAS STILL couldn't believe the report. It wasn't that he thought the men were lying. Nor did he have trouble accepting the idea that a group of ghouls could overpower a few of his men. He just couldn't accept how he could have been stupid enough to let it happen.

It's not my fault. I warned him, damn it, but he just wouldn't listen. Thomas forced himself to calm down and think things through. The archbishop had just been doing his job. Jenkins had wanted to set a good example for the rest of the men. Thomas had tried to warn him, but Jenkins had decided that the risk was worth taking. Sometimes things just happen that are beyond control.

"Who am I kidding?" Thomas mumbled to himself as he dropped his head into his hands. "The archbishop put me in charge of everything relating to combat. I could have argued with him about his plans a bit more strongly." Thomas really didn't think that it would have changed anything in the end, but he didn't even try. If blame could be placed anywhere, it would be with him.

Enough, he thought to himself. *What's done is done, and blaming myself isn't going to change a damn thing.* One of the things that made Thomas an excellent leader was his ability to solve problems, no matter how complex or sensitive. It was an ability he needed to utilize now.

The biggest problem they would face now would be morale. Since the victory at the blood bank, the men had finally been growing more positive about their chances at emerging victorious against the abominations. When news of the archbishop's capture got out, morale would plummet lower than ever. He couldn't even offer much hope about their chances of rescuing him. The abominations would mostly likely kill the archbishop long before he could be found and rescued.

The men would need another victory soon—something big enough to make them believe that no matter what happened, they would emerge victorious. *Maybe I can even make this incident work for us. If I can make Jenkins into a martyr, the men will do anything to avenge him.* Suddenly all guilt Thomas had felt over the incident evaporated, and a new plan started forming in his mind.

There was only one thing left to do before he could really get back to work: the archbishop's capture would have to be reported to their superiors. It was something Thomas really did not want to do, but they would find out soon enough anyway. *Who knows, maybe I can use this as an excuse to ask for even more reinforcements.* In any event, he knew he couldn't put off his next task any longer.

Time to call the Vatican.

Chapter 17

JENKINS AWOKE with a start to the sound of knocking. It took him a moment to remember where he was and why it was so dark. The lack of windows or even a watch made it difficult to guess the time, but it was most likely after sunset. Whoever was at the door was probably going to escort him to see the vampires. If he lived through the next hour, then he should be able to consider his mission a success. If the way he had been treated so far was any indication, however, he had nothing to worry about.

The trek through the sewers had been difficult to accomplish blindfolded, but once they had reached their destination, things had gone surprisingly well. It was true that he was locked in a small room with no windows, but that was understandable. The ghouls needed to wait for their masters to wake and tell them what to do with him. Until then, they couldn't afford to take any chances.

It wasn't as if he had been mistreated. On the contrary, he had been given everything that he might need. The ghouls had provided him with food, a comfortable bed and chair, a restroom, a change of clothes, and even a small table on which to place the things he had brought along. After about an hour, he had decided to test the hospitality.

Jenkins had been a bit sore from the trip through the sewers, so he had asked his guard if he might have something to alleviate the discomfort. Less than five minutes later, someone had come by with medication for him. They even offered to check his ankles and knees for injury. The way he was being treated convinced Jenkins even more that he had made the right decision.

Once alone, he had settled in and prayed for a short time for guidance, and then he decided to take a nap. What else was he going to do? Besides, he had been tired even before he spent an hour roaming through the sewers.

The knocking came again, a bit louder this time, and Jenkins shook his head briefly to bring his thoughts back to the present.

"Come in," Jenkins said to his visitor. The door opened slowly, and he saw a ghoul standing in the hallway. Jenkins smiled at him. "What can I do for you?"

"The masters will see you now. I'm here to escort you to them." There was something familiar about the ghoul.

"Is that you, Martin?"

The ghoul grinned.

"You guessed it. How'd you know? It's not like you got a good view of me while you were blindfolded."

"Your voice."

"Oh, I didn't even think of that. Anyway, I can see you just woke up. Would you like a couple minutes to get yourself together?"

"Definitely, but only if you think my tardiness won't upset them."

Martin dismissed his concern with a wave of his hand. "Nah, just don't take too long."

Jenkins nodded. "Do you mind if I ask you a question, Martin?"

"Go ahead, but I can't promise an answer." The ghoul probably thought he was sniffing around for info on his masters.

"Why did you knock on my door?"

There was a brief pause.

"I don't understand." Jenkins could hear the confusion in his voice.

"I mean, why didn't you just come in? I am just a prisoner here. What difference would it make?"

"That would have been rude. What if you had been changing or in the bathroom? You know that you're our prisoner. We know it. By now even your people should know it. Why add insult to injury? If we're rude to you, or mistreat you, does that make you any more of a prisoner? On the contrary, doing things like that make prisoners even harder to control.

"It's not possible for you to escape us, so we don't lose anything by being nice to you and seeing that your needs are met. Besides, you might be dead very soon. The least we can do is preserve your dignity." The answer was much more thought out than Jenkins had been expecting. Even more proof that he wasn't surrounded by demons.

"Well, thank you, Martin. I really do appreciate that." Jenkins went to the bathroom and quickly washed his face and hands. His hair was a bit mussed, but it would have to do. He wasn't about to press his luck by taking the time necessary to fix it. "I'm as ready as I'm going to be," he said, leaving the bathroom.

Martin looked him up and down and nodded his approval, but he made no move to lead him out.

"A couple bits of advice first. It goes without saying that they'll kill you if you lie."

Jenkins had already figured as much, but he was an honest man. "I'm not worried about that. My job demands honesty above all else."

"Good. Just as importantly though, don't do anything to annoy the female; she's still not happy about the ambush your people set for her a few weeks ago. She understands the asset you can be, but if you push her, she'll kill you. The others can restrain her, but they wouldn't be able to prevent her from striking at least once. Don't even look at her the wrong way."

"Thanks for the warning, Martin. I'll do my best." The ghoul nodded and motioned toward the door.

"Good, let's go."

* * *

"WAIT HERE." Martin had led him to a closed door. Jenkins did as instructed, while the ghoul entered the room. *Probably doing some sort of introduction*, he guessed. A few moments went by before Martin came back out into the hallway. "They're ready for you. Good luck, priest."

"Thank you, Martin." Jenkins put out a hand, which the ghoul accepted before turning to walk away. He watched as the ghoul disappeared down the hallway, and then he turned back to the closed door. As confident as Jenkins was, he couldn't help but wonder if he would ever leave the room he was about to enter. *Whatever happens, I know that I'm making the right decision.* Jenkins put his faith in God and opened the door.

He entered what appeared to be a small conference room. It was beautifully decorated, with comfortable-looking chairs, plush carpet, and skillfully crafted wall hangings. The decor, however, was not the first thing to grab Jenkins's attention.

He had expected to be meeting alone with the two vampires, but the room held nearly a dozen people. Most notable was a small group of a five, who stood whispering to each other on the other side of the room. He recognized one of the males and the female as the pair he'd been expecting to see, but the other three males were a mystery to him. As he closed the door, they stopped talking and looked over at him, and Jenkins swore he could feel his heart stop. Every one of them was a vampire.

"There're five of you?" Jenkins reflexively blurted. Of all the things he had considered saying to make a positive first impression, a shocked question hadn't been on his list of options. Fortunately, the male vampire that he recognized grinned and motioned him toward a half dozen chairs that had been arranged in a circle. Jenkins took a seat in the closest one, and the vampires followed suit. Then they all quietly studied each other for several minutes.

The male who seemed to be in charge continued to smile, while the female stared at him with barely contained rage. When he looked into her eyes, Jenkins immediately felt a sort of tugging at the edges of his mind. Obviously, her vampiric abilities included at least one form of mind control. Either she wasn't strong enough to completely penetrate his fortified mind or she was so powerful that he noticed her mental touch without her even trying. Given what he had seen of her abilities thus far, he was inclined to believe the latter.

The other three males remained a complete mystery to Jenkins. Two were eyeing him with interest, while the third was wearing a completely neutral expression. He experienced a moment of self-doubt when he considered that the vampires might be doing exactly what Arch-Templar Andrews had feared; gathering more of their own kind to wage a full-scale war against the SOG. He pushed the thoughts from his mind. The time for second-guessing himself was long past.

"As deep as my patience and appreciation for silence runs, we don't have the time to simply sit and stare at each other," the first male said, breaking the silence. "My ghouls tell me that you came quietly, and that from the way you acted, it seemed you were waiting to be captured." He let the statement hang, inviting response.

"That is correct." Jenkins decided that simply trying to blurt everything out all at once would not be the proper way to handle the situation.

"Why?" Jenkins knew that he needed to choose his next words very carefully if he wanted to survive the night.

"I've come to realize that I'm on the wrong side in this conflict, and I wish to help you." The vampires exchanged quick glances, and it was clear that they didn't trust him.

"You'll understand, and forgive me, if I don't start leaping for joy at our good fortune." The sarcasm was so thick that, had the vampire been mortal, he would've choked on it. Jenkins wisely chose to remain silent. "Here's the deal. Start from the beginning, and tell us why you're here. Be aware that my wife will be examining your mind the entire time. And if you lie to us, you will die."

Jenkins almost fell out of his chair when the vampire said the word "wife." Sure enough, upon closer inspection, he could see that both the male and the female had gold wedding bands. He did his best to cover his surprise at the possibility that vampires could be married. The female already looked ready to gut him, and he saw no point in actually giving her reason to. If they accepted him, there would be plenty of time later for explanations. Speaking of which, they were all awaiting his explanation.

"Understood." Jenkins acknowledged their terms, but before he could begin, the male held up a hand to halt him.

"Hold on a moment." The vampire looked past Jenkins and motioned for someone to approach.

The archbishop remained silent as he watched a pair of ghouls set a few trays down at a side table. The trays held six glasses and several pitchers. A single pitcher seemed to contain water, while the others were filled with a red liquid. Jenkins felt bile begin to rise in his throat as he realized what the contents of the other pitchers was. Human blood.

He struggled to stay calm as the ghouls began filling glasses and serving their masters. He automatically accepted the glass of water that was offered to him. It was all Jenkins could do to control his revulsion.

Get a hold of yourself. You know that they're vampires. What did you think they'd be drinking? Unfortunately, logic didn't seem to offer him much comfort. Understanding something and seeing it were two very different things. He realized that the only way he was going to get through this was if he didn't allow anything else to distract him. Also, it probably wouldn't hurt to show a little backbone. He sat up a bit straighter, took a drink of water, and looked the male square in the eye.

"May I begin?" The male grinned and nodded assent. He also raised his glass to Jenkins in a mock toast. It would seem that he had passed a test of some kind. Even the female was looking at him differently, although her gaze would still be considered hostile.

Jenkins took a deep breath and began his tale. Starting with the first incident between the female and Arch-Templar Andrews, he went over everything that he thought was important. He also volunteered juicy bits of information every now and then to help lend credence to how serious he was and how much he had to offer. It took about an hour for him to finish, and, surprisingly, none of the vampires had interrupted him a single time.

There was nothing left for him to do but sit back and wait for the vampires to respond. As he waited, he began to study them more carefully. There were subtle differences between them that he hadn't noticed before.

The pair he recognized appeared perfectly human so long as he didn't look them directly in the eye. Their skin even had a slight rosy glow to it. By contrast, the other three males seemed a bit pale. Their skin tone had improved since they had started drinking at the beginning of the meeting, but it still didn't look quite as normal as the first two. Jenkins wondered if that had anything to do with how old or powerful they were.

"Well?" The first male finally spoke up, but he wasn't speaking to Jenkins.

"He's telling the truth. He honestly does want to help us." The female almost looked disappointed as she spoke, but at least she no longer seemed ready to kill him.

"Good. That's going to make things much easier." He turned his attention back to Jenkins. "I guess it's time for us to make proper introductions. My name is John, and this is my wife, Danielle." John proceeded to introduce the other three males, and Jenkins nodded to each in turn. "I can't say that I ever expected us to be working together quite like this, but I'm hopeful about what we can accomplish.

"For what it's worth, archbishop, I applaud your courage in coming to us. I'm sure that you have questions you'd like to ask." He paused as a ghoul refilled his glass. "Please feel free to do so."

"Thank you, and yes, I am very curious about a few things." It was a huge understatement, but he didn't want to push his luck.

Jenkins spent the next thirty minutes or so learning things about vampires that no one else in the SOG would probably ever believe. John and Danielle spoke wistfully about their wedding and when they were both still mortals. They explained how rarely they actually needed to use violence to solve their problems, and that most of the blood they drank came from blood banks. He also learned about

Sam's recent transformation from ghoul to vampire in order to save him from wounds sustained in one of the battles with SOG forces.

The more Jenkins learned, the more fascinated he became. He continued asking question after question, throwing caution to the wind. He was literally on the edge of his seat. The vampires, for their part, seemed almost delighted to indulge his curiosity. With the small exception of the blood-filled glasses, it was almost as if he were mingling with random people. They were certainly a far cry from the evil abominations he had learned about in the SOG.

"That's enough for now," John said as a way to politely forestall his next question. "I for one would love to sit back and talk all night about past adventures, and separating myth from fact. Unfortunately, we should really be getting down to business." Jenkins nodded a reluctant agreement.

"I guess that I should admit I'm not really sure what to do. I know that I want to help in any way I can, but I honestly hadn't formed any plans beyond getting to meet you and not being killed." The vampires grinned at the thought but did their best to keep their fangs hidden. After all, they didn't want to be rude.

"That's perfectly all right; we've already decided what to do. Your presence will just make things much simpler, especially due to your high rank within the SOG. Speaking of which, archbishop, what exactly is your position anyway?"

"Please, call me Matthew, or Jenkins." He was feeling much more comfortable now. "To answer your question, I'm in overall command of all SOG operations along the East Coast, or rather I *was*. I only took direct command in this area in order to oversee the conflict that had begun between us." There was a note of pride in Jenkins's voice as he answered the question, but it was well-deserved. He was relatively young to hold such a high position within the SOG.

"Is that good?" The question came from Jose. "I mean, how much do we really know about the organization of the leaders in the SOG? Maybe the East Coast is some sort of training area or something."

"I don't know, Jose," Chris was speaking now. "The East Coast is a pretty important area. It doesn't make much sense that anyone would use it as a training ground for anything." Jenkins was about to confirm what Chris had said, but Jose cut him off.

"Well I'm just saying that it's a possibility," Jose said, getting a bit defensive.

"No, what you're saying is that you're stupid and don't think things through." Chris bared his fangs after finishing the verbal jab.

"At least I check to see if my blood's tainted before drinking it," Jose shot back. Chris couldn't help but shudder at the memory Jose had dredged up.

Jenkins sat back, speechless, as the two elder vampires continued to hurl insults at one another as if they were bickering teenagers. He was afraid they would attack each other at any moment; however, the other vampires seemed to think the situation was hilarious. After a few minutes, however, John seemed to have had enough.

"Have you two quite finished?" The bickering stopped immediately. There was definitely no question of who was in charge. "How about we stop arguing long enough for Matthew here to elaborate on his old job?" There was a series of agreements, and then John motioned for Jenkins to pick up where he left off.

"Well, actually, the title—rank if you will—of archbishop is very broad in the SOG. Rank is a only a small factor in your standing within the organization. Your importance is shown more by what you're in charge of. For example, a newly promoted archbishop might only be tasked with overseeing a single large city. This person technically has the same rank as every other archbishop, but far less prestige and almost no say in what goes on around him." Jenkins paused for a drink of water and to clear his throat.

When he looked back up, he was too astonished to continue speaking. The vampires were all waiting patiently for him to continue and not even trying to hide their interest. The appeared as interested in what he had to say as he was when they were speaking earlier. Jenkins couldn't believe he was holding the honest interest of five vampires all at the same time. Afraid that they might grow impatient, he quickly reorganized his thoughts and went on.

"Even when taking the entire world into consideration, the East Coast is a very important area. It's one of the highest commands you can have in the SOG and still actually be a commander. Any higher, and you basically just sit around reading reports from other commanders instead of actually doing anything. When you factor in my relatively young age, I'm considered quite the rising star within the organization. If I hadn't ... I guess you can say 'defected,' I'd probably be overseeing all of North America within ten years."

While he was making his old position clear, Jenkins swore that he saw pure excitement in John and Danielle's eyes. It was enough to almost unnerve him. There could be a very simple explanation. He was sure the discovery that a very prominent enemy leader had come over to your side willingly was a pleasant one, but it almost seemed more than that. In the end Jenkins decided that it didn't matter very much. It was just one more thing that he didn't understand yet.

When it became obvious that Jenkins was finished, the vampires began to discuss something among themselves. At least, that's what he assumed they were doing. Their lips were all moving, but he couldn't hear anything but a low hiss. He guessed they were deciding what to do with him and were purposefully keeping their voices below mortal hearing.

"I think I speak for all of us when I say that we definitely have use for you on our side." John was speaking in a normal tone once again, and the other vampires were nodding their agreement. "Who knows, we may even become friends. You have to appreciate the irony in that." They all shared a brief chuckle, and this time it was Jenkins who tried to get everyone back on track.

"I'm still not sure exactly what you want me to do. You said that you already had a plan, and I'm guessing that I fall into it somewhere." John nodded but didn't speak, so he continued. "So once you fill me in, I guess I'll have a better idea how to help."

"That's where it gets a bit complicated. We can't tell you anything of our main plans yet." John waited for Jenkins to make the obvious response.

"I don't understand." Jenkins wasn't sure whether he should be concerned or not, and his voice betrayed his thoughts.

"There's a lot you don't understand yet about the situation. Unfortunately, if we tried to explain it to you, I doubt you'd believe us. On the contrary, it would probably convince you that you were wrong in coming to us at all. If you'll trust us enough to be a little patient, however, you'll understand."

"How patient?"

"In two days Danielle and I will be taking you to see someone very important in Europe. Everything will be explained to you then." Jenkins was unsure, but he desperately wanted to trust them, even if it did seem a bit odd.

"All right, I guess I can agree to that. All in all this whole experience has gone much better than I expected, so I guess I can work with a few uncertainties. In the meantime, there's got to be some way I can help out. If not, I'm sure there's more I can learn that'll make me a more effective asset." Danielle started clearing her throat, obviously getting impatient.

"It would seem that my wife has a suggestion." John leaned back with his drink, an indication for Danielle to take the floor.

"I think Matthew would of great assistance helping us sort through the data we stole. Jasmine still isn't sure which symbols mean what on those maps."

"That's right, you guys made off with tons of intel when you raided our outpost recently." Jenkins felt a brief pang of sorrow for the lives lost during that raid but quickly stifled it. "If you show me what you've got, I'm sure I can make sense of it for you." A thought suddenly occurred to him that brought an onslaught of panic in its wake.

"I should get one thing straight before I help out with anything though. I came to you so I could help end this conflict, not escalate it. I will *not* provide information that will make it easier for you to slaughter more of my men." Anger flashed in Danielle's eyes, and Jenkins wondered if maybe there was a better way he could have worded things.

"Why, you insolent little—" John cut her off with a glare.

"Sorry for that, Matthew, but you should take care how you word things when talking to my wife." It was an echo of Martin's earlier warning—a warning that Jenkins silently cursed himself for forgetting. "Perhaps we should make something clear as well." John's face grew hard, and now there was no mistaking him for a normal human.

"We have the ability to strip any piece of information that we wish from your mind. Things that you don't even know that you know, we can take from you. We can leave you an empty, brain-dead husk of a human if we wish, and there's nothing you can do about it." John paused a moment, mainly for dramatic effect, before continuing.

"I have no wish to do that to you. You came to us of your own free will, and we believe that your intentions are good. You deserve the opportunity to answer our questions on your own, and we plan to give it to you. Just don't push your luck.

"If it'll help put your mind at ease, know this. We have no intention of directing any attacks against SOG soldiers. Facilities yes, but we promised the same person that you're going to meet soon that we would avoid unnecessary bloodshed. You have our word on that."

"May I ask to whom you made this promise?" The confusion in Jenkins's voice was evident.

"Yes, but you won't get an answer. You'll meet him in two days. Basically, we agreed to follow his plan and see what happens. In the meantime, we're free to defend ourselves, but we won't hunt your people. The only exception we're making to that promise is in regard to werewolves.

"The hatred between vampires and werewolves is older than even we are. The only reason they even work with the SOG at all is because it makes it easier for them to kill vampires. Also, they are the only portions of the entire organization that can realistically threaten us. We will hunt down and destroy every werewolf that we can, at our own discretion. If you hold back on us on that subject, we *will* rip the information out of your mind." A few moments of silence went by before Jenkins realized John was waiting for him to officially agree to his terms.

Jenkins was not a fan of bloodshed in general, whether it be human or werewolf, but he did need to be realistic. The vampires were not going to sit back and allow themselves to be destroyed. They had every right to fight back. They had also proven, on more than one occasion, that they valued life. So could he find fault with their willingness to attack werewolves?

The only reason that the SOG employed them in the first place was because they stood no chance against vampires without them. In the eyes of the SOG leadership, werewolves were just the lesser of two evils. Once vampires were wiped out, they would probably simply turn on the werewolves. How hypocritical would it be to try to protect them just because he didn't want *anyone* to be hurt? This conflict would not be resolved overnight, no matter what he did.

It was also true that every werewolf posed a threat to every vampire. Jenkins knew that any werewolf who encountered a vampire would attack, even if the werewolf in question knew it stood no chance of surviving the fight. There was no gray area in this case.

"Okay, I do apologize for getting a little carried away earlier. I can't say that I'm thrilled at the prospect of any bloodshed, but I'm no fool either. So far, you've shown far more restraint than my people have, and I do understand why you don't want to hold back when it comes to the werewolves." He paused and thought for a few moments. "In the interests of working together peacefully, I'll agree to help with whatever you need."

"Good, because we intend to launch an assault against the werewolves in the area tomorrow night. We figure that if we eliminate the werewolves, the SOG forces in this area won't be able to threaten us until they receive large numbers of reinforcements. By then, we hope our main plan will take most of the pressure off. We just have no idea where to attack." He glanced over at his wife. "Danielle, take him to see Jasmine and get the symbols on those maps figured out. You two," he indicated Chris and Jose, "the first blood shipments should be in;

make sure everything's running smoothly. If anyone needs me, Sam and I will be on the roof working on his training." He was about to dismiss the meeting when Danielle spoke up.

"Hold on, I almost forgot something. I've been experimenting with something for a little while that I finally got to work." Danielle made sure she had everyone's attention. "We're all aware of how useless conventional melee weapons are against werewolves—and other vampires, for that matter." John already knew where she was going with this, but the others seemed very interested in what she would say next.

"I think I've found a way to enhance our regular weapons with magic, to make them more powerful. If it works, they'll be just as effective as our claws."

"That's great!"

"Really?!"

"Awesome!"

The others all started talking at once, excited about the prospect. No one had to tell them how much of an advantage it would be, to be able to fight a werewolf with an effective sword.

A strong, experienced vampire could overcome a werewolf's physical advantages, but it was very difficult. Their size alone gave werewolves an extra advantage in reach. Even with claws fully extended, a vampire had to get much closer to strike. It was the main reason most vampires would stick to ranged attacks, relying on magic or modern weapons, to bring down a werewolf.

The other difficulty was blood consumption. It wasn't easy for a vampire to use magic for long periods of time uninterrupted. Also, it should be taken into consideration that while using his claws to fight a werewolf, a vampire would also be using extra strength and speed. It was even worse if he had to do all of these things at once. To top it all off, it was rare to be attacked by a lone werewolf.

The ability to use a sword would solve many of these problems. The sword would give the vampire longer reach, making claws an option rather than a necessity. Speed and strength would still take their toll eventually, but every little bit helped a great deal when combating the wolves.

"There *is* one complication." Danielle had to raise her voice to be heard. "Since I've never done this before, we really have no way of knowing whether it's going to work. Until one of us strikes a werewolf with an enhanced blade tomorrow night, this is all just hoping for the best." The others sobered and nodded their understanding.

"Thanks, love. I'd almost forgotten about your experiments. Anyway, you all know what to do. It's a little after 2230." John had always found a twenty-four hour clock to be more efficient when addressing larger groups. "Let's meet back here at 0100. At that time, we'll go over battle plans and turn over all the weapons we want enchanted to Danielle. That should leave enough time before sunrise to finish preparing. Now, if no one has anything else to add, you're all dismissed."

* * *

JENKINS FOUND himself standing in some sort of office filled with computers and ghouls. It was just one example of the impressive organization these two vampires had put together. Sure, it was nothing compared to the SOG, but the SOG was a worldwide organization of hundreds of thousands. This was all the work of two individuals.

At the moment he was just trying to stay out of everyone's way. No one was really paying any attention to him, but that was hardly surprising. Danielle had escorted him to the room, and no one was likely to argue with her. They all seemed too busy to be bothered with random distractions anyway.

"Hey, Matt, wake up!" Jenkins nearly jumped out of his skin at the command. "Have a daydreaming problem, do we?" He must've been contemplating his surroundings a bit too deeply, as he hadn't even realized Danielle was speaking until she raised her voice.

Great, first I annoy her and then I ignore her. It's like I'm begging her to kill me. He was a bit concerned that Danielle wasn't pleased, but there seemed to be more humor in her voice than malice.

"Oh, sorry. It's just shocking to see the infrastructure that you two have set up for yourselves here. What were you saying?" She let out a very human-sounding sigh.

"Anyway, as I was saying, Matthew, this is Jasmine." Danielle indicated the ghoul standing next to her. "She's the one we placed in charge of making sense of all the data we stole from your outpost. You'll be assisting her with whatever she needs." He nodded, and Danielle turned to the ghoul.

"Jasmine, this is Archbishop Matthew Jenkins. He defected to us from the SOG and will be assisting us with whatever we need. Get those maps figured out first; we plan on striking tomorrow night. After that's finished, feel free to just use your own discretion."

"Understood, mistress." As Danielle turned to leave, Jenkins noticed that Jasmine was eyeing him very unhappily. He hoped that there wouldn't be problems working alongside the ghoul.

"Oh, Jasmine, one more thing." Danielle had stopped before leaving the room. "Don't kill or torture him. If you need me, call me." She left before Jasmine could reply verbally, but the ghoul still bowed in the direction she had gone.

Well, that was certainly nice of her, Jenkins thought to himself, *even if it was a bit extreme.* When Jasmine rose from her bow, however, Jenkins saw the look on her face, and his opinion quickly changed. *God help me, she looks disappointed.* Danielle's final warning no longer seemed quite so extreme. Jenkins was beginning to realize that the vampires were not the only ones he needed to worry about gaining acceptance with.

* * *

BY THE TIME Jenkins got back to the conference room, the vampires were all already there. He quickly took the last remaining empty chair, while the ghoul who was escorting him bowed and left. There was a pitcher of water on the table next to his chair, and he helped himself while John got the meeting started.

"Are you hungry?" At first Jenkins didn't realize John was addressing him.

"Yes, a little. I was too nervous to eat much yesterday."

"Do you have any special dietary requirements we need to take into consideration?" Jenkins shook his head.

"Other than not eating meat on Fridays, of course."

"I'll have some sandwiches brought up for you." He looked at a ghoul, who nodded his understanding, bowed, and left. "I'm sorry I didn't ask earlier. I'm not really used to being around people in my haven who require food. When we're all finished here, I'll have Marcus show you the kitchen and introduce you to the cooks." Jenkins was confused until he remembered Jasmine telling him that their haven was actually a very successful hotel.

"That would be great, thank you."

"You'll learn that we're very fair. Until you give us a reason to doubt you, all of your needs will be met. Now, on to business. What've you got for us?" John obviously didn't want to waste any more time.

"Well, I didn't get a chance to see too much of the intel you have. Despite your approval, Jasmine doesn't seem to trust me very much. I can't say that I blame her, and I'm sure she'll get over it. By the time I left for this meeting, I noticed that she was starting to relax around me." He paused to sip at his water.

"I'm not really surprised, either," Danielle cut in. "In retrospect, I should've stayed with you. Jasmine's one of my ghouls, as were the ones working in the blood bank. Ghouls made by the same vampire tend to share a bond with each other. Losing so many at once, especially when they were not even soldiers, has taken its toll on her.

"Not that it's any excuse. I'll talk to her later. We don't have time to deal with that sort of thing." John waited until he was sure Danielle had finished before continuing.

"You were able to decipher the maps though?"

"Oh yes, that was no problem. But I do understand why you were having difficulties with them. The symbols that we use on our maps aren't really a code, and most of the time they have nothing to do with what they represent. Whoever came up with them originally just picked them at random when making our map system. At least that's what we think."

"You don't know?"

"Of course not, because no one cares. Anyone with inside information or knowledge knows what they all mean, so what difference does it make? Making it more difficult to translate when it's stolen is just a positive by-product.

"Every time you talk to someone, do you use a special language to protect your privacy from eavesdroppers? No. Why? Because normally, unless the eavesdropper knows what you're talking about, your conversation is meaningless to them."

"Once you put it that way, it does make sense. But does this mean it's going to be a pain to translate every map we have?" The annoyance in John's voice was almost tangible.

"No, no, not at all. The symbols are universal." Jenkins actually chuckled. "Our own people would never be able to remember different sets of symbols for different maps. All I had to do was tell Jasmine what each symbol meant, and she was able to do the rest. Anytime you guys see an unfamiliar symbol on a new map, just ask and I'll tell you what it means."

John was about to point out that Jenkins had just said the symbols were universal when he realized what he had meant. Not every map was the same. The symbol for a hill might be the same on every map with a hill, but not every map would have one to see. He nodded for Jenkins to get on with his report.

"The location you're looking for is Oak Terrace. It's a housing development on the outskirts of town. That's where all the werewolves that operate in this area are supposed to stay." John thought about it for a moment.

"I think I know exactly where you're talking about, but an entire housing development?"

"It's not as bad as you're probably thinking. As you can imagine, werewolves are much harder to keep under control than regular soldiers. They refuse to be placed in barracks-type structures, so we put them in housing developments to give them more space."

"Got it, although I'm sure even a housing development feels like a closet to a werewolf. So now that we know where to strike, what about opposition?"

"That's a little more complicated." Before Jenkins could elaborate, there was a knock at the door. He waited while one of the ghouls answered it and let in another carrying a tray of food. As the tray was placed next to him, John indicated that he should just help himself.

Jenkins took a moment to examine what had been brought for him and was quite satisfied. There was a small pile of sandwiches, which appeared to be roast beef and turkey, and several small serving bowls of various condiments. They had even given him half a head of lettuce and two fresh tomatoes. Jenkins began to prepare his first sandwich as he returned to the current conversation.

"As I was saying, I'm not really sure how many werewolves you might be facing. As of two days ago, there were about two dozen left in the area, but we've been getting heavy reinforcements lately. There could be as many as three dozen by the time you attack. Minus the couple of wolves that will be out on patrol, you should plan on facing thirty of them at minimum." There were a few gasps from the younger vampires, but the ancients just nodded.

"What about soldiers?"

"Hmm? Soldiers?" Jenkins was busy chewing and wasn't sure if had heard properly.

"Yes, how many regular mortal soldiers will be there?"

"None." It was obvious that Jenkins was confused by the question, but the vampires could only guess as to the reason. "As a matter of fact," he continued, between bites, "if you do detect a single mortal in the development, call off your attack immediately." Technically speaking, werewolves were mortal, but they all knew what he meant.

"I thought we made it clear earlier that we didn't appreciate being instructed not to harm your precious soldiers." Danielle sounded a bit threatening, and Jenkins's confusion only deepened.

"What are you talking about? I'm only trying to help you all survive." His defense seemed to have an effect opposite what he had been hoping for.

"How dare you—" In the blink of an eye, John seemed to vanish from his chair and reappear in front of his wife, who was now standing in a very threatening pose.

"Sit down!" She obeyed without hesitation. "If you threaten him again, I swear I'll smack you." John sounded as if he were scolding a child. "As you said earlier, we don't have time to deal with this sort of thing."

Before she could respond, John had returned to his seat. "Matthew, please explain what you meant. Why should we be concerned about the presence of regular mortals at the development?"

"I'm sorry about the misunderstanding." Jenkins finally realized what Danielle thought he had been talking about. "I meant that no soldiers should be there at all. The werewolves don't like soldiers on their turf, and they have no real reason to be there. There are actually rules preventing SOG soldiers from entering werewolf territory, even if it's territory that the SOG provides for them.

"So if there are any soldiers there, it means one of two things. Either they know you're coming and have set a trap or something very abnormal is going on. Either way, you should call off the attack and try to figure things out first." Jenkins went back to eating while the others digested this new insight.

"I owe you an apology, Matthew. It was I who overreacted and spoke poorly this time."

"No hard feelings. We're getting along so well that I keep forgetting we started out on opposite sides. I keep expecting you to know what I'm referring to without having to explain it." She nodded, and Jenkins poured himself a fresh glass of water.

"Okay, so we know where to strike and roughly what we'll be facing." John got the meeting back on track, and Jenkins just sat back and listened. There wasn't much input he could offer in a tactical sense, so he just waited while the vampires planned out their attack.

About twenty minutes later, as he was admiring a particularly colorful painting, Jenkins heard them begin discussing their weapons. He remembered Danielle saying that she was going to try enchanting them. Jenkins perked up, since he found the whole thing wondrously fascinating.

"You all brought the weapons you wanted me to work on, right?" The other vampires nodded and began placing them next to Danielle's chair. "Good, but first I want to test the sword I enchanted for John." She reached behind her chair and pulled out the sword she had given him recently.

"Once I got Matthew working with Jasmine, I went to work on this. It should be finished, but it occurred to me that we can actually test it."

"I didn't think we had time to go hunting tonight."

"We don't, Chris, but that's not what I meant. If the blade will cut John or me, then it'll definitely work on anything. How about it, husband? Mind if I slice and dice you?" Jenkins noted how different she sounded when talking to her husband. He had believed vampires incapable of love, but that sure seemed a fallacy with these two.

"Why not? Just be careful. If it doesn't work, I don't want the blade to snap; and if it does, I don't want to lose an arm."

"Speaking of the blade," Jose interrupted, "that sword is beautiful. Did you just get it?"

"Yeah, there's a new weapons shop in town. The owner actually crafts many of the decorative swords he sells. Turns out he makes a fine battle-worthy blade as well. Just look at this craftsmanship." The test was forgotten for a few moments as Chris and Jose examined the sword. Jenkins had to admit that it was very detailed, the handle especially, and he could see why John wouldn't want it accidentally broken.

"All right, guys. Stand back so my wife can cut my arm off."

"Very funny, dear. Did you forget who was holding the sword?"

The other vampires got out of the way, and John held his arm out. Danielle very carefully drew the blade across his forearm and then put the weapon aside. Sure enough, a thin stream of blood was left in the blade's wake.

"It worked!" The others congratulated her while John healed himself.

"Was it supposed to burn?" John was absently rubbing the area where the wound had been a moment before.

"Oh, I forgot to mention that part," she answered, giving her husband a quick wink. "Something else I added in, but I wasn't sure if it would work or not. Since I wanted to test it on you first, I kept that enchantment mild. Now that we know it works, rest assured that it will be much worse when you use it on others."

"That's great, but is there time to do that to everyone's weapons before sunrise?"

"Should be, but I need to get started now, and I can't be bothered until I'm finished." John nodded, and she started gathering up the weapons that needed work.

"I guess we're done. You guys go do whatever you want. Just be back before sunrise. Sam, we've got more work to do." Chris and Jose left to go hunting, while Sam headed up to the roof. "If you feel up to it, Matthew, you can join Sam and me. As a spectator only, of course."

Jenkins was surprised at the offer.

"Why, I'd be delighted." A chance to watch one vampire training another? What a fascinating prospect. He eased himself out of his chair and followed John.

As he left the room, he passed Martin in the hallway. The ghoul gave him a thumbs-up, seeming genuinely happy that he was still alive. Jenkins waved back and smiled.

Things were going remarkably well. Not only was he still alive, he was more certain than ever that he had made the right decision. Except for a few physical differences, it was just like getting to know anyone. Even the way they bickered and joked, it was all perfectly normal. The SOG would have you believe that all vampires ran around foaming at the mouth while eating babies.

Jenkins vaguely wondered what else the Vatican was being less than honest about when it came to the SOG. These thoughts brought back to mind the trip to Europe John had mentioned. He was curious to find out who was important enough to these two ancient vampires to inspire their promises of nonviolence toward the SOG.

I wonder if they're taking me to meet some head vampire or something? If Jenkins remembered his suspicions in two days, he would certainly appreciate the irony.

Chapter 18

"I HAVE TO ADMIT, John, I don't like the way this smells." Chris always was the most cautious of the group.

"What's to like? It stinks like wolves here, but that's the whole point." The five vampires were concealed on a hill overlooking the housing development that the archbishop had said housed the werewolf force for the area.

Thirty ghouls were on standby about a quarter mile away, in case things didn't go as planned. John doubted that they would be needed, but Marcus insisted, and it was always better to err on the side of caution. It was always possible that there could be more werewolves than they could handle, or it could be a trap. In either case, the ghouls would move in to back them up.

"That's not really what I meant," Chris continued. "The smell I can understand, but I didn't expect it to be so quiet. We're either about to take them completely by surprise or about to walk into a trap." John couldn't fault his logic.

"You've got a point, but I'm inclined to think we've taken them by surprise. Besides, even if they did try to set a trap for us, I don't think it would work. They don't know there're five of us now, and they couldn't handle Danielle by herself." Chris nodded to concede the point. That had been a carefully-planned-out ambush, and Danielle had survived. There was no way they could set a successful trap for what they didn't know was coming.

"We've wasted enough time looking around. Let's get started." John watched with a note of satisfaction as the others took up the positions he had assigned to them earlier.

They all accepted John as their leader in battle, but you could never be sure where vampires were concerned. Once the blood started to spill, especially when werewolves were involved, most vampires tended to just follow their own instincts. It was the reason most vampires didn't survive their first encounter with a werewolf. It was also the reason John had been a bit concerned while they were planning this attack.

The element of surprise aside, they were in for a very tough fight and would have to fight smart if they wanted to win. Fortunately, this was not the first time they had fought together, although Sam hadn't been a vampire back then. They all had their specialties, and John had done his best to form their battle plan around them.

Chris and Jose, like John, preferred to fight hand to hand. The three of them might carry firearms, but they would rather rush into the fray wielding swords and claws. They would be getting the most benefit from the newly enchanted swords. It was decided that, after the initial attack, they would charge off in three different directions, causing as much damage and confusion as possible.

Danielle, on the other hand, preferred to keep her distance in combat. She might not be as strong or as fast as John, but she was far more adept at combining magic with her vampiric abilities. Fire, lightning, and mind control were her specialties in combat. Her job would be the most difficult of all.

Once the real fight started, she would be responsible for keeping track of the others and directing her attacks accordingly. It wouldn't do any good if she took down a werewolf that was attacking John, if

Chris was the one who needed help. She was also experimenting with a telepathic link that would allow the five of them to communicate with each other by thought alone. That would be the only possible way to communicate throughout the fight, as the battle would be moving far too fast for speech. Establishing the connection wouldn't be a problem; however, she was concerned that she wouldn't be able to maintain the link once the battle heated up. Fortunately, she wouldn't have to worry about her own defense, so it was the perfect time to test it out.

That's where Sam came in.

Since Sam hadn't yet mastered most of his new abilities, John decided to give him a job he would feel more comfortable with. Armed with a pair of combat shotguns loaded with phosphorous ammunition, he would be defending Danielle. This way he would be able to use his abilities to enhance the skills he already possessed. It was also one less thing that Danielle had to worry about, which would make things a little easier for her.

Tactically speaking, the five of them actually made for a very well-balanced team, and they all knew their roles backward and forward. Unfortunately, the first casualty in any engagement was always the battle plan. They all knew that after the first few minutes the battle would quickly degrade into a bloody free for all. If Danielle's telepathic link worked it would help, but there was still a good chance at least one of them wouldn't survive the night.

Is this telepathic thing working, or am I just thinking to myself? John decided a quick test was in order before they attacked.

I hear you, but it sounds odd.

Same here.

Yep.

I can hear everyone. You'll have to forgive how we all sound; I'm still learning this telepathy garbage. So long as we can tell each other apart, we should be fine. John tended to agree with his wife, but it was still strange.

All right, I just wanted to make sure this worked before we started. You think you'll be able to keep this up?

As long as Sam can keep me safe.

No problems there, ma'am.

Aww, so formal.

Shut up, Jose.

Make me, fledgling.

All of you shut up! I've got enough voices in my head as it is. John was starting to get a headache, and that bothered him. Vampires usually didn't get headaches, unless, of course, pieces of their head were missing.

Hey, John?

Yeah. He was pretty sure it was Chris talking.

I'm starting to think this was a bad idea. It's hard to focus with everyone else talking in my head. I can only imagine what it's like for Danielle. Maybe we should've practiced this earlier, before we were about to go into battle.

Chris was absolutely right, and John couldn't believe it had slipped his mind. They had all been so excited about the enhanced weapons that he had completely forgotten Danielle mentioning the telepathic link until they got here.

I agree, but we have to be able to communicate. Let's try this. Danielle, focus the link to only pass on directed thoughts. That way we'll only hear each other if we're actually trying to communicate. As for the rest of you, only use the link when calling for assistance.

The only reason we're even bothering with this is so Danielle will have a better idea where to focus her attacks if she can't see us. If we're able to assist each other, that's great, but it's mainly for Danielle's benefit. Feel free to ignore the link completely until you need it. Sound good? There was a string of agreements, and John nodded to himself.

Good. In that case we better get this show on the road before we're discovered. Last chance for arguments. As expected there were none. Even Jose was getting serious in preparation for the coming battle. *All right, Danielle, you ready?*

Always.

You take the left, and I'll start from the right.

Say the word.

Attack.

There had been a lot of debate earlier about the best way to initiate the attack. The element of surprise wouldn't last long against werewolves, so it would be important to capitalize on it as much as possible.

John decided the best approach would be for Danielle and him to just start blasting as many houses as they could. With this many werewolves in close proximity, it was impossible to tell which houses were occupied and which were empty, so they would just attack them at random. Hopefully they would get in at least a few good hits.

Simply setting fire to a house wouldn't be enough to kill a werewolf, but that wasn't really the intent. Danielle and John's objective was confusion. As the occupants stumbled out of the flaming wrecks, Jose and Chris would rush in for the kill. Once the wolves started trying to fight back, John would join Jose and Chris while Danielle kept the fireworks going. One way or another, they were all about to find out how good their planning really was.

John and Danielle split the darkness with their first fireballs at nearly the same time. In the time it took the blasts to reach their targets, both vampires had thrown out two more. The first line of houses in the development exploded in rapid succession. The vampires hadn't really expected the explosions, but they weren't about to complain.

John followed up his initial attack by spraying fire at random, trying to cause as much damage as possible. A few loud cracks and bright flashes resulted from Danielle calling down lightning in the middle of the development. It was impossible to tell if she was hitting anything, but it was making one hell of a racket.

Within seconds they could see bodies jumping out of windows and bursting through doors. Jose and Chris drew their swords and vanished into the flames. It seemed reckless since fire was even more dangerous to vampires than it was to wolves, but they were very skilled at what they did.

One entire side of the development was enveloped in flames when they heard the first howls. John could see wolves bursting out of their houses already transformed. He took a final look at his wife and rushed in the direction of the closest howling.

He had barely gone fifty feet before he instinctively leapt over the claws swiping at him. Spinning around in midair, John drew his sword and slashed in the direction of his attacker. Any remaining doubts he had about the enchanted swords quickly vanished as the werewolf's head spun off into the night.

A werewolf that had been rushing to attack John froze when he saw his comrade get beheaded by a regular blade. Capitalizing on the beast's shock and indecision, John punched a clawed hand through its chest and removed its heart.

John was about to reflexively toss the heart aside, but the smell of fresh blood reminded him of what he was holding. This was no ordinary mortal's heart. He decided that he could spare a moment, and without further consideration, he tore into the still warm heart.

Suddenly it felt as if fire were shooting through his veins. The wolf had been young, but compared to mortal blood, it was ambrosia. Even the small amount of blood inside the heart was enough to replenish what he had already used that night.

He decided it would be nice to get another heart for Danielle. With all the energy she was expending, the boost in strength would come in handy. Oddly enough, however, he couldn't find any more wolves that still had their hearts intact. Now that he thought about it, he hadn't really seen many wolves at all.

This is too easy.

Tell me about it. The voice startled him for a moment. His thought was intended as a personal one, but he must've been concentrating hard enough to activate the link. However, the response did intrigue him.

Elaborate.

I haven't found as many as we thought we should, and the few I did kill were all pups.

Don't mean to butt in, but I've noticed the same thing. I've only got one confirmed kill, and he barely even fought back.

All right, you two are on recon. Figure out what's going on. Danielle, ease up on the fire and lightning. You're mostly just wasting blood now anyway. All the fire and lightning, mixed with the fresh blood from the few kills they did make, was driving John's senses wild. He was hoping Jose and Chris would see something somewhere else in the development that would explain what was going on.

Not wanting to waste a free moment, John went back to the spot where he was last attacked and grabbed the two freshest werewolf bodies. Danielle and Sam were both carrying as much extra blood as they could manage, but they might as well enjoy the spoils of war. In seconds he was back with his wife and Sam, bodies in tow.

"Thought you guys could use a snack." Danielle needed no further prompting, and she immediately tore open the throat of the closest body. John invited Sam to share the other one with him, but he held up a finger in warning.

"This is different from mortal blood, Sam, and this is not the time for you to go into a blood frenzy on us. I'm only offering you a bite at all because I have a feeling we're all going to need every bit of help we can get." Sam had learned the hard way that John wasn't overstating the danger. If anything, he was probably playing it down a bit. Nevertheless, he was confident that he could handle it.

John made sure to keep an eye on him as he bit into the corpse. When his body started to convulse, John wasn't concerned. It was just a side effect of the infusion of so much intense power. It soon became clear that Sam wasn't going to lose control; however, it was a good thing he wouldn't have to worry about leaving this victim alive.

Aw, hell. It sounded like Chris, and he didn't sound happy.

What's wrong?

We found the rest of the werewolves, and it's not good. John had to hold back from demanding answers. Chris would pass along any information that he thought was important. *They're all gathering on the other side of the development. We just couldn't see them before because of all the fire in the way.*

Trap?

I don't think so. It just looks like there're a lot of elders trying to organize the rest and figure out what's going on. John realized he was nodding despite Chris's inability to see him. He had been afraid that there was a trap set for them, but it just sounded like there were enough elders to keep most of the younger pups from charging blindly into the fire. Unfortunately, being heavily outnumbered might be worse than falling into a trap.

How many?

Not sure. Jose went in closer to try and get a count.

Somewhere between a lot and a shitload.

This is no time for jokes. Sometimes Jose's annoying sense of humor tried even John's immense patience.

I didn't mean that as a joke. I seriously can't tell. All I can see is fur, fangs, and movement. The elders seem to be keeping them all under control, but they can't keep them still. I think I even see a few dazed ones that haven't transformed yet. What do you want us to do?

More frightening than Jose's report was how serious he sounded all the sudden. Retreat wasn't really a viable option anymore. Danielle and he would probably be able to escape, but there was no way the others were capable of outrunning so many wolves. They still had a good chance if they made good use of the situation. There was no way the wolves really knew what they were facing yet.

Get back here now. John had barely finished issuing the command before the two elders were back at his side, each toting a fresh corpse.

"I see you had the same idea we did," John said, indicating the werewolf bodies.

"No sense in letting them go to waste."

"Agreed, but eat quickly. We need to make our move before the wolves attack." Jose and Chris dropped their meals and started draining them.

"So how should we play this?" John turned to Danielle, who was licking the last of her werewolf's blood off her fingers. Sam had finished his as well, but he was just sitting next to the body with a euphoric expression on his face.

"We have to attack, hard and fast, before they finish getting organized. As soon as those two are ready we'll charge."

"What about the ghouls? We could definitely use the support."

"No." John had already considered that possibility. "If we call them in now, they'll only be slaughtered." Seeing that Danielle was ready to argue the point, he decided to meet her halfway. "Tell them to move in, but to not engage the wolves. Wait for them to get involved with us first. Hopefully it'll keep them from mounting a coordinated counterattack against our ghouls." She nodded and began relaying the new orders.

In the meantime the others had finished, and Jose was busy trying to get Sam's attention. He was actually trying to be nice about it but ended up just slapping him. Once Sam was standing up again, Jose nodded that they were ready.

"All set, Danielle?"

"Yeah, the ghouls should be in position in about ten minutes. They'll wait for my signal and then hit'em with everything they've got."

"Good. Stay behind us and pump as much fire and lightning as you can into them. Sam, are you going to be able to defend my wife?"

"Right now I feel like I can take them all single-handedly." They all smiled, feeling the same power flowing through their own bodies.

"All right, let's move." They instantly became five blurs, nearly invisible in the darkness. Even moving slow enough to prevent Sam from falling behind, they were in position in a matter of seconds.

Danielle didn't waste any time pouring vengeful fire and lightning into the werewolves' position. The advantage to having so many targets was that she didn't have to stop and aim. Every stream of fire and every bolt of lightning couldn't help but hit something, and it wasn't long before the entire mass of wolves was roaring in anger and pain.

The fire was too spread out to do much more than piss the wolves off; however, the lightning bolts were having far more effective results. Since lightning was much more difficult to call forth than fire, Danielle wasn't normally capable of such a sustained barrage. The werewolf blood was adding to her power, however, and she was taking advantage of every ounce.

Once she began concentrating her attacks toward the center of the werewolves' ranks, the other vampires took their cues and attacked. Jose and Chris rushed to either side, while John circled around to attack them from behind. Meanwhile, Sam readied his shotguns and just tried to stay a few steps ahead of Danielle.

At first the werewolves were too disorganized to successfully defend themselves. They tried to avoid the fire and lightning raining down on them, only to be cut down by the vampires harassing the edges of their ranks. The elders were trying to keep control, but their efforts were actually working against them. If they had just simply charged, they'd probably have been able to overwhelm the attacking vampires. Of course, they had no way of knowing that there were only five of them.

John was surprised at how well the attack was progressing. Unfortunately, there were more wolves than he could count, and many of them were the size of bulldozers. Once they finally got their act together, things could go bad very quickly. Ironically, it was as he was considering the possibility that the fight began to turn.

It began when Danielle's attacks became more directed than they had been before. She was beginning to pick targets more carefully, because she could no longer afford to sustain a general barrage. It was a lull that allowed several of the wolves to begin tracking the source of these attacks.

As John disemboweled his latest attacker, a unifying roar went up among the rest of the werewolves. They suddenly charged in all directions. Most ran toward Danielle, but enough went after the others to prevent them from coming to her assistance. The battle was finally joined.

* * *

SAM'S CONFIDENCE quickly waned when he saw the mass of wolves heading for his position. Confident or not, however, he still aimed his shotguns and let them have it. His enhanced strength was more than enough to hold the weapons steady as they emptied themselves.

Sixteen phosphorous rounds slammed into three different werewolves. All three went down, screaming in agony, but one managed to climb back to its feet and continue charging. While Sam worked quickly to reload, Danielle sent several streams of fire directly in front of them in an attempt to break up the charge.

Sam was able to empty his weapons and reload two more times before the wolves began getting dangerously close, and Danielle never let up with the fire. Unfortunately, it wasn't working. They had easily killed over a dozen wolves, at least two of which were elders, but it wouldn't save them from the twenty or more that were still coming.

There was time for Sam to put down one last target before he had to drop his guns, and draw his sword. In an instant Danielle was next to him, her own sword in hand. She looked far more confident than he felt. Of course, she'd been doing this for centuries.

"We can't stand here. We've got to split up and hit them on the move."

"Not a chance. John told me to protect you, and that's what I'm going to do."

"Now isn't that sweet." Before Sam could react, he felt himself being lifted up. He knew it would be useless to resist, so he just tried to not drop his sword as he was literally thrown one way while Danielle ran in another.

Sam reflexively rolled into a fighting stance, but there were no wolves around his new position. Danielle had been right, of course: now that they were going hand to hand, Sam could no longer protect her. It would end up being the other way around.

Everyone form up on Danielle. The silent command came from John, and Sam quietly cursed the crazy woman. Now he'd have to fight his way back to where he had already been. Getting annoyed at the situation wouldn't accomplish anything, however, so Sam turned his free hand into a set of claws and charged back into the fray.

Jose and Chris had managed to find one another and were now more or less fighting side by side. When they heard John's command, they began trying to locate everyone else. Despite having found each other, they had no idea where they were. Even young werewolves were pretty big animals and being nearly buried in them made it difficult to be sure of your surroundings.

The fight was also growing more difficult now that the shock of their enhanced weapons had worn off. Since most werewolves were all but immune to most conventional weapons, they didn't bother trying to avoid most attacks. That had allowed the vampires to cut many of them down before the wolves as a whole realized what was going on.

Now that the werewolves had figured out to avoid their swords as well as their claws, things were no longer as one-sided. Both Jose and Chris had taken small injuries already, and things didn't look like they were going to get much better any time soon. Linking up with the others was starting to sound like their only chance for survival.

"Hey, Chris! You know where we are?" Jose was guessing they were close enough to hear each other.

"Not a clue," Chris answered, pulling his sword out of a werewolf's chest. His instincts suddenly kicked in, and he rolled to the left, barely avoiding the claws of an elder werewolf. His counterstrike was swift, but the elder easily avoided the blade.

Chris didn't let up on his attacks, but the elder was faster. Every strike was evaded, and Chris tried more complicated attacks, using his claws as well as his blade. It wasn't having the desired effect, but at least he was keeping the elder on the defensive.

The werewolf leapt back once again to avoid Chris's blade, and at the same time, it struck out with its own claws. Chris managed to block the blow, but its force drove him to his knees. He was barely able to move, and other wolves were closing in on all sides.

Fortunately, even an elder werewolf could get distracted by bloodlust every now and then. Thoughts of a fresh kill overcame better judgment, and the wolf failed to notice the presence of the other vampire. Jose easily severed the elder's spine as it moved in for the kill. It wasn't technically dead, but it could do nothing more than flop around until it did finally die. Chris reacted by spinning around and gutting the younger wolf that had been blocking his escape.

"What took you so long?" Chris demanded, climbing back to his feet.

"You're welcome," Jose answered smartly, stepping over the elder's still-twitching corpse. They quickly stood back to back and tried to survey the situation. There were still a few wolves surrounding them, but the death of their elder had them spooked, and they were keeping their distance for the moment.

"We need to find the others, but I've got no clue which way to go." Jose had to agree. His senses were going completely haywire. He could barely even sense Chris standing right behind him. All he could sense was fire and werewolves.

"Maybe we should just pick a direction and charge." Standing still was making them both very uncomfortable. There were still a lot of elders out there, and they both preferred the idea of facing them alongside John and Danielle.

"Better than nothing I guess." As if on cue, a short burst of fire shot into the air from their left. Neither vampire had to say anything; they both knew it was a signal from one of the ancients and immediately ran in the indicated direction. They stayed side by side to better defend themselves, but they mostly avoided conflict. The sooner the five of them were in one spot, the sooner they could end this.

John had been getting worried about Chris and Jose. It had taken them so long to show up, he was beginning to think they hadn't made it. On a whim, he had sent a stream of fire into the air, thinking that maybe they had gotten turned around. Sure enough, both elders showed up seconds later looking relatively unharmed.

Now that all five of them were together, they were starting to coordinate their attacks. Danielle was able to go back to ranged attacks, since she had four bodyguards now. For the moment, the wolves were being kept at bay.

Seems everything's going quite well.

Don't hold your breath, Sam. The elders haven't really committed themselves to the fight yet.

Why not? You'd think they would try to overrun us. There was logic in that, but he was forgetting how intelligent elder werewolves were, even after they transformed.

They know that if they attack us now they might win, but most of them would die along with us. Chris cut in to explain things before John had a chance. *Right now they're just sending in cannon fodder in the hopes that we use up most of our blood fighting them off. That way they can move in when we're weakened. My guess is they'll charge the instant it looks like Danielle can no longer use fire and lightning against them.*

Oh, and you guys are all okay with that?

Not much we can do about it. Besides, our ghouls are ready to jump in when we need them. Don't worry about it, Sam. Just pay attention and don't let any of them by you. They could all sense Sam's agreement, as the mental chatter ceased and they turned their full attention to the battle once again.

No human eye could follow what was going on. Even a ghoul would find it difficult to follow the blurs that were werewolf and vampire, striking and counterstriking at each other. The only clues present that a mortal would understand were the fires and the bodies. Werewolves reverted back to their original human forms upon death, which made the whole development look like a human slaughterhouse.

John, Chris, and Jose were trying to keep the werewolves off guard by leaping back and forth, constantly switching targets and changing their styles of attacks. Their movements were perfectly coordinated from centuries of fighting together. Sam couldn't hope to keep up with them, so he went back to being Danielle's last line of defense.

The fighting went on like this for what seemed like an eternity, but in reality it was only a few minutes. The ground at the vampires' feet was soaked in blood, not all of it belonging to their enemies. Every successful strike by a werewolf required more blood to heal, blood that the elders were quickly running out of.

John knew the others couldn't last as long as he could. Sam was beginning to slow down, and Chris and Jose's skin was much paler than usual. Not even Danielle would be able to keep up her pace of attacks much longer.

Danielle, stop using your magic and go hand to hand, John silently ordered. *Save whatever you've got left for when the elders attack.* She didn't waste any energy replying, but soon joined them, sword at the ready.

By now there were very few younger werewolves left. Normally they would have scattered, but all of the blood and death in the air had driven them into a frenzy. In the end they practically threw themselves onto the vampires' blades.

The sudden silence was deafening, but the vampires didn't waste an instant. There were bodies and blood everywhere, and they only had a matter of seconds to try and replace what they had used. Even Sam instinctively leapt onto the closest body and began draining it.

Realizing that they could wait no longer, thirteen elder werewolves roared and charged. No words can truly describe what it is like to have a wave of elder werewolves bearing down on you. The closest comparison mortals might understand would be if an entire row of large storage sheds suddenly sprouted claws and fangs and began to chase them through the neighborhood. Even that didn't convey the sheer terror that werewolves instilled in everything around them. Experience was the only thing that helped when faced with such a sight.

John raised his dark blade as his friends reluctantly pulled themselves away from their meals and took up fighting positions beside him. The ground began to shake with the charge, and he hoped that they would be able to survive nearly three-to-one odds. Although, they did still have a few trump cards to play.

Get down! Danielle directed the mental command as strongly as she could, and the others dove for cover. She called upon the power of all the blood she had been holding back and thrust her hands at the oncoming wolves.

Bolts of lightning began firing directly from her fingertips as she howled in defiance at the charging wolves. Danielle concentrated her fire at the trio of elders at the head of the charge, and John watched in awe as all three were reduced to charred bones. He'd never seen her use lightning in such a fashion, but he wasn't going to complain.

The elders might have misjudged their abilities, but they were already committed to the charge. Besides, they realized that Danielle would have continued her strike had she had enough power to do so. Two to one was still very favorable odds if the vampires had to go hand to hand.

Once the lightning ceased, the vampires leapt back into their fighting positions and met the elders' charge. Jose and Chris attacked the same wolf, attempting to finish it off quickly. John and Danielle had the same idea, while Sam just tried to stay in one piece.

The one big advantage they all had was size and speed. As long as they didn't hold still, it would be difficult for the werewolves to strike them without hitting each other. It wasn't the best way to fight off werewolves, but it was the only one they could come up with.

John distracted a wolf with a few quick strikes while Danielle rushed from behind it and cut a chunk from its left leg. The elder yelped in pain and backed away, but it was by no means out of the fight for good.

Jose and Chris attempted a similar attack, but with Chris leaping onto the wolf's back to go for the kill. It was a risky maneuver, but it looked like they would pull it off. When Chris was about to drive his sword through the elder's neck, however, another wolf swatted him aside as if he were a simple pest. It wasn't a fatal blow, but it would take a lot of blood to repair his shattered ribcage.

Sam, for his part, was quick to avenge him. He had managed to retrieve and reload his shotguns, and he sent a full load of phosphorous rounds into the elder that attacked Chris. The beast didn't go down right away, but it was obvious that it had been fatally wounded. It would just take a few extra seconds for the phosphorous to finish melting through its hide. It was quite an impressive display coming from the weakest of their group. It also made him a target, and Sam quickly vanished into the night to escape the coming retaliation.

The vampires continued trying to coordinate their attacks as best as they could, but it wasn't easy. It took a lot more to kill an elder than a regular werewolf. Anything short of decapitation, severing their spines, or burning them to a crisp was almost wasted effort.

Technically, it took much more to kill an elder vampire than it did an elder werewolf, but that still didn't give them much of an advantage. It would be pretty easy for the werewolves to toss them around and crush them if they weren't careful—far from fatal for a powerful vampire, but not exactly something that would put the vampire in a strong position for a counterattack.

John knew that he should tell their ghouls to move in, but if he had a single weakness, it was his respect for his friends' lives. If their ghouls joined the fight, he knew that the werewolves wouldn't stand a chance. He also knew that there was an excellent chance a single elder werewolf could slaughter half of them. He refused to throw his ghouls away so easily. If they could reduce the werewolves' numbers a bit more, he would feel more comfortable calling the ghouls in to finish the rest. It didn't really occur to him that if he was destroyed in the meantime, all his ghouls would be doomed anyway.

He had to remind himself to stop thinking so much and focus on the fight at hand, as a werewolf's counterattack nearly took his head off. Danielle lunged at the wolf from the left, but the elder evaded her attack. It wasn't like her to react so slowly. The fight was definitely taking its toll.

As John moved to help Danielle bring the wolf down, Chris finally rejoined the fight. He wasn't pleased about being flung nearly fifty meters and having his chest smashed in, and he went after the closest wolf with renewed fury. As Chris split his new target down the middle, it started to look like they were gaining the upper hand. That is, until Jose misjudged a leaping strike and ended up letting a wolf catch his right leg in its jaws.

Jose howled in agony as the beast clamped down, severing the appendage. Despite the leg turning to ash nearly instantly, the wolf tasted enough blood to drive it into a frenzy. Sam rushed to get Jose a safe distance away, while Chris got between them and the wolf. John was about to lend a helping hand as well but was distracted by the sudden breakdown of their telepathic link. He wasn't sure exactly how he knew, but he did, and that could only mean one thing: his wife was in trouble.

Danielle had been trading blows with her own wolf when Jose had gotten injured, and his howl had distracted her. It was only for an instant, but that was all the wolf needed. The elder werewolf punched a clawed fist almost the size of a beach ball completely through her chest. It wasn't the fatal blow it would have been to a less powerful vampire, but it was damn close.

John saw the elder lifting his wife off the ground and rushed to her aide. He didn't get very far before being tackled by a pair of werewolves. A burst of speed allowed him to quickly decapitate one of them, but the other bore him to the ground. John knew that no matter how quickly he killed this wolf, he wouldn't get to Danielle in time.

* * *

DANIELLE'S MIND was so filled with pain that she could barely concentrate. She could feel herself being lifted off the ground. The beast's arm was the size of a small tree trunk, and she could feel it twisting around inside her chest. If the wolf had been any larger, its arm would have split her torso in half.

It was clear that the beast was toying with her. She couldn't even stop the bleeding, since the slightest movement of the wolf's arm would rip open any seal she could form around the opening. The physical presence of the wolf's arm in her chest was also making it impossible for her to regenerate her spine, so she had no control over her lower body.

Danielle might still be conscious, but she was a bloody mess. The only thing she had managed to do was hold on to her sword—not that it was going to do her any good, since she could barely move her arm. As the wolf brought her to its gaping maw, she could feel her eyes begin to close.

"*No!* I will *not* be killed by an *animal*!" Danielle shouted, fury overcoming weakness. She thrust her free hand at the elder's head, opened her eyes, and sent a stream of fire into the beast's face. The werewolf howled in agony and began shaking its arm violently in an attempt to either get rid of the vampire or rip it to pieces.

Despite being tossed about, Danielle kept blasting fire directly into the wolf's head. If not for her tough hide, her body would have already been jerked apart. The wolf's movements were successful in causing her to lose a dangerous amount of blood, however, so she quickly severed its arm.

Danielle had no idea where all of her energy was coming from, but she wasn't about to argue with it. The elder's arm was still stuck through her chest, but she didn't really care about that either. Anyway, she knew that removing the appendage now would only make things worse. Since the arm was no longer moving, the wound had completely sealed around it.

The elder's headless corpse had collapsed by now, but Danielle didn't seem to notice. She didn't even notice that, for the first time, her fire was beginning to burn her own hands. She merely adjusted her aim and began melting through the werewolf's chest. All she noticed was that killing things had never before filled her with such sheer pleasure.

* * *

JOHN FINALLY managed to ram his sword through his attacker's chest. The elder was a particularly powerful one, so he tore its throat out for good measure. Pulling his blade free, he was finally able to see what had happened to his wife, and he took an involuntary step back.

Danielle was hovering in midair, sending a stream of fire at what used to be a werewolf. He could see the arm going through her chest and was amazed that she could still muster that much fire—not to mention that he still didn't know how she was able to hover.

The sight confused more than concerned him, until he looked more closely. Upon closer inspection, John could see that her hand was smoldering, which was definitely not normal. Even when they first started learning how to use magic, they were never burned by their own fire.

It also wasn't like her to waste energy like she was doing now. The werewolf was barely more than charred flesh and bone, yet she wouldn't let up. It was as if she was in a frenzy, but that couldn't be the case. Her attack was too calm and directed for that to make sense.

"Danielle, that is enough!" Since their link had been broken, John tried shouting, but she didn't answer. He saw that the fire was beginning to consume her forearm, but she still didn't seem to notice. The idea of physically stopping her wasn't very appealing, but John saw no other way. Rushing to her position, he signaled for the ghouls to move in. It was time they ended this.

Once he was close enough, John sheathed his sword and leapt at his wife. At this point, brute force was the only way he could really think of to handle the situation. He was hoping that colliding with his wife would force her down and snap her out of whatever trance had come over her. The shock of the actual collision, however, caused Danielle to lose control over her fire, and they both went down in flames.

John, ignoring the flames that were charring his skin, grabbed Danielle and began rolling her back and forth. It didn't help that, not only was she continuing to spew fire, but she was shrieking like a banshee. He actually thought he saw small tongues of flame coming from her eyes.

Unsure of what else to do, John directed a hard slap to her left temple. Anyone listening would've actually heard Danielle's skull crack with the blow. It was nearly impossible to render a strong vampire unconscious without draining their blood first, but John knew what he was doing. He knew that any nonlethal injury wouldn't have any lasting effect, so cracking his wife's skull didn't really bother him.

Regardless of how much control Danielle did or did not have over her powers, she had to be conscious in order to maintain them. The instant her body went still the fire ceased, and John was quickly able to put out the lingering flames on both of them. He then threw her limp body over his shoulder and moved to the outskirts of the development, where the others were waiting.

"Master, are you all right?" John looked up to see Marcus running toward him. He gently set his wife, werewolf arm still through her chest, on the ground, and stood to meet his ghoul. John still had enough blood in his system that, by the time Marcus reached him, most of his burns and claw wounds had healed.

Marcus saw Danielle's broken form lying motionless on the ground, but he pretended not to. There would be time for questions later. For now, he had to make his report. Besides, he knew that as long as Danielle wasn't a pile of ash, she'd be fine.

In all the excitement of preventing Danielle from self-immolation, John hadn't realized that the battle was over. It only took a moment to go over the details, and he listened as his ghoul filled him in. It was nothing really unexpected or spectacular.

Once the remaining elder werewolves saw that the vampires were preoccupied with their own wounded, they all moved in for the kill. They were so distracted that the ghouls attacked completely unopposed. A hail of phosphorous shells, with a couple grenades added to the mix, easily put the wolves down. Only a single elder was able to turn and see where the new attack was coming from before the flesh was literally melted from its bones.

It was all very straightforward, and he dismissed the ghoul once he was satisfied that none of them had been hurt. Marcus bowed slightly and ran off to supervise the cleanup tasks that had to be done. John watched him go for a moment before seeing to his own tasks. It was time to assess the damage.

"Is everyone all right?" John asked the question as he turned around. The vampires had all gathered in a loose huddle to tend to their wounds and await his orders. John noticed that the werewolf's arm had been removed from Danielle's chest, and a bandage was in its place.

Since she was unconscious, Danielle wouldn't heal as quickly. Bandaging her chest would prevent unnecessary blood loss until the wound healed on its own, or until she regained consciousness and was able to control the process herself. It was a good idea, and John had to admit that he himself would never have thought of it. Mortal first aid had never really occurred to him as an effective method to assist in vampiric healing. The idea had to have been Sam's. He most likely did it by reflex, and John was silently grateful.

"We're fine. Danielle's the one unconscious," Jose growled in obvious pain.

"Oh, grow up!" Chris shot back. "You know as well as the rest of us that as long as she isn't ash, she'll be fine. You should be more concerned about that stump you've got for a leg." John took their bickering as a good sign. Sam was the one he was concerned about.

While Chris and Jose were bickering, Sam was just sitting next to Danielle's body, eyes fixed in an empty stare. John noticed that he hadn't even allowed his hands to revert back to normal. It was probably nothing, but he still wanted to make sure that Sam was okay. Unfortunately, they all heard something that quickly took priority over anything that could possibly be said. Sirens.

One thing a vampire never wanted to hear was sirens, and judging from the sudden silence all around him, the others heard them too. It was obvious enough what was necessary that there was no need for John to hand out orders to the others. Chris helped Jose, while Sam lifted Danielle, and the four were gone in seconds, heading back to the haven. The only thing that remained was for John to give Marcus his instructions. When he went to do so, however, he saw his ghoul already running around and shouting orders to everyone. Sam had obviously done a fine job of passing his responsibilities on to the new head ghoul.

There was still some time before the authorities would arrive on the scene. It might be too risky for the vampires to stay, but the ghouls could risk it in order to clean the area. Body parts needed to be thrown into the already raging fires, shell casings needed to be collected, and false evidence needed to be planted.

It wouldn't be possible to get everything perfect, but when a werewolf had a limb severed, that limb didn't always revert back to its human form. The implications of werewolf heads and arms showing up on the morning news would be disastrous to say the least. Unfortunately, nothing they did would be able to conceal the slaughter that had just taken place. If they were able to conceal all of the supernatural evidence, however, the authorities might settle on gang violence as a reason for the night's horrific events.

In any event, the ghouls were professionals. John had no doubt they would leave themselves plenty of time to disappear before the various emergency vehicles arrived. Getting themselves arrested would defeat the whole purpose of the cleanup operation they were performing.

John took one final look around. Satisfied that there was nothing left for him to do, he vanished into the night.

Chapter 19

JOHN COULD COUNT on one hand the number of times he and Danielle had stayed awake on a plane. The main reason they traveled during the day was to help ensure that they would remain unconscious for the duration of the trip. They hated to admit it, but flying made them both very nervous.

The ability to fly had been around for only a short time in comparison to their total life spans, and they were still getting used to the concept. Danielle was bothered mostly by the idea that she had no control over what was going on, and John didn't like not knowing if they could even survive a plane crash. Unfortunately, flying was the only way for them to cross long distances in a timely fashion.

As he looked out the window, however, John had to admit that no matter how nervous he was about being twenty-five thousand feet above ground, he loved the view. Most people enjoyed seeing the way things looked from far above, but they didn't know the half of it. With his vampiric sight, John was able to see everything far more clearly, including things that mortals could never see at all.

Their pilots had standing orders to fly through clouds whenever possible. A mortal might not be able to see through the white haze, but to a vampire it was breathtaking—at least to a vampire that had enough humanity left to be able to appreciate it. And with his wife resting, John needed something to take his mind off of the flight itself. Of course, it would have been easier had Jenkins not spent the entire trip thus far staring intently at him.

"You realize that you'll be just as useful to us if I decide to remove your eyes, yes?" Even a mortal could tell that he wasn't serious, and Jenkins just smiled.

"It's all right; I used to feel the same way about flying."

"Is it that obvious?" John asked, not turning away from the window.

"Well, I wouldn't call it obvious, except maybe to someone else who's gone through it." Jenkins waited for John to continue the conversation, but all he got in response was a grunt. "If you don't mind me asking," he wasn't quite ready to give up on conversation yet, "wouldn't you be more comfortable in the other room with your wife?"

"What makes you say that?"

"Nothing really." Jenkins shrugged. "It's just that you two seem inseparable most of the time."

"She is still weak from her injuries. It's better for her to rest and heal naturally than to waste blood forcing it." John was purposefully keeping his answers as short as possible, in an effort to hint that he wanted to be left alone.

"Really? I didn't think that vampires could sleep at night." Obviously Jenkins either didn't get it or just didn't care.

"We can sleep whenever we choose," John answered, finally giving in and turning to face the archbishop. "It's just that our bodies are practically useless during the day, so most vampires choose that time to sleep. It's not quite that simple, but that's the short version.

"Now, is there any particular reason why you're pestering me?" John asked, leaning back and arching an eyebrow.

"Well," Jenkins seemed to actually consider the question for a few moments, "if I had to narrow it down to only one specific reason, then I'd have to say fascination." The archbishop was clearly satisfied with his answer, and he waited to see what John would have to say about it.

"Okay, you win. Why am I so fascinating?" He only seemed to be half-serious, but it was enough for Jenkins.

"You're joking right?" Jenkins sounded genuinely surprised. "I've been taught that all vampires are demonic animals, and I've seen enough to believe that to be true. Then you two come along and change everything. In addition to being the two oldest vampires I've ever heard of, you don't seem that different from any regular married couple.

"Now, here I am on a plane with you, headed who knows where, and you wonder why I'm fascinated? Speaking of which, I don't suppose that there's a chance of you filling me in on our destination?" The first question may have been rhetorical, but the second one wasn't, and the archbishop gave an expectant look.

"Not a chance, but nice try," John sighed. "Even if I did tell you, you wouldn't completely believe it." Jenkins seemed disappointed but not surprised.

"Look," John started, rolling his eyes, "I do understand what you were saying about being fascinated, and I admit that in your position I would probably feel the same way." He was trying his best to sound sympathetic, but it wasn't something that he was used to doing naturally.

"There's still some time before we fly into the sun, and you've already noticed how much I enjoy flying, so I suppose answering any questions that you have about us will help to pass the time. Oh and if you're hungry, there are some sandwiches and drinks in the compartment above you."

Jenkins had seemed ready to speak, but now he got up and began rummaging around in the indicated refrigerated compartment.

"Is there a reason why the thermoses here are two different colors?" Given the very different dietary requirements between vampires, ghouls, and mortals, it seemed a pertinent question to ask.

"The silver thermoses are safe for you, but the red ones are ours. Speaking of which ..." John trailed off and held out a hand expectantly. Jenkins retrieved one of the red thermoses and tossed it to him with surprisingly little hesitation. "Thanks. I wasn't sure if you would comfortable with me feeding in your presence or not." Jenkins shrugged his shoulders as he sniffed at the contents of one of the "safe" thermoses.

"Well, it's no secret to me that you require blood for sustenance, and this is about the most subtle way you can go about drinking it. I admit that it does feel a bit odd watching you do it, but I think it's important for me to learn to get used to things like that." John nodded appreciatively and took a drink while the archbishop selected a pair of sandwiches.

"Okay then, Archbishop Jenkins, what would you like to know?" he asked as the archbishop finally made his choices and began to eat.

"To be honest, I want to know everything; however, there is one area in particular where I would like to start. We were always taught that vampires were demons, but the teachings did not get any more specific than that in regard to the origins of vampires. It was the only area in which we seemed to lack any real information, and that was something that always bothered me. Our teachings seemed to imply that vampires simply appeared one day as abominations sent by Satan to cause havoc throughout the world, and our lack of evidence was in reality proof of this, rather than a reason to question it.

"Since most vampires seem to act in a more or less demonic fashion, no one questioned the teachings, despite their lack of any factual basis. I realize that man is not meant to know all things, and that I should have faith, but then you two came along and changed everything." He paused briefly to wash down a mouthful of turkey and cheese. "I am uncertain of many things right now, but one thing I know for sure is that neither you nor your wife is a demon. That realization has me questioning all of our teachings about vampires once again. So my question to you is just what exactly are you, and where did your kind come from?"

"Well, that was officially the most long-winded way that you could have asked that question."

"So sue me for having a lot on my mind." After sharing a very brief chuckle, Jenkins noticed John's smile turn to a look of sorrow. "What's wrong?"

"Nothing serious, just that I knew you would eventually ask that question, and I don't know the answer. I know that we are vampires, but I don't know what that means anymore. Until recently, I was inclined to agree that we are demons. I am honest enough to admit that Danielle and I do not display any of the normal qualities one would expect from demons, but I didn't think that mattered. In other words, I have no idea what we are.

"Unfortunately, your second question is not going to have any better answer. I know how one vampire makes another, but I don't know how we originated as a species, if species is even the right word for us." John paused in his answer to drink, and Jenkins took the opportunity to press on.

"You and your wife both seem to be very educated and in possession of vast resources. Surely you have researched the matter over the years." Jenkins's tone betrayed that he was a bit disheartened but wasn't ready to give up just yet.

"Of course we have. Discovering our origins has been a goal for us ever since we decided to accept this *un*life. Unfortunately, this was no easy task, since there are no written records containing the kind of information that we seek—at least none that we know of anyway.

"We tried to work our way backward through time, starting with ourselves. We began to make a sort of 'vampire family tree,' starting with us at the bottom. Danielle and I date back to the eleventh century, and we have managed to trace vampires back nearly a millennium before that; however, I'm afraid that's where the trail runs cold.

"You see, we've been forced to do most of our research by word of mouth. We find out who sired a particular vampire and then find the sire, and then we find out who sired him, and so forth. It didn't really matter where we started, since theoretically all vampiric bloodlines will eventually lead back to wherever we came from."

"That seems sensible, but what happens when you can't find a particular vampire?"

"Normally we just start over somewhere else. All vampires are related to some extent, so the more we find and record, the easier it is to figure out where the missing pieces should be. The difficultly we are having is that we haven't been able to find a single vampire from before the time period we have gotten to in nearly three centuries. We're starting to think that there just aren't any ancient vampires left except for us, which is naturally going to make our search damn near impossible to complete."

"Maybe you made it to the end already, and that's why you can't find any more of them." Even as he said it, Jenkins knew how useless his comment was. If they had made it to the end of their search, not only would they have some answers, but they wouldn't have spent the last three centuries continuing to look. If John was annoyed at his trivial comment, he gave no sign of it.

"Unfortunately, the only thing we know for sure is that we aren't at the end, but rather the beginning. We have the names of several vampires from the period; we just can't find them. If it was the same name repeated over and over, we would have grounds to think we'd found the first one, but it looks like just another level on our tree. To make matters worse, written records from the time period are far too vague for us to use. Sorry, but for all of our research, we still don't know."

"Well, so much for my first two questions." Jenkins sighed.

"True, but I'm sure you have many more where they came from."

"Good point." Jenkins spent the next two hours letting loose a tidal wave of questions that John could barely keep up with. Most of the questions made sense, but a few of them seemed so random that John couldn't believe that Jenkins had really come up with them. The archbishop had actually asked John if he stretched as a matter of habit from when he was human, or if a vampire's muscles really need to be loosened up from time to time.

"Fifteen minutes until daylight, master." This announcement over the plane's intercom system succeeded in interrupting their conversation.

"Sorry, Archbishop," John held up a hand to stay any further questions, "but that's my cue to leave."

"I understand, but can you at least tell me how much longer it will be before we land?"

"I suppose there's no harm in telling you that much. It'll be about another four hours, which raises an interesting point. We'll be landing during the day, so things are going to have to be done very carefully. You will need to play the part of a supervisor while the ghouls do the necessary work.

"Once we land just go with the flow and act like you're in charge. We'll be in a hangar, which will cut down on prying eyes, but you can never be too careful. For obvious reasons, Danielle and I will need to stay on the plane until sunset, but the rest of you are free to mill about until then, so long as you don't break cover."

"What is our cover?"

"Very simple. We carry several crates filled with random nonsense for situations like this. The ghouls will unload the crates into the hangar, and it will be your job to keep an eye on the shipment until someone comes to pick it up. In essence, you just have to do what you are told and wait for sunset. The ghouls will brief you more thoroughly before we land."

"Okay, sounds like a plan."

"All right then, I'll see you tonight. If you need anything, just ask one of the ghouls." John got up and crossed over to the section of the plane that was sealed off from the sun. He was starting to open the door when he remembered one last thing. "Oh, and don't bother my pilot. He's under orders not to tell you where we're going. That goes for all of the ghouls."

The annoyed look on Jenkins's face merely confirmed that he had been planning to do exactly that.

"Very well. I suppose I can live with the occasional small surprise."

John's expression broke into one of mischievous glee. "Oh, this surprise is anything but small."

Jenkins's curiosity was practically burning a hole in his brain. "What's that supposed to mean?" As expected, John merely winked and, without answering, closed the door behind him.

Chapter 20

"I HAVE TO ADMIT that out of all the possible ways I saw this playing out, you two still managed to surprise me," Pope Stevens commented as he sipped his tea.

Since the vampires' return was expected, they had seen no need to sneak into the pope's room through the window again. Since that approach would have also been further complicated by the blindfolded mortal they had in tow, it was decided that they would simply knock. Danielle had been prepared to control whoever opened the door, but it turned out to not be necessary. The quiet servant had looked them both up and down and simply motioned for them to follow. No attention was given to Jenkins, who was blindly trying to maintain his footing while clutching John's shoulder. Only when they were all comfortably seated in the pope's private chambers did John allow Jenkins to remove his blindfold, and the result was more than worth the wait.

Jenkins clearly knew that he was in no danger, so he took his time examining his surroundings. Although the lighting was dim, he had been wearing the blindfold for quite some time, and his mortal eyes needed time to adjust. The quaint and humble surroundings seemed to intrigue the archbishop at first, and his initial reaction was rather disappointing. It wasn't until his gaze focused on the third individual in the room that his eyes widened in shock.

Pope Stevens was physically very unimposing, and he was not wearing anything that gave away his office. These two factors, along with the low lighting, would have made it difficult for the average man to recognize who was in the room; however, he *was* the pope, and Jenkins an archbishop with the SOG, so recognition was nearly immediate.

At first he assumed it was all a joke and he was dealing with some sort of look-alike, but that did not fit the situation. The ancients were acting as if this meeting was important, and the current situation very serious for all three of them. No, there was no time for that sort of foolishness, which meant ... he really was in a room with Pope Stevens. Jenkins's jaw hit the floor.

The archbishop was not the only surprised individual in the room. Stevens noticed not only the lack of restraints on the prisoner but the laid back attitudes of both vampires. He supposed it was possible the ancients were using mind control to keep him in line, but the situation did not feel that way to him. It almost seemed as if they were all on equal footing, which was strange, but he was clearly not as surprised at the situation as the prisoner was, and it was a bit difficult to keep from smiling at his shocked reaction.

"We do try to keep things interesting, don't we, love?" Danielle agreed with her husband's statement by stifling an all too girlish giggle.

"Indeed." The ancients spent a moment enjoying the humans' reactions before responding to the pope's comment.

"Honestly though," John decided to get down to business, "we were a bit surprised ourselves at how things went down. Long story short, this man is Archbishop Jenkins. He is the highest ranking SOG official on the American East Coast, and he surrendered himself to us willingly. Apparently, he's decided that he's on the wrong side. Over the last couple of days, he has assisted us enough to earn our trust, even had we not been able to read his mind, so hopefully this will help things progress more smoothly."

"I see. Well, this is definitely an interesting development, but it should help to—" The pope was interrupted by Jenkins grabbing his hand. The archbishop had recovered from his surprise enough to show proper respect. He had fallen to his knees and was trying to kiss the pope's ring while at the same time mumbling something about honor and worthiness. In retrospect it should have been expected, and the pope gave him a moment before coughing lightly to get his attention.

"Please be seated and try to relax. I suppose this means you were not expecting to see me tonight, were you, my son?"

"That would be an accurate assumption, Your Excellency. Not that I am not deeply honored to meet you, but I find this situation extremely confusing."

Jenkins had managed to relax enough to realize how strange the situation was. Why were the vampires and the pope in the same room and acting so friendly toward one another? The pope was of course a nonviolent individual, and the vampires had proven themselves to be full of surprises, but they were supposed to be mortal enemies. Not only were they not at each other's throats, but there was absolutely no tension in the room, and this, to Jenkins's mind, was possibly the oddest thing about the entire situation.

"As confused as you are right now, it is good that you are here by choice. I have a story to tell you, my son, which will come as a tremendous shock. All you need remember is that I speak the truth, and it is a truth you need to know if we are going to be able to make plans for the future." While the pope spent the next hour explaining the true history of the SOG, the vampires carefully studied Jenkins's reactions.

Clearly what Jenkins had been taught matched up well with the true origins of his organization, and he seemed a little confused at being forced to sit through the schoolboy-style lecture. This changed very abruptly the instant Pope Stevens mentioned the SOG being ordered disbanded centuries ago, and how he had no knowledge of the organization prior to the vampires' previous visit. Despite his eyes widening at learning this, his reaction was not nearly as severe as anyone in the room had expected.

"You don't seem very surprised by this news, my son."

"To be honest, Excellency, I am feeling many things right now, but surprise is no longer one of them. There is a reason why I am here by choice." Jenkins closed his eyes briefly and took a deep breath. "I have been trained to interpret God's will and taught to act on it, no matter what He desires. Lately I have been plagued with feelings that I was no longer acting according to His will. John and Danielle here have acted contrary to everything I had been taught to expect from vampires.

"In the past I had always been so sure of myself and the SOG's mission, but that began to change as our conflict with these two escalated. It began to seem more and more as if we were the ones in the wrong. The only thing that we could say in our defense was that they were demons so anything goes, but they never acted particularly demonic. The whole situation just didn't feel right to me, and I was quite uneasy about it. My unease eventually led me to believe I was perhaps on the wrong side.

"Listening to your story merely proves I was right. Rather than surprise, I feel tremendous relief that I made the right decision in defecting. I was never truly certain until this moment. Unfortunately, I also feel a large amount of disgrace for the years of service I did provide for the organization. I take solace in this new knowledge, that the corruption I feared had gripped the entire Church is limited to the organization itself." The pope leaned back and contemplated what had been said thus far.

"You should not feel disgrace for your past actions, my son. Your job was to administer to men's souls, and it is a job I am sure you did quite well. All of you were being led astray, but it was not you doing the leading. In fact, you followed your faith and your heart and left nearly the instant you realized things were not as they seemed, and now you wish to be part of the solution. You should be proud of yourself, not disgraced." Jenkins looked down at his teacup and silently nodded.

"Of course, you do realize that you were not brought here simply for us to tell you the truth behind the SOG."

Again Jenkins nodded. "No doubt you have some questions for me."

"Precisely, we need to figure out a way to shut down what may very well be the most powerful organization in the world. The first thing we need to know is who is pulling the strings. You have confirmed what we already suspected, and that is that the common soldiers and line-level priests do not know the truth. What, may I ask, is your exact position within the SOG?"

"I was the archbishop in command of the American East Coast."

"What exactly does that mean, as far as the SOG's hierarchy is concerned?"

"Well, basically the SOG uses priests and high priests as line-level supervisors. They stick to a single post and essentially stay in place. Next there are bishops, who take responsibility for several posts in the same geographical area. The same is true for archbishops, the difference being mainly in the size or importance of the area in question. Some archbishops are responsible for entire countries, or multiple countries, because those countries themselves are small or otherwise easy to monitor.

"The eastern coast of America may not seem overly large; however, because of its strategic importance and industrial might, it is a very prestigious posting for someone as young as I am."

"Yet you were unaware of the truth behind the organization?"

"Yes."

"Do you believe this to be true of the other archbishops?"

"That is difficult to say. There are about one hundred and sixty archbishops throughout the organization, but we are technically all equal in rank. I have met many throughout the years, and I would say they are as in the dark as I am about the situation. However, there are archbishops who have been in very prestigious posts for decades. It is possible they have either figured out the truth or been told by their superiors. Every organization seems to have that particular clique of people who know the truth regardless of rank." The vampires were listening intently to the conversation but had agreed earlier that is was best to let the pope handle the questioning.

"Okay, so even if a few of them are aware of the truth, we can assume that it is not information given out freely upon attaining the rank of archbishop. So what is the next level? To whom do you report?"

"I report to Cardinal McWilliams. He shares responsibility for North America with one other cardinal. Cardinals are placed more based on the number of archbishops, about twenty archbishops will report to the same cardinal, than geographical location. There are only eighteen cardinals throughout the organization, versus the one hundred sixty people sharing my title, and they are the highest-ranking individuals in the SOG. I was always told that the individual cardinals simply report the necessary information on their sectors to the Vatican."

"Okay, so we know that does not happen, but it doesn't mean that they aren't reporting to someone. That person, or group of people, could even be close to us here. Or, those cardinals could be running things." Pope Stevens stopped when he noticed Jenkins shaking his head.

"No, it is possible that the cardinals know what is going on, but there has to be someone above them. Their positions change too often for them to be the top rung on the ladder. You can't take an archbishop who doesn't know the truth and promote him to one of the people holding the reins. It would never work. One mouthy person who didn't like what he was told would blow the whole thing."

"I disagree." John jumped into the conversation for the first time. "You already said there were archbishops holding down long-term posts. These individuals could be being groomed to eventually take the place of a cardinal. It would be an easy enough task to make the archbishop disappear if it looked as if he would not go along with it. The cardinals don't all have to be in on it either. A small handful of them could know the truth and be pulling the strings for the rest."

"He has a point." Danielle couldn't stay silent any longer. "This organization is supposed to be the best-kept secret of the Catholic Church. That is a huge advantage to anyone pulling the strings from behind the scenes. No one questions the lack of visible leadership or recognition from above, because it is all a big secret. Most of the cardinals may be just as ignorant as the archbishops. You only need a very small number of people who know the truth. Let's face it, when you're dealing with religious fanatics, they don't ask a lot of questions. No offense, guys."

"None taken," the pope and archbishop echoed each other.

"There's only one very big problem with this theory," Danielle went on. "Ignorant or not, the cardinals are the highest rank in the SOG, but they are supposed to report to someone. So if they are ignorant, who are they reporting to? We may be talking about fanatics, but that does not mean they are stupid. Keeping a secret this big for this long implies that these are all very intelligent people."

"I think I know where you're going with this, love. Simple solution says there is a mole somewhere in the Vatican—a single individual who isn't necessarily anyone important within the SOG but is on the other end of the line every time an ignorant leader calls or otherwise contacts the Vatican to report. This person could easily shuffle the information to the cardinals who were pulling the strings. The ignorant cardinals would never know that their counterparts in other areas of the world were really the ones to whom they were reporting." The pope did not appear pleased at the implications the vampires were beginning to hint at, but he made no effort to argue the point.

"Unfortunately, I have to admit that your logic is sound. I may have never considered the possibility because it means someone close to me is involved with this. Thankfully you two are not blinded by such bias. Of course, this is all just speculation. We are essentially making it up as we go along, and we could be terribly far from the truth."

"Agreed, but I think it is a good start. The more people who know a secret, the more likely it is for that secret to be let out. It therefore seems very unlikely that all of the cardinals in the organization know the whole truth. So either a few of them do or none of them do. Either way we have several of them who are reporting to the Vatican on a regular basis. If there wasn't someone here for them report to, I think eventually one of them would start to notice that something wasn't right." There was a series of nods around the room, although not all of them pleasant.

"Okay, point taken." The pope held his hand up to regain everyone's attention. "It sounds to me like we have two main objectives at the moment. We need to topple the organization as a whole, and we need to discover who the mole at the Vatican is, if such a mole exists. I agree to the logic of your arguments, but, despite my age, I also know a thing or two about technology. It would not be impossible to use technology to gain the same results." John and Danielle were both forced to concede that point.

"Whether or not the mole exists, the more important challenge here is how to deal with the SOG as a whole. I think we can all agree that it isn't plausible for the two of you to rampage around the globe toppling the SOG completely on your own. No doubt you have considerable resources, but attrition would eventually wear you down. This conflict is either all or nothing. If you fail to topple the entire organization, then it doesn't matter how much damage you cause. We need to find another way."

"You won't get any argument from us on that point. We do have help beyond our own resources, but nothing on the scale that would be necessary to combat an organization of this size. We also have no desire to go into hiding, which causes a bit of a problem for us. We're open to suggestions on how we should proceed from this point.

"With all the information we now possess, maybe we can work our way from the top down. If we eliminate all these cardinals you mentioned, that may be akin to cutting the head off the snake. However, we did promise to keep the violence down to a minimum. There is also the problem of continuing to maintain the cover we now have. Our actions have already been extremely risky, and we've been lucky to keep conventional law enforcement off our backs."

Jenkins held up a finger. "Well, to be honest, you've had some help on that front. Remember that the SOG has just as much invested at remaining a secret as you do. They've been doing their best to cover their tracks and help cover the indications of battle. Between your efforts and theirs, your cover is safe for now. If your secret gets out, it becomes more likely that theirs will. The SOG wants to expose your secrets for themselves, not for the general public."

"I guess that makes sense, but you'll understand if we're not inclined to send them any thank-you cards any time soon." The weak attempt at humor brought a few grins from around the room.

Pope Stevens spoke next. "Well, not to bore anyone by getting back to business, but I have an idea. I've been studying the information you gave me on your first visit, and I must say that you really hit a treasure trove. I can't believe you were able to access that much information just by raiding a single outpost."

"I wouldn't say it was easy, but we were surprised as well by how linked all of their systems were. Maybe they never considered it possible for someone to not only break in but be able to hack as deeply and as quickly as we did. As powerful as we are, we barely made it out. You were saying something about having an idea?"

"Yes, right. Well, as you no doubt already know, part of the information you got away with was essentially a map of SOG facilities throughout the entire world, complete with what cover is being used at each facility. There's no list of members, although most of the important individuals are indicated in other files. Now, I have thought about how to handle this situation for some time now. All of my prayers and meditation has told me that I have the right idea, although all three of you are going to think I'm insane."

"Get to the point, old man." Jenkins was appalled at Danielle's statement, but it was clear she meant it playfully. He had to keep in mind that these two didn't see Pope Stevens in the way that he did.

"Patience is a virtue, my child, but as you wish. I am going to schedule a press conference in which I will go public with all the information you gave me." A pin drop would have sounded like an explosion in the silence that followed.

"Your right," John pointed out, "you are insane. Why don't all four of us just schedule an appearance on *Jerry Springer*? They could march in a few of the head cardinals, and we'll throw chairs at them." The pope let him rant for another moment before signaling for silence.

"I am serious." Even without any mind reading abilities, it was clear from his expression that he was in fact serious. "Hear me out. We already established that direct confrontation will not work, and that secrecy is the only thing that has allowed the SOG to operate for this long. Once I remove that secrecy, the organization will crumble. Think about it. I will report all locations, along with the names and locations of as many of the organization's leadership as we know, so that local authorities can deal with them.

"There will always be some vestige of them in existence somewhere, but their power and size will be gone. They will no longer be able to carry out large-scale operations, so the organization will no longer pose a threat to you. Most of their leadership will be gone, and I believe the vast majority of the members will simply turn themselves in. We've already discussed that nearly the entire SOG believes they are doing the right thing. When I publicly denounce them, I feel the organization's cohesiveness will crumble."

"I admit that there is logic to what you are saying, but it just seems so, I don't know, easy I guess. How can the solution be as simple as that?" Danielle and John seemed unconvinced but at least willing to consider the merits of the idea. "What do you think?"

"Huh?" It took Jenkins a moment to realize the vampires were addressing him. "Actually, I think it's a brilliant plan, and by far the best option we have at the moment." John smiled at Jenkins's casual use of "we" rather than "you."

"Well of course he's going to agree. Anything that the pope says is going to be gospel for him," Danielle interjected. "No pun or offense intended."

"None taken, but seriously, that's not it; I truly think this is the best possible plan for us. Secrecy is the SOG's greatest asset, so by removing that, we will be dealing them a serious blow. Remember also that I've been a member of the SOG for over a decade now. I have an idea how this will work in the minds of most of the organization. A few weeks ago I was convinced you were both demons and I was doing God's work, and I changed my mind before even learning the truth. I can only imagine how many members will immediately quit upon learning what is really going on. There will definitely be mass confusion, but confusion is easy to deal with, and since most of the leaders don't know the truth either, they will be unprepared to deal with the inevitable questions, which will in turn lend even more weight to the real truth.

"If we're successful in capturing most of the high-level leaders, we may very easily eliminate the SOG as a threat altogether. The only thing I'm a bit concerned about is the werewolves. The werewolves don't care about the truth of the SOG, one way or the other; they just want to hunt and kill vampires. The SOG has been identifying and organizing werewolves for centuries, and currently there are literally thousands of werewolves on the SOG's total roster, all of—"

"Holy shit!" Danielle shocked the room with her sudden outburst. "Oh, excuse me, but that number sort of surprised me. Those are just the werewolves the SOG knows about? How could there be so many?"

"Oh, well not to get too off topic, but there's a simple explanation for that. The SOG has been hunting down and destroying vampires for centuries, but we don't bother werewolves. The only real predator a werewolf has to worry about is a vampire. We're weeding out their opponents, so they are able to flourish more easily than would otherwise be possible.

"Anyway," Jenkins paused briefly to ensure he had satisfied Danielle's curiosity, "my point was that the werewolves won't care about the truth one way or another, so we'll still have to worry about them." Pope Stevens seemed thoughtful while considering Jenkins's point.

After a brief pause, John spoke next. "Actually, I don't think that'll be much of a problem. Secrecy is just as important to a werewolf as it is to the SOG. The pope may not be discussing werewolves and vampires to the press, but drawing attention to the SOG as a whole makes that organization a very dangerous cover for them. Since they have no loyalty to the SOG anyway, I'm betting on them deserting the organization immediately after its existence is made public.

"Honestly, now that I've had a moment to think about it, this may work. One way or another, the werewolves will almost definitely abandon the SOG, and they are the only true threat to us. Whatever the humans do is almost irrelevant at that point, and we can expect continued resistance simply because all these humans do know of our existence and may continue to hunt us on their own. All in all though, I can't think of any better ideas."

"Okay, so I'll take that as agreement to my plan. Unfortunately, I'm not certain of the best way to expose the mole, if any, here at the Vatican."

"That's actually the easiest part," Danielle chimed in. "Just let us interview all the cardinals you apprehend. We can easily glean the necessary information from their minds. We just need to catch at least one who knows the truth in order to find out what is really going on. The only problem will be in the apprehension."

"That shouldn't pose too much of a problem. Most of the necessary information can be found in the material you retrieved. Rest assured that all our assets will be in place before the official press conference so that we can make the apprehensions immediately."

"Wow, it sounds to me like we may just have a plan here. When did you plan on scheduling this press conference?"

"Very soon. I am going to make this my top priority, so it should only take a few days to set everything up. So if we're all agreed, I'm an old man and need to get to sleep." The vampires nodded at the intended dismissal and began to rise to leave. "Oh wait, I almost forgot." The pope took a small package from behind his chair and handed it to Jenkins.

"That's a cell phone. I want you to keep it close at hand. I don't understand how, but, for security purposes, it has been programmed to send and receive calls to and from only one number. This way you all won't have to keep making this trip if anything important develops."

"Good idea, thanks," John nodded, impressed at his forethought.

"Um, Excellency, there is one more thing I would like to ask you." It was Jenkins who spoke.

"Yes, my son?"

"Well, what is to become of me? I realize my time with the SOG has been misguided, but in my heart I still wish to serve the Lord." Stevens seemed sympathetic and unsurprised at the question. He had not expected the vampires to find a willing prisoner, but from the moment Jenkins had explained his situation, the pope had known this question would come.

"My son, I was merely waiting for you to ask. As you already know, your title of archbishop cannot be recognized by the Church;

however, you were already an ordained priest when the SOG took you into their fold. You also followed your heart and, in the end, made the right decision on your own, even though at the time you felt as if you were betraying the Church as a whole. There is no reason why you could not return to us as the priest you were. In fact, I wish all priests were as dedicated to the Lord as you have proven yourself to be. I would even go so far as to say that you may be a bishop again someday."

"Why, thank you, Excellency," Jenkins muttered after a moment of disbelief. It was hard to not feel a small amount of sorrow over the loss of his rank, as he had always been very proud. On the other hand, the knowledge that he would not only not be thrown out of the Church but even allowed to remain in the priesthood was more than he could have hoped for, and he bowed deeply.

"What's more, I even have your first posting." That statement drew the attention of all three of his guests, and Stevens grinned. "These two," the pope waved in John and Danielle's direction, "are confused. They think they are demons without souls and with no hope of redemption. They both want desperately to be saved but are too afraid to ask. Someone needs to show them that they were never lost. I can think of no one better suited to the task, and what a perfect penance for your years of service to the SOG."

"Yes, Excellency, I agree. It will be my personal mission." The glint in his eye betrayed just how pleased Jenkins was at the choice of assignment he had been given. The vampires remained silent but offered curt nods as they headed for the door. John paused before leaving to allow Jenkins, who had bent to kiss the pope's ring, to catch up.

"Good luck to us all then?" John offered.

"We don't need luck, my son. God is on our side." The vampires seemed unconvinced but offered no further comment as they all left and began the journey home.

Chapter 21

"YOU SENT FOR ME, Initiate?" Andrews was displeased to have been summoned by an initiate, but the messenger had been quite insistent. In the days since the archbishop's capture, morale had been at an all-time low, and the massive defeat suffered by their werewolves had everyone a little jumpy. He was willing to forgive the minor protocol infraction, provided there was a good reason behind it.

"Yes, sir." The initiate jumped to attention only to be immediately waved back to his seat. "I apologize for insisting that you come to me, sir, but some of this information you need to see as I make my report. Sir, we found it." Andrews cocked an eyebrow, as it appeared that the initiate's head was about to explode with excitement.

"Okay, found what?" The initiate seemed confused by Andrews's lack of interest until it finally occurred to him that no one knew what he was looking for except the senior initiate who had given him the assignment.

"Oh right, sir, sorry. My excitement seems to be getting the best of me." Andrews had to refrain from visibly shaking his head. The poor kid was even out of breath, but from what?

"Okay," he glanced at the initiate's name badge, "Leonard. Why don't you slow down, take a deep breath, and tell me what you found? Your discovery is meaningless if you pass out before revealing it."

"Good point, sir." Leo closed his eyes briefly and got his breathing under control. "The haven, sir. I know where it is." Andrews's expression grew serious, and he had to fight to control his own breathing.

"The demons' haven?"

"Yes, sir," Leo answered with an ear-to-ear smile.

"I don't understand. I thought the odds of us finding the haven were astronomical?" The excitement was beginning to set in, and Andrews was beginning to feel a bit light-headed.

"Sir, please have a seat and I'll show you what I found. I admit that I had a bit of trouble standing up myself after realizing what I had uncovered." Andrews took the offered chair as the initiate sat down and rotated the monitor to face him.

"Okay, even though it was determined that we weren't going to find the demons' haven through simple investigation, we had to try. A few of us were assigned to the task, much in the same way that a team was assigned to find their blood bank. Well, needless to say, we were not having much luck. Once we successfully found the blood bank, however, I began to make a few assumptions to narrow my search parameters." Leo paused and waited for Andrews to indicate that he was still following him.

"Well, I got my first idea from us actually. A few days ago, during evening services, I was praying for the souls lost in the attack on Lori's Bed and Breakfast when I came to a realization. We were using Lori's as not only an outpost but also a barracks facility. However, Lori's was actually a public establishment, a real bed-and-breakfast.

"I remembered that the demons were not alone. They had to have a significant number of minions. When you consider how many of their minions we have encountered in battle, and as employees at their former blood bank, who knows how many they have? Well, where do you think they are all staying? What if they were doing the same thing as we are and using a public place as a secret barracks? If this is true, then nothing as small as Lori's would be able to accommodate them all. Logically I considered a hotel as the natural upgrade, at least as far as capacity goes."

Andrews raised a finger to interrupt Leo's explanation. "I understand, but why would they necessarily need to have a public place? There's plenty of space underground, or even abandoned buildings they could use that would be very secretive."

"Honestly, sir, we did think of that but agreed that it's too cliché. We know that these two demons are very old and have access to significant resources; do you really think they would settle for living underground? Personally, if I were immortal, I would want to be comfortable at the very least. If I were rich, I may not necessarily flaunt it, but I would want my standard of living to reflect it. SOG research actually shows that most of the havens we've discovered are what you'd expect to find if searching for the home of a mortal. The more 'normal' a vampire's surroundings the harder they are to find."

"Okay, I'll concede that point, and if we're going to follow that train of logic, it is sensible that we'd be looking for a hotel, but there's got to be hundreds of them in the city."

"True, but I applied some of the same filters that we used when looking for the blood bank. Unfortunately, it didn't work out very well. I knew the hotel would have to be privately owned, so that narrowed it down a lot, but nothing else seemed to help. Studying hotel employees didn't yield the same success as with the blood bank, so I had to make another assumption to narrow things down more.

"I decided that the vampires would make good use of their resources, and whatever hotel they were using would have to be five-star. The problem now was proving it, and there weren't many options for me to choose. We do know what they look like, however, so I took a long shot and have been searching through photos of all the hotel owners in the city."

"Seriously?" Andrews hadn't intended to interrupt Leo, but his last comment had surprised him. "Photographs are one of the easiest pieces of evidence to fake, and what if they simply never had a photo on file? They clearly aren't stupid." Realizing he had cut Leo off, Andrews forced himself to stop. "Sorry, please continue."

"Well, I did say I knew it was a long shot. I didn't have any other ideas to work with, and no one really expected any success anyway, so I just went with it. No one could be as surprised as I was when the idea actually worked. They made a single mistake nearly twenty years ago. Check this out." Leo opened the file he had been compiling earlier and showed it to Andrews.

It was a small newspaper article from 1992 about the change in ownership for Pinnacle Towers, one of the most exclusive hotels in the city. The article had a small photograph of a young couple shaking hands with the original owner. The brief article merely mentioned how the original owner had grown too old for the responsibility and had sold the property to the young couple, Mr. and Mrs. Johnson. The photograph was not the best quality, but there was no mistaking the pair of vampires that they had all gotten to know so well.

"That's amazing. I'm looking right at the proof, and I still can't believe that they would have made such an obvious error. Are we sure this is legit?"

"That is a valid concern, sir. You may find it interesting to know that I have found records of the hotel's ownership being changed six more times since the date of this article. The current owner is a man named Reginald Garrison. There are even photographs to go along with all the changes. By all appearances, the vampires are no longer there."

"What do you make of it?"

"Well, there are only two options. Either they're there or they aren't. It's possible that this whole thing is a fake to throw off anyone who might be researching their location, but I don't think so. I think the original photo and article are real, and all the follow-up changes are the fakes to make people think they have moved on. We obviously know that they are still in the area, so it seems logical that they are still there.

"Also, this was not easy to find. This article didn't just fall into my lap the way you'd expect fake evidence to. I only found it because I insisted on searching records from the date of each hotel's construction until the present, and I searched *every* record. It's always possible that we're being duped, but if you want my professional opinion, this is the real thing." Leo leaned back in his chair and let Andrews finish studying the picture and his notes.

"I'm inclined to agree with you, and this truly is an amazing find. You're to be commended, Leo. You may have just saved us all."

"Thank you, sir, but I must admit that there was a decent amount of luck involved, especially with all the assumptions I had to make." Andrews actually smiled in response, something he hadn't done in days.

"What you call luck, I call divine guidance. If I'm going to be honest, I'd have to say that I was beginning to lose faith. Our losses recently, and the capture of the archbishop, have gotten me to start questioning the path we should take. I have a feeling that a higher power had a hand in guiding you to what you needed to see." Leo began to nod his agreement.

"Yes, sir. We needed a miracle, and here it is." Standing up, Andrews patted the initiate on the shoulder.

"Keep up the excellent work, Leo; I have a briefing to assemble."

* * *

"WELL, GENTLEMEN, you now know everything I do." Andrews's statement was met by a series of nods and very sober expressions. "Questions?"

After listening to Initiate Leonard's report, Templar Commander Andrews had immediately gathered up his senior staff for a briefing to decide how to proceed. The meeting only consisted of six other individuals, which was a grim reminder of how serious their losses had been recently. Five line-level commanders and a single administrative aide were the only ones in attendance, and it hadn't taken long for him to bring everyone up to speed.

"I assume we are going to attack as soon as possible, but how do we verify the information without tipping our hand?"

"Excellent question. Any ideas? Remember that I've only had this information for about ten minutes longer than all of you. I haven't had a chance to work out little details like that yet."

"I have an idea, sir."

"Okay, Jack, let's hear it."

"Well, it is safe to assume that the staff of any location the vampires are using will almost entirely be made up of ghouls."

"You mean like the blood bank."

"Yes, exactly. Ghouls are more difficult to sense than vampires, but not in close proximity. Let's pick a couple of Templars and get them a room for a night or two. They can wander the hotel, meet some of the staff, ask a few touristy-type questions here and there, and all while arousing zero suspicion.

"They'll be able to tell if the staff are normal mortals or not. It isn't suspicious for people to wander around a hotel where they staying, especially if they do so as a couple." Everyone seemed to like the idea, including Andrews.

"I like it. It wouldn't hurt to get a rough layout of the building either."

"Um, excuse me sir?" Andrews hadn't been finished, but his aide wouldn't have interrupted him had it not been important.

"What is it, Megan?"

"If you're concerned about the layout, keep in mind this is a public building. We can get detailed blueprints whenever you want."

"Okay, good point. We can assume that the vampires would be using either the top or the bottom few levels as their haven. Our infiltrators may be able to verify that information, but their first priority is stealth. Sounds like a plan to me. Now we need to be ready to move immediately. Let's assume the information pans out. How do we proceed?"

"And what kind of security can we expect?"

"Obviously every ghoul they have left is going to be there."

"True, but that number is much lower now than it was."

"Right, but what about static defenses and metal detectors?"

Andrews let his people discuss the variables for a few moments. This was the most important part of the briefing. He would listen to his people brainstorm, all the while gleaning the most important information from each statement. His final decision would end up being a product of everyone's input.

"Okay, here's the plan." The discussion had reached the point of a debate, so Andrews knew it was time to cut everyone off in order to have the final say. "I like the idea of sending in a pair of spies. Megan, see to those arrangements and get them a room starting tomorrow."

"Yes, sir."

"Now, assuming they confirm our suspicions, we need to be ready to move the following morning. We won't need the same subtlety we used at the blood bank. I want every soldier we have, and I want them armed as heavily as possible.

“We know that there will be visible security; all hotels of this caliber have that in some form or another. We also know that, in this case, it is just for show, and our concern will be the employees themselves. Static defenses likely won’t be a concern, as I doubt they would have such a thing. Even a metal detector would be considered a ‘turnoff’ by the types of people who stay in a place like this one. I do admit that concealed x-rays and metal detectors are possible.

“Even if they get suspicious over the number of people coming that morning, and they definitely will, they may be slow to act. Remember that secrecy is paramount to them; the ghouls will not break cover in front of witnesses until they are sure what is going on. This will allow us to take them by surprise and make the first several moves before meeting any true resistance.

“We want to minimize the risk to civilians, so no one will actually attack anyone unless attacked first. However, once combat is initiated, the one and only priority is to get to the objective and destroy the vampires. Everyone will also need to keep an eye out for the archbishop. Most likely he’ll be locked in a room or cell somewhere, and we can search for him after the battle, but we don’t want to take any chances of having him getting caught in the crossfire.

“Unfortunately, we can’t make a lot of detailed plans until we get blueprints and have an idea of where in the building to direct our assault. That’ll be your jobs. Come up with as many variations as you can, and as we get more info, you can settle on a plan of attack.” His commanders all nodded understanding. “This is basically a search-and-destroy mission. We’ll move in slow and get as close as we can to the objective, but once the balloon goes up, we’ll unleash the wrath of heaven on these demons.” An outside observer could have easily mistaken the group of mortals sitting around the table for a pack of wolves. “Well then, you all have your orders. It ends here.”

Chapter 22

"WHAT DO YOU say, love, been an interesting couple of days?" Danielle asked as she came out of the shower.

"I'd have to agree with you on that note. I like having a plan, but I don't like just sitting around waiting for things to happen."

"That's true, but there isn't a whole lot left for us to do since we already destroyed all the werewolves in the area. Pope Stevens's press conference is going to be in a few days, and there simply isn't any point in us doing anything until then. It's not like the SOG mortals are any true threat to us." Danielle sat on the bed next to John as she finished wrapping a towel around her hair.

"Yeah, but we shouldn't underestimate them. I don't like the idea of having known enemies literally in our backyard and essentially ignoring them. We know that they're planning and plotting away, and we're just assuming that they aren't a real threat. Let's hope that Stevens's address will come before the SOG *can* become a bigger threat to us." Danielle's expression made it clear that she wanted him to drop the subject. "So, where is everyone anyway?"

"Chris and Jose said something about catching a movie, and Sam is out hunting somewhere." John was about to protest Sam going out alone, but she cut him off. "Stop being so protective; he proved himself during the battle. He'll either control himself or he won't."

"Yeah, you have a point. I'm sure he'll be fine. There is something I have been meaning to ask you though. With all the excitement, it keeps slipping my mind, but it's been bothering me more and more lately." He sat up as she motioned for him to continue. "Your abilities seem to be different lately. I don't know if they're getting stronger or just changing, but there has been a definite difference."

"What do you mean?" she asked guardedly.

"Well, I've noticed a couple things lately. Hovering for one seems to be new. I know that you have occasionally managed to glide or even fly over short distances given the right conditions, but I have never seen you simply hover in midair before. Your magical attacks seem to have also increased in intensity. Your fire attacks especially have me concerned, since I've never known you to be burned by your own fire, and the attacks themselves seem less controlled. You can't tell me you haven't noticed any difference."

"No, I have," she sighed. "I've been thinking a lot about it actually, but I don't have any real answers. I think I'm just getting stronger. I mean we're both very old, and we don't know any other vampires older than we are, so we don't really know what to expect. We do know that for vampires, older means stronger, but we just have no true gauge to go by.

"As for the control, that's most likely just due to the situation. It's been ages since we've faced a true threat like this one, and I guess I'm out of practice. Plus they did almost succeed in killing me once already. In these last few battles, I haven't been holding back. It's seems reasonable that I would have difficulty controlling my powers under those circumstances, especially since they seem to be getting stronger at the same time.

"I can't be sure, but I do believe the simplest solution is most often the correct one. On the other hand, if I'm right, you should be having similar difficulties." She raised an eyebrow inviting a response.

"I hadn't really thought about it until now, but you may be right." John replayed a few moments from the recent battles in his mind before adding to his reply. "You always were better at mental control and magic than I was, but my physical abilities do seem to be stronger. I have noticed that certain things seem to be easier than they were. My speed and strength seem to have increased, and I was able to shrug off damage a bit easier than I remembered being able to.

"I didn't really put much thought into it until now. Like you said, it's been a long time since we have fought without holding back, and there was plenty of anger to fuel my strength. I don't seem to be having any control issues, but I have noticed more difficulty in keeping my thirst at bay when we fight, so maybe that's it. Hearing your theory makes me wonder though.

"If you're right, it's a good thing. I don't think either of us is ever going to complain about getting stronger. We just need to be careful and maybe spend a bit more time practicing our control. We don't need you burning yourself to a crisp and me running through the city in a frenzy, now do we?" She smirked at the thought.

"If I agree with you, can we stop talking about it?"

"Excuse me?"

"Well, it sounds like we've decided it's a positive change that just needs to be handled carefully, so I think it's time to move on to more pressing matters."

"Like?"

"Like the fact that we have the place to ourselves until morning, yet for some stupid reason your pants are still on." Danielle's leer was unmistakable as she dimmed the light.

"Ah, you always were the brains of the operation."

"Shut up."

* * *

"WAKE UP!" Marcus couldn't understand how John and Danielle could still be asleep with the sound of gunfire and explosions so close. To his knowledge, no one had tried to forcibly awaken them before, but it didn't look like there was any other choice, so he rushed to their bedside.

"Please, master, get up!" He tried shaking John gently but began using more force when he didn't get a response.

"Sir, is that really a good idea?"

"No choice. Get Jenkins in here. We have to move now! You, get some water to toss on them or something." More ghouls burst into the room, some of them noticeably injured and covered in blood.

"They're close. Sam made it out on the other side of the building, and everyone else is trying to slow them down."

"Chris and Jose?"

"Chris is with Sam, but he's badly hurt. Jose is ash." Marcus had always liked Jose, but there was no time to mourn now.

"How long?"

"Minutes, maybe less. We're holding them for now, but there are a lot, and they don't seem to care about civilian casualties this time. What's the problem with them?"

"I can't wake them, and the water didn't work. We'll have to try to carry them out."

"Okay, should we—" The ghoul's head exploded in midsentence as the first SOG soldiers appeared in the hall. Return fire scattered them, but not before another ghoul took a round in the arm. Jenkins and the ghoul sent to fetch him appeared from the side room, and Marcus knew they had to move now.

"We are officially out of time. You two, pick them up and go. Jenkins, follow them. The rest of you, take defensive positions.

* * *

"HMM?" JOHN MUMBLED incoherently as he started to roll over. There seemed to be a lot of commotion, but it was probably just his imagination, as his dreams had a tendency to be rather vivid. But why did he feel wet? There was also a vague sense that there were others in the room and they were in danger. The noise was also deafening, but none of it was real.

"Master! Get up!" The ghouls had noticed his movement, and they rushed to continue jostling him awake.

"Wha ... what's going on?" Being forced awake was very disorienting, but John trusted his ghouls and was content to allow them to take the lead. A glance at Danielle showed her in a similar state of bewilderment, and a series of loud noises only added to his growing confusion.

"They found us. Master, please, we need to move." The ghouls were hustling them through rooms as quickly as possible, but the vampires were not making things easy for them.

"Huh, who? Where are you taking us?" They were moving, but too slowly, and Marcus knew the soldiers would soon catch up to them. At least Jenkins was following quietly and trying to just stay out of the way.

"We're being attacked. I'm begging you both to please just trust me and move."

"Attacked?" Danielle stopped walking. "That's stupid; I'm going back to bed." Marcus couldn't believe what he was seeing. Both ancients were acting like stupid children. How could they be ignoring their senses so strongly? They couldn't fight the SOG and their masters at the same time.

Jenkins had joined in the effort to drag John and Danielle away, but it was doomed to failure. The vampires were just looking at them like the ghouls had all lost their minds. While Marcus was trying to figure out what to do, a trio of grenades rolled into the room.

One of the ghouls immediately leapt into action and successfully kicked two of the grenades back toward the attacking soldiers. The third grenade, however, had been cooking for too long and detonated. The ghoul was able to absorb most of the explosion by sacrificing himself, but a few pieces of shrapnel got by and bit into John's unprotected chest. The wound was minor, but it succeeded in snapping him out of his stupor.

"What are we waiting for, people? Let's move." Danielle was not as lucid as John, but she was responding to his voice, so Marcus was more than happy to let his master take the lead. They were now easily able to outpace the mortals pursuing them, but it wasn't long before they ran out of running room.

"Now what?" There were plenty of secret doors hidden around their palatial suite, but the escape elevator was on the other side of the floor. Fighting was out of the question, since the vampires' abilities were clearly limited. They needed a plan and fast.

"Easy, Danielle and I are going to wrap ourselves in blankets and jump out the window. The fall won't injure us too badly, and there's a manhole cover less than a block down the street. Our exposure will be limited, so we'll survive, but it's going to hurt like hell.

"You guys use the roof access in the next room. Take the fire escape down and meet us underground." John had been wrapping himself and Danielle up while he was issuing his instructions, and without waiting for acknowledgment, both of them jumped through the window.

Marcus waited just long enough to see the vampires hit the ground and begin moving again before leading everyone into the next room. The instant the vampires jumped, they were out of danger. Marcus's new job was safeguarding as many ghouls as possible while they made their escape.

* * *

"NO, DO NOT pursue them. Interview witnesses and tear that place apart for evidence, but under no circumstances are you to pursue them. Is that understood?"

"Yes, sir."

Andrews put down the radio with mixed feelings. By all definitions, the assault had been a total victory. The vampires' haven was destroyed, along with most of their ghouls. It also looked as if they had found a significant amount of computer equipment, which could be holding all sorts of treasures waiting to be uncovered. Most importantly, while they had taken losses, those losses had been very light.

It had been too much to hope that they would be able to destroy the vampires outright. The ghouls had thrown everything they could into protecting their masters. At no point did they truly fight back. It was an escape attempt from the beginning, and there was confirmation of the destruction of at least one of the demons.

A normal military commander may have ordered a pursuit, since the enemy had clearly been routed. However, you never follow a vampire underground, much less two ancients, unless it's part of a grander scheme. Andrews had no wish to spoil the victory by ordering his men to their deaths.

With the destruction of their blood bank and now their haven, the ancients' infrastructure had been removed. Reestablishing themselves would be very difficult, since their ghouls had been so drastically reduced in number. It was over.

The smartest thing the demons could do now would be to run, but they had their pictures. More importantly, once their computers had been hacked, they would have access to all the personal information they would ever need to track them down. No matter where they went or what they did, they would be detected and eventually hunted down. Plastic surgery did not work on a vampire, so it was only a matter of time. Given the choice, Andrews would have preferred to run his fingers through the ash that was all that was left of the ancients, but victory was victory.

Chapter 23

"IF THIS DOESN'T work, we're going to be in trouble."

"Love, we're in trouble no matter what. We already knew this wouldn't be a blanket solution. Whatever's left of the SOG after this is still going to be after us, and we have a lot of rebuilding to do." It had been nearly a week since the disaster at their haven, and everyone was gathered in one of the safe houses they had established throughout the city. Barely more than an abandoned warehouse with electricity, it was never intended for long-term use, and they needed to decide on their next move.

It had been difficult to focus on the future having lost so much so recently, but John was getting the feeling that they were running out of time. Chris had been brooding since the attack, and most of the ghouls were blaming themselves. Jenkins had originally tried comforting them; however, after one nearly fatal incident, he realized that he represented too convenient a target for their anger. To top everything off, Sam was under the impression that the whole situation was his fault. He was convinced that had he still been a ghoul, and thus awake and running things, the assault could have been prevented.

The one positive note was that there had been enough warning for the ghouls to wipe all the hard drives in the building. By the time the SOG took control of the hotel, all the computers in it were as useless as paperweights. Their accounts and the majority of their resources were as untouchable as ever; it was just their infrastructure that would need to be rebuilt.

It had been difficult to not succumb to the urge to seek revenge that had permeated the group since the attack, but John had been the voice of reason. Their focus had to be survival, not just simple revenge. The cycle of attack and counterattack was not solving any of their problems, and the SOG had officially gained the upper hand. Their only logical choice was to run and concentrate on starting over somewhere else.

They had been arguing over possible locations when they heard about a special press conference from the Vatican on the evening news. Apparently Pope Stevens had set a date, and they agreed to not make any final decisions until after his speech. None of them expected their problems to instantly disappear, but they were all curious as to how aggressive he would be.

* * *

"I'M SURPRISED that Chris and Sam aren't here to see this."

"They may just be uncomfortable being around me." Jenkins wouldn't miss this press conference for anything, but he was careful to stay close to the ancients in case either Chris or Sam decided he was still on the wrong side again.

"I guess it doesn't matter either way, so long as they aren't doing anything stupid." Danielle grimaced at the thought and pointed at the small television in the room. John checked the time and grabbed the remote control to turn on the evening news, which had already started.

"—speculation about the subject of tonight's press conference. What do you think, Jim?"

"Honestly, Susan, I couldn't even begin to guess. The announcement came literally out of the blue two days ago, and ever since, the air has been full of theories. Unfortunately, in light of the Church's rocky waters these past few years, most speculation tends to be leaning in the negative direction."

"An unfortunate truth indeed, Jim. For those of you just joining us, about two days ago we received an announcement from Pope Stevens concerning a very important live press conference scheduled to begin any moment now. We weren't given any details, and since the original announcement, the Vatican has been very tight-lipped about the whole affair. The only thing that we do know is that no live audience was allowed in the conference, with the notable exception of news personnel. While this may be common for many occasions, it is a rarity for the pope to refuse public attendance."

"Their expressions are priceless." In spite of everything, it was hard not to find humor in the situation. It was rare to be reporting a story live that you knew nothing about, and that cluelessness was evident in the interplay between the two news anchors. Also evident was the excitement of hearing something new at the same time as everyone else. It was a refreshing difference from the regurgitated nonsense that they were stuck reporting most nights, and the vampires were easily able to pick up on their subtle nuances.

"Yeah, Stevens really didn't give them anything but a date and time. This is going to be worth it if for no other reason than to see their expressions when it is all over." John grunted in reply, while Jenkins remained silent.

"Well, Susan, it looks like we're about to get our answers."

"That's right, Jim. We're going now to Kevin, who's reporting live from the Vatican. Kevin, are you there?" The scene switched from that of the anchors to a medium-sized conference room crammed full of news reporters and camera equipment.

"Yes, Susan, I'm here," Kevin replied after a brief delay. "I hope that the listeners at home can hear me okay. We've been asked to stay as quiet as possible, and we're doing our best to comply." It explained why the reporter was talking barely above a whisper, but his voice still came through loud and clear.

"Well, you're coming through loud and clear on our end. Can you describe the scene and atmosphere for us? It looks a bit crowded in there."

"That it is, Susan. As you already know, this conference is closed to the public. There are a few other major news networks here, but that's it. Each of us was allowed to bring only a single cameraman, so there are only about a dozen of us in the room, but this room clearly wasn't designed for camera equipment.

"The atmosphere here can best be described as one of tense excitement. No one here has any idea what we are about to hear, but it must be important. This level of—Wait, Pope Stevens is about to enter the room. I need to take my seat while Jason readjusts the cameras to give you guys the best view."

With that, the reporter nodded once to the camera and joined the other reporters in occupying one of the few chairs that had been set before the room's podium. They didn't have to wait long, as Stevens entered the room with a single aide a brief moment later.

"Wow, is it me, or does he look a lot younger on camera?"

"That's his aide, stupid."

"Very funny." Despite Danielle's verbal jab, John did have point. Fully garbed in his impressive array of vestments, Stevens did look much younger than the frail old man with whom they had twice met. Of course a lot of that was probably a combination of makeup and the iron resolve that was clearly emanating from his eyes.

"Good evening, and may God bless all of you," Stevens began upon reaching the podium and clearing his throat. "I realize that many of you have been wondering what this conference is all about, and I regret the secrecy that was necessary in its planning." John found this to be a humorous beginning, since in reality he was guessing that most people couldn't care less what the pope had to say and had already changed the channel. It was simply a truth of the times.

In the long run it didn't matter. When the pope was finished, the shock factor of what he had to say would be enough to ensure that everyone would want to hear it. The conference would surely be rebroadcast several times, and millions would be searching for it online within twenty-four hours. He was also completely certain that every single member of the SOG was now riveted to his seat, waiting to hear what the pope had to say, and that was all that really mattered.

"There is no easy way for me to explain what it is I invited you all to hear, so I will simply tell you the truth as I know it now. I assure you that everything I have to say is true and has been verified by Church officials, although I am certain that the majority of you will not believe any it. However, given the information in question, the Church cannot and will not remain silent." John had to admit that he was finding it difficult to turn away from Stevens's steely gaze.

"It is no secret that many centuries ago we lived in a much more superstitious time. Instead of using science to explain the unexplainable, people turned to solutions of a more supernatural nature. Even Mother Church was not immune to this way of thinking and was responsible for Her share of atrocities." John and Danielle were both visibly shocked by how Stevens was phrasing his speech, and Jenkins nearly fell out of his chair. Church officials were usually not very open about the mistakes of the past, yet here the pope was throwing out words like "atrocity."

"He's proving his honesty," Jenkins mumbled.

"Huh?"

He turned to face the ancients and shook his head slightly. "The Church is always being criticized for not revealing, or admitting, the entire truth. This is especially true when something pops up that could make us look bad. It's gotten to the point where people don't seem to take anything we say seriously anymore. By being so openly honest about the Church's own negative history, I think he hopes to prove that he's serious about telling the truth. Seriously, I don't think I've ever heard anyone from the Church use the word 'atrocity' to describe anything the Church has ever done in any official capacity, and I'm betting that statement alone bought him at least a few thousand pairs of ears." Jenkins's theory seemed sensible, but now was not the time to discuss it. They listened as Pope Stevens spent a few moments outlining some of the more well-known atrocities for which the Church had been responsible.

The speech as a whole followed along the lines they had all expected. Stevens described the original SOG and the circumstances under which the organization was disbanded, and then he went on to the matter of its members continuing to act in secret. Kevin wasn't even attempting to throw in any soft-spoken commentary, and his expression was one of shocked disbelief. Even if the reporter was useless, the cameraman was at least occasionally panning around the room, so the viewers at home could see the matching expressions from everyone else in the room.

The pope went on describing the evidence he had been given access to, and he issued a promise to distribute all of it to agencies around the world. He ended by sending a plea, phrased more like an order, for all members of the SOG to turn themselves in peacefully. Church assistance was also promised to all necessary agencies in an effort to ease the possible congestion.

"That was decidedly unsatisfying," Danielle mumbled as the pope left the podium.

"You said it," John answered as he turned off the television, "but to be fair, we already knew what was happening."

"Try to be a little positive. Whatever the results are of this press conference, even you have to admit that he followed through on his promise. I mean, you can't doubt that he went into this knowing that he'll get into some kind of trouble for being so ... verbally brutal, but he did it anyway. You can't say that he didn't try his best," Jenkins' voice was close to pleading.

"Agreed, and I do believe this will actually come out fairly positive. I mean, think of all the scandals in the Church lately, and consider how weak and sporadic the Church's response to them has been. Simply put, people are getting tired of the Church ignoring its own dirty laundry. Yes, Stevens was pretty nasty, but he described a nasty situation.

"Most people probably won't even believe anything he said, but those who do will most likely respect his harshness. The Church is finally scooping up its own shit. I wouldn't be surprised if that little speech even buys back a few followers." John and Danielle both looked to Jenkins, who reluctantly gave a small nod.

"I hate to admit it, but I think you're right," Danielle added. "So what do we do now?"

"There's honestly not much we can do until we either see or hear what effect this has on the situation. In the meantime, we'll continue with our preparations to move. Do you still want to find a place in New York?"

"Well, that does seem to be..." As the vampires went back to discussing the details of their upcoming move, Jenkins leaned back and let his mind wander over the possible implications of the speech they had just heard.

Chapter 24

"GUYS! GUYS! Hey, guys!" Jenkins was shouting like an insane child as he burst into the room. The four vampires were standing around a table studying a pile of maps and blueprints, but only John looked up at his intrusion.

"We're busy. Go away." Jenkins was taken aback by John's rebuke. It had been four days since the pope's broadcast, and the vampires had finally gotten back to the business of moving and planning the next stage of their battle against the SOG. The mood had been growing increasingly serious, and they apparently had no time for his foolishness.

"Seriously, this is important." Jenkins had begun to get used to the way the vampires regarded him, but if he persisted, they normally paid attention.

"Seriously, leave us alone, or I'll let Chris kill you." John did have an odd sense of humor, but Jenkins didn't much care for the pleased expression on Chris's face. He could understand that when the vampires were up to something serious, they tended to assume that all mortals were simply obstacles or a waste of time, but on this he was going to be heard, whether they wanted to listen or not.

"All right, Goddammit, this is important, so shut the hell up and listen to me!" Expressions of annoyance turned to shock as the priest very loudly took the Lord's name in vain.

"Um, okay. I didn't think you guys could talk like that."

"I'll do penance later. What I've been trying to say is that the Vatican finally got in touch with me about the results of the press conference." Chris and Sam were clearly unimpressed, but he knew that John would want to hear more.

"Okay, fine, but make it quick."

"Well," Jenkins pulled up a chair, "there's good news and bad news."

"My, how cliché. May as well get the bad news out of the way first."

"Figured you would say that, but the bad news won't make any sense unless you hear the good news first. It's over." He paused, inviting a response, and John's eyes narrowed.

"What do you mean?"

"I mean, it's over. The SOG is no more. The members have completely disbanded." He noticed that even Sam and Chris were suddenly giving him their undivided attention. "Okay, I see I have your attention now, so I'm just going to tell you what I was just told.

"First, His Excellency apologizes for taking so long in getting in touch, but the situation quickly got out of control. Within twenty-four hours of the press conference's first broadcast, every member of the SOG turned himself in. When I say every member, I mean that quite literally. The Vatican said it would probably take weeks for them to finish cataloging everyone's names, but so far it appears to be 100 percent.

"The thirteen cardinals heading the SOG even turned themselves in before they could be apprehended, and five of them have already admitted to knowing full well the true nature of the SOG. They even found the mole." Danielle arched an eyebrow.

"Yep, you both were right. Someone at the Vatican was helping to coordinate everything. As it turns out he was just a low-level priest with amazing computer skills. The cardinals were clearly the ones in charge; he apparently acted as everyone's secretary. Anyone who communicated with the Vatican was really talking to the mole, who would then distribute the information as necessary. Something like that anyway. They don't quite understand it all yet, but the important thing is that the mole was actually waiting to turn himself in the moment the broadcast ended." Even seeing how serious Jenkins's expression was, John glanced to his wife, who confirmed that he was telling the truth.

"That's great, but it doesn't make sense," Chris chimed in. "Wait, what was the bad news?"

"You hit it on the head. It doesn't make sense. We know for a confirmed fact that the SOG essentially dissolved overnight, but no one knows why. We hoped to have massive defections following the press conference, but that was just a hope. None of us expected the whole organization to simply go away. Plus the pope made plans to apprehend the main leadership, yet they turned themselves in as well.

"More significant to me is that the Vatican confirmed Thomas Andrews as one of the soldiers who turned himself in." Jenkins saw that the name meant nothing to any of them. "Okay, Danielle, he's the guy who attacked you and started this whole mess." Realization dawned in four sets of eyes.

"As you know, he was badly injured in the attack. I promoted him to military commander of the area. He is essentially the one who has been planning the attacks and ambushes ever since. Now, I know in my heart that he would sell his soul to Lucifer himself if it meant a chance to continue hunting you both down. So why would he immediately turn himself in? We're missing something here, and it has everyone at the Vatican on edge."

"Ah, they're afraid the SOG is trying to pull the same crap they did before."

"I think that is a major concern, but they're keeping a very close eye on it all. It's just a big question mark, and no one can figure out what it means." His information dispensed, Jenkins sat back and sipped a beer one of the ghouls had brought him.

"Okay, well I'm content to just call this a victory for the moment, but it doesn't change our immediate concerns. We still need to move, and New York seems to be our best option." John pushed a few blueprints over to Jenkins. "I'd like to get your opinion on a few properties we're looking at."

"John," Danielle got her husband's attention, "we can't ignore the implications of what we just learned."

"I'm not, but one thing at a time. The only thing we know for sure is that something is going on, but we don't know what, and it's pointless to waste time focusing on it without more information. If you want my opinion though," John's eye narrowed as his fangs protruded, "something else is pulling the strings."

* * *

THIRTY MILES OFF the east coast of the Euphrates River, and about five hundred meters underground, is an extensive network of unexplored caverns. Deep within these caverns, an ancient eye opened, and lips aged beyond recognition curled into a smile that would cause demons to flee.

Epilogue

"*MY GOD*! Ma'am, you can't keep doing this to me. I'm an old man, after all." Jason had closed up shop for the day over an hour before, yet he came out of the storeroom to find Danielle sitting comfortably with her feet up on the counter examining one of his knives.

"Oh, sorry. Hope you don't mind," she set the knife gingerly on the counter, "but that blade caught my eye. How are you, Jason?"

"How I am is sure that I locked the door and lowered the gate, just like last time. Yet here you sit."

"Here I sit." Danielle wasn't sure the best way to approach the topic she came to discuss, so she coaxed the conversation a little to see what Jason would say about her. "The sword is unbelievable by the way. My husband swears he has never used a finer weapon."

"Now I am certain that the sword I made was intended for combat, so your statement carries all sorts of implications." Danielle didn't take the bait. "Well, it's none of my business. I'm just happy that you were both pleased with my work."

"Hmm, you seem to be tactfully ignoring what's really on your mind." She would force the issue if necessary.

"Well, to be honest, I know there is something about you that isn't normal. But like I said before, it's none of my business."

"You said it yourself, you know that I've broken into your shop twice now without a trace of an explanation how. I asked you to make me an instrument of death and later told you how well it performed. Have you not added these facts together?"

"I have, but it's—"

"None of your business." Jason smiled as she finished the sentence. She rose and stood next to his chair. The temperature in the room dropped noticeably, and there was something different about her gaze. "Are you afraid?"

"No." Jason seemed confused by the question. "Look, all I know is that for the first time in a very long while, someone asked me for a weapon that I was proud to make—something real and not just pretty to look at. I don't really care about anything else to be honest with you, so if you need to 'tie up' any loose ends, get on with it."

Danielle smiled and almost laughed out loud. *Oh my God, he thinks I'm some kind of mobster come to kill him so he doesn't lead back to me.*

"Wow, I wasn't sure what you would make of me, but you certainly made it worth the wait. I did not see that one coming. Tell me, are you so willing to accept death because you simply don't care anymore or because you only have a year before the cancer kills you."

Jason nearly fell out of his chair.

"The doctors say it could be two years or more."

"But you don't believe them, and, quite frankly, I think you're right."

"Okay, friendly banter aside, you have officially gotten my attention. I never told you any of that, and now I'm afraid I'm going to have to ask you to explain yourself."

Danielle nodded, relieved that she had finally gotten him on the same page. "Essentially, I came here to offer you a job that would involve an entirely new life."

Jason chuckled softly at her statement. "Look, whatever game you're playing, I appreciate the offer and consideration, but I'm happy here and way too old to start a new life."

"Ah, but you misunderstand me; I meant new life very literally. And you can't lie to me. I know that the only thing that makes you happy is working with weapons, and that the combination of cancer and arthritis makes it nearly impossible to truly work your craft. Come work for me. Join my family, and you'll have everything you could ever want ... including time." Jason knew that she was being ridiculous, but she sounded so serious.

"You're not making any sense, and it's getting late. We really need to wrap this up."

"Okay, I'll cut to the chase. I have something to tell you that you are not going to believe. Then I'm going to prove it to you and make you an offer I doubt you'll be able to refuse.

"I was born in the year 1070 AD, and I am a vampire."